CALIFORNIA STATE UNIVERSITY, HAYWARD
LIBRARY

Utopian Literature

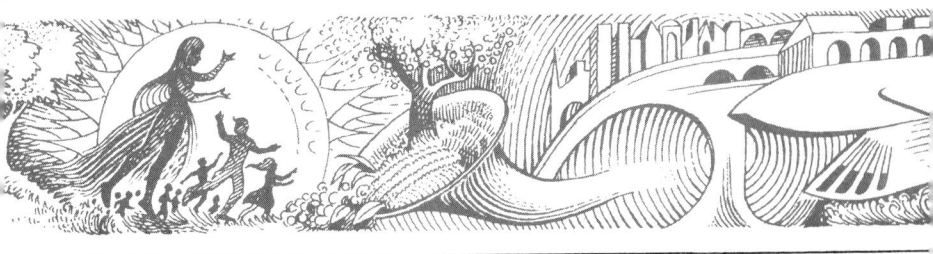

Advisory Editor:
ARTHUR ORCUTT LEWIS, JR.
  Professor of English
The Pennsylvania State University

A.D. 2000

Alvarado M. Fuller

Introduction by Arthur O. Lewis, Jr

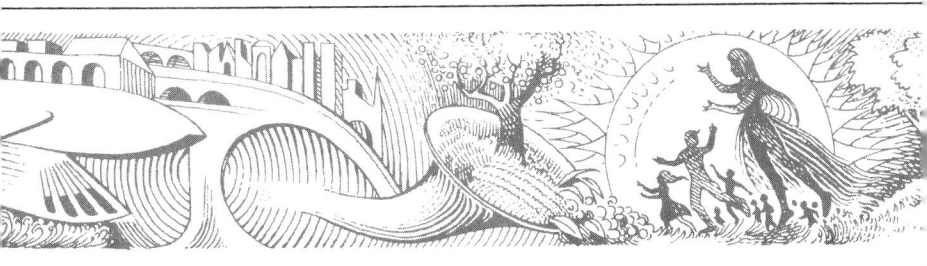

ARNO PRESS & THE NEW YORK TIMES
NEW YORK • 1971

PS
1724
F28
A7
1971

Reprint Edition 1971 by Arno Press Inc.
Introduction Copyright 1971 by Arno Press Inc.

Reprinted from a copy in The Pennsylvania State University Library

LC# 71-154441
ISBN 0-405-03524-1

Utopian Literature
ISBN for complete set: 0-405-03510-1

Manufactured in the United States of America

Publisher's Note: This edition was reprinted from the best available copy

CALIFORNIA STATE UNIVERSITY, HAYWARD
LIBRARY

INTRODUCTION

For Alvarado M. Fuller (1851-1924), as for so many American utopian writers, tomorrow's world would be immediately better if only the good, natively intelligent American people were permitted to go their own way under wise and proper leadership. In *A.D. 2000* this better world has been achieved in only three generations, for Fuller's inventive army lieutenant, Junius Cobb, awakens after 113 years to find a prospering, happy, democratic United States stretching from pole to pole, led by the great grandsons of friends he had left behind when he undertook his dangerous experiment in suspended animation. For the imaginative Cobb, little of what he sees, after his slight initial confusion, causes any real surprise. The changes in government and economic policy and the new technological achievements appear to him as completely reasonable outgrowths of activities in his own time. No doubt Fuller himself, career army officer and dabbler in science and invention, would have reacted in the same way.

A.D. 2000 was first "Entered according to act of Congress in the year eighteen hundred and ninety," and its publication in this banner year in the production of American utopias, especially those written in reaction to Edward Bellamy's *Looking Backward, 2000-1887*

(1888), raises the inevitable question of Fuller's debt to Bellamy. There are some interesting parallels. The most obvious is in the methods used to move the hero into the future: Bellamy's Julian West goes to sleep in May 1887, and awakens in September 2000; Fuller's Junius Cobb sleeps from December 1887, to June 2000. Neither had intended so long a sleep: West, through hypnotism, only overnight; Cobb, using himself as guinea pig in a scientific experiment, only until 1989. Both remain hidden and sleeping beyond the intended time, the one because of a fire, the other because of a bureaucratic blunder. Among other similarities are the heroic Roman first names which are nearly identical and the treatment of the loneliness of the heroes even in a world where they find new and sympathetic friends. Both cling to the thought of their beloved of earlier times: Julian West marries her great granddaughter; Junius Cobb has his true love herself restored to him through the devotion of her father and the wonders of science. Still another similarity is the doubling of the penalty for one found guilty of a crime after pleading not guilty in Bellamy's novel which is somewhat like the doubling of the penalty for one whose appeal is denied in Fuller's.

One outstanding difference between the two novels and one over which neither writer had any control is their reception by the public. Bellamy's has been reprinted hundreds of times in many countries and influenced the course of world history. Fuller's has appeared only in the original edition; in a volume entitled *Back to Life (A.D. 2000), A Thrilling Novel,* "Copyright 1911";

and in the present reprint. (It is probable that the version of 1911 is made from the same plates as that of 1890, with only cover, title page, and frontispiece changed.) Fuller dismissed any influence from Bellamy, perhaps protesting too much: "Lest originality of title and theme be denied, it is but justice to myself to state that both were assumed in November 1887." A closer inspection of the two works would doubtless reveal the truth of the matter.

Fuller, unlike Richard Michaelis (*Looking Further Forward*), W. W. Satterlee (*Looking Backward and What I Saw*), and Arthur Dudley Vinton (*Looking Further Backward*) who also published utopian novels in 1890, made no overt attack on Bellamy. Whatever the truth may be in regard to his knowledge of *Looking Backward*, his novel can stand in its own right both as a work representative of several strands of utopian thinking and for several interesting characteristics of its own. *A.D. 2000* is partial to the military, much concerned with technology, respectful of wealth and accomplishment, and patriotically adventurous.

Thus, Fuller's pride in the army runs through the entire book. The title page proclaims *Lieut.* Alvarado M. Fuller as author. Almost the first prize of the hero's new life is to be named Lieutenant-Colonel in his old regiment, the Second Cavalry, and told that as "a Lieutenant-Colonel, at thirty-three, the youngest in the army, you will one day command the army of the United States." Military officers are obviously the cream of the crop, chosen after long training from the non-commissioned ranks, and service seems to have become almost hereditary: the Secretary of State is descended from a Brigadier General known to Junius Cobb; President Emory Craft is the great grandson of Cobb's dear friend Lieut. Hugh Craft (one of the two who helped in his experiment), killed as a major at the Battle of Ottawa in 1917 ("A soldier's death! A noble ending to a noble man!"), and his son, Capt. Hugh Craft, becomes one of Cobb's two closest friends in his new life. Among Cobb's earliest discussions after his arrival in Washington are those with President Craft regarding the nation's rearmament and subsequent defeat of the British, and with the Secretary of War about the composition of the nation's military forces. On the next to last page, the great rewards are military in nature: Cobb is commissioned "Admiral of the Aërial Navy of the United States," Craft becomes "Commodore in the Aërial Navy," and Capt. Lester Hathaway, descendant of Cobb's other friend and helper, receives "A colonelcy in the army."

It is only fair to note that Fuller's pride did not extend to worship of the military. Cobb's remarks about "the state of promotion in 1887," although typical of junior officers in any army at any time, are scathing: "Promotion at that time was slow beyond measure—stagnated. Old men with grown-up families were still Lieutenants, while the majority of Captains were old, rheumatic, and unable to perform their duty. Lieutenants did all the work." Nor was he a militarist—not when he called for an army of 148,000 for a **nation of** over 500,000,000 population, even though he provided for a draft to make up the difference between the number of volunteers available and the army's total needs.

Fuller's interest in science and invention—he is known to have invented a submarine and to have been interested in communications and in calendar reform, for example—is clearly reflected in the novel, sometimes to the detriment of the plot. Frequently the action stops to permit explanation of a scientific point or a technological marvel. For example, Cobb, still weak and barely able to hold a pencil in his hand, tarries in his tomb long enough to demonstrate mathematically to his fascinated rescuers why he had failed to awaken as planned in 1988 [sic], and would not have awakened until 2198, except for the fortuitous discovery of his letter and the accidental slipping of a workman's crowbar in 2000. As he goes about the new world, he listens avidly to explanations of the workings of the pneumatic railroad, the submarine, calendar reform, "sympathetic telegraphy," and malleable glass (in the latter case making his own tests to prove the accuracy of the explanation). Later, although he first must learn about the difficulty of producing a large enough supply of hydrogen to keep the "aërial ships" aloft, he is able to develop a system which enables him and his two friends to reach the North Pole, and it is Cobb who, at great length, explains how to locate the right course for leaving the Pole to go home. There is, in fact, so much of this scientific and pseudoscientific emphasis that the reader begins to feel as if the proper title for the book might well be *Tom Swift and His Pneumatic Railroad,* or *Tom Swift and His Amazing Submersible* or, better still, *Junius Cobb and His Ozone Machine.* The hero is, in many ways, a superscientist, for not only does he understand and, as in the case of the aërial navy, improve upon the technology of the year 2000, he is also, despite assumption of his rights by a dishonest clerk, responsible for the excellent explosive in general use and for development of the superfuel which powers the fastest ships.

Perhaps an even better analogy than Tom Swift would be to a Horatio Alger story. The rise of an impecunious army lieutenant to the kind of wealth that permits him to divide five million dollars between his two friends as a wedding gift and his wife-to-be to give their fiancées handfuls of jewelry is Algeresque and, as so often in Alger, occurs on the last page. Similarly reminiscent are his being more or less adopted by the President, and his receipt of high military command, with its promise of even better things to come.

As utopias go, *A.D. 2000* has no unusual proposals. Basic to the new society are equal taxation, limitation of both profits and wages, and a reformed judicial system—all ideas amply demonstrated by other writers. Even such scientific wonders as wide use of electricity, glass buildings, double-decker city streets, balloons, control of climate (although damming the Gulf Stream is not the usual method) are found, if not always together, in numerous other utopias of the late nineteenth century. The specifics of streamlined government, expanded civil service, limitation of time in public office, and public operation of railroads and postal and telegraph services are not unusual. The existence of the Central Sea—not found elsewhere—is not integral to either society or plot and appears to be little more than an excuse to describe the hazards of industrial carelessness and the operation of submarines.

What makes *A.D. 2000* worth reading is the wide-eyed, somewhat stuffy but likable, Junius Cobb, who, as the story progresses, becomes more and more Fuller's alter ego. His new life is to be one of wealth and prestige in a world where respect for these attributes is still strong. If one has sufficient talent (it also helps to belong to a good family) he can achieve high rank in the military, in government, in society, and he can expect the common folk to adulate him, the newspapers to praise him, and his peers to conform to his every wish. (Where else could a young woman commandeer a navy cruiser and divert it from its assigned mission simply by identifying herself—through a personal letter from her father to her aunt, at that—as a daughter of the President?) And for Cobb, as for his creator, such a situation is only the appropriate reward for a man of talent, as had all too often not been the case in 1887.

Whenever Cobb seems most know-it-all—*he* invented meteorite; *he* wins the race to the North Pole; *he* has studied J. M. Scheyer's Volapük, the artificial language which had become the language of diplomacy—one remembers that this intelligent, imaginative, and adventurous young man had taken the biggest chance of all and that his slight, completely human, mistake had almost cost him his life. It is difficult to dislike him for long. The hero wins through to fame and fortune, and the reader gives him grudging admiration while at the same time absorbing the author's version of tomorrow.

If the novel seems at times like little more than an early twentieth-century pulp magazine, it is at the same time attractive evidence of the never-ending faith of the inventive Projector (to use an eighteenth-century term) that a better world can be developed if only we put our minds to it. If Fuller's prophesies of technological progress and political change were not always completely accurate, he was able, nonetheless, to show a world which has many resemblances to our own, and, by A.D. 2000, it may look much more like his than now appears to be the case. As patriotic American and as utopian reformer, what more could he wish for?

ARTHUR O. LEWIS
MAY 1971

A. D. 2000

A. D. 2000

A NOVEL

BY

LIEUT. ALVARADO M. FULLER
U. S. ARMY

CHICAGO:
LAIRD & LEE, PUBLISHERS

Entered according to act of Congress in the year eighteen hundred and ninety, by LAIRD & LEE, in the office of the librarian of Congress at Washington.

(All rights reserved.)

PREFACE

Lest originality of title and theme be denied, it is but justice to myself to state that both were assumed in November, 1887. My thanks are due to Lieutenant D. L. Brainard, Second Cavalry, for the true copy of the record of the Greely party left in the cairn at the farthest point on the globe ever reached by man—83 degrees 24 minutes North Latitude, 40 degrees 46 minutes West Longitude.

THE AUTHOR

CONTENTS

CHAPTER I
Junius Cobb's Marvelous Discovery.......... 9

CHAPTER II
A Startling Proposition..................... 31

CHAPTER III
Preparing for the Test..................... 45

CHAPTER IV
Jean Colchis, Conspirator and Savant....... 61

CHAPTER V
On the Eve of a Century's Sleep............ 80

CHAPTER VI
Faithful unto Death........................ 101

CHAPTER VII
"You Say this is A. D. 2000?".............. 108

CHAPTER VIII
San Francisco in the Twenty-First Century.. 130

CHAPTER IX
The Central Pneumatic Railroad............ 150

CHAPTER X
Under the Central Sea..................... 168

CHAPTER XI
The Army of Instruction................... 199

CHAPTER XII
Junius Cobb Reads a Newspaper............. 235

CONTENTS

CHAPTER XIII
NEW YORK CITY—POPULATION 4,000,000 245

CHAPTER XIV
THE LAW OF THE LAND 261

CHAPTER XV
THE SYMPATHETIC TELEGRAPH 278

CHAPTER XVI
CHICAGO THE METROPOLIS OF THE COUNTRY 299

CHAPTER XVII
NIAGARA FALLS HARNESSED 309

CHAPTER XVIII
THE MYSTERY OF THE COPPER CYLINDER 315

CHAPTER XIX
RESURRECTED 332

CHAPTER XX
AN AERIAL VOYAGE 347

CHAPTER XXI
THE TRANSATLANTIC LIFE-SAVING STATIONS 363

CHAPTER XXII
LOCATING THE NORTH POLE 380

CHAPTER XXIII
UNITED AT LAST 396

CHAPTER XXIV
CONCLUSION 404

A. D. 2000

CHAPTER I

"Number three! half-past eleven o'clock—and all's well!"

"All is well!" came the response from the sentry at the guard-house, while the sharp click of his piece as he brought it to his shoulder and the heavy tread of his retreating footsteps were all that was heard to break the stillness that reigned supreme throughout the garrison.

It was a dark, dreary, foggy night. The heavy atmosphere seemed laden with great masses of fleeting vapor, and the walks of the post and the ground surrounding them were as wet as if a heavy shower had just spent its force.

Such was the Presidio of San Francisco, California, a military post of the United States government, on the night of November 17th, 1887. The lights of the garrison made little effect upon that thick and saturated atmosphere; yet the little that they did make only seemed to add more to the depth of the surrounding gloom.

In the officers' club-room, near the main parade,

was gathered a jolly party of old and young officers. The rooms were handsomely, even superbly, furnished. The billiard-tables were in full blast; the card-tables were occupied; while many sat and chatted upon the various military topics which are ever a part of the soldier's life.

In a set of officers' quarters, some distance away from the main parade, were assembled three subalterns of the line. The room was bright and cheerful, and the decanters upon the table showed that they knew of the good cheer of the world. The furniture upon which the officers sat and reclined, as also about the room, gave evidence of refinement and education; while the cases stacked with books, near the entrance, bespoke a tendency and desire on the part of the occupant of the quarters for the improvement of his mind. A grate fire in the angle threw its cheerful rays upon those present, while the luxuriousness and warmth of the whole room was in direct contrast with the gloominess and cold without.

Opening from the main room through a curtained door was a second room, the inside of which was a study. There was no carpet upon the floor, and the boards gave evidence of having been used by many feet. Tables containing jars and many curious vessels, wires in every direction, bottles filled and empty, maps and drawings, and instruments of peculiar form and shape, were seen about the room.

In one corner was a large Holtz machine, whose

great disc of glass reflected back the rays from the lights in the front room.

The three men were soldiers and officers of the army.

In the center of the room, by a small table upon which was a roll of paper, with one hand holding down the pages, while the other was raised in a commanding gesture, stood Junius Cobb, a lieutenant in the cavalry arm of the service. Sitting in an easy-chair near the fire, with his legs on the fender and his eyes watching every movement of the speaker, reclined Lester Hathaway; while midway between the table and the right side of the room, in a large rocker, sat Hugh Craft.

Lester Hathaway was a graduate of the military academy of the United States, as was also Hugh Craft; both were lieutenants in the army—the former in the infantry, and the latter in the artillery branch of the service.

Lester Hathaway was about twenty-eight years of age, tall and slim, fair-haired, a pleasing face, languid air, and a blasé style. To him the world was one grand sphere for enjoyment; it was his life, his almost every thought, as to how he could pass his time in an easy and amusing manner. Balls, parties, and dances were his special vocations. With him there was no thought of the true hardships of life.

Young and handsome, courted by the ladies, he could not understand how it was that others should occupy their minds with subjects of research and study.

Hugh Craft was of a different type; yet, like Hathaway, he was tall and thin, and about the same age; but here the likeness terminated. He was darker than his companion, with sharp features, an aquiline nose, and a chin denoting great firmness. His eye was piercing, and wandered from one object to another with the rapidity of lightning. He was much more of a student than Hathaway. delighting in all that portion of the sciences touching the marvelous; a good listener to the views of others. Altogether, Hugh Craft was a man worthy to be the partner of a scientific man in a great enterprise.

Junius Cobb, the central figure in the room, deserves more than a passing description. He was a man about thirty-three years of age, of medium height, but of a full and well-developed form, black eyes, a pleasing countenance, a dark mustache nearly covering his lips, square chin, and eyebrows meeting in the center of the face—all tokens of a great firmness and decision. He was one who had given many of his days and nights to hard study in science, in political economy, and, in fact, had taken a deep interest in almost all of the various progressive undertakings of his day.

Outside of his duties, Junius Cobb had employed every spare moment of his time in experimenting in chemistry and electricity. The room off the sitting-room, where the three gentlemen were gathered this dark and foggy night, was his workshop, into which no man was permitted to go save he himself. Its mysterious contents were known to no other person.

His friends would come and visit him, and sit for hours talking and chatting, but no invitation was ever accorded them to enter that single room.

"Craft," and Cobb pointed his finger at that personage in an impatient manner, "we have often discussed these matters, I will admit, but it is a theme I like to talk upon. Do you believe in the immortality of the soul?"

"Why, of course," replied that person, looking surprised.

"And you, too, Hathaway?" continued Cobb, addressing the other.

"Most certainly I do," was the reply.

"Now, do either of you believe that the living body can be so prepared that it will continue to hold the soul within its fleshly portals for years without losing that great and unknown essence?" and Cobb fixed his sparkling eyes upon his listeners.

"Yes," answered Craft; "but by God alone."

"I do not mean by God," quickly returned the other. "God is all powerful; but by man?"

"Then, of course, I would say that it cannot be done."

"But if I were to show you that it was a fact, an

accomplished fact, you would, of course, admit it?"

"No, Cobb. Look here, old fellow," pettishly exclaimed Hathaway, rising from his chair, "what is all this about, anyway?"

Cobb glanced at him with an expression of pity and quickly replied:

"I mean, Hathaway, that it is in my power to hold the life of mortal man within its living body for an unlimited time. I mean that I can take your body, Hathaway, and so manipulate it that you will be, to all appearance, dead; but your soul, or whatever you choose to call it, will still be in your body; and further, that after a certain time you will again come to life, having all your former freshness and youth."

Cobb stood at the table with his hand upon the pages of his book, and a smile upon his face which seemed to say, "Deny it if you can."

Hathaway and Craft looked at him in amazement. These men had known Cobb to be a student, but neither of them had ever thought him demented.

The proposition advanced by him seemed so terribly contrary to all the principles of science, natural law, and life, that neither of them could believe that the man was in earnest.

Both Hathaway and Craft had often come to Cobb's quarters, and exchanged ideas with him concerning various and many topics; both knew him to be a student of chemistry and philosophy, and that he worked many hours in his little back room

They knew that he worked with chemicals and electricity, and both knew him to be a very peculiar man, yet neither of them had ever before seemed to be imbued with the belief that the man was of unsound mind. The grave and startling statement advanced by Cobb had so astonished them that it was impossible to think him sane.

"Yes," continued Cobb, "I have found this power. I have no doubt that it strikes you with amazement that I should even suggest such an almost preposterous theory. I have no doubt that you almost think me insane; but my researches in the past few years have been rewarded by the most startling discoveries. We have all imagined, for many years, that as soon as the body was deprived of air for a considerable time, life would become extinct, or, in other words, that life could not exist without air. Such is not the case—ah! do not start," he exclaimed, seeing both Hathaway and Craft bend forward inquiringly in their chairs. "I repeat, such is not the case. Without the oxygen in the air, the blood of man would be white, yet it would possess all the properties necessary to continue life. But one thing must not be confounded with this statement: oxygen is necessary for life *with* action, but not necessary for life *without* action. A strange statement, is it not? Am I tedious?" he asked, looking at his listeners.

"No; not at all," they both exclaimed. "Please continue, for we are very much interested."

"Well," and Cobb's eyes flashed as he warmed up to his subject, "it was long ago discovered that there was a peculiar odor arising upon the passage of a current of electricity through oxygen gas; this was also perceived even in working an electrical machine. This odor was named ozone. Both of you gentlemen are sufficiently proficient in chemistry for me to pass over the various methods by which ozone can be manufactured, yet I think it quite necessary that I should state a few facts about this very remarkable gas, if, indeed, it can be called a gas; it is really allotropic oxygen. Now, oxygen can be put into a liquid state, or even into a solid state; yet it is most difficult to keep it in either of those conditions—so much so that it would be of no use for the purposes for which I desire to use it. Oxygen is contracted by passing an electric spark through it, and ozone is perceived by the peculiar odor arising therefrom. If the intensity of the current is increased sufficiently, the oxygen is proportionately decreased in bulk. Suffice it to say that oxygen can be reduced millions of times in bulk by this simple method, always provided that the electrical energy was sufficient at starting. You will perceive," and he hastily quitted the room, entered his workshop, and returned with a small bottle fitted with a tight stopper, and containing apparently a stick of camphor—"you will perceive," he continued, "when I open this bottle, a most peculiar odor, a lightness in the atmosphere, a seeming renewal of life, and a sense of languidness passing over you."

Saying this, he took out the glass stopper and passed the bottle two or three times in front of Hathaway and Craft. As the bottle was moved from side to side, both of them experienced a strange sensation; it seemed that the air was heavily charged with a something that gave them feelings of unutterable lightness, of calm repose, and intense satisfaction. The lights danced about in thousands of forms, yet each appeared to possess some true and beautiful shape. They moved, they walked and ran, yet no effort seemed to be required. It was as if they were a part of some living thing, yet not a part: a part of it in that they moved and had feelings coincident with it, yet not a part because no effort was required, of brain or muscle, to be a part of it. For a moment it seemed to each of them that a state of exertionless existence had been reached, and then each knew no more. They lay in their chairs apparently lifeless.

Cobb quickly replaced the stopper in the bottle, and took from his nostrils two small pieces of sponge, which had been saturated in some kind of solution.

Returning to the back room, he replaced the bottle on the shelf from which he had taken it, and came back to his position by the table.

He watched Hathaway and Craft a few minutes, when, seeing no appearance of reviving, he arose and opened the windows and wheeled their chairs around so that the cool night air could strike them full in the face. This done, he sat himself down near the table and seemed to watch with great earnestness the countenances of his two friends.

He had sat this way but a moment, when a sigh escaped the lips of Craft, his eyes opened, and he gazed about him with a most puzzled and dazed expression.

Cobb sprang quickly to his side, and presented a glass of wine to his lips.

"There," he said, "take some of that, old fellow; you will feel like your former self in a moment."

Craft drank the liquor without saying a word; then, raising himself, he looked Cobb in the eyes, and asked:

"Have I been asleep, Cobb, or what is the matter? I feel as if I had just awakened from a most delicious slumber, a most refreshing one, and yet I had no dreams, nor does it seem that I am fatigued in the least."

At this moment Hathaway opened his eyes, and also in a dazed manner viewed his surroundings.

"Why, bless me, I have been asleep!" he exclaimed.

Cobb quickly filled a second glass of wine and gave it to him, saying: "Drink that; you will feel all right in a jiffy."

Hathaway emptied the glass, and then, looking at Craft, said:

"I know now; it was the bottle, or rather the contents, that has caused us both to fall asleep."

"Yes," said Cobb, "it was the contents of that bottle that has caused you both to enter the first stages of death."

"How long has this sleep continued?" asked Craft.

"About ten minutes."

"And was I also asleep as long?" asked Hathaway.

"Yes; a little longer," returned Cobb. "Craft awoke first."

Pausing to light a cigar, he then resumed:

"How do you feel—sick or languid?"

"Oh, as for me, not at all," spoke up Craft. "I cannot say that I feel any ill effect from the drug."

"Nor I," said Hathaway, "except that I am a little dry," with a laugh.

"Then take some of this wine," and Cobb filled a glass for each of them. "It will brace up your nerves."

They drank the wine, and appeared to suffer no evil effects from their enforced sleep.

"Will you not smoke, also?" asked Cobb, as he passed over a box of fine Havana cigars. Each took one, and Cobb laid the box aside.

Soon the clouds of smoke rising to the ceiling renewed the scene of warmth and sociability which had prevailed before the uncorking of the bottle of ozone.

"You, gentlemen," said Cobb, drawing his chair

to the fire, and taking a seat near the others, "have seen pure ozone in its solid state, and you both have felt its effect. It is the life-giving principle of oxygen. Ozone is everywhere; in the air, of course; in all creation, in fact. I do not wish to tire you, but if you desire, I will explain why I said that I had the power to hold life in the human body for an indefinite time."

"You will not tire us. Pray go on; I, for one, am most anxious to know more of this wonderful discovery of yours," quickly returned Craft.

"I also car listen for hours to your words," answered Hathaway.

"Then, I will explain to you my researches in this direction;" and Cobb arose and entered his little back room, soon returning with a good-sized box, which he laid upon the table.

Craft and Hathaway watched him with an earnestness which gave evidence of the interest they took in the strange theories which he had advanced. Indeed, it was a most strange, not to say terrible, power for a man to possess—that of holding the soul of man within its fleshly portals during his pleasure.

After Cobb had placed the box upon the table, he opened the roll of papers which he had before him at the time he got the bottle of ozone. Referring to one of the pages, he looked toward Hathaway and said:

"Can you tell me how many cubic feet of air the

average man requires in every twenty-four hours?"

Hathaway, taken by surprise, hesitated, blushed, and admitted that he had forgotten the exact amount.

"Well," continued the other, quickly, "it is not to be supposed that you should remember the answer to such a question, so I will tell you. A healthy man, in action, consumes about 686,000 cubic inches in every twenty-four hours. Now, what I wish to have you understand by that, is this: that the average man requires about 137,200 cubic inches of oxygen in every twenty-four hours. This is the accepted way of putting it; in reality, he needs the ozone contained in that amount of oxygen. I do not desire that you should receive the impression that the oxygen is not needed for the man, but that the ozone only is required for the continuance of life where there is no action. I may surprise you when I say that each of you draws into your lungs, every day, over seven pounds of oxygen gas, but such is the case. Now, in those seven pounds of oxygen there are just two grains of pure ozone. Do not interrupt me," as Craft attempted to speak; "I know what you would say—that that is contrary to the accepted opinion on the subject, and that the amount is much greater—but let me tell you that my researches have found it entirely different: two grains only, to seven pounds of oxygen, or thirty-five pounds of common air. You will perceive by the above that each of you requires nearly two grains of ozone per day, or about 700 grains per year. Now, if by any freak of nature you could remain in a perfectly passive state, doing nothing, exercising no action at all, this amount of 700 grains would fall to about 400 grains; that is, the blood would require that amount to continue to perform its vital functions. Thus you see that you would require for the maintenance of life for a hundred years, 40,000 grains. This is equivalent to nearly seven pounds of ozone. Ozone, as you have already ascertained, cannot be taken into the system through the nostrils without serious consequences. It is too powerful, and would soon cause paralysis and death; but it can be taken into the system through the pores of the body without danger to life. Again, ozone can be kept in the solid state under the pressure of two atmospheres; reduce this pressure, and it will begin to evaporate. Crystals of stronetic acid, you both know, quickly decompose carbonic acid gas. Now, the whole secret is this: If insensibility is first produced by any of the various means at our command, and the subject is then placed in a receptacle sufficiently strong to withstand a pressure of over two atmospheres, and surrounded by crystals of ozone and stronetic acid in certain proportions, insensibility will continue, and the subject will in no way change, save a slight decrease in weight. Life is there, and will continue there until the ozone is entirely exhausted. To compensate for the loss in weight, the subject is bound about the abdomen with cloths saturated in certain oils and preparations which I have ascertained will furnish all the nourishment required for a given period."

Craft and Hathaway could not help looking at this man in amazement.

Was this the man with whom they had played billiards, with whom they had drank and associated, never dreaming that he was engaged in any such investigations? Was he, indeed, crazy? and were they the listeners to a lunatic's chattering discourse?

Such were the thoughts that passed through the minds of both.

Cobb stood watching the effect of his words upon them. He noted every change in their countenances; he read every thought as it came to their minds. He spoke not a word, waiting for them to give utterance to the skeptical ideas which he knew they entertained.

"It is too strange! It is too contrary to natural law and science! It is impossible!" and Craft arose as if to go.

"Yes, Cobb," said Hathaway, "this is too much; it is a fancy you have gotten, but a fancy which can never be realized. You have allowed your theories to become shadows, your shadows to become tangible, but the tangibility is apparent to no one but yourself." He too arose from his chair.

A smile played upon the lips of Cobb, a smile of

perfect self-satisfaction. His eyes shone as if his very soul centered in them.

"Look!" he cried; "look! and behold for yourselves whether my words are worthy of consideration!"

Saying this, he raised the lid of the box on the table; then, stepping back and pointing his finger at it, exclaimed, in a tone of command, a tone of majestic confidence in his own power:

"Look! Behold life in death; death in life!"

Craft took a step forward, and glanced into the box. A puzzled and ludicrous expression came over his face, his lips parted, then, finally, his white teeth showed themselves as he gave vent to a loud and prolonged laugh.

Hathaway had by this time advanced and obtained a view of the contents of the box.

"A cat, by all that's holy!" he exclaimed; "a poor dead cat!" and he too joined in the merriment of his friend.

Cobb stood still, not in the least endeavoring to check their hilarity, but waiting for them to get through.

Again the others looked at the cat in the box, and again they laughed heartily; but seeing Cobb so quiet, it at last dawned upon them that there was something peculiar in the surroundings of the animal.

In the box which had been brought out and placed upon the table was a large Maltese cat, lying upon its side on an asbestos pillow. The head of the animal was wrapped with bandages, as was also the under part of the body for a space of about two inches above its thighs. The cushion upon which it lay was placed within what appeared to be a zinc coffin of something under ten inches in height. At the head of the cat was a small saucer-shaped vessel with a perforated top, while surrounding the whole was a space of over four inches in width. In this space were the remains of a few crystals of some white substance. The box seemed to be lined with glass, and a glass top covered the whole, its sides seemingly glued to the sides of the box.

"Come," said Craft, noticing that Cobb was waiting for some remark from one or the other of them; "tell us, Cobb, why you have that cat lying in that box. Is this the principle you have been speaking of? Are we really to believe that you have in that case an animal undergoing the treatment you have spoken of?"

"Gentlemen," answered Cobb, with a feeling of pride, "you have guessed it. One year ago to-night, at twelve o'clock, I caused this poor animal to become insensible; then placing it in this case, with its mouth and nostrils covered, with bandages of nourishment about its loins, with a cup of stronetic acid at its head, and crystals of ozone surrounding the body, I hermetically sealed the case. From my experiments, I ascertained that the amount of ozone necessary for the continuance of life in an animal of this size, and for a period of one year, was 1,425 grains. This amount I put into the case. You can easily see how near correct I was in my calculations, for there are not over ten grains of ozone left on the floor of the box to-night. I asked you here, gentlemen, not only to listen to my lecture on ozone, but to witness the return to life of this animal."

All laughter in Hathaway and Craft had changed to a grave attention to all that was said by their friend.

At last it seemed to them that there was something, indeed, in the theory he advanced. In an attitude of intense expectation, they awaited his next move.

"As I have said," continued Cobb, "that cat was placed in this condition one year ago to-night. It is my intention to bring it to life again this evening; but before we begin, let us take a glass of wine and light our cigars, and then to business."

He filled their glasses from the decanter on the table, and each took a fresh cigar from the box.

Craft again sat himself down in his chair and leisurely puffed clouds of smoke from his mouth, while Hathaway stood with his back to the fire.

Both were now prepared for anything which Cobb might advance, for it seemed to each of them that it was no longer a question of "Is it true?" but a "fact only to be proved."

Cobb, having left the room, soon returned with a small box containing six cells of Grenet battery and about ten feet of wire attached to two pieces of copper. These he placed upon the table.

Taking the box containing the cat, he carried it to the front window and set it upon a chair. Entering once again his little work-room, he brought out three sponges and as many strips of common linen, and then from a bottle in his hand he sprinkled the sponges well. Approaching Craft, he said:

"Let me bind this upon your nostrils, and at the same time caution you not to open your mouth, but to breathe through the linen bandage and sponge."

Craft arose and submitted to the operation of having his face below the eyes covered by the sponge and bandages.

Cobb then approached Hathaway and treated him in like manner.

This having been finished, he wrapped his own face carefully with the third bandage. His mouth was purposely left free that he might explain the few remaining acts in his strange comedy.

Going across the room, he threw open the window to its full extent; then coming back again, he opened the window before which stood the chair containing the box. Turning to his friends, he answered their mute inquiries by stating that he took these precautions lest the remaining ozone in the case should, in escaping, overpower them. The air passing through the room from the back window would quickly carry out the evaporating ozone.

"I will break the glass top of the case," he said, "and quickly seize the cat, withdraw it, and throw the box out of the window."

Cobb now adjusted the cloth about his mouth, while the others came closer to him that they might not miss any part of the proceedings. Taking a small hammer from a shelf near by, he struck the glass a smart blow, shattering it into many pieces; quickly seizing the cat, he drew it out of the case and threw the latter out of the window. Next, tearing off the bandages about its loins and head, he clapped the two copper discs against the body of the animal—one upon its back and one upon its breast, just over the heart; then dropping the zincs into the fluid of the battery, completed the circuit by touching a push-button.

The effect was startling: the poor animal gave a gasp, a shiver ran through its frame, its chest heaved a moment, and it breathed.

Quickly taking it to the fire, he rubbed it briskly with a towel for a couple of minutes, and then laid it down upon the warm rug near the grate, that its body might receive the heat from the fire.

The animal lay but a moment where he had placed it; it soon arose on its legs, walked around once or twice, and then quietly lay down in a new position.

Taking the bandages from his face, Cobb told the others to do likewise. The air in the room was only slightly impregnated with the odor of ozone.

The windows being closed, a saucer of milk was placed before the cat, and the animal instantly arose and lapped its contents.

It seemed to all present as if the animal had just arisen from a sound sleep. There was no indication in its manner that it had undergone any new or unusual treatment.

It was strange! It was more than strange—it was marvelous!

No longer was there any doubt in the mind of either Craft or Hathaway. The theory had been plainly and truly demonstrated. Cobb had become possessed of a power unknown to any other living man. What would he do with this power? was the question that immediately came to the mind of each. Would he use it for good, or for evil? Was it a plaything that he had discovered? or had he worked out this problem for some great and grand undertaking?

"What next?" inquired Hathaway. "What is the next act in this drama?"

"To bed," said Cobb, glancing up at the clock. "It is now ten minutes past one. To-morrow evening meet me here. Say nothing, not even a word, about what you both have witnessed and heard to-night. Have I your word?" he asked, inquiringly.

"Yes, certainly," they replied together; "if you wish us not to speak of it."

"I do indeed wish it, and trust that nothing will cause you to divulge a single part of this evening's occurrences. Good-night!"

Shaking their hands at the door, he again said good-night as they descended the stairway.

Returning, he filled the grate with more coal, and threw himself down, without undressing, upon the cot in the corner of the room. A moment later, the deep sound of his breathing and the low purring of the cat on the rug were the only sounds heard in the room.

CHAPTER II

The next evening, Junius Cobb again welcomed the arrival of his friends to his apartments.

The November rains had set in in reality, and like the preceding evening, the post wore an aspect of moistened gloom.

Cobb's friends had come earlier than usual, for the events of the previous evening were so vividly before their minds that it was impossible to await the arrival of the conventional hour for calling upon their friend.

They rattled up the stairs, knocked respectfully at his door, and entered without waiting for his well-known voice.

He was sitting in his easy-chair, but arose at the first sound of their approach, and as they entered, cordially grasped the hand of each.

"Boys, I am glad you came earlier than is your custom," he said, motioning them to chairs.

"We could not wait for nine o'clock," replied Hathaway, breathless from running up the stairs.

"No; we couldn't wait," chimed in Craft. "I do believe I dreamed of nothing but ozone, dead cats, chemistry, and the like, all night. I am, in fact, weary for want of sleep."

Cobb did the honors of his house, and soon all

three were quietly sitting, and sending clouds of smoke airily toward the ceiling.

"Any news at the club?" inquired Cobb of Craft.

"Nothing out of the usual run. Dilly, the young one from the Point, and the others are working hard at a game of cinch."

"A good night for a quiet game, or for a quiet chat, too," said Hathaway.

"Yes," said Cobb; "but would you rather play cinch to remaining here and listening to what I have to say?"

"Oh, no, my dear boy; excuse us. I left them all in their glory, and hunted up Craft, that we might the sooner get here, for I have no doubt that you have some remarkable disclosures to make tonight."

"You are right; I have—and some that will probably strike you as being the most fanciful and, perhaps, untenable, you have ever heard," returned the other, looking his two listeners in the eye.

"Let that be seen in the future," they both exclaimed.

"What is your pay?" abruptly asked Cobb, after a moment's silence.

"You ought to know—$1,500 a year."

"And yours the same?" to Craft, "both being dismounted officers."

"Certainly; and a mighty small sum for a man to put on style, go to parties, and send bouquets and the like, I assure you," returned that personage.

"And mine is but a trifle more. We are all poor, is pecunious gentlemen, are we not?"

"Yes, decidedly so, I fear; for I am not aware that either of us has anything outside of his pay," answered Craft.

"And what are our chances for promotion? The way things go now, I will have to serve fifty years to become a colonel. Of course, I cannot serve that long, as I would be over the maximum age," gloomily broke in Hathaway.

"It is even so, gentlemen," and Cobb knocked the ashes from his cigar. "Promotion in the army is so exceedingly slow that none of us can expect to reach a colonelcy; in fact, the most that is before us is a majority. Here we are, gentlemen of thirty and thirty-five years of age, giving our lives and brains to this government for a paltry $2,000 a year. I, for one, intend to remedy this sad state of affairs," and he arose and walked across the room in an impatient manner.

The others watched him curiously. His manner of action spoke volumes, and indicated plainly that there was something he had to tell them in conjunction with his remarks.

Cobb strode nervously across the room for a minute, then suddenly approaching the table, he filled to the brim a glass with whisky from one of the decanters. Raising it to his lips to drink its contents, he suddenly paused, and begging the pardon of his guests, invited them to join him. His thoughts were not upon his actions.

"Listen," he exclaimed, as their glasses were laid upon the table; "are you ready to give me your strictest attention?"

"We are all ears, and will gladly listen to all you have to say," answered Craft, while Hathaway's eyes and manner betokened the curiosity he could not conceal.

"Are you both willing to give your oaths that what I tell you to-night will never, under any circumstances, be divulged by either of you to a living soul, or ever put in writing, or in any manner made possible to be known?"

Both of the men gave him this promise.

Cobb arose and took a small Bible from the mantel over the grate, and advancing to the table, held it in his right hand, requesting each of the others to place his hand upon it. They arose from their chairs and placed their hands upon the sacred volume.

"Repeat after me," said Cobb: "I swear by all that I hold sacred, by my hope of salvation in the after life, and by my belief in a just and good God, that I will not divulge or disclose, by tone of voice, or writing, or other symbol, that which may be communicated to me this night; so help me God."

His words were slowly and solemnly spoken, and the repetition of them by the others was in a manner indicative of the sincerity and truth they both felt in the obligation taken.

"Good!" and Cobb laid the book upon the table.

"I might now go on and tell you of that for which I asked you to meet me here to-night, but there would be no use in communicating to you these secrets unless you agree to assist me. It is your help that I desire."

"Cobb," and Craft's manner indicated that he felt hurt by his friend's hesitation, "I have known you for quite a long time. I have admired and respected you, and if I can be of any assistance to you in any way, you have but to ask me."

"Then, if I tell you that that which I ask of you can be performed without any neglect of the duties you owe to your God, your country, or yourself—that it will harm no one, nor will anyone have cause to complain of your action—will you swear it?"

"Yes!" they both exclaimed.

Again Cobb took the sacred volume from the mantel; again was the oath administered, and again was it taken freely and unreservedly.

"Gentlemen, I thank you," and an expression of gratitude came into Cobb's eyes. "Such friendship is worthy of you!"

After some ordinary conversation, he wheeled his chair nearer the others, and thus addressed them:

"For many years I have served this government honestly and well, but my salary has never seemed to me sufficient for the actual needs of a man in the position of an army officer. The government requires too much for the pay it gives. Again, a man is required to serve too many years in the lower grades; he is an old man by the time he is a captain. This is certainly contrary to the principles of a good and efficient government. As a captain, he should not be over thirty years of age, at the most. Here am I, who will be only a captain at fifty, if even then. This discourages the average young man. It keeps many from entering the service, because they say, 'I can do better outside.' I am ambitious, and desire to gain rank and wealth. But one thing I have found: *Life is too short.* I propose to lengthen it. You do not yet comprehend the import of my words *I propose to enter life again a hundred years hence!* I know this statement startles you, but such is my intention. I propose to put myself in the condition in which you have seen that Maltese cat. I will sleep a hundred years. My arrangements are all made; my property, small though it is, is so fixed that it will not be lost to me in that time. But I must hold my commission in the army—that is the hard problem. What do you think of my scheme?" and he put his hands behind him, and stood watching the effects of his proposition.

To say that his listeners were surprised, would ill interpret their feelings. They were dumbfounded. They could not believe that this man would dare to undergo the risk of death for the mere possibility of again living at a future day. He certainly was joking! He had asked them there to see if they would be such fools as to accept his remarks as given in earnest and good faith!

As soon as Craft could get his breath, he exclaimed, vehemently:

"You are certainly not going to subject yourself to such a test!"

Hathaway could not speak; he simply sat and looked at this man in amazement.

"Yes," and Cobb laughed at the horrified expressions upon their faces. "Yes, I do most certainly intend this very thing. I have nothing to lose; I have everything to gain. My theories will be tested, my suppositions proved. I have invested all my wealth except a sufficient amount to carry out my programme, in such a manner that in a hundred years it must, or my calculations are very much out of the way, increase in a way to make me a rich man. If I can hold my rank in the army, I will be a colonel, probably. With wealth and rank, I can again enter the world in a position to gratify my ambitions and desires. If I succeed, all will be well; if I fail, why, that is the end of it. Without chick or soul in this world dependent upon me, why should I hesitate to advance the sciences by undergoing the ordeal of that which I have advocated? No one but I ought to be called upon to prove the theory I have originated. If I fail, what is the consequence? I simply die! On this earth, a human being dies every second; does it interfere with the steady and slow movement of the machinery of life? No, not at all! Though 32,000,000 die every year, they are not missed! Do we know what the future is? Do we know it to be worse than the present? No! Then, why care if we die to-day or to-morrow? I am resolved to take this opportunity of demonstrating that man can live longer than the allotted time accorded him. I have always longed to know what this world would be like in a hundred years: it certainly will be a strange world! Most men think that we have reached a state of perfection already, and that it is almost impossible for man to improve upon the present condition of life, surrounded, as we are, by so many and great inventions. I, for one, do not think that way. I believe we are but in our infancy to what we will be in a hundred years. You have each given me your sacred promise that you will assist me in my undertaking. I hold you to it. I am, in reality, going to die, as regards all my friends, all my associations, and as regards the very present itself. I think I can almost understand the feelings of the condemned criminal on the scaffold, who is about to leave behind him all that is dear, all that is sacred to him. Yet I am buoyed up by other feelings that that poor wretch has not; I will live again. I do not believe that either of you can quite understand my feelings in this matter.

It is too new to you both. There are many cases on record where men have given up life for various reasons—given it up cheerfully and without a murmur; and those men never expected to live again—at least, in the flesh. Why should I falter? I, who go but to come again; to again enjoy the pleasures of life; to walk, see, speak, and associate with mankind!"

Cobb ceased speaking, and paced the floor in an excited manner. It was evident that this man, much as he talked of severing his connections with the present, was still loath to attempt this terrible ordeal. Yet, it was also apparent to both that he would not hesitate in his purpose. He was a man of too strong will; he would make the sacrifice.

His friends knew it and felt it.

Ceasing his walk, Cobb faced them and said:

"Before I leave, before I enter this dormant state, I must secure my position in the army beyond the possibility of losing it. How I am to do this, has long been a problem. If I am dead, I will be dropped from the rolls of the army; if I go on leave, I must return at the expiration of that leave, or, failing to do so, be declared a deserter. There seems to be but one way for me to accomplish my object. I will explain it."

Cobb now entered his little room, and soon returned with a small sporting rifle and a paper box.

It was an ordinary thirty-calibre rifle, such as is used in sporting galleries.

Approaching his friends, he opened the box and showed them a row of small cartridges. They differed very little from those used in the ordinary rifle.

Handing one to Craft, he said:

"Do you notice anything peculiar about that cartridge?"

"Well," and Craft examined it critically, turning it over and over, "it seems to be nothing but a solid thirty-calibre bullet. I cannot see that it is a cartridge at all," and he handed it to Hathaway.

The latter examined it closely. It was, indeed, to all appearance, but an ordinary bullet with the base filled flush with some black substance; in length it was only seven-tenths of an inch; in calibre, thirty one-hundredths.

Taking one of them between his thumb and forefinger, Cobb twirled it about and said:

"This is one of my new cartridges for use in actual service. It seems to you, no doubt, very small, very inadequate to the needs of actual warfare. You would both naturally say that it is too small for long range, too small for executive work; that it is altogether unfit for the purposes for which bullets are made." A smile played about his lips. Then, continuing, as he held up one of these bullets: "This is an ordinary thirty-calibre bullet, but the grand principle is in the explosive used with it. Heretofore it has required about fifty grains of powder to send such a missile on an effective mission. Now, fifty grains of powder require quite a good-sized space; it requires a case to hold it, and all this lengthens out the cartridge. If a magazine gun is used, but few such cartridges can be placed in the magazine. I have overcome all this by using a new explosive of my own manufacture. I take the ordinary bullet and simply fill the hollow end with one grain of my new compound, covering the whole with a fine and durable cement. All this saves space, and enables me to put about forty cartridges in my gun. Do you comprehend the drift of my remarks?"

Both of his listeners nodded assent.

Cobb loaded the gun with one of the ordinary cartridges, and then placed a bundle of common wrapping-paper on end at the other side of the room. Taking a position in the further corner, he discharged the piece at this improvised target.

The bullet entered the paper and penetrated through about forty sheets. Then, loading with one of his own cartridges, he again took the same position, and again discharged the piece.

Upon examination, it was found that over ninety-seven sheets of paper had been perforated. Cobb laid the gun on the table and said:

"You see the effect of the two cartridges! Which is the superior of the two? Of course, mine; and in effect as forty is to ninety-seven, or even more, perhaps. This is the power that will grant me my leave! This explosive is my own invention. You have seen its power. If we put gunpowder at one and that of gun-cotton at four, then that of meteorite, my new compound, would be nearly forty-six.

Like gun-cotton, there is little or no smoke upon discharge, as you have witnessed; but, unlike gun-cotton or nitro-glycerine, the explosion is not instantaneous, but similar to that of gunpowder. Now, the amount of gas evolved upon the explosion of one grain of gunpowder is, in volume, about three hundred of carbonic acid and nitrogen, but the true volume, considering the heat, is about fifteen hundred times that of the original charge. Meteorite has a rate of combustion three times slower than gunpowder, while the volume of gas liberated is more than sixty-six times that of the latter, or about one hundred thousand times its original bulk. This is the power, as I have said, that gives me my leave of absence. On the 22d of last month I sent an application to the War Department for a leave for the purpose of perfecting a gun in which to use these cartridges. With the application I sent some of the cartridges. I also sent a sealed packet containing the formula for making the explosive, but with the positive directions that the formula should not be made known until I had perfected my experiments. I asked for leave until I had completed my work. Through the little influence I possessed, I pressed this application to be granted in the manner I asked. Yesterday I received my leave, and here it is;" and he handed Craft the following paper:

"WAR DEPARTMENT, A.-G. O.,
WASHINGTON, November 9, 1887.

"Special Orders,
No. 156. [Extract.]

"5. Leave of absence is hereby granted First Lieutenant Junius Cobb, Second Cavalry, from December 1, 1887, until surrendered by him in writing, or upon his return to duty, for purposes which he has communicated to this department.

"By command of Lieut.-Gen. Sheridan

"R. C. DRUM,
"*Adjutant-General.*"

"I had this leave," said Cobb, as he took it from Craft, after the latter had read it, "while I was talking to you last night, but I preferred not to show it to you until this evening. Any time after the first of next month I can leave the service and return when I wish, and my commission will be secured to me."

Craft and Hathaway both told him that though they thought his undertaking was a very foolish one, nevertheless they would give him all the assistance in their power, as they had promised.

Cobb and his friends talked a little longer on various things to be done, and finally separated for the night; the two latter going home to wonder over this great scheme of their friend, the former seating himself in his easy-chair to deliberate upon the thousand and one incidentals necessary to carry it out.

CHAPTER III

In order to carry into effect this great and ambitious idea, Cobb had commenced operations as early as July.

He knew that he must find some place in which to lay his body, that would be perfectly safe from any possible disturbance. It would not do to select any house, or any particular piece of ground, nor could he go to any island or distant part of the globe.

A hundred years would make such changes that it was impossible to foretell what places would not be disturbed in that time. It was a most difficult problem to solve.

Was there a place on earth that he was sure would not be reached by human hands, and its contents and secrets made known, in a hundred years!

It was imperative that he should find such a place, and with all the assurance that one has in life of anything, that it would remain unmolested. What would not happen in a hundred years! Were he to take the most unfrequented and out-of-the-way place he could conceive of, it might be the very place of all others that would be the first to be explored by some enterprising genius in the future.

Cobb knew this, and realized the necessity of selecting such a spot as would give the utmost assurance that no one would desire to destroy, enter, or molest it in any way.

After many hours of reflection upon the subject, he at last decided upon what he considered to be the best place possible to select—the place that would, in all probability, remain in its primitive state for the period desired.

There was being built upon Mount Olympus, some three miles from the city of San Francisco, by a Mr. Sutro, a generous gentleman of that city, a reduced copy of the statue of "Liberty Enlightening the World," then in position on Bedloe's Island, New York harbor.

This statue was to be about thirty feet in height, resting upon a pedestal some forty by thirty feet in area, and twenty-five feet high.

Cobb conceived the idea that such a piece of work would, in all likelihood, remain undisturbed by any and every person for the period necessary for his long sleep. No sooner had this belief taken possession of him than he at once took measures to communicate with the gentleman who had charge of its construction.

A Mr. Bennett was the supervising architect, and this gentleman was easily induced, for a consideration, to undertake the construction of a small chamber within the base of the pedestal. He also agreed that the chamber should be reached through the side by a hinged block of marble fitting perfectly, but movable with ease from the inside, and that the purpose for which it was constructed should never be made known by him.

Mr. Bennett was not aware of Cobb's true intentions regarding the chamber; it was simply a contract between them that such a piece of work should be performed. Bennett was a man of his word, and was well known to Cobb, who placed the utmost confidence in him; yet, to make it still more binding, he placed him under a sacred oath not to enter the chamber after it was built, or communicate his knowledge of its existence to any living soul, nor to leave any information of it at his death.

While the pedestal was being built, Bennett had one of the largest marble slabs taken out, at night, by workmen brought there blindfolded, and replaced upon hinges, so it would easily open and shut by the pressure of a finger on a concealed spring.

This part of the work having been accomplished, it was very easy to carry out the remainder.

The pedestal being finished and solid, he took workmen there every night, blindfolded, and opening the slab door, cut out the masonry, hauling away the material as fast as it was taken out. Cobb desired that the chamber should be as deep as possible below the center of the pedestal, for security; Bennett made it so by digging down, after entering the base, and lining the sides with heavy brick-work.

The interior of the chamber, after construction, was fourteen by eighteen feet, and in height nine feet and six inches. The floor was made very smooth by a liberal use of Portland cement. The door was so constructed that after an inside catch had been set, it would lock itself upon being closed, and no amount of skill could open it without breaking the marble slab. There was no inlet for light, nor was there any entrance or exit for air.

Such was the finished condition of the chamber, as turned over by Mr. Bennett to Cobb, on the 15th of November, 1887.

Cobb had not been negligent in the meantime, but had gotten many of the necessary things into shape which he knew would be required, for his chamber was to have a great many and a great variety of instruments, all of which would be absolutely necessary to insure success.

Nothing could be done before the 24th of November, for on that day the Statue of Liberty was to be unveiled and turned over to the city of San Francisco by Mr. Sutro.

At last the 24th arrived, and the ceremonies of dedication were over.

As the last citizen left the vicinity of the statue a man came up the hill to view the surroundings. That man was Junius Cobb.

He approached the pedestal and looked carefully over its sides. Yes, it was all right; no one had

had an inkling of the secret entrance, or a thought that it was to be used for anything save that for which it had been erected.

Satisfied with his inspection, he passed down the hill, and took the Haight-street cars to the city, leaving them at the corner of Market and Montgomery. With rapid strides he quickly passed down that street to the Occidental Hotel.

Near the entrance of that noted army resort, whipping his legs with a small cane in a most impatient manner, stood Hathaway, as if awaiting the arrival of some expected person.

Cobb at once walked up to him and cried:

"Hello! Hathaway; on time, I see; but where is Craft?"

"Playing billiards in the other room—at least he was there a minute ago; but do you want us to-night?" inquiringly.

"Of course! did I not ask you to meet me here?"

"Yes, I know; but are you going to work so soon? What is the use of doing anything to-night? You know I have a partial engagement for this evening, and would like to keep it;" and Hathaway looked beseechingly toward his companion.

"To me this is business, and I cannot postpone it; if your social duties are so pressing, why, I will have to excuse you."

Cobb showed the displeasure he felt at the apparent want of interest displayed by the other in what to him was the greatest undertaking a man could engage in.

"Oh, no," quickly replied Hathaway, noticing the effect of his words upon Cobb; "you do not understand me. I am ready now and at all times to give you my earnest assistance. What shall I do?"

"Go and find Craft, and meet me here in ten minutes;" and Cobb turned on his heel, and passed down the street. Proceeding a few blocks, he hailed the driver of a passing express wagon, who pulled up his team at the curb-stone near where Cobb was standing.

"Are you engaged?" quickly asked Cobb.

"No," the man replied.

"Do you wish to earn twenty dollars?"

"Do I? try me!" The man's face gave evidence of his sincerity.

"Will you work all night for that amount?"

"Yes, sir."

"And go wherever I wish?"

"Yes; so I get back by morning."

"And will you permit me to take your team, after you have gone a certain distance, and drive the remainder of the way, you to remain with one of my men until I return?"

"Well, as to that, is it not a little peculiar to ask a man to let his team be driven off by unknown parties without a guarantee that it will be returned?" and the expression of his countenance indicated that he was in a quandary, for he did not like to lose the twenty dollars, nor did he like the idea of letting his team be driven away by strangers.

"You need have no fear as to that; your team will be returned; but, to satisfy you, I will leave two hundred dollars with you as security until I return it."

"That alters the case," said the man. "I am with you."

"Then, be at the corner of California street in ten minutes;" and Cobb turned and walked back to the Occidental.

Craft and Hathaway were awaiting him at the door of the hotel, the former puffing away at a cigar which the kindness of some friend had furnished.

"Ah, here you are, both of you. Good! And now to business."

Cobb seemed as if he was in a hurry to get to work, yet he showed no signs of excitement.

They passed up Bush street to the works of the electrical supply company, where, entering the place, Cobb asked if the stores and apparatus which he had ordered had been packed and were ready for shipment.

Receiving an affirmative reply, he told his friends to await him there, and quickly descended the stairs. Proceeding to the corner of California street, he met the expressman whom he had engaged; mounting the driver's seat, he directed him up Bush street, and stopped the team where he had left his friends. Giving the man orders to wait for him, he again ascended the stairs. The work of removing the boxes was at once commenced.

First, there was a long box, looking much like a coffin, being some eight feet by three, and over eighteen inches in depth. This was carefully taken down-stairs and placed in the wagon; then followed five boxes of various shapes and weights.

All things being safely placed in the wagon, Cobb mounted to the seat, telling Craft and Hathaway to get in and sit upon the boxes, as there was no room for them in front. Then, turning to the driver, he said:

"Drive up into Kearney, and thence into Market toward the park; take Haight street at the junction."

Away rattled the wagon, passing through the crowded streets and by the flashing windows filled with all the holiday goods, ready for the Christmas season.

The night was quite dark; a slight drizzling rain which was falling, was very favorable to the scheme which Cobb and his friends had on hand. Passing up Haight street to within about half a mile of Mt. Olympus, Cobb ordered the driver to pull up his team. He then directed Hathaway to remain with the driver while he and Craft took the outfit to its destination.

The place where they had stopped was a side street, close to and off of Haight street, and it was impossible for the driver, as much as he strained his eyes, to determine his surroundings.

Cobb handed the expressman ten twenty dollar gold pieces, with the understanding that they were to be returned when he brought back the team.

Leaving Hathaway with positive orders not to permit the driver to leave that particular spot until their return, Cobb mounted the seat again, Craft sitting beside him.

Turning once more into Haight street, for the purpose of throwing the driver off of their true course, they proceeded down that street for a couple of blocks, and turned sharp to the right, and drove quickly toward Mt. Olympus.

Not a soul was in sight, and the many wagon-tracks made by the artillery and carriages, which had attended the unveiling of the statue, would conceal all indication that another carriage had gone up to the pedestal that evening.

Driving close to the side of the base, Cobb pulled up, and both dismounted from the wagon.

The secret spring of the door was quickly touched, and the heavy marble slab swung upon its hinges; then, with all dispatch, the boxes were unloaded and carried into the interior of the chamber. The large box required all the strength of the two men, but it was finally gotten inside. This being finished, Craft took the reins, and quickly drove the team back to where Hathaway was impatiently awaiting him.

The money was returned by the driver, who then hurriedly departed for the city.

Seeing the man well out of sight, Craft and Hathaway carefully made their way back to the statue, and were soon inside of the pedestal. The slab door was then nearly closed, leaving but a slight aperture for the entrance of air, the opening covered by boxes, to prevent the rays of their lights being seen by any chance visitors to that neighborhood.

During their absence, Cobb had taken out two lanterns from one of the boxes, and now a bright light made everything quite clear within the chamber.

"Now," said Cobb to Hathaway, "take that hatchet and open all of the boxes."

The lids were quickly torn off and thrown to one side.

The contents of these boxes needed careful inspection. The large one was first emptied. The sides of this box were wrenched off, disclosing a large glass case, seven feet six inches by two feet eight inches, and sixteen inches in height. This glass coffin—for such, indeed, it resembled—was carefully taken out and set upon the floor. Then followed, from the same box, an ordinary set of single bedsprings, or woven-wire mattress, such as are used on single beds. Cobb then took from one of the smaller boxes a pair of iron horses or trestles, and placed them in one corner of the room, with their legs firmly fixed into the cemented floor. Carefully lifting the glass case, he and Craft set it upon the trestles, leaving a space of about thirty inches between it and the floor. Next they hinged the wire mattress to the trestles, so that there were full twenty inches between it and the bottom of the glass case. From the next box unpacked were taken seventy five cells of Grenet battery. These cells were of peculiar construction, and differed from the regular style in that the zincs were drawn up and held clear of the electropoion fluid by slight fastenings, which terminated in glass bulbs blown in the tops. Cobb had selected this battery on account of its great strength, and for the reason that it would remain inactive for an indefinite time, provided the zincs were kept out of the fluid. Placing an iron stand near the head of the case, he and Hathaway arranged the jars upon it, and connected the various cells for intensity.

The wires were then run through small holes in the top glass of the large case, being insulated with a special covering that would withstand age without deteriorating.

The next thing was to set in position, over the row of battery cells, an iron beam, with a fall of about four inches, the fall terminating in two sockets. This beam was held over and in position by a pulley, over which ran a wire rope composed of aluminum strands, and having attached to it a fifty-pound weight. Connected to the two poles of the battery were insulated wires, terminating in flat discs of copper.

These wires were about thirty feet long, and passed through the holes in the top of the glass case, the copper discs being inside.

From another box were taken two bottles of fine old French brandy, two bottles of whisky, a small bottle of Valentine's beef juice, and several cans of preserved meats, which had been prepared by Cobb, and the cans made of aluminum for the purpose. An alcohol heater was also taken out and set up in such a manner that a glass reservoir could, upon being turned on, feed it with alcohol. Through this heater ran wires joined to a platinum strip and connected with twenty cells of the battery. A cup and saucer, knife, fork, can-opener, spoon, and a couple of stew-pans, were next taken out and laid by the heater.

All these things having been put in order, Cobb, with the assistance of Hathaway, carefully lifted from a large box a heavy glass case, two feet nine inches high by three feet square. This case was set in the further corner of the chamber.

Through a door in the top, which Cobb opened, both Craft and Hathaway saw a number of wheel and pinion works, while at the bottom of the case was a circular piece of bright aluminum divided into equal divisions. The center of the ring was sunk into the glass bottom half an inch, and on one side of the ring was a number of small wheels and rods; the whole presenting the aspect of very fine and delicate mechanism.

Cobb now took out of the last box a large and very elegant compass, two feet in diameter and with a heavy needle; this he placed in the sunken center of the glass case.

Craft noticed that there was no iron or steel in the works in this box; nothing but aluminum, save the needle itself.

Through the sides of the case, Cobb adjusted an aluminum rod connecting with the pulley and weight attached to the beam over the batteries.

By this time the needle in the compass had settled and the positive pole pointed to 283 on the aluminum scale.

Both Craft and Hathaway had asked but few questions during all this work, curbing their curiosity until such time as their companion would enlighten them as to the meaning of all this apparatus. They had been on the point, a number of times, of asking for some information, but the other had, by a look, quickly given them to understand that he was not yet ready to explain things. But it was impossible for Craft to hold in any longer; he had to ask the use of this last glass case, with its many wheels and delicate machinery.

"Wait! You will understand it all soon," answered Cobb. "There is little more to do to-night." Then, taking a paper from his pocket, he scanned it for fully five minutes, making a few notes upon it with his pencil during the time.

At last, seeming satisfied, he bent over the compass in the box, and by a small screw in its side turned the whole delicately adjusted works around until a fine pointer, from which projected a tiny hook, became flush with the figures 260 from the zero of the scale, or to a reading of 4 degrees 20 minutes; then turning the whole compass-box around, he carefully adjusted it so that the needle should point exactly to the figures 993, equivalent to a reading of 16 degrees 33 minutes, the magnetic variation east, of San Francisco, California, in December, 1887.

It was easy to see that the little hook which hung down from the overlapping works would become engaged with the needle of the compass if the latter were to retrograde in arc 12 degrees 13 minutes.

Unscrewing a cap on the top of the case, he applied a small air-pump, which he had taken out of the box, to the opening, and screwed it firmly on; then, closing the glass door, he placed cement along the junction of the door and sides, from a bottle which he had brought for that purpose. In a few moments, the cement had set, and then, working the air-pump, he soon exhausted the air from the case; finally unscrewing the pump, he replaced the cap and laid the pump in the corner of the chamber.

All this being finished to his satisfaction, he announced that the work for the night was completed.

Looking at his watch, Cobb said:

"It is now four o'clock in the morning, and time that we should get out of this if we don't wish to be seen departing. We have done all that it is possible to do for the present; let us at once start for town; besides, you have to be at the post by six o'clock."

"Yes, that is true," returned Hathaway; "we are due at that hour. We have done a good deal of work, but for the life of me, I am totally ignorant of the purposes of all this apparatus. I would like to have you explain some of it to me," and his eyes turned inquiringly toward the large case with its wheels and compass.

"All in good time!" and Cobb cautiously opened the swinging panel.

The coast was clear; not a single person was in sight.

"Now, then, be lively!" and he stepped out, the others following quickly. In another moment the door was closed, and not a sign was left to indicate that the pedestal of the Statue of Liberty held within its interior the apparatus necessary for prolonging the life of a human being.

The three friends passed down the hill, and took the Haight-street cars for the city. It was the first car for the day, and not another passenger was on board.

Arriving at the Occidental, Cobb said:

"You are expected to be at reveille this morning, but I have no duties until retreat. There are a few things that I wish to attend to; so I will leave you here. Be sure to be at my quarters at 9:30 to-night. Good-bye!" and he left them without waiting for a reply.

It was nearly eight o'clock, and after a hearty breakfast, when Cobb left the hotel, passed down Montgomery street into Washington, and made his way to a small-sized house at the foot of an alley leading from that thoroughfare.

The windows of the house were all closed by shutters, and the whole building bore an aspect of dilapidation.

Ascending the four rickety steps that led to the door, he gave a sharp knock, repeating it after a moment, as no answer was obtained.

"Who knocks?"

"It is I, Colchis! Open the door."

The door swung open, and Cobb entered, the door closing behind him with a bang.

CHAPTER IV

It is necessary to go back a few months in our story, and introduce a new character, the inhabitant of the little old, dilapidated house in the lane.

On the evening of December 10, 1886, as Cobb was coming out of the Cosmos, a favorite club of the young gentlemen of San Francisco, he had run into an old and crippled man who was passing down the street. Cobb was in a hurry as he emerged from the place, and did not notice the poor pedestrian in time to avoid a collision. The consequences were that the old man was knocked to the ground, and appeared to be badly hurt. Cobb at once stopped and lifted the man up to ascertain the extent of his injuries, and finding him still insensible, had called a hack to convey him to the nearest druggist.

The man was about sixty years of age, his right leg partially paralyzed, the sight of his right eye gone, and deep scars upon his face and neck. His clothes were shabby and much worn, yet there were indications that the man had seen better days.

That portion of his face which was not scarred and seamed, gave evidence of quickness and perception, and a general appearance of knowledge and former refinement was plainly noticeable. His hands, too, were not those of a man accustomed to hard work.

This man was Jean Colchis, a native of France, but a refugee from that country. He had, in his time, been a great chemist; he had been noted, far and near, as a man greatly gifted in the sciences, and one who had given much to his native country in the way of scientific invention; but, at a later day in his life, he had been led away by the persuasion of others to engage in a plot against the ruling power of his land. This plot being discovered, he was sentenced to death, but, escaping, had taken refuge in the United States.

He was the recipient of a small pension from the members of his family who had not joined in the conspiracy, and upon this small pension Jean Colchis lived in the humble and rickety house in Duke's Lane.

The pension was sufficient for all the needs of the old man and his only daughter, a lovely girl of seventeen years; it gave them their daily sustenance and life, and a slight margin from which to purchase the few things he needed to continue the one hobby of his life, chemical analysis.

When Cobb had taken the old man to the druggist's, an examination had shown that nothing but a slight contusion of the side of the head had resulted from the unexpected knock-down he had received. He soon regained his senses, but was in a weak and helpless condition.

Learning from him the place of his abode, Cobb at once took him there in a hack, and carefully attended him during the remainder of that evening.

Such was the introduction of Junius Cobb to Jean Colchis.

Cobb's kindness to the old Frenchman was rewarded by an invitation to call again, and as he descended the stairs of the old, rain-beaten house, he resolved to come the next evening.

He did come, and many evenings after, and it was from this old man that Cobb first learned the art of making ozone in quantities. It was not a difficult matter for them to ascertain the various hobbies each possessed. Their conversation soon gave each an insight into the desires of the other for a knowledge of the many things yet unknown, but yet imagined. Their desires being so assimilated, their tendencies so coincident, it was only natural that each should take more than a common liking to the other.

But, though he had worked with Colchis in the manufacture and uses of ozone, the latter never had any idea of the grand scheme his friend had in view, for Cobb would not communicate the secret to him for fear that he might divulge it to others.

The door of the old house had opened to admit Cobb, and had closed again, leaving him in the hall. There was no light to guide him, but his knowledge of the place and surroundings was such that he found no difficulty in ascending to the little back parlor where Colchis usually sat when not at work.

Opening the door, he entered, and was quickly clasped about the neck by a pair of plump white arms, while a face, radiantly beautiful, looked into his, and a red pouting mouth invited the kiss which he quickly bestowed upon it.

"Oh, Mr. Cobb, I am so glad you have come! I heard you at the door, and have surprised you! Now, have I not? Say yes; for you know I have!" and the sweet little maiden released him, and shook her delicate finger in a menacing gesture, as if her command could not be disobeyed.

Marie Colchis was the only child of Jean Colchis —a beautiful, fair-skinned girl of seventeen, with long, heavy blonde hair; plump in form, with small, fine hands; loving in disposition, with most winsome ways; innocent as a new-born babe.

Jean Colchis had kept this sweet girl close to him with a jealous care. She knew no one, scarcely, save her father and Junius Cobb. Witty and bright beyond her years, yet gentle and innocent as a lamb, she had from the very first conceived a girlish love for her father's visitor. And Junius Cobb loved the girl dearly; loved to hear her girlish talk and watch her innocent ways; loved to stroke her hair, and loved to kiss her lips and feel her arms about him. Was there any harm? He was thirty-three, and she was but seventeen.

Jean Colchis noted their peculiar love, and

smiled. No man was closer to the heart of Jean Colchis than Junius Cobb. Nothing could the latter ask that the old man in Duke's Lane would not have given him—even his daughter, should he seek her. But this, of course, the old man knew was beyond expectation. It would have pleased his old heart, but the disparity of years caused him to believe it to be impossible.

And Marie—what were her thoughts and feelings?

She loved Junius Cobb—loved him, young as she was, as a mature woman loves the man she would call husband. She loved him with her whole heart, with her very soul.

Cobb knew this, and reproached himself many times for causing her affectionate heart to entertain the hope that she would sometime be his wife.

It had come by degrees, unseen by either, until each had felt that the brightness of the world was centered in the other. He could not marry her; this he knew, for she was too young. He could not wait until she had bloomed into the magnificent woman that he knew nature had destined her to become, for he would then be dead to the world. He could not tell her the truth! He did what thousands of others have done—he temporized.

"Marie," and he took both of her hands in his, and looked long and lovingly into her eyes; "Marie, you are not a child, you are a woman. You are far beyond your years. What I tell you to-night will cause you pain, but it must be said."

"O, Mr. Cobb!" she cried, and the tears flooded her eyes; "are you going to tell me that I am no longer your little Marie! that an—an—another is going to take you away from your little girl?" and she buried her head in his hands and cried piteously.

"No, Marie, not that!" he quickly returned. "But I am going to leave you; am going far away; I may never return!"

"And you will meet other and beautiful women, and will forget your Marie!" she said, still sobbing.

"No! darling little Marie! Will it give you pleasure if I tell you that I swear to be true to you—to wait until you have grown to womanhood? that I will marry no other woman living but you?" and he stroked her beautiful hair and raised her face to his.

"If you swear this, you do love me!" she cried through her tears; then, brightening up, she threw her arms about him, and murmured: "Though it will grieve me to the heart to see you leave me, yet your promise will ever tend to dull the sorrow of your absence, and will be a beacon light for me to look forward to. A few years, and you will come and claim me, will you not, Junius?" and as the words left her lips, she blushed and dropped her eyes from before his gaze.

Somehow, she had never before used his first name. It seemed to her that he was too far above her, too much older, for such a liberty on her part.

And how had their love ripened, these two of years so wide apart? Simply and easily enough. In one of his loving moods, Junius Cobb, in kissing her good-night, had said:

"Marie, I will wait until you grow up, and marry you!"

"Will you?" she had replied, laughing, yet earnestly. "Then, I accept you, Mr. Cobb, and will grow just as fast as I can."

Very simple, and very easy.

"Marie, little darling," and Cobb's voice was sad and low, "to-night I go far away. To-night we must part; but my sacred promise I give you, my girl darling, that when I return, you shall be my wife, *if living*."

He knew his deception, but it was better, he thought, to let her live without the knowledge of the utter impossibility of the fulfillment of her hopes, than to tell her the truth, and break her heart. She would outgrow her girlish love, he argued, and time would soften, if not deaden, the sorrow of his continued absence.

For a half-hour they talked, they loved, this man of thirty-three and the girl of seventeen.

Who can fathom the mysteries of love!

Leaving her in sorrow at his coming departure, but hopeful for the future, he moved toward the workshop of Colchis, while a choking sensation surrounded his heart, and tears filled his eyes.

Turning the knob of the last door at the end of

the hall, Cobb entered, and found his friend moving toward him.

The room was lighted by four Edison incandescent lamps, one in each corner, besides an arc light directly over a large and peculiar machine from which sparks were incessantly being emitted.

Like all true workers in electricity, Colchis apartments were a net-work of wires, while the various parts of the house were connected, in one way or another, for quick communication. The answer to the summons which Cobb had made at the door was given by a speaking-tube, while the door itself opened and closed by magnets; thus Colchis was enabled to remain in his room while answering the calls at his door made by the few who had occasion to visit him.

"Ah, Junius, my boy, welcome to the shop!" and the old man grasped the latter's hand. "I was expecting you this morning, sure; for it is now over forty-eight hours since you were here. What has kept you away?"

"Duty, master; duty." Cobb had early used the term master, in token of the ability of his old but generous friend.

"I was engaged the past two nights, and it was impossible for me to get here; but how progresses the work? Are you making a good showing, for you know the time is drawing near when I shall want the full amount."

"Yes; there are nearly eight pounds ready for you when you desire to take them."

"Good! It is close to the amount, I must say; and the batteries are still at it, I see."

"Will you take a look at the work of the day?"

"Yes; but yet, master, you know that I do not pretend to pass upon your work. I am too well satisfied that it is being well done."

They moved toward the sparkling and crackling instrument near the further corner of the room.

In reality, it was not what would be called an instrument, but a veritable manufacturing machine, turning out its products, small though they were, in the most perfect manner, and ceasing in its work but for a brief time during the whole twenty-four hours. This was the decomposing machine which Colchis and Cobb had devised and made for the concentrating of the ozone in the air. It was a rude affair, in one sense of the word, for neither of them had had any experience in making such machinery before; yet it was marvelous in other respects, for it accurately performed the duty for which it had been constructed. Standing upon four legs, was a glass case, about sixteen inches square by twenty deep, in the upper portion of which was a separate compartment with a glass bottom, having a hole some eight inches square through its center; on each side of this hole, with the points about one-sixteenth of an inch apart, were ten platinum wires, while the opening in the top terminated in a common stove-pipe, which was run into the chimney. Entering at the bottom of the case was a two-inch pipe, connected with a large double-cylinder air-pump, which in turn was coupled to a pony motor worked by storage batteries.

Along the other side of the room were twenty-four cases, each containing four accumulators of under .005-ohm internal resistance. These batteries were, individually, capable of developing 350 ampere hours of work, and each cell had an electromotive force of eight volts. A part of this battery was attached to the platinum points in the inside of the case, while the remainder was used to work the pump, feed the lamps in the house, etc.

The pump was an ordinary compressor of two cylinders, each cylinder having a capacity of 1,000 cubic inches. The total power exerted was 3,000 pounds every six-tenths of a second, or about thirteen actual horse power.

The air being received into the cylinder, was forced into the glass case through the pipe in the bottom, and under a pressure of two atmospheres; thus delivering, every three minutes, 200,000 cubic inches of air. The air, in rising, passed through the aperture above and out through the pipe, which was provided with a valve opening at a pressure of thirty-five pounds per square inch. Between the platinum points, by means of an automatic break, were continually being sent a series of electric sparks, causing the air to be deprived of its ozone.

which fell in vapor to the bottom of the glass case, and there formed into crystals of various sizes.

The machinery which Colchis and Cobb had erected was not perfect by any means, and the consequence was that they could not save all of the ozone in any given quantity of air. They did the best they could, saving about fifty per cent.

The air-pumps were capable of driving through the reduction chamber over 80,000,000 cubic inches, or 4,000 pounds of air in every twenty hours; but this vast amount yielded only 400 grains of ozone. The expenditure of force for the result obtained was enormous; but there was no other method for them to get the amount of ozone required, except with greater power and cost.

Early in July, Cobb had gained the assistance of Colchis to manufacture these crystals, and had put in the reducer, pumps, and motor immediately after.

Every evening at six o'clock, and every morning at five, a team drove up to Colchis' back gate, delivering new storage batteries and taking away the old ones.

Day after day, from seven in the morning until five in the afternoon, and from seven in the afternoon until five in the morning, since the 5th of August, the manufacture had been going on; making one hundred and twelve days' work up to the morning in question—November 25, 1887.

"Master, this is the 25th of August, is it not?"

"Yes, Junius."

"And you say the quantity that I asked for is nearly ready?"

"Nearly. At five o'clock to-morrow morning I will have 45,000 grains."

"Good! That is the amount, exactly."

"But at first you desired only seven pounds; I would have had that some time ago."

"Yes, master; but I did not care to have you stop at the exact amount; circumstances might cause me to wish for more, at the last moment."

"It has been incessant work for the machines, I can assure you; but they have done splendidly;" and Colchis laid his hand lovingly upon the reducer, near which he was standing.

"Colchis, how can I ever repay you for the time you have given to the manufacture of these crystals?" and Cobb took up a glass bottle with a sealed top containing a pound of ozone, the result of over two weeks' constant work.

"Say nothing about pay, my dear boy; it has cost you enough already, I fear; for the continual recharging of all these accumulators must take no small sum."

"True; it has taken quite a little fortune, to me at least, to obtain these eight pounds of ozone; but I hope the money has been well expended.

"Junius," and Colchis laid his hand upon the other's shoulder, "you have never told me what you are going to do with all this ozone. Is there a secret about it? If there is, my boy, you need not say a word; perhaps I ought not to ask you, but leave you to tell me, or not, as you wish."

"Colchis, my dear old friend, I ought to be more confiding, and tell you why I sought your assistance, why I have used your time, why I have taken your knowledge and used it to my own advantage; but it is impossible to make you acquainted with this one great object. Ask no more, I pray you!" and he turned away as if he had refused that which the other was justly entitled to request.

Putting his arm about Cobb's neck, Colchis looked him in the eyes with a kind and loving expression:

"Say no more; make no excuses; I surely would not pry into your secrets. We all have undertakings, we all have periods of our lives concerning which we do not care to communicate to the world. Your secrets are yours, Junius; I do not feel hurt in the least that you enlighten me not upon them."

"But I know your curiosity has been aroused, and you naturally have wondered why I have wanted all this ozone, especially when it has taken such an expenditure of money and time to procure it."

"Yes, it has; but it is gone now. I no longer have any curiosity on the subject. To-morrow morning I will have the full amount that you have requested, 45,000 grains."

"How much have I had already?"

"In August, a year ago, you had about ninety

grains, and in the following October, a little over 1,500 more."

"Yes; that was for the experiment with the cat."
He had spoken without thinking.

Colchis looked up, surprised; a curious expression came over his face, but he said nothing.

"Yes," he continued, "I remember now. There were about 1,600 grains made by the old process. Had we been compelled to follow that method, we would never have completed our task."

"True, my boy! It was a lucky day for you, I have no doubt, when we hit upon the idea we have since employed."

"Come," said Cobb, "let us sit down. I have a little more to speak of ere we part for the night."

They passed through the door into a smaller but neater room.

The furniture was plain and scarce, but the fire in the grate gave the room an agreeable appearance. Colchis touched a button, and instantly a bright light shone out from a pair of Edison lamps; then, handing Cobb a glass and bottle, taken from a pile of books and papers on the table, he said:

"Brighten up, Junius, with some of this old cognac; it is good, I can assure you, for we Frenchmen know what is good brandy. Had I a cigar, I would offer you one; but I do not smoke, so you will have to provide yourself with that article, if you smoke at all. Now, sit down," as Cobb finished his glass of brandy, "and tell me what it is that appears to worry you. Why are you so sad tonight?"

"There is not much to tell, master, except that this will be my last night to pass with you, my dear old friend; I am going on a long and dangerous journey, one from which I will never return—that is, to my friends now living. I go not to escape the consequences of any crime or wrong-doing, but to gratify my ambition alone. It would give me much pleasure, much happiness, could I but take with me such a dear friend as you have been; but it cannot be. Do not look startled, dear Colchis; I am not going to commit suicide; and yet, again, I am—suicide as regards all present, but not as regards the future. I will say no more, nor must you ask me any questions. For your kindness, I have only thanks to offer, unless you will confer a favor upon me by taking this check for $2,000 as a partial recompense for your labors in my behalf," and he laid the check upon the table.

Colchis arose from his chair, seized the check, and tore it into a hundred pieces; his eyes looked deep into those of his young friend, and then the tears came, and the old man sunk back into his chair. The friendship which had been so romantically begun between these two men was then, by Cobb, to be ended, and the sore healed by a money consideration!

"Junius, I did not believe that you would insult me in this manner! Our friendship has been one of the brightest spots in my life. Let it end if it must, but let it end with the feeling that each has aided the other to the best of his ability, and without hope of other recompense than the knowledge that the assistance was spontaneously and willingly given. You are about to embark in some new and great enterprise; of that I feel assured, yet I do not ask its import. If you must leave the old man, never again to see him—if you must sever the friendship that has been a Godsend to the refugee from his native land—so be it; I can say no word against it, believing you would not do it were it possible to do otherwise. Let us say no more upon the subject. At six o'clock to-morrow morning send to me, and I will have the ozone ready to be delivered to your man. There will be eight pounds of it, in as many bottles."

"Then, there is nothing more for me to do but to take your hand, dear, kind old master, and bid you a lasting but sorrowful farewell. May a good God watch over you, Colchis, is the last wish of your friend and pupil. Good-bye!" and, saying this, Cobb pressed the old cripple to his heart.

"Good-bye! my darling boy," sobbed the old man. "But, Junius, does Marie know this? The child loves you. She talks of you continually. Does she know you are going away forever?" and he put both hands on the shoulders of the young man and looked him in the eyes.

"Ah! master, master! Like a coward, like a cur,

am I running away! I have seen her! I have lied to her! lied, I tell you; lied to her! and because I had not strength to tell the truth!" He buried his face in his hands, and sobbed like a child.

"My son, cry not at what I am convinced you did for the best interests of that dear girl. My faith in you is not shaken. Let God alone judge our motives; mankind can do it not!"

"O master! I cannot leave you in this manner! To leave you now with the simple knowledge that I will never return, would be to provoke all manner of thoughts detrimental to my honesty and sincerity of character. You shall know all! I will confide in you my secret!"

Then by the side of this grand old man, Cobb sat and told him of his great undertaking, and of his love for his daughter.

Half an hour after, the door opened, and Colchis, with a face grave and sad, called to his daughter Marie.

Entering the room, she looked from one to the other, as if seeking some explanation of the quiet, sad expression of each.

Junius Cobb bowed his head, and the hot tears fell upon his hands. Colchis turned his face away.

Quickly going to her lover, Marie knelt at his feet, and gently raised his head until their eyes met.

"Do not cry, Junius; do not cry. I know you cannot help yourself. Duty calls you away, and you must go. Such, you have told me, is a soldier's fortune."

He clasped her to his heart.

"Marie," gravely and sadly spoke her father, "he leaves us to-night. When he returns, no man can tell. But let this comfort you: he has asked for your hand; your heart, I know, is his already. I have given my consent, and gladly. Let him go to his duty cheerfully, and await his return. If you are constant in the love you profess as a girl, you shall marry Junius Cobb, or no other. I swear it, as I hope for salvation hereafter," and he raised his hand toward Heaven in token of his oath.

Cobb raised his eyes inquiringly to those of his friend.

What did he mean by those words? Was he, too, imposing upon the girl's innocence? A strange light, a gleam of hope, of inspiration, shone in the eyes of Jean Colchis as he once more bade Cobb good-bye, and left the room.

Marie and Cobb were alone—alone for the last time: she, hopeful for the future; he, brokenhearted from a knowledge of what that future was to be.

"Junius, my own," she murmured, "go, and do your duty. God be with you, as will always my prayers. But go with this knowledge: that I swear by the God my mother taught me to adore, that I will wait till you come to me, will be true to you forever; will marry none on earth but you."

How beautiful, heavenly beautiful, was this girl, standing there under the electric light.

None can tell the passions that moved that man's heart.

Would he give up his great undertaking, and live and marry this Hebe, this angel? Too late! too late! The die was cast; he must meet his destiny!

With an aching heart, he kissed her good-bye—kissed her good-bye, and forever.

Into the chilly morning air he went, but there was no chill like the chill at his heart. Turning once toward the old house, he cried in his anguish:

"God watch over you and take you, for you are lost to me forever!"

CHAPTER V

It was the night of December 1st, and torrents of rain poured down, flooding the streets of the city and the grounds of the Presidio.

Seven had just struck from the little, old-fashioned clock on Cobb's mantel.

But few changes had taken place in that room since the last evening we saw our friends there.

The lights shone just as brightly, and the fire in the grate glowed with all its former heat and cheerfulness, yet an air of depression seemed to pervade the whole room and its occupants.

Cobb walked the floor with a quick and jerky step, while Craft sat silently watching the embers in the grate, as if trying to solve some abstruse problem by their aid. Hathaway lay at full length upon the long sofa, near the further wall, puffing a cigar and sending out the circles of smoke in a manner peculiar to men who are in a nervous mood.

From the time that his comrades came that evening, with the exception of a few words of welcome, Cobb had appeared in this abstracted manner, and had seemed to be totally oblivious to his surroundings. His friends had, with great perception, understood his feelings, and had remained in their chairs, preserving a dead silence, waiting for him to open the conversation.

At last, with a quick movement, he stepped toward a side-table and filled a glass tumbler with whisky, and drank it to the bottom; then, setting down the glass, seemed to be again absorbed in his thoughts.

Only a minute, however, did he remain in this position; for it seemed that the liquor had revived him and the depressing sense of gloom was passing off. Turning to his friends, he exclaimed:

"Am I not a coward, thus to seek energy and strength in that bottle of liquor? But I cannot help it; I am in the saddest mood of my life! Until this moment I have had only a longing for the time to come for me to make the experiment; but now that the time has arrived, I must admit that I am terribly loath to undertake the ordeal. O my friends!" he cried, "it is certainly impossible for you to understand my feelings! I am like the condemned man on the scaffold about to leave this world, with its pleasures and sorrows, never again to see those whom he loves; never again to associate with those who have been dear and kind to him. I am to enter into a strange condition; and when I again move, and walk, and see, if, indeed, I ever do, it will be to find that those who were dear to me are but dust."

Saying this, he buried his face in his hands, bowed his head, and wept.

His friends said no word, their own feelings almost overcoming them, but waited the passing of this transitory outbreak of the man's feelings.

"There, dear boy," said Hathaway, rising and putting his arms about the latter; "there, let it pass. We are convinced, that if it was required of you, you would undertake this task; but it is not required, so let it end here and forever."

"Yes;" and Craft joined his voice with that of his friend. "Yes; there is no need for you to suffer, no need for you to imperil your life for the sake of advancing the sciences. Let it end!"

Cobb brushed away the tears, and looked at them a minute in silence; then, with a quick, jerky tone, said:

"No, it is too late! My fate ordains it! I will— I will, I say, go through this ordeal! Were I to stop now, what would you think of me? that I was a coward and afraid to carry out my boasted theory!"

He paused a moment, and then his face brightened.

"Enough!" he cried. "It's all over now, and I am Cobb once more! Were I never again to see the light of day, yet would I venture this uncertain existence!"

The old fire of his eyes flashed forth.

Craft and Hathaway saw that it was useless to argue the question with him, and reluctantly submitted to the inevitable.

Striking a match, the latter said:

"So be it, Cobb; I deplore your undertaking, but I admire your pluck."

"Then to business," returned Cobb, "for this is my last night with you. Now, listen and understand well your instructions: My leave is here; countersigned this morning," and he touched his blouse pocket; "so to all inquiring friends to-morrow you are to say that I left last evening. All my property in this house is to be divided between you two, and to be yours forever, for I will have no use for any of it again, excepting a few things which I will take with me when I leave here to-night. The iron box which you see in the corner goes with us, as it contains papers and valuables which I hope to again see and use. This valise is packed with a few articles necessary upon our arrival at the chamber; with these exceptions, everything in all my rooms belongs henceforth to you both. In my laboratory you will find many interesting works and many valuable instruments; make such use of them as will improve your minds. My manuscripts are there also, and you will find much information in them. I wish you, Hathaway, to go to town and get the same teamster that we had before—you will find him at Neeland's, and his number is fifty-six. Drive to this address," giving him a paper. "where you will receive certain packages which will be ready; then drive to the old place where Craft remained with the driver before, and await his arrival. You must not go to the address until

11:30 o'clock, nor must you be at the rendezvous an instant before 12:30. Craft will meet you there at that time, and remain with the driver, while you will continue on to the pedestal. I will be at the latter place. Is that perfectly understood?"

Both signified assent.

"There is one other subject," he continued, "which is of the most vital importance, and concerning which I pray you make no mistake. At 127 Market street is a medium-sized safe, within which is a full account of all that which has transpired up to this morning, as well as a full account of what will take place, as regards myself, to-night. It contains all information necessary to enable the person who may open it, a hundred years hence, to locate my body and bring me to life, should my arrangements fail to fulfill my expectations. This safe has been sealed, and the key thrown away by me. Upon the door is the legend: 'Intrusted to the care of the Treasurer of the United States, and to be opened by him in the presence of the President and his cabinet, on January 1st, 1988.' With this safe is a letter explaining that the contents are of the greatest importance, and that it will be for the good of the nation that the same be well taken care of; and further, that it is desired and requested that it be deposited in the Treasury vaults until the day set for its opening. This safe will be transferred to you upon presentation of this order," and Cobb handed Craft a large envelope which he had taken from his inside pocket. "I charge you, upon your oath, to deliver it safely at the vault doors of the Treasury. Draw lots to see which of you shall take a leave of absence and take it to Washington. Gentlemen, be sure in this; it may be life or death to me."

Both of the others reiterated their promises to carry out every detail as desired by him, not only in this, but in all other things connected with the work he had in hand.

"Good! And now, Hathaway, away upon your mission. Craft and I will await the arrival of the hack."

Hathaway at once left the room, and passed out into the storm, while Craft settled himself down in an easy-chair by the fire.

Cobb wrote a P. P. C. card, and laid it upon the table.

"Give that," he said, "to the boys at the mess; it will be for a longer time than any of them think, I guess. When they read it, little will they think that that card will be faded, musty, and, perhaps, crumbling into dust when its owner calls at the club again. Ah, Craft, never before did I leave a farewell card with such feelings of sadness! They will take it in their hands, read it, and cast it aside with the single remark, 'Well, he'll be back soon.' Will be back soon! Yes: when their bones are dust; when their souls have passed out to their Maker; when they have each solved the grand problem of life!" Seizing the card in his trembling hand, he kissed it-"a brother's kiss, a parting kiss to those who are dear to me," he cried. "Ah, Craft, perhaps before theirs will my bones be mingled with the dust of the earth!"

Dropping the card from his hand, he bowed his head in sad contemplation of the future. His thoughts were turning back, once more, into a gloomy channel.

"Cheer up, Junius, and let us trust, dear boy, that you will successfully pass through the ordeal and live among men again. Have you completed everything that is necessary to be done? or are there some few things yet to be gotten ready?" Craft hoped to change the current of his friend's thoughts.

"Nothing. Everything is ready for me, and I hope—aye, I know—I am ready myself;" and he raised his eyes glittering with his powerful will.

"And to-night is your last with us? Oh, Cobb, I wish you would give this up!" imploringly said the other.

"No, no; oh, press me not, Craft!" and he looked beseechingly at his friend. "I must advance to my task; it is impossible to retrace my steps, yet God knows the heart-pains which rack my breast; He alone can fathom the utter misery of my position. From father, mother, brother, and sister, and from friends most dear I am soon to be parted forever— forever, *forever!* Hear you the word? *forever!*"

Like a wail of deepest anguish, prolonged and heart-breaking, came the last words, ending in a sob, as he sank into his chair and pressed his hands to his streaming eyes.

Let him not be called weak. He who could face death with a smile upon his lips, now cried at simple separation. But, alas! how much meant the word, separation—forever, *forever!*

The sound of carriage-wheels caused Cobb to start from his brooding. Raising his head, he glanced through the window just as the bright lights of a hack flashed along the road.

"Our time is up!" he exclaimed, with a strong effort at firmness; "there is our hack. Take that box and your coats, while I will take this valise."

Saying this, he arose and put the things together near the door; then entering the other room, he put out the lights. Returning to the front room, he and Craft took their several loads, turned down the lamps, and descended the stairs to the hack.

Could anyone have seen Cobb's eyes in that dark hall, he would have seen the tears falling many and fast. His anguish was great, and it was all that he could do to refrain from crying out in his pain. The quarters that had sheltered him for many a day and many a night, were being left behind, never again to be occupied by him. His books and instruments, the companions of many happy hours, were to be used no more. He had taken his last look upon them. Oh, it was hard! and his strength was sublime to overcome the tendencies to a complete breakdown, and a bursting into a flood of tears.

"Good-bye, dear old rooms! Good-bye to all that is in them—again, good-bye!"

Craft heard his sobs as he uttered the words, and his eyes filled to overflowing.

Down the walk they went without another word, and to the hack which was standing in the pouring rain, with its lights flashing out upon the night. There was no thought of the water that was streaming down upon them; other feelings filled their breasts. The door was thrown open, and Cobb motioned Craft to enter, and then followed himself.

"Drive according to your instructions," he said to the driver; and the door was closed upon them.

As they started away, Cobb turned to the glass window, raised his hand gently toward his old quarters and murmured sadly: "Good-bye! good-bye!"

Away they rattled down the road toward the main gate.

"It's a bad night, Craft." Cobb's voice was hard and forced, but it was evident that he was desirous of bringing his thoughts to other things.

"Yes, indeed it is; but good for us, nevertheless. How much warmer and drier are we in this hack than if we were outside to-night!" trying to put his thoughts into another channel.

"Number two! Half-past eleven o'clock—and all's well!"

"Number three! Half-past eleven o'clock—and all's well!"

And the cry was repeated on to all the posts, the answers coming clear and sweet to this poor, departing soul.

As the last sentinel gave his call, the carriage passed through the outer gate by the main guardhouse, where number one was walking his lonely and solitary beat. As they passed the porch, the sentinel repeated the round of posts, crying, in a sharp and pleasing tone:

"A-l-l's well!"

"A good omen, by the gods!" and Cobb half sprang up in his seat. "A good omen, and it is for me! I feel it! I know it! Away, then, with all sorrow, and let me feel that this is my bridal trip, instead of my funeral voyage. Come, Craft, we are clear of the post; sing me the old song of 'Benny Havens.' It will cheer us up and I want to hear the words once more."

"All right!" and soon Craft's soft, melodious voice swelled forth in the strains of that old song so dear to the hearts of every man from West Point. Softly, but with power, came the words:

> "Come, fill your glasses, fellows, and stand up in a row;
> To singing sentimentally, we're going for to go.
> In the army there's sobriety promotion's very slow;
> So we'll sing our reminiscences of Benny Havens, oh!"

And then Cobb's full voice joined in the chorus:

"Oh! Benny Havens, oh! Oh! Benny Havens, oh!
So we'll sing our reminiscences of Benny Havens, oh!"

As the last words of the chorus were sung, the lamps of California street shot their rays into the carriage.

On they went, but a silence again ensued, and neither spoke until the hack had reached McAllister street. Here Cobb caused the driver to pull up, and alighted, telling Craft to continue on until he came to where Hathaway was waiting for him.

He was then to transfer the iron box into the express wagon, dismiss the hack, and send on the team.

"You will find me at the appointed place," he said, as he passed down the hill.

The hack soon passed out of sight, and Cobb continued on until he had arrived at the pedestal. Seeing no one in view, he applied his hand to the spring, and was soon inside of the chamber. Striking a light, he was enabled to ascertain that everything was just as he had left it. Turning to the compass box, he was satisfied that it had not been disturbed, for the needle still pointed to 993.

Opening his valise, he took from it the eight bottles of ozone, a two-quart bottle of a thick, dark-brown liquor, several rolls of silk bandages, three or four small boxes, and a tumbler and sponge.

By the time these preparations had been completed, Hathaway drove up with the express wagon.

Dismounting quickly, the two men unloaded the contents, and carried them inside.

First there were two iron boxes; these Cobb laid at the head of the case on the trestles. Next was a very heavy iron cylinder, and then a barrel of plaster of Paris and a ten-gallon keg of water; finally, a wooden frame-work with a large screw and wheel to it, was brought in.

All things being gotten into the chamber, Hathaway drove back to where Craft was in waiting with the driver. The team was quickly transferred, and the driver dismissed, and watched until well on his way to the city. The two men then joined Cobb in the chamber.

It was now one o'clock in the morning of December 2, 1887.

Cobb turned some alcohol into the asbestos lining of the heater, and soon a bright and cheerful fire made the room quite comfortable.

The bottom of the glass case, which was hung upon hinges, was then taken off and laid upon the smooth floor, then some of the old boxing was laid out to form a mixing-board for the plaster. These things being satisfactorily arranged, the plaster was mixed by Hathaway and Craft, while Cobb commenced undressing. Stripping himself to the skin, he bound his hair back with bands of flannel, and then thoroughly oiled himself from his head to his feet, that the plaster might not adhere to his naked body.

"Is the plaster ready to set?" he asked, as he stood with his back to the fire.

"Yes," answered Craft, adding a little more water to the mass.

"Now spread the plaster upon the glass door, to the depth of two inches."

This was done, and in a minute it had set; then another spreading was made to a depth of three inches. As soon as this was laid upon the former mass, Cobb carefully stretched himself upon the whole and placed his hands by his side. The plaster gave way a little as his form sunk in it.

"Now," he said, "pile up the plaster until you have made it about five inches high, and I will remain in this position until it has set."

They did so, and in about five minutes Cobb arose from the door, leaving a perfect mold of his body.

Next, he bound his head and body with wide strips of cloth, surrounding the loins, and up to the lower parts of the breasts, with some fifteen wrappings. This being satisfactorily accomplished, he threw a greatcoat over his shoulders, and said:

"I will now explain the working of the various apparatus which we have placed in position. After I have wrapped my face, as I will show you later on, I will lie down within this mold; you will then place the door, supporting me upon it, on its hinges and close the catch. Through the small glass door in the upper part of the case, you will arrange this platinum tube from my mouth to the orifice in the side of the case, just here where this wheel is," and he pointed to a little wheel made on the end of a projecting tube through the side of the case. "Opening the small door, you will have free access to my body, and you will attach the bandages upon my face to the little spring catch which you see upon the inside of the case, near the upper part. Cover my face and bandages well with plaster of Paris, so that no entrance may be given to the ozone. Take those eight bottles of ozone, and quickly empty the contents upon both sides of my body, into the side troughs which you see, and at once close the door. I will take this position at 2:30 o'clock, and immediately take a dose of five grains of opium. In twenty minutes after, by your watches, you will turn this wheel on the side, one point, and every minute thereafter a point, until the forty-five points, or full revolution of the wheel, have been passed over. This is to shut off the supply of air gradually as the ozone commences to enter through the pores of my body. Have some fresh plaster ready, so that the instant this is accomplished, you can, by quickly opening the little door, pull out the tube from my mouth, and cover the opening with a spoonful of plaster; then, as quickly as possible, withdraw your hand, leaving the pipe inside, and close the door again and seal it with Portland cement. Before the ozone is placed within the case, see that the lower door upon which I lie is sealed by this preparation," and he took a medium-sized bottle, and gave it to Craft. "Now, as regards the compass-needle, I will explain its action." He moved over toward the instrument as he spoke, but suddenly started back upon discovering that the needle no longer pointed to the figures 993.

With a troubled look upon his face he gazed upon it. The needle now pointed to 1,007.8, or to a reading of 16 degrees 47.8 minutes.

"This is caused by some local attraction," he said, looking around. Then, suddenly: "Ah! I see it! It is caused by those two iron chests. But I fear it cannot be helped; for if they are moved into any other position, the attraction, though it might not be so great now, would be greater at some future time. It cannot be helped! I am sorry, for it will add nearly a year to my stay in this chamber. You perceive that the needle of that compass points to 1,007.8, or 16 degrees 47.8 minutes. That is the magnetic variation, plus 14.8 minutes for those iron boxes, of this place at the present moment. The magnetic pole is moving slowly toward the west; very slowly, indeed, but fast enough for me to utilize its movement. At present it is moving but 0.3 minutes per year, but this movement is increasing in a direct ratio of 0.145 minutes per year, which will bring the change in the variation, in 1988, to within 14.85 minutes of where the little hanging catch now is. My calculations were for one hundred years, but those iron boxes will carry it just one year longer, or to January 1, 1989. As I said, the needle will move 0.445 minutes toward the west this year, and 0.590 minutes next, and so on, arriving at 4 degrees 34.85 minutes on January 1, 1988; but this will be still 14.85 minutes from the little catch which you see hanging down. In one year from that time, it will strike it. The instant that it does do so, the fine wheel-work is released, and the heavy weight will cause it to move; this movement will drop the large beam upon the glass bulbs of the batteries, break them, and drop the zinc into the electropoion fluid. The batteries will then work, and I will have my power. The flask of alcohol is broken, its contents saturating the asbestos feeder, while a current heating to a white heat the platinum strip, starts the fire. At the same time the same current through these magnets withdraws the bolt holding the under door of the glass case in which I am: it falls by my weight, and I roll upon the bed-springs, while the door, relieved of its weight, closes again, thus shutting off the escape of the ozone. In descending through the bottom of the case, the bandages are torn off of my face, and another current of electricity passes through my heart by means of the proper discs. Thus, you see, I am released from my ozone prison into good and fresh air; the ozone is shut off, and my life is brought back by the shock of electricity. From the alcohol heater, which is by this time all aglow, I receive the warmth necessary to again set my blood circulating properly through my veins. Of course, I am weak, very weak; so I at once commence refreshing myself from the liquors in those bottles. After that I prepare some of the beef juice, clothe myself in one of the suits I have in that small iron chest, and I am a new man. If the air in the chamber is not pure enough for me, I have plenty in that cylinder, and can turn it on at any time, for it contains 8,000 cubic inches of air under pressure of twelve atmospheres, or, in round numbers, 96,000 cubic inches; giving me plenty of air for over five hours, without counting that which may be in the chamber. Before that time I will be out of the place. Last comes the wooden frame and wheel; that we will now set in position. I had this made for fear that I might not have the necessary strength to open the door when the time came; with it in position I can bring a pressure to bear upon the slab door of this chamber and burst it open, if need be. Do you understand it all now?" and he smiled at the curious expression on their faces.

"Yes," said Hathaway; "but why have you gone to all this trouble with that compass, when you could have put in good-sized springs, as well?"

"That is just it, my boy. I could not have put in a spring just as well. Had I used a spring, it might be rusted or broken by the time I would want it to work. Batteries could not be thought of at all, a they would not keep so long. In fact, I had to get something that was as sure in its work as the earth is in its movement around the sun. Nothing is more sure than that the compass needle will slowly turn back toward the west. It is simple and sure; why, then, should I seek for anything different?"

"I understand it all; your explanation is quite clear," said Craft. "It is a most marvelous and ingenious combination of natural laws with human auxiliaries."

Taking his watch out of his pocket, Cobb then said:

"The time is passing; let us at once to our work. You both know your duties; so commence."

At exactly thirty minutes past two, Cobb had taken the opium and had his nostrils, and mouth between the lips and teeth, filled with fine asbestos cloth, while strips of the same material were placed over his whole face, leaving but a small opening for the platinum tube between his lips. He had previously thoroughly saturated the bandages about his loins and body with the brown compound which he took from the bottles, and which he had informed them was the nourishment to give sustenance to his system during the period of his inanimation.

Lying down within the plaster mold, he told them to place the door in its position. Craft and Hathaway, by hard work, got it on to the hinges, and fastened the catch; then opening the little top door, asked Cobb if it was all right so far.

"Yes," answered Cobb, partly opening his mouth, and speaking through the filling. "Yes; it is all right. And now, no tears, no show of grief; let me say a lasting farewell. I thank you, dear boys, for all your kindness to me, and it grieves me sorely that I will never again see you; but such is fate! May God bless you a thousand fold, and watch over you through life, is my last wish! Take my hand, each of you; there, that is right; good-bye! Now fit the plaster well over my face, and look to your watches."

"Good-bye, dear old friend!" they both exclaimed, while the tears streamed down their cheeks. "Again good-bye! and God be with you!"

Craft then quickly broke the seals of the ozone bottles, while Hathaway placed the perforated vessel containing the stronetic acid at Cobb's head.

Craft then placed all of the eight bottles of ozone in the case, and, wrapping his coat about his arm to cover the hole and prevent the escape of the ozone gas, scattered the contents on either side of the body, but not touching the door upon which Cobb lay. Taking his arm out, the door was fastened, and their attention was given to watching for the time when they should commence turning the small wheel at the side of the case.

Save a slight raising of his finger in token of recognition of their last farewell, Cobb had not moved since the closing of the door.

At 2:41 his chest was rising and falling in a regular manner, while a slight tremor of the case denoted his heavy breathing.

As their watches showed 2:51, Craft turned the wheel its first notch. From that moment on, not a word was spoken by either of them, nor a sound made, save the sharp click of the wheel as it turned onward toward the 45th division.

They watched their friend through the glass cover; the heaving of the chest became less and less, the breathing lower and lower, while a purple hue settled upon his body.

At thirty-six minutes past four, the last division of the wheel had been reached. Craft then took a spoonful of plaster, and, inserting his hand carefully inside of the case, pulled out the tube from Cobb's mouth, and poured the half-liquid plaster into the hole in the cast.

Taking his hand out, the door was carefully fastened and cemented around its edges; the same thing was done around the edges of the lower door. They then put out the fire in the heater, and set the inside spring of the slab door of the pedestal.

Going to the case, Craft laid his hand upon it, and then, kneeling at its side, gave way to his grief, and the tears came thick and fast.

"Come, Craft," said Hathaway, whose eyes were also filled to overflowing; "come, old boy; it is all over. We have performed our part, and, perhaps, are accessories to a man's suicide. God be with him! he was a noble man, a true friend, and one we will never cease missing."

Craft arose, and they passed out into the cool morning air. The marble door swung back upon its hinges, the inside catch gave a sharp sound as it closed upon the latch, and Junius Cobb was entombed alive.

Quickly applying the cement to the edges of this door, as they had done to the glass case inside, the two friends, seeing that it was perfectly set, descended the hill and passed out of sight.

CHAPTER VI

For nearly five years, Jean and Marie Colchis occupied the old house in Duke's Lane.

The old man worked hard, and long hours were passed in arduous experiments. The ozone machine had performed its mission, and was a thing of the past. The hair on Colchis' brows was whiter, the lines of care on his face deeper, and his gait slower.

Fortune had smiled upon him. Money had rolled in, and the interior of the dilapidated old building was in strange contrast with the exterior. The rooms were handsomely furnished: bric-a-brac, books, a piano, and a thousand and one little *joujous* dear to the feminine heart, gave evidence of the hand that had wrought this change—Marie Colchis.

The seventeen-year-old girl to whom Junius Cobb had bidden a tearful adieu, had become a highly educated woman of twenty-one. The beauty of her youth grew with her years. Her disposition was commensurate with her beauty. The solace of her father in his age, the pride of his heart, she became the one object for which he lived and labored.

Often and often had this sweet girl asked of her father some knowledge of Junius Cobb. When would he come? Was it known where he was? and did her father think that he still remembered his old friends in Duke's Lane? Then, as her thoughts wandered to their last interview, with its sad parting, tears filled her eyes, and her bosom heaved and fell with deep, sorrowing emotion.

She still loved him; time had wrought no change. Her father saw it, knew it; and while a shade of sadness passed over his brow, he simply muttered:

"It must be done!"

Thus time passed.

A great invention was Colchis at work upon. It would astonish the world; it would make him famous for life; his wealth would become vast in the extreme. But none of these thoughts disturbed the calm equanimity of this great man.

He cared not for fame and honor, for his life was about run out. But wealth! Ah! that was another thing! He did want it; but for whom? Not himself? Who knows?

"They will want it, will want all I can give them," he said to himself many times.

Later on, there came many visitors to the house in Duke's Lane. They came singly, and sometimes in pairs. They remained a while closeted with the old man, and then they went away. They were scientists sent by the government to report upon the invention of Jean Colchis.

One day, after a more lengthy visit than usual

from one of these gentlemen, Colchis entered the little parlor where Marie sat reclining in a large chair, reading a book of poems.

Upon his approach, she quickly arose, and greeted him with warm affection.

"My daughter," he commenced, as he led her to a chair and seated himself by her side, "we are going to leave Duke's Lane. I believe the time has come when you should see more of the world; should mix in society, and take the place which your talents, beauty, and moral attainments give you by right. You are nearly twenty-one years old, highly educated, and exquisitely beautiful. You will make friends wherever you go, and you will have suitors by the score. With wealth, position, wit, and beauty, what more can you desire? Do not interrupt me, darling," as his daughter was about to speak; "I know what you would say: that your heart is given to Junius Cobb, and that you want no other suitors. I have had fears, Marie, that Junius would never come back to us in this world—that, perhaps, he is dead."

A cry of anguish burst from the poor girl's lips:

"Oh! do not, do not say that! He is not dead! You know it, father! Oh! tell me he is not dead!" and she sank at her father's feet, overcome with grief.

"O, God!" breathed the old man between his set teeth; "I fear it must be done!" Then, leaning over and stroking the golden locks of his daughter, he said:

"Marie, look up."

Her eyes, glistening with tiny tear-crystals, were turned up to his.

"Look into my eyes, my child, and listen well to my words. Do you love Junius Cobb as fondly now as when you were a girl, on the night when he said good-bye and left you? Answer me as your heart dictates."

"O, father! can you doubt it?" A heavenly look appeared in her eyes. "Would to God I could be with him in this life, or in death!" Her head fell upon her father's bosom.

"Then, life without your lover is worse than death?" and her father fixed his eyes in a hoping, expecting, desiring expression upon his daughter.

"Yes!" burst from her lips; "a thousand times yes! for what is life without him? If I be not with him in death, then death is oblivion!"

"My noble, true-hearted daughter!" and he folded her to his heart. "Your lover is true to you—that I can swear. Await with patience, my child, till God wills your union. Now, once more listen to my words: it is my desire that you enter the world of life and fashion, rule my house as its mistress; entertain, make friends, and let no worry enter thy heart. Do this, and if at the end of four years more, you ask for Junius Cobb, your betrothed, he shall come to you. I swear to you, my daughter, that my words are true."

"Father, I will do thy bidding." She wept tears of hope as she sank into her chair.

Soon the world of fashion, the society of money and brains, began to chipper-chapper of the new Crœsus and his divine daughter, who had suddenly come into their midst.

The Colchis mansion was among the finest of those beautiful homes which have made San Francisco famous as a city of palaces. His hospitality was prodigal; his entertainments fit for kings. He and his beautiful daughter were objects around which fluttered the culture, the fashion, and the wealth of the city.

Men came, saw the divinity, and worshiped at the shrine. Suitors implored her love, begged it, but without success. To all was Marie Colchis kind, honorable, and lovely, but to none gave she the slightest encouragement.

Time passed, and still she was the same. Suitors still persevered, but without success. Against her no word of disrespect could be uttered, none could bear feelings save of love and admiration; all spoke of her as the frozen sunbeam.

Colchis père saw it, and understood it; she could never change.

Then Jean Colchis arose one morning, and told his daughter that he must go away on important duty. His stay might be protracted to months, he could not tell her how long. She was to remain, and under the guardianship of her housekeeper, she should find what amusement she chose.

Their adieus were spoken, and Colchis sailed out of the Golden Gate in a ship of his own.

Months passed, and Marie Colchis grew sad and disconsolate. Her lover gone, and her father away, there was nothing to live for. Hours upon hours she sat and wept—wept tears of such sadness as only a heart bowed down by the most intense sorrow could cause to flow.

The house on the hill was closed to the world, and Marie lived but in the past, and with slight hopes for the future.

It was the 13th of March, 1897, and Jean Colchis had arrived home to his child. There was sadness in his eyes as he clasped his darling daughter to his heart; but a firm, determined expression overspread his countenance, as though he had fought some great battle, and felt himself the victor.

"Never again, dear old father, can I open this house to the world," she said to him, as they sat and spoke of the past.

"And never again shall you, my child," he had returned, holding her in a loving embrace.

"Let me leave the world and all it contains! Let me go and bury my body as I have my love! Father, I am dying!"

The time had come. Jean Colchis saw that not an hour was to be lost. Fate had ordained it; he must comply, though he murdered his beloved child!

"Grieve not, my child," he tenderly said, "the future is bright and assured. I am going to take you to your husband!"

Like a burst of the sun through a dark and dreary sky, her eyes lighted up, and she sprang toward him, clasped him around the neck, and covered his face with kisses. Then she arose, staggered, and fainted. The good news was too sudden.

Two weeks after this eventful day, Jean Colchis and his daughter sailed away in the ship which had once before borne him out of the harbor. As the vessel passed through the Golden Gate, the father and daughter stood at the rail and took one last look at the life behind them.

"See! dear father," Marie exclaimed, pointing to the shore on the south, while a bright smile illumined her face. "See! there is the Presidio, with its little houses! Junius lived there, once—Junius, my own, and to whom we are now hastening. God watch over him!"

"Amen!"

The words came sadly from the old man's lips. Thus they sailed away, and never more was word heard of them by the living world.

The years came and passed, but these two loving hearts came not again to the haunts of man.

And the other—Junius Cobb? He lay an inert mass in the pedestal of the Statue of Liberty, on Mt Olympus.

CHAPTER VII

A beautiful day it was, this 19th of June, A.D. 2000; to be sure, the sun was sending down its rays with a trifle more heat than was agreeable, but all things considered, it was one of those lovely days which one sees, in the month of June, in Washington.

The heads of the various departments had not yet left the city for their summer vacations in the country, but were hard pressed by the business required of them by Congress; for that body was still in session, as the national legislature did not end its work until the first of July.

In the Treasury building, Treasury Square, all was bustle and activity, and clerks and messengers were flying in every direction.

At his desk in the sumptuous office provided for him, sat Mr. Brett, the Treasurer of the United States; while near him, quietly smoking a cigar, sat Mr. Peck, the first assistant to the Treasurer.

They were quietly discussing matters pertaining to their department, and evidently had plenty of time on their hands.

It was 14:10 by the large dial on the wall, and near the time when the Secretary of the Treasury would ask for the final papers for signature for the day. A huge stack lay upon the table awaiting this call, and the two chiefs were only remaining to send them to him.

As the hands of the dial marked 14:15, a sharp knock was made upon the door, and immediately after, Mr. Lane, the second assistant, entered the room accompanied by Mr. Howell, a subordinate officer in the Treasury Department.

"Well, Mr. Lane, what is it? Have you any more business?" asked the Treasurer, looking up.

"Yes, sir," answered that gentleman, with apparent excitement. "Yes, sir; I have some papers here which I think may be of very great importance. As Mr. Howell was going through the old store-room containing the records at the close of the administration of 1908, he found this bundle, marked as you will see by looking at it. Deeming it my duty, sir, to at once acquaint you with the fact, I have brought it here." Saying which, he handed the Treasurer a small package of papers, bearing upon the brief-side this indorsement:

"TREASURY DEPARTMENT,
WASHINGTON, January 29, 1888.

"This paper is this day deposited with the Treasurer of the United States, by Hugh Craft, Second Lieutenant in the First Artillery. With it is also deposited an iron safe, presumably containing the papers referred to in the body of the communication. Entry of the papers is made in book 'C,' folio 476. This document is to be transmitted from Treasurer to Treasurer, as they may be appointed, until its contents can be complied with; which will be by the Treasurer serving in 1988.

"CONRAD N. JORDAN,
"Treasurer of the United States."

The Treasurer took the paper in an unconcerned manner and glanced over the brief. Looking over his glasses, he said:

"Well, Mr. Howell, I see nothing about these papers that requires my attention. Undoubtedly they have been long ago acted upon by the proper authorities," and he handed them toward that gentleman.

"But the inside, sir," quickly returned Howell. "I must admit I read it, and so found out that it was of importance, even at this late day. It contains an account of a safe to be opened in 1988, and which has been deposited in the vaults since 1888. Now, if such a safe had been opened in this department in 1988, or since, I would have known it; for, as you know, sir, I have been here over fifteen years. I think, sir, that this communication has been mislaid long before the time set for opening the safe, if, indeed, any such article is in the vaults, and that it might require investigation."

Mr. Brett seemed a little more interested in the matter, as he again turned the document over in his hand; then opening it he read its contents.

In silence his subordinates watched him, and noticed an increasing excitement in his manner as he progressed.

This was the letter which Cobb had written and sent with the safe, and of which he had spoken to Craft and Hathaway.

Having read the main document, the Treasurer returned to the briefs and saw that it had been transmitted by five Secretaries, as their indorsements were upon it; but after the year 1904 no more indorsements were made, and it was apparent that the paper had been mislaid since then. Handing the bundle to Mr. Peck, the Treasurer said:

"That is a most curious document, I must say. Can you make anything out of it?"

The latter perused it carefully, and also looked at its indorsements.

"If such a safe is now in the vaults," he answered, returning the communication, "it should be looked after at once, for the time has long since passed when it should have been opened. Perhaps you did not notice that the last indorsement says that the safe was deposited in the certificate vaults on January 7, 1904, by Treasurer Chamberlin. I think it would be well to look into this matter; and if you wish it, I will at once attend to searching that vault."

"I quite agree with you, Mr. Peck, that we ought not to let this matter drop without at least trying to discover if the safe mentioned in the paper is now in this department. I wish you would take the matter in hand and thoroughly search the old vaults, especially the one mentioned as containing the safe on January 7, 1904. Notify me if your labors are rewarded by success. Good morning," and the Treasurer bowed to Mr. Peck as the latter left the office. In passing out, Peck motioned to Mr. Howell to follow him.

The vaults of the Treasury were cut up into many small and minor vaults. Some had been used for the storage of old documents of the department which had no further value than that, by law, they could not be destroyed. One series of these latter were the certificate vaults containing the stacks of fraudulent certificates used by the Chinese, in the latter part of the nineteenth century, to gain admission into the country, and in one of which the safe was supposed to have been deposited.

An investigation was at once made by Peck and Howell in these vaults, and resulted in complete success; for, hidden behind huge piles of papers and boxes of documents, was found the small safe taken to Washington in 1888, by Hugh Craft.

It had taken several hours for the two men, with the aid of a couple of janitors, to unearth, or rather unpaper, the iron box; but it was there, nevertheless, and they read the legend painted upon it with many expressions of wonder.

At 10:30 the next morning, when the Treasurer came to his desk, they reported the result of their search, and informed him that they had gotten the safe out into the main corridor of the vault, awaiting his orders.

Mr. Brett immediately accompanied Peck down to the vaults, and saw for himself the safe. He read the legend upon it, and could not conceal his astonishment: the letter was genuine, and the safe was there.

The contents of that iron box had been placed in it over one hundred and thirteen years ago! What were the secrets it contained? Why was it sent to the Treasurer of the United States, with instructions not to be opened before a hundred years had passed? Why was it not opened at the proper time?

All these thoughts quickly passed through the Treasurer's mind.

Carefully noting the inscription upon the door of the safe, he informed Mr. Peck that he would at once communicate with the President upon the subject. He then went back to his office.

At 11:15 that morning the President was informed that the Treasurer of the United States had most important business with him, and desired an immediate audience; it was granted him. The President was sitting in his private office, in the executive mansion, and received the Treasurer with a kind smile of welcome as he entered.

Mr. Brett immediately communicated the purport of his mission, and handed the President the letter which had been found.

Mr. Craft, the President, seemed greatly surprised at the communication, and taking the letter, read it carefully—both it and its indorsements.

"Delivered by Hugh Craft, of the army," he read, to himself; then aloud:

"Why, a namesake of mine! I have had relatives in the army for many years; I wonder if this man could have been one of my ancestors?"

Taking down a large volume from an upper shelf of his book-case, he quickly turned the pages under the date of 1888. "Yes; yes, it is here," and he followed on for several pages more; then, referring back, read:

"'Hugh Craft, Second Lieutenant, First Artillery, July 1, 1886; First Lieutenant, September 15, 1891; Captain, October 6, 1906; Major, October 14, 1916; killed at the battle of Ottawa, August 5, 1917. Married Augustine Phelps, May 28, 1890. Children: Edward, born September 12, 1891; Harry, born May 4, 1894; Mabel, born December 11, 1906.'"

Then, turning over the pages, he continued:

"'Edward married in 1916 and died December 22, 1937, leaving three sons; one of whom, Arthur, married in 1940. Arthur died in 1981, leaving one son, Emory D., born June 19, 1941.' And that man is myself. It is most strange that I should at this late day receive a communication signed by my great-grandfather. Whatever the contents of this safe may be, they are in some manner connected with me, and I am most anxious to at once unravel the mystery."

Rising from his chair, he touched an electric bell, and upon its being answered by an orderly in the uniform of the President's guards, sent a summons to his Cabinet to immediately meet him at the Treasury building, he then called for his wraps and signified his intention of at once proceeding with Mr. Brett to the Treasury and opening the safe.

In about an hour afterwards there were gathered in the office of the Treasurer the President and all the members of his Cabinet, and Mr. Brett, the Treasurer. The gentlemen, upon request of the President, then proceeded to where the safe had been drawn out into the corridor.

There it stood, apparently in as good condition as when first sent to the Treasury, save a slight discoloration caused by time. The legend was still plain, and the party surveyed it with much curiosity. The combination of the lock, of course, was unknown to any of them, and the key-hole was of no use, as none had a key to fit it. The services of a couple of machinists were soon procured, and the outer door quickly yielded to their efforts, and was torn from its hinges, exposing a large plate-glass door, behind which were plainly seen several articles.

Breaking open this door, for it was cemented around its edges, the contents of the safe were soon in the possession of the President.

First was a bundle of papers, then some newspapers of 1887, and finally three photographs in well-preserved condition, though brown with age.

The bundle of papers was first examined. They

gave the whole secret of Cobb's intention of undergoing the ordeal of the cataleptic state, together with all that which had taken place up to the evening of December 1st, 1887, as well as what would follow on that night, and complete directions as to what was necessary to be done to again bring him to life should he not gain his natural state by the means he had prepared. Full mention, with the names of Craft and Hathaway, was made of their share in the work, and the photographs were of himself and his two friends. His leave of absence, also, was among the papers, and proved, by its signatures, its genuineness.

Upon intimation from the President, the whole party repaired to the office of the Secretary of War, where the papers were carefully read, and a deliberate consideration of the matter undertaken.

The records of the War Department for the years 1887 to 1950 were then sent for, and the record of Cobb and the other two found.

Opposite Craft's name was the entry, "Killed at the battle of Ottawa, August 5, 1917;" after Hathaway's name, "Died of wounds received at Bovispe Hacienda, Mexico, March 17, 1915;" while after Cobb's name were the words, "Dropped from the rolls of the army as a deserter, to date from December 1, 1904, under the provisions of section 1229 of the Revised Statutes, no report having been received from him since December 1, 1887."

All those present read the instructions contained

in the bundle of papers all saw the photographs, and all read portions of the newspapers which were found in the safe. The signatures of both Craft and Cobb were carefully compared with those which were made in the old signature papers attached to the record-book, and found to correspond exactly.

All present agreed that everything was perfectly genuine, and that the articles had been placed in the safe about the time specified.

"This is a very remarkable affair, gentlemen!" finally exclaimed the President, after again looking over the documents. "This paper directs that the place of entombment be opened by the first of January, 1988, or as soon thereafter as possible. It is now the 20th of June, A. D. 2000; quite a long time after that set by Mr. Cobb for giving him assistance is it not? If he has done what he says he has, in my opinion, the man is long since dead. The mislaying of the first document was a culpable act on the part of the administration of 1908; but it is our duty to remedy it, if possible. I know of nothing to do but to send at once to California and open the statue spoken of in this letter. If the man is dead, we may at least learn something more of his strange undertaking. I feel a personal interest, aside from that of my office, in this matter; for it appears that my great-grandfather was an accessory to this man's foolish venture, and I would do all in my power to repair his wrong-doing. Mr. Miles, I desire that you take measures at once to solve this mystery and, if possible, render some aid to the man Cobb, if, indeed, it be not too late."

The Secretary of State answered that everything would be done that was possible, and that men would that afternoon leave on the Central Pneumatic for California. He arose, bowed to those present, and retired.

At 16:30 that afternoon, two men, with grips and coats, left Washington on the Central Pneumatic for California.

The distance was a little over 3,600 miles, and the party arrived at its destination at 11:25 the next day.

An immediate call was made upon the mayor and council of the city, and the purport of their mission disclosed. Full arrangements were soon made for going to the Statue of Liberty, which still occupied Mt. Olympus, and was apparently in as good condition as when placed there in 1887, and ascertaining if the disclosures contained in the safe were true or not.

San Francisco had grown so much that the statue no longer occupied an isolated position on the outskirts, but was entirely surrounded by large and beautiful dwellings, and that part of the city was now densely populated.

As it would not be well to have the mission of the party known while working into the base of the pedestal, it was decided that no entry should be attempted before the following midnight. The two gentlemen, having taken dinner, proceeded with their arrangements, and soon had procured the services of four strong men to open the supposed chamber.

As the dial struck the hour of twenty-two that evening, two hacks passed quickly up Haight street, and thence to the foot of Mt. Olympus, which, though surrounded by residences, was yet bare upon its top. Leaving the carriage in two parties, the occupants cautiously proceeded to the statue.

It was a quiet night, and in that part of the city few persons were about, and none in the vicinity of the top of the hill. The moon was in its first quarter, shedding very little light, and in consequence dark-lanterns had been provided.

Albert Rawolle, the chief of the party which had left Washington, and who had charge of all the preparations, was a cool and quiet man, and well fitted to superintend such a piece of work. Stationing two of his men in position to guard against surprise, he commenced operations on the northeast corner of the base. He had made a careful survey of the whole structure, but could find no signs of an entrance, so had selected that corner as affording an easier task for his men.

At 23:55 the work was commenced, and the picks were driven into the hard joints with quickness and dispatch, soon making a large breach in the wall. At 1:25 one of the men drove his bar through the side, piercing the wall into the chamber. Quickly enlarging the opening, bull's-eye lanterns were held to the hole, and the interior was bared to view.

As their eyes gradually became accustomed to the gloom, all the contents of the chamber were brought to their vision: the cases, the batteries, the boxes, and all the many things which Cobb had placed therein a hundred years before.

There were no signs of life, however; everything was as cold and silent as the grave.

The first moments of their excitement being over, the men went to work with increased vigor; for there was, indeed, something more than ordinary in this place—something true in the letter of instructions left in the safe; there was about to be disclosed to the world a most marvelous fact in the history of mankind.

With alacrity the men worked and toiled at the breach, and soon it was opened to a full foot in diameter. A moment later, as one of the men gave a rather more powerful blow than usual, his bar slipped from his hand and went crashing into the chamber.

With the exclamation of the man came a sharp, crashing sound from within, followed by a flood of light. Everyone jumped to the opening, and gazed within the chamber, while a superstitious shudder ran through each, and it seemed to them as if their very hair was rising on end.

"My God! Look!" excitedly exclaimed Rawolle

to the others, and his voice seemed hoarse and hollow. "Look! there is a man moving inside the chamber!"

With eyes almost protruding from their sockets, the men gazed through the breach. Indeed, it was enough to try a man's nerves; for within that chamber which but a moment before was wrapped in total darkness, in cold, and apparent death, was now light and life, and a man was slowly rising from his bed, with his hands pressed against his breast. They watched him as he moved feebly toward the fire, which they could not see, but which they knew was there by its reflection.

They could not speak, so strained were their nerves; but their eyes followed every motion he made. They saw him turn to the fire and slowly rub himself with his hands; then take a bottle, and striking its top against the side of the fire-place, break it open and take a deep draught of its contents, giving no heed to its broken and ragged edges. They saw him open a chest and take from it what appeared to be a quilt and throw it around him, and then, seating himself at the fire, continue the rubbing as before.

Lyman, Rawolle's assistant, was about to speak, but the latter motioned him to silence, saying, under his breath:

"Hush! let us see what this all means—what this man will do; for it is a scene that may never again be enacted upon this earth."

Cobb, for he it was, as is already surmised, did not sit long in front of the fire, but soon arose and took from his breast and back the two copper discs which were held in place by a band; then tearing off the bandages from the lower part of his body, he threw them to one side; next he placed upon the fire a small stew-pan, filling it with the liquor from another bottle which he had taken up and opened.

In a minute the savory odor of cooking meat came to the nostrils of the watchers, while Cobb, taking it from the fire, poured it into a cup and began drinking it. Five minutes longer they watched him, during which time he had finished his repast, and had partially arrayed himself in clothing which he took from one of the boxes.

No longer able to restrain himself, Rawolle placed his head within the breach, and in a quiet tone of voice, so as not to startle Cobb, said:

"Your friends are here and waiting to assist you; what shall we do? See! we are at this hole which we have made endeavoring to gain entrance to your cell."

As the words were spoken, the sound seemed to startle even the speaker, as well as the others, and Cobb turned, and for a moment shook as if some terrible vision had passed before his eyes; but, as the faces of the men were distinctly visible by the reflection from the fire and the incandescent lamp above it, he soon regained his composure, and in a weak voice asked:

"Who are you that have dared to break into this place? By what misfortune am I thus disturbed and my plans upset? By whose authority do you come? Have you gained the knowledge through Mr. Craft or Mr. Hathaway?"

"It is by the order of the former, sir, that we have broken into this chamber," replied Rawolle, not knowing the exact import of Cobb's question.

"Alas!" murmured Cobb, "are there no true friends on earth?"

With trembling limbs he sank down upon a box near the fire, but just in view of the others.

"We are ordered to rescue you, Mr. Cobb," added Rawolle; "and your weak condition demands immediate succor. Waste no time, we implore. It is the President's order."

"Whose order?" quickly exclaimed Cobb.

"President Craft's."

Weak as he was, Cobb sprang toward the opening through which Rawolle was speaking, and excitedly cried:

"Is it not 1887? Who is President Craft? I never heard of him. Tell me, what is the year? Are we in 1800 or 1900?"

"Neither, sir," answered Rawolle. "It is A. D. 2000."

"My God! Have I been asleep since 1887?" and he pressed his hands to his brow, clutching his hair as if endeavoring to tear aside the veil of the past, that a realization of the moment might be made plain to him. "Have I slept a hundred and thirteen years? Am I now alive? or is this some terrible nightmare? No! no! I heard your voices! I live! I live again! Thank God! I have not failed in my undertaking." He looked around him in a dazed manner.

"But can we not help you?" broke in Rawolle; "you have no time to lose in your weak condition. Tell us at once what we are to do; it will take over an hour to enlarge this breach. Have you no door, or mode of entrance?"

"Yes; there was a door, but it was sealed up after I entered this place. Go to the other side of the pedestal, and I will try to open it."

They all passed around as directed, and Cobb applied himself to the wheel and gearing. Weak as he was, it became somewhat of a difficult task for him to turn the screw, but the mechanism had been so perfectly adjusted that it revolved even by his feeble strength. Lifting up the spring catch, he slowly turned the screw, and the door opened upon its rusty hinges.

A moment later, all were in the chamber of the Statue of Liberty.

Astonishment was depicted upon the countenances of all, as they beheld the interior of the chamber and its peculiar contents. But Rawolle gave no heed to the strange condition of the place; his thoughts were upon Cobb, who lay upon the floor, where he had fallen, unconscious, after opening the door. Quickly seizing him, they bore his body to the fire and rubbed back the departing life. His legs and arms were stiff from long inaction; his face was wan and his form somewhat emaciated. Their work was soon rewarded by a return to consciousness of their patient. Rawolle opened the box from which he had seen the clothing taken, and soon Cobb was clad in warm, comfortable garments. Ten minutes were consumed in preparing fresh broth and administering to the weak man's wants.

Cobb's strength returned quickly to him, thanks to the liquor and beef juice, and he moved from the fire toward the compass case.

"You say it is A. D. 2000?" he asked again; "are you not joking me? Is it indeed that year? or, rather, is A. D. 2000 this year?"

"For a fact," answered Rawolle. "It is as I tell you; and we are now in the year 2000."

All the others joined Rawolle in assuring Cobb that he was not the subject of any jest; it was just as had been told him.

"I cannot understand it; I cannot see why I have lain so long. I should have been awake years ago, in 1988; something has gone wrong," and he moved closer to the compass case. "It must be here, if anywhere," and he leaned over the box and gazed upon the needle and wheel-work. An instant only he looked, and then he sprang back and exclaimed:

"Ah! what is this?" and an expression of blank astonishment came over his face. "What is this?

The needle of the compass not at 260, but still far away to the east of it!" and he examined it most carefully.

There it was, not at 260, but away to the east of those figures—at 899, or to the reading of 14 degrees 59 minutes. There was some mystery about this that sorely puzzled the brain of Cobb.

As the others attempted to speak, he bade them be silent until he could solve this problem.

Looking down, his eye fell upon the iron bar which the workman had let slip through his hand in opening the breach. It rested just under the aluminum rod attached to the wheel-work. From the bar his eyes wandered inquiringly from one to the other.

"It shlipped out of me hond in making ther hule," said the man who had dropped it into the chamber.

The mystery was solved. The iron bar, in slipping through the workman's hands into the chamber, had struck the aluminum rod and set the wheel-work in motion; everything else had worked perfectly, and as Cobb had designed that it should work. But one other thing troubled him very much, and that was why did the compass-needle mark 899 instead of 260, as it ought to do?

"Give me a pencil and paper," he said to Rawolle, "and be still but a moment, and I will answer your questions."

The materials were given to him, and he busied himself a moment in putting down some figures.

"Yes, as I thought," he soon exclaimed, throwing down the pencil. "It was I who made the mistake. Gentlemen, you see that needle marking 899," and he pointed it to them. "Well, a hundred and thirteen years ago, or, more accurately, in December, 1887, it marked 1,007.8. I computed that it would move to where that catch now is, at 260, in one hundred years; but, like many another man, I made a most simple error. In my work, I read 14.355, instead of 1.4355—the mere misplacing of the decimal point. It came near costing me my life. Instead of the needle moving 732.7 points, as I thought it would, it moved but 73.27 points in the hundred years that I anticipated remaining here. It has moved only 108.7 points in one hundred and thirteen years."

It was well that Cobb had made this great mistake, for the movement of the magnetic meridian was, in reality, so slow on the meridian of San Francisco, that he could not have used it with any degree of safety. One hundred and eight points, or an arc of 1 degree 48 minutes, was too small to work upon, as any great magnetic storm, earthquake, or other disturbance might have caused it to oscillate over such a small arc and spring the wheel-work. In fact, the needle, as Cobb had set it, would not have arrived at the little catch before the middle of June, A. D. 2198.

Without losing another moment, Cobb wrapped himself in a heavy overcoat taken from the iron box, and requested Rawolle to take the other box with him, and to take him to a hotel at once, as he needed rest and refreshment.

The party then left the chamber which had been Cobb's abiding-place for so many years, and proceeded to the Occidental Hotel, leaving a man to guard the place and its contents.

Arriving at the hotel, Cobb was at once shown to his room, and refreshments ordered; later on he detailed the whole story of his long and death-like sleep, and received, in return, all the information concerning the finding of the safe and the mission of Rawolle and Lyman.

Despite the secrecy with which all had been done, the papers of the next day contained the following:

"MOST WONDERFUL!

"IS IT A HOAX? IS IT TRUE?

"ONE HUNDRED AND THIRTEEN YEARS ASLEEP, BUT NOW ALIVE!

"Junius Cobb, a Lieutenant in the Army in 1887, was Last Night Taken from a Chamber Cut in the Solid Masonry of the Statue of Liberty on Mt. Olympus.

"The Rescue Made by a Party Sent from Washington.

"The Paraphernalia Still in the Base of the Pedestal.

"The Story of the Guard Who was Left to Prevent Entrance into the Interior.

"The Man Now at the Occidental Hotel.

"Copy of the Dispatches sent by the Chief to the President of the United States."

And then followed column after column of the news, which startled all San Francisco at nine the next morning, when the extra edition was sent into the streets.

Thousands upon thousands of people visited Mt. Olympus after twelve had struck that day, and by midnight of that 22d of June, A. D. 2000, the whole world had heard the news, and wondered and wondered.

CHAPTER VIII

The sun was streaming into Cobb's eyes; he was restless; he awoke. The room was empty, not a soul in sight, and he lay in his bed, all alone. How long he had lain there he could not tell, but he knew it must have been some time, for his bones felt sore, and he had a great desire to get up and stretch himself. The room was the same that he had entered the night before; of that he felt assured as he glanced around.

For some time he lay half awake and half asleep, his thoughts running in a most confused channel. In memory he wandered back to his old friends, Craft and Hathaway. He was living, but where were they? And his kindred, where were they? Dead! all of them! Not a single soul of all those whom he had known and associated with were living. Indeed, he was alone in the world! In his mind, once again he viewed the longings and cravings which he had cherished for a knowledge of what the world would be at a future day, and the vision materialized into a full knowledge that at last he had the power he so long had desired. What a wonderful experience! What a remarkable transition he had passed through! He had become a king, an emperor, a very god, for he had annihilated time, and passed, in a second, over many score of years. Was he to find such changes in the world as he had anticipated? Was he to be satisfied with things as he should find them now? Had he thrown away a life of quiet enjoyment and comparative ease, among his friends and kindred, for a new life in which he would be dissatisfied, miserable? Was the light worth the candle? All these and many more were the questions he asked himself as he lay there awaiting the approach of some one from whom he might possibly receive an answer. He could lie there no longer; he must arise and be about. Had they all deserted him, that he was thus left alone? No, that was hardly possible; they would soon come. He rose upon his elbow and looked about the room.

No sooner had he raised himself in his bed than a door opened and a man entered and quickly approached his bed.

It was Lyman, and Cobb instantly recognized him, though he appeared to be so differently dressed from the style which he was accustomed to seeing that it made him doubt his identity.

Approaching close to him, Lyman looked into his eyes with a searching expression, as if endeavoring to fathom his very thoughts.

Still upon his elbow, Cobb returned his gaze and asked:

"Well! is it time to get up? Why do you look at me in such a manner?" and a feeling of fear ran through him that he might be laboring under a hideous dream, and that he was not only alive again, but had never been dead to the world, as he thought.

The sorrowful expression of Lyman's eyes disappeared, and a glad smile parted his lips.

"Thank God, my boy, you are yourself again! We have watched you for a long time, hoping for this return to consciousness. Do you indeed know me?" and he leaned over and took the other's hand.

"Of course I know you. Have I been sick? have I lain here long? Has everything been a dream? or am I awake in the new era?" and as he asked the question, he sat up in bed.

"You are laboring under no delusion, Mr. Cobb," Lyman replied, smiling at the man's eagerness on the subject. "You are the same man whom we rescued from the pedestal of Sutro's statue, and you are still in the land of the living, after years of inanimation. You have had a long and most severe struggle for your life since being brought here on the night we dug you out of the pedestal. It is now the 16th of September, almost three months since your release, and you have lain upon your bed or sat in your chair nearly all the time. Your mind has wandered, and you have known no one until to-day. We have sat near you for hours, and for hours have listened to the history of your life."

As he ceased speaking, he arose and filled a glass with wine, and gave it to the other, saying that it was necessary that he should get well as soon as possible, now that he was himself again.

"And I have lain here since June 22d?" Cobb asked again.

"Yes; lain, sat, and walked—for you did walk a very little of late."

"It is strange! But, really, is it A. D. 2000?"

"In truth, it is."

"And Rawolle; where is he?"

"Out; but he will soon be back, for he has not left your side, except for brief periods, since we brought you here. One of us has always been near you."

Cobb looked at him a moment, and then asked:

"Will you please explain why you are wearing such outlandish clothing, for it is entirely different from anything I have been accustomed to seeing," and he surveyed the other from head to foot.

Lyman smiled, and took a step backward that a better view of him might be obtained.

"All in good time, my boy," he answered. "Suffice it to say that this is the custom, or style, now. We have got a full suit for you as soon as you are able to put it on."

Saying this, he went across the room and threw open the doors of a wardrobe, disclosing a number of articles of wearing apparel hanging therein.

To Cobb, he presented an appearance quite out of the general order of dress, and an aspect quite comical; yet, the more he looked at him, the more he was inclined to admit that his dress was becoming, and, no doubt, very comfortable. It seemed to him that he had seen styles similar to that his friend wore, depicted in the old prints as worn by his forefathers. The main features were: tight-fitting knee-breeches, but coming a little lower down than those of the old style; black silk stockings and low-cut shoes, the shoes having large gilded buckles upon the instep; vest low in front, but closing at the neck; close-fitting cutaway coat without tails, unbuttoned in front, but held together by frogs; neither collars nor cuffs, but in their place small and neat rufflings. There was no shirt-front visible.

His glance was but momentary, yet it was long enough for him to note these few changes and minor details in Lyman's dress.

"Come, Cobb," said Lyman, "get up and dress. I will bring you your clothing."

With the aid of Lyman, it was but a few minutes ere he was thoroughly arrayed and fitted out in the prevailing style of the day.

Handing him a fine pair of boots of very light material, Lyman said:

"Put these on, for it is wet outside; the low shoes are worn only during dry weather."

Putting on the boots, which fitted him perfectly, Cobb surveyed himself in the glass. He liked the change from the old style. It was indeed a comfortable substitute for the heavy and loose-fitting trousers and long-tailed coats formerly worn. No collars to cut one's ears, nor cuffs to hang down over one's hands. It was handsome withal, and permitted a free action of the limbs.

"Is this now the prevailing style?" he asked Lyman.

"Yes. No other style of clothing but this is worn by men," was the answer.

"And how long has this been the custom?"

"A great many years—how many I cannot say. It has been the style since I was born. I believe I have heard that it was inaugurated in 1910. Certain gentlemen in the city of Chicago were the first to start the movement, as near as I remember it. Anyway, the change was made, and now it is the only style of gentlemen's wearing apparel in the United States. Of course, there are certain modifications of it, as for summer and winter, and in certain trades, but the one main idea is adhered to, namely: close-fitting clothing and knee-breeches, with shoes for dry and boots for wet weather."

"I think it a jolly change. It seems like old times, when I dressed for mounted duty with my troop." And Cobb took a turn around the room, bringing back the memories of the days when he had, in his top-boots, swung the belle of a frontier town.

At this moment Rawolle entered the room, and started at seeing Cobb up and dressed. With unfeigned pleasure he rushed up to him and grasped his hand, crying:

"Cobb, I congratulate you on your return to consciousness!"

"Pray don't mention it. I am just as glad to be up and around as you are to see me."

"And how do you feel? Have you had a good rest?"

"Good rest! Well, I like that! I should say I have. I hope you don't think a man can sleep three months without being satisfied, do you?"

"No. You ought to be ready to get up by this time, I must admit; but that is not to the point: are you in condition to start for Washington to-day?"

"Yes; any time you desire."

"How glad I am!" Rawolle quickly returned. "I have been away from home so long that I am most anxious to get back to my family. I will look into the matter and see if we cannot go to-day. In the meantime, look over the morning paper," and he tossed the paper which he had in his hand to him.

"Yes," said Lyman, going over to the other side of the room and taking up a large grip; "busy yourself with the news while I get our traps into shape for traveling."

Cobb took the paper as it fell into his hand, and opened it. It was a very large daily, and seemed to contain a vast amount of information. Looking at the heading of the paper, he saw that it was the "Daily American." At the first glance over it, he perceived that it was quite different from the papers which he had seen in former days. Leaning back in his chair, he carefully looked it over.

It was not headed San Francisco, as he thought it would be, but America; and the date was the 16th of September. Where was America? he asked himself; he knew of no such place. It must be some new and very large city close by, else the paper could not have reached them so soon. No paper that he had ever before seen contained the amount of news that this did. There was news from all parts of the world; not scant and close-cut, either, but full and elaborate accounts. What appeared to him as very peculiar was that each column had its own heading, as, "From Europe," "From Asia," "From South America," etc. Another thing that appeared very remarkable was that there were no advertisements, nor time-tables of transportation, nor lists of places of amusement. In fact, there was nothing local in the paper that he could ascertain. It was just such a combination of news as would as quickly interest a man in New York as one in San Francisco. He also noticed that the printing was peculiar; that but two or three kinds of type were used in the body of the paper, and that the ends of lines were not, as formerly, flush with the ruling of the next column.

All this was so very strange to him that he was on the point of asking for information from Lyman, when his eyes met the word "Cobb," in big headline letters. Of course he must read what was said of him before asking any questions regarding the paper in which the account was given. He read:

"COBB!

"S. F., 15, 22 D.—The physicians in charge of Junius Cobb report no change in their patient during the day. Food is administered at regular intervals, and taken with apparent relish by the sick man. Mr. Cobb has gained rapidly in flesh, and his health seems to be almost perfect, save the one remarkable condition of insensibility to surrounding objects. The physicians in charge have strong hopes that another week will bring forth great and marked improvement, and that the man's mind will return to him."

And again, further on:

"JUNIUS COBB.

"WASHINGTON, 15, 11 D.—In the Cabinet meeting to-day, the President said, referring to the peculiar condition of Junius Cobb, the Lieutenant taken from the tomb in San Francisco last June, 'that if his condition did not soon show some signs of improvement, he thought that it would be to the best interests of the man, as well as the nation, that he should be brought to Washington for treatment.' He further said, 'that all of the apparatus used by Cobb in his experiment had been received at the State Department, and was there held until Cobb would be able to arrive and explain its use.'"

And still further on:

"LIEUTENANT COBB!

S. F., 15, 5 D.—The excitement in the case of Lieutenant Cobb has not in the least abated. Crowds of people have, for weeks, endeavored to gain admission to his room, but have been prohibited by the doctors. The Lieutenant has shown wonderful vitality in passing through the fever which followed his resurrection from the dead. Rawolle, the President's messenger, has shown most commendable skill in keeping his patient quiet and holding back the crowds of reporters who wished to gain admission."

He dropped the paper, closed his eyes, and sat in a kind of dreamy state, revolving over the extracts which he had read. The world had not forgotten him yet. He was still an object of interest, and his condition was the subject of special telegrams to the papers. What would be the next dispatch sent out to the world, when it was found that he was up and in his right mind; was able to start for the capital city—was, in fact, on his way? How would he be received when he reached there? Whom would he meet? and what would his future be?

His reveries were broken into by the entrance of Rawolle, who took a telegram from his pocket, saying: "We are going to-day. I have just received this dispatch, and will read it to you:

"WAR DEPARTMENT,
WASHINGTON, 16, 13 D.
"*To Albert Rawolle, Occidental Hotel, S. F.*

"Telegram received. If Cobb can travel, give him the orders of the President to report with you at once in Washington. The President has read your dispatches with the greatest interest, and awaits further information in the matter. Notify me of the hour of your departure. Acknowledge receipt.

"N. A. MILES,
"*Secretary of State.*"

Cobb listened attentively to the reading of the message.

"Miles, Secretary of State; and the same initials," he mused. Then aloud:

"Is this Miles, who is signed here as Secretary of State, any relation to Brigadier General Miles, of 1887?"

"Not to Brigadier-General Miles, Mr. Cobb, but to General Miles, who died in 1918. He is a great-grandson of that noble and illustrious general."

"And who is President now?"

"Emory D. Craft, of Illinois."

"Craft, did you say?" Cobb quickly asked, and he went back to his old friend of the artillery, who had so nobly aided him in his work.

"Yes; but why does it seem to interest you so much? you do not know him;" and Rawolle looked puzzled.

"Perhaps not," smiling; "but I may have known

his great-grandfather; in fact, I may possibly have been an intimate friend of his—who knows?"

"True. Your status is so different from that of any other man, that I would not be surprised if you had been his bosom friend."

Then turning to Lyman, he continued:

"Come; it is time we were attending to business. Let us go at once and see about our transportation and check. Cobb will excuse us for a few minutes, will you not?" to the latter.

"Certainly. By all means get our tickets as soon as possible, for I will then feel that we are soon to be on the road."

Saying this, he lighted a cigar and watched them depart.

A few moments later he went to the window and pulled aside the heavy lace curtains and gazed out upon the busy street below him. This was his first view of the outside world, in daylight, since 1887. A hundred and thirteen years ago he had had rooms at this very same hotel. Was it possible that he was not dreaming? Was he, in fact, alive and well, and again standing in a place that had known him so many years ago—that had been his home at a time so long since that every mortal man who then lived was now dead and crumbling into dust? His thoughts wandered back to the years long past, to his old friends, to the happy days passed in their society; and then to the darling girl whom he had left in Duke's Lane—his betrothed. Alas! they were no more! But he: he was here, and alone in the world!

So many years must have made a great change in the history of his country and in the manners and condition of the people. Until he should have learned them, he would be practically a stranger in a strange land. He remembered how he had sat, those many nights before entering the pedestal on Mt. Olympus, and wondered upon the future, and what that future would bring forth to him, if he was fortunate enough to survive the ordeal and live again. He remembered with what delight he had anticipated coming again into life among a new people and among scenes of great advancement and of wonderful progress. His hopes had been realized, and he lived again; yes, he who had lain a hundred years in a comatose state, now breathed, walked, and had his being once more. His theory had been most remarkably proved—proved by the man who had first advanced it, and the world should demand no further proof. What would be his reputation in Washington? Would there be any difficulty in proving that he was what he claimed to be— a man who had lived in 1887? No! it could not be; for there were the proofs in the safe, and such proofs as no man could dispute—letters written years ago by men long since dead—aye, dead before a man of his apparent age could have been born. No! He quickly dispelled the idea that it would be difficult for him to prove everything.

Recovering from his sombre chain of thought, he turned his attention to the street beneath his window.

He gazed again and again up and down the street and across the way. Was this the Montgomery street he had so often walked upon? It differed so from its former appearance that he felt that he was dreaming. Great, massive buildings, in all the most artistic styles, met his eyes on every side. Beautiful stores, with huge plate-glass windows. extended as far as the eye could reach. The sidewalks, as well as he could tell, were clean and in perfect condition; and where he had in former times noticed the peanut-vender, the fruit-seller, the blind and the lame with their excruciating music-boxes, and the scores of others obstructing the sidewalks, was now clear, clean, and wholly for the use of the pedestrian. He noticed that that which people had to sell was kept within their stores, and not on the sidewalk; that there were no signs hanging over the heads of the passers-by to fall and, perhaps, break their bones; nor were there any posts of all and every description along the streets. There were no telegraph or telephone wires in view, nor were visible many other things which had formerly been eye-sores to people of taste.

The streets were paved with some new kind of material; what it was, he could not tell from where he stood, but it was such as gave very little sound from the passing vehicles. It was smooth and clean, and free from the many holes which had formerly rendered traveling so uncertain, even dangerous.

A hundred years had made very little change in the heterogeneous assortment of vehicles one sees in a great city. There were many fine and elegant equipages, with and without horses, the latter driven, as Cobb presumed, by electric motors. Yet of this class there were not very many, as San Francisco is a city of hills, and not well adapted for anything but horse or attachment propulsion.

The attire of the pedestrians was that which struck him as the most peculiar. All the women wore short dresses, none reaching lower than within eight inches of the ground. Their feet were covered with low-cut shoes, in some instances; in others, with small, neat patent-leather top-boots, the top of the boot just hidden under the dress. He noticed very few silks worn, most of the dresses being of heavy goods.

No bustles were worn, and the dresses were close-fitting with jacket basques in most cases. Hats were the prevailing style.

It seemed to Cobb, as he looked at his own new clothing and that of the gentler sex, that the very acme of simplicity and good, sound common sense was seen in this new order of raiment.

Cobb knew that there were many things for him to learn, now that he was so new to the world, and that there would be so many peculiar and remarkable inventions that he ought not to evince much surprise when he should behold them for the first time. There was much that demanded immediate attention and study, if he wished to be upon an equal footing with the rest of mankind.

At this moment Lyman entered the room, followed by Rawolle.

"We have been a little longer than we anticipated," exclaimed the latter, throwing off his coat; "but there was really no need of hurrying too much. We have plenty of time to reach Washington by to-morrow morning."

"To-morrow morning!" cried Cobb, in surprise.

"Certainly, to-morrow morning. I think we will be there at 6 dial," nonchalantly knocking the ashes from the end of a cigar which he was smoking.

"Mr. Rawolle, I am prepared for many new and, to me, quite startling statements, but this of yours is a little too strong, is it not? We are over three thousand miles from Washington, and I very much doubt your ability to overcome that distance by to-morrow morning, though you may have made great strides toward its achievement."

"My dear Cobb, it is just as I tell you; at least, as near as I can remember. Let me look at the schedule and I will give it to you, exactly."

Rawolle took the time-card out of his pocket, and, quickly running over it, said:

"No; I am a little out of the way. If we leave here at 16 dial to-day, we will be in Washington at 8 dial to-morrow."

"Enough!" pettishly exclaimed Cobb. "I will not question you any more. Go ahead and do it, that is all, and then I will be satisfied."

It piqued him to think that they were making sport of his ignorance; he lighted a cigar and walked to the other side of the room.

"Now, Cobb," continued Rawolle, "we have our tickets here, and will leave for Washington on the 16-dial train. I have had a trunk fully furnished with all the necessary articles that you will need for the first few days in Washington, so you will not have to immediately look after such things upon your arrival. It is now 13 dial, and we have three hours until train-time."

"But tell me, Rawolle, why do you speak of 16 dial and 13 dial? Of course, I know you refer to the time; but what has been the change in the calendar that you should employ such terms?"

Both Rawolle and Lyman smiled.

"True! you cannot know of the changes which have occurred."

Rawolle drew his chair closer to Cobb, and continued:

"The calendar has been somewhat revised since you were on earth before, or rather, since you so unceremoniously skipped from the society of your friends; and I suppose you have not kept note of the changes in time?" looking at him in a quizzical manner. Cobb laughingly acknowledged the sally, and requested him to continue.

"It was as long ago as 1920," proceeded Rawolle, "that the new order of time went into effect. In that year, a commission of scientific gentlemen was convened by direction of the national legislature for the purpose of considering the feasibility of making such a change in our calendar as would simplify it and make it more uniform. The result was that the calendar, as we use it to-day, is quite different from that which was in vogue during your time. We now divide the whole day into twenty-four hours, as formerly, but number them from one to twenty-four. Our time-pieces have two hands, but they are not used as were those of old time; one hand marks the minutes, and the other marks the seconds. The hours are marked by numbers showing themselves through a circular slot in the dial, changing every hour. One hour after midnight the dial shows the figure 1; and so on up to 24, which is the close of the day. Thus: 12 o'clock, old style, is 12 dial, new style; and 5 o'clock, old style, is 17 dial, new style. We do not use the word 'o'clock' any more, but employ the word 'dial,' instead. The word 'dial,' however, is usually omitted, the customary expression for time being simply the numerals of the hours and fractions thereof. The commission could not ignore the fact that the excess of 57.2 minutes per day over the 86,400 used in the computation must still be carried forward as an excess to be afterward accounted for; for 86,400 was the nearest number to the whole which was a common multiple for three numbers, representing seconds, minutes, and hours. The excess, being 5 hours 48 minutes and 47.8 seconds per year, is still carried forward to the fourth year, where it is taken up as an extra day, and is called 'Old-Year-Day.' The year, as now divided, consists of 13 months of 28 days each, and one day over. The year has 365 days, as of old, but the first day is not counted as a day of any month; it is called 'New-Year's-Day,' the next day being January first. There are 28 days in each month, with a new month, *Finis*, added. New-Year's-Day is neither Monday nor Tuesday, nor any other day of the week; but simply New-Year's-Day; and January first is always Monday. The advantages of this system are, that every month commences on Monday and ends on Sunday, having just four weeks. In leap-year the additional day is called 'Old-Year-Day,' and is just before New-Year's-Day; these days are legal holidays. This, with some other minor alterations, is the way the calendar stands in every civilized nation to-day."

"But is it not a little confusing to you, this change from the old to the new style?"

"You forget that I never used any other," laughingly returned Rawolle.

"True; I had forgotten that fact. But does not

this extra day interfere in many ways with the dates of bills, notes, and other legal documents?"

"Not at all. The extra day is simply New-Year's-Day—a day of time to fill in the year, but not for any other purpose. In regard to the dating of official papers, they are dated the next day, and this day is as if it never existed. Do you comprehend?"

"Yes, I comprehend your statements, but not having had any experience in the use of this new order oi dates, I cannot say that I am fully aware of how it works."

"You will find no difficulty in its application, I assure you."

Without speaking further on the subject, all busied themselves in their preparations for the journey eastward.

CHAPTER IX

At 15:42, as Rawolle named it, but at 42 minutes past 3, as Cobb persisted in calling it, their arrangements had been completed and they were at the front entrance to the Occidental.

At the curb stood an elegant four-seated carriage of very light construction, with a driver upon the seat. There were no horses attached to the vehicle, which was very low in build, and with wheels of fair size. The driver sat in the rear, on a sort of raised single seat, with a small wheel, like a tiller-wheel, in front of him.

It was an electric drag, with the storage batteries underneath the seat. There were many passers-by at the time, but, thanks to Rawolle's care, none knew who were getting into the carriage, else there would have been a crowd in a few minutes.

Taking their seats, the driver started the current, and the carriage rolled rapidly down toward Market street.

"What do you think of this for a carriage, Mr. Cobb?" asked Rawolle.

"It is a most decided advance upon anything we had in old days," the other returned, looking admiringly over it. "This is, no doubt, an electric carriage?"

"It is an electric drag, and the style of all the first-class carriages in the city, except those which are used for hill travel. These carriages run up grades of three hundred feet to the mile with ease."

"Are they expensive? and how long will their batteries last?"

"No; far less expensive than horses. The batteries, or accumulators, are very small, but with great power. The weight carried by such a carriage as this, in accumulators, is about fifteen pounds, and the energy is the equivalent of two horses for six hours, or a greater number of horses for a less time. The accumulators are charged at the rate of about fifty cents per set, which is a six-hour run. The great saving is that when the carriage is not in use, there is no expense."

The carriage was going at a good round gait, but the motion was easy and steady.

Passing into Market street, Cobb was astonished at the magnificence of the buildings. He could not remember ever having seen a single building then standing as being there during his time. The architecture was grand in the extreme; beauty was not lacking, but was combined with strength.

He saw horses, electric motors, and cable cars, but the latter no longer ran upon tracks on the street; the trucks were all underneath the roadbed, while the cars were held aloft by thin but strong steel supports. The cars, moreover, were lighter built and set closer to the ground.

He saw no horse-cars. The pavement was everywhere of the same material—clean smooth, and elastic; and he rejoiced to think that at last mankind had awakened to the fact that it was not only cruel, but costly, to cause horses to run upon cobble-stones, and pavements of similar construction. He did not have time to note all the many changes which had taken place and then in view, ere the carriage stopped at the gate of a most imposing edifice.

Alighting from his seat, Rawolle assisted him down, saying:

"Here we are, Mr. Cobb."

Having gotten out, they all went into the depot, for such Cobb was informed it was. He was surprised at the grandeur of the building. It far exceeded anything he had ever seen for similar purposes. Rawolle took him around and showed him the various waiting, toilet, dining, and other rooms.

The depot was on the site formerly occupied by the old station, at the corner of Third and Townsend streets.

Passing into the main hall, he perceived a stream of people coming from the left. The interior of the depot, after passing through the main hall, was a vast space with a great arched roof. The ground was paved with marble slabs, and divided by iron fencing into five large compartments; the first running from side to side of the building, while the others were set at right angles to it. Each of the four divisions had a great slot or opening through its floor, of about two hundred feet in length by twelve in width. The last opening was filled by a train which had just arrived.

The people were flocking out, and through the gates into the main hall, or, as Cobb called it, the fifth compartment.

His attention was riveted to the train as it stood upon the track. It was so different from anything in the railway line that he had ever seen before, that he was most anxious to learn something about it.

It was a train of five cars, each about forty feet long, and of circular construction. It rested upon innumerable little runners, and was set quite close to the ground. The end of each car was a huge circular disc of a diameter a little greater than that of the car, and having an elliptical opening of some seven feet in the long diameter. Along each side of the cars was another set of runners, while two more sets were upon the tops.

There were no windows to the cars, and they looked plain iron cylinders of vast size, set upon a lot of little iron legs.

Standing there a moment, Cobb watched the last passenger leave the hall, and soon heard the guard cry for the gates to be closed. Almost immediately the gate of that compartment was dropped, and he saw the huge train sink into the opening and disappear from sight.

Turning toward Rawolle, who had been watching him with a curious expression, he exclaimed:

"Rawolle, tell me what kind of transportation is this that I have just seen? It is something that beats my time, and I am at a loss to understand its working."

"I do not wonder at your expression of astonishment, my dear boy;" then pointing toward the third opening, and looking at his watch, he continued: "You will see a similar train soon come up; watch carefully."

Cobb did as directed, and in a moment saw a train of cars, in all respects similar to the train which he had seen disappear through the left-hand slot, rise from below. It came up gradually, and at last stood, as its mate had stood, flush with the floor of the room; but, unlike the former, it had no passengers to disembark. There it stood, silent and empty.

As the train reached the level, a placard was dropped from the top of the gate, bearing the words "Omaha, 16 D.," in large letters.

"That is our train, Cobb," said Rawolle, following the eyes of the other to the sign. "Let us get our traps together and get aboard."

Approaching the gate, which had by this time been thrown open, and through which many people were passing, Rawolle showed the tickets, and the three men passed in and proceeded along the train to the second carriage. Curbing his impatience to learn more of his peculiar surroundings. Cobb followed Rawolle and Lyman into the car.

The car resembled the sleepers of former years, except that it was decorated in a grander style and had no windows. It was lighted by electric lamps, which made it as bright as day. The seats were somewhat differently constructed from those of the old kind, but the general appearance of the interior was quite the same.

A porter met them at the door, and after seeing their tickets, showed them to their section

Throwing down his grip and coat, Rawolle said:

"Come, Cobb, there are a few minutes before the train leaves; let me show you about."

"All right; I am at your service."

"Mr. Cobb, I think you will find this train a most decided improvement upon those used in your day," remarked Lyman. "Of course it is old to us, but I can imagine your surprise at many of the improvements you see about you."

"Right you are," returned Cobb; "there are so many new and peculiar contrivances around me that I am like a man who has just awakened in a land of fairies. I am not going to be too curious, but await developments, for I have no doubt that I will be satisfactorily informed concerning them all at the proper time."

"This is the pneumatic train," continued Lyman, motioning toward the train on the track.

"Now, hold on," interrupted Rawolle, quickly; "all in good time. It is better to explain all this to Mr. Cobb in detail. Let him first see what there is to be seen, and then we will explain it to him afterward."

Passing into the first car of the train, Cobb was shown the smoker; and here he found a hundred little inventions which had been made with a tendency to increase the comfort of the traveler across the continent.

"This is the Central Pneumatic, or Continental Express," said Rawolle, "excepting the baggage-cars; they are below, receiving the baggage as it arrives."

At this moment the sound of a deep-toned gong was heard, and Rawolle said they must hurry back, as that was the signal for the gates above to be closed preparatory to starting.

A moment later, they were all standing on the platform between the cars, and an instant afterward the whole train began to sink, and soon had left the opening far above them. The train rested upon a sort of hydraulic lift which came to rest as soon as it had reached a level some twenty-five feet below the floor of the depot. They were in a subterranean chamber, or rather a series of chambers, which were brilliantly lighted by electric lamps.

There were many tracks in every direction, with moving trains upon them.

Leaning out to the side of his car, Cobb saw an engine, or what he took to be such, move up and couple to his train, and soon he felt it being rapidly hauled away.

This subterranean labyrinth of roads was similar to the yard of a great railroad center. Men were in every direction, turning switches, coupling cars, clearing tracks, etc.

Their train was taken about a mile underground, and then run into a great iron tunnel. A peculiar sighing sound, like that of a great storm a long distance off, now fell upon his ears. Turning inquiringly to Rawolle, he asked the meaning of it.

"Air—sucking air," was the answer.

"Yes; I presumed as much," Cobb returned, piqued at the brevity of the answer.

"Observe all you can, Mr. Cobb, for you have but a few minutes more. I will explain it after we are in the car," noticing the impatience of the other.

The tunnel in which they then were was, like the great lower chambers, well lighted up. At one side, and opposite to where they stood, was a recessed chamber containing what appeared to be very powerful machinery. Cobb saw the motor disconnect from the train at this point, but he was not permitted to notice further the working of this most remarkable invention, for the guards ordered them into the car, and the door was closed and bolted.

Going back to the smoker, they lighted their cigars and settled themselves comfortably among the cushions.

"Now," exclaimed Rawolle, sending up a cloud of smoke, "now I am at your service."

"Then, tell me all about that which I have seen," Cobb impatiently asked. "Don't you see how anxious I am?"

"Very well. Let us commence at the beginning: In the first place, this that you have seen is the pneumatic railway. Its official designation is 'The Central Pneumatic.' There are, in the United States, quite a number of these roads. From San Francisco run three, as follows: one to the north, one to the south, and this one to the east. Here is a map showing all these roads in the country;" and he took from his pocket an official railway guide, and handed it to his listener. "As the word implies, air is the motive power—not compressed, but atmospheric pressure against a surface, on the other side of which a partial vacuum has been created by exhaustion. This is the method in the tunnels only. After the trains leave the great tunnels, they are moved about the yards, which you saw were all underground, by electric motors. Hydraulic lifts take them up to the station and lower them again. Everything is underground until the train rises through its opening in the floor of the depot. When the guard ordered us into the car, and bolted the door, we had been pushed into the receiving section of the main tunnel. The main tunnel is a complete iron and stone structure, extending between San Francisco and Salt Lake without break. At Salt Lake are the engines which exhaust the air from this tunnel, the pressure of the external air being the propelling power to move the train forward to its destination. The tunnels are twelve feet in diameter, and the rear car of the train carries a shield, or end-piece, which almost fills the cross-section of the tunnel; in fact, there is but the hundredth part of an inch between the edge of the shield and the interior side of the tunnel. The engines, as I said, are constantly pumping out the air, but this is carried to such a degree that the external pressure on the tubing of the tunnel is always under one pound per square inch. A series of valves at the end of the tunnel farthest away from the engines, permits ingress to the air which acts against the rear end of the train to move it forward. The train is first placed in a movable section of this tunnel, and, everything being ready, this section is moved upon rollers into connection with the main tunnel—a sort of valve action. The instant this is done, the air is permitted to enter *in front* of the train, and then gradually shut off until, the train having acquired its normal speed, the valves are closed altogether, and the air permitted to enter the tunnel *behind* the train only. It is very simple, and works to perfection. There are inlets through the rear shield of the train, to which are connected tubes running to each car. These are the air-tubes of the train. As the pressure of the air against the rear shield is one pound per square inch, a like pressure is exerted at the orifice of each tube; but, as there is no resistance to its ingress, it passes through into the cars. causing an internal pressure of the atmosphere of nearly one pound per square inch. Valves opening in *front* of the rear shield, and at a pressure of a little less than one pound per square inch, permit of the escape of the vitiated air into the tunnel *ahead* of the rear shield. Thus a steady stream of pure air is maintained throughout the whole train. The trains are received at their destination upon compressed-air receivers, and gradually come to a stand-still. At Salt Lake, forty five minutes are allowed for this train to transfer passengers and for supper, and then the train starts onward for Omaha. At that city the train is again made up and starts upon its new course for Chicago, New York, New Orleans, Minneapolis, or other point, as the case may be. Now, our train was placed, as I said, in an auxiliary tunnel, which was, by simple mechanical means, brought into position as the segment of the main tunnel. You, of course, noticed that each car was fitted at its end with a circular disc, covering the whole end excepting the door which leads into the next car. Well, this circular disc covers the end car completely. When our train was brought into the main tunnel, the pressure upon its end-section would have been, if suddenly exerted, so great that we would have started off with a great shock, but the air is allowed to enter behind the car gradually, as I have explained. When the full momentum is reached the full pressure of the external air is allowed to exert itself against the end of the train."

"And how long does it take to gain this full momentum?" Cobb asked.

"But a few moments. Are you aware that you are now traveling at the rate of two hundred and forty miles per hour, or four miles per minute?"

He smiled at the look of incredulity which his words evoked. Cobb was loath to believe he was in earnest, for he felt no shock of starting, nor did he experience any motion such as he would naturally associate with such a terrific speed.

"Such a rate must make the wheels spin," from Cobb.

Lyman looked at him, while Rawolle burst into a laugh.

"I do not see anything to laugh at," the other retorted, a little nettled.

"No, no, Mr. Cobb; do not be displeased. We really meant no discourtesy; but your remark is not what you would have made had you thought a moment, for we know you to be a man of education. We do not use wheels on the pneumatic roads. These trains run upon the many little runners which you saw under the cars. Were we to use wheels," he continued, after a pause, "centrifugal force would tear them into pieces in no time. Take the case of a wheel four feet in diameter: the circumference of such a wheel is a little over twelve feet. At the rate of four miles per minute, it would have to revolve 1,760 times. No wheel that can be made would stand such a test. It would fly into fragments inside of the first mile. A wheel of the above dimensions and at that rate of revolution would have a centrifugal force equal to 1,000,000 pounds. Now, as the centripetal force is the tensile strength of the material only, and that of the best steel wire only 160,000 pounds, it will readily be seen that the centrifugal force would instantly cause the wheel to fly into fragments."

"You are right," Cobb answered, going over the figures in his mind. "Wheels would never do; I can see it plainly."

"Even were we to use a smaller wheel to decrease the centrifugal force, we would have to increase the number of revolutions, so there would be no gain in so doing. Our trains run upon two peculiarly constructed rails, and the runners are flanged to exactly fit the rail. There is, in addition, on either side of the tunnel, another rail of similar shape, while upon the upper part are two more. The car has runners for all of these rails, and the position of them is such that the car cannot jump the track, or swing or sway from side to side. It travels as if in a groove, and the little runners, separate from one another, conform to the curves of the tunnel."

"It must take powerful engines to exhaust the air from such a long tunnel, does it not?"

"Yes, very powerful ones. But what is different from any other mode of propulsion, the same engine can do as much service for a line 2,000 miles long as for one of 200 miles in length, rate of speed being the same. The reason for stations at intervals of about 500 miles, is because more trains can be kept in motion on medium short lines than on very long ones. There are at Salt Lake, at the receiving end of this line, fifteen engines of 5,000 horse-power each; ten at work all the time, with five in reserve.'

"A pretty strong set of engines for a single railroad, I would say; and a costly motive power, too."

"Not so costly as you would think," he returned. "If you take into consideration that these engines are worked by electricity, and not by steam, and that the electricity is furnished by water-power, you will perceive that they can be worked quite cheaply."

"Give me some of the statistics, please," said Cobb.

"Certainly. The tunnel is twelve feet in diameter, which gives it a superficial area of 17,712 square inches. Now, at a pressure of one pound to the square inch, a train has a pushing force at its end of the same number of pounds. A train weighs 50,000 pounds. The heaviest grades on the line are some of two hundred feet to the mile. The power required to push this train up such grades is 2,000 pounds, for the matter of friction is not taken into consideration, being, by our arrangements, reduced to the minimum. Thus the pressure in the tunnel is always sufficient to move eight trains. If a train moves four miles in a minute, then the volume of air in the tunnel to be displaced is equivalent to the area multiplied by the length, which gives 2,600,000 cubic feet; but, under a pressure of one pound, this volume becomes 3,000,000. The pumps at each station are ten in number, each of thirty feet diameter by ten-foot stroke, with a volume for each of 7,060 cubic feet. These pumps make thirty strokes per minute, which is equivalent to sixty single strokes. Thus the volume of air displaced by the pumps is 7,060 x 60 x 10 = 4,236,000 cubic feet, an amount far in excess of that required."

"Then, judging from your remarks, there is practically no limit to the speed which can be obtained by this method of propulsion?"

"On the contrary," Rawolle returned, "the limit is reached when the friction on the runners generates such an amount of heat that they begin to disintegrate. At three hundred miles per hour they become very hot. As it is, we have to use a very peculiar kind of alloy for runners, and during all the time of running, keep a stream of oil flowing just in front of each runner.

"But," asked Cobb, "does not this oil congeal upon the rail in cold weather?"

"It does, most certainly; but there are little scrapers just in front of each runner which cut away the congealed oil to the merest fraction of an inch from the rail. These cutters must, by the train running between its upper and lower rails, always be just so far away, and no farther, from the rails."

It seemed to Cobb that he could advance nothing but what this man had a ready explanation for its action or cause. It was, indeed, a most marvelous invention. Here he was traveling at the rate of two hundred and forty miles per hour, and scarcely felt the motion.

"Where is the electricity for these powerful engines generated?" he inquired.

"For the Central and Northern, as well as for the Pacific Pneumatic and Mountain lines, the dynamos are at the Shoshone Falls, in Idaho. These falls furnish an immense water-power, estimated at over 300,000 horse-power. The current is delivered at the station in great cables of peculiar construction, and well insulated."

"Do you have any accidents on the roads? At such a rate of speed, an accident would be fraught with frightful consequences," Cobb continued.

Rawolle smiled as he said:

"During your time, accidents were not uncommon—in fact, I might say quite common, judging from the old chronicles; but we have never had an accident yet upon any of our lines. There have been, of course, breaks and delays; but as each train is in communication with each other, and with each end, and with the chief of the exhausting department, everything is known at all times regarding the position of trains and their condition."

Striking a match, he continued:

"No train could run into the one ahead of it, for the reason that there will always be a cushion of air between them; and further, were any ordinary number of runners to break at one time, the train would not be affected by the loss."

"How wonderful, yet how simple!" exclaimed Cobb, lost in admiration. "But I am at a loss to understand why the people of my time did not discover and put into operation the same project."

"Perhaps someone did discover the principle, but had not the means to test his theory," Rawolle returned.

"How long has this system been in operation?"

"About thirty years," he replied, after a moment's thought.

"Tell me one other thing," said Cobb; "has the pneumatic railroad superseded all other kinds?"

"Oh, no; by no means. There are railroads all over the United States, and very much the same style of your day, excepting the great improvements which have been made, and also the one other most important fact, that all engines are run by electricity. The pneumatic lines are through lines only, and are for rapid transit between very distant points, and only for passengers, mail, and express. All freight is sent by the other roads."

"Then, the towns, excepting the great centers, are connected by electric railroads for inter-transportation?"

"Yes, the pneumatic is only an auxiliary to the rest of the roads—a means only of overcoming great distances quickly."

"And what is considered good speed for the electric roads?"

"Seventy-five miles per hour for passenger trains, and fifty for freights."

"Then, they must be very differently constructed from those of old," exclaimed Cobb.

"They have very different roadbeds, and, of course, different engines. But enough for the present," looking at his watch. "It is 18 dial, and we had better get into the sleeper and prepare for supper, for we are almost at Salt Lake."

CHAPTER X

After supper, and when settled back once again in the cushions of their sleeper, Cobb immediately resumed the conversation about the pneumatic roads.

"They must be very rich and powerful corporations, these which own such lines as this?"

"No," returned Rawolle; "for they are not owned by individuals, but by the government. All railroads in the United States are in the hands of the government, and are operated with a view to just covering expenses."

"Are the rates of passage high?"

"We do not consider them so. There is one fixed rate throughout the country of one cent per mile."

"But," musingly inquired Cobb, "is not there a difference in operating the roads? Are not some more expensive to the government than others?"

"Certainly," answered Rawolle. "But, like postage on letters, a universal rate is found to be the best; the larger and more patronized roads paying the losses incurred by the smaller and country routes."

"I presume," said Cobb, "that there can be but few changes in the general management, supervision, etc., of the roads from those in vogue in my time?"

"There you make a mistake," quickly returned the other; "for, having been connected with the pneumatic lines, I am well posted in what is done to-day and what was the manner of operating railroads during the first part of the twentieth century. Nearly every detail of to-day's management differs from that in vogue a hundred years ago. It would tire you for me to go into details. A few facts, though, I will give you: All freight is of two classes, and is sent at so much per pound per mile. At the sending point it is stamped similarly to a letter, showing date, place of shipment, destination, etc. The same rule is followed in regard to baggage of individuals, the owner having a duplicate of the stamp placed upon his baggage. There are no tickets shown or taken up on the pneumatic lines, but the names of passengers to depart from the train at intermediate points are telegraphed ahead, and the persons are looked after by the inspectors. On all lines the tracks are double, trains passing but one way on each line of rail. There are no whistles or bells to the locomotives of the service lines; no tender with its coal and water; no cab in the rear for the engineer; no furnace and fireman. The locomotive is an electric one, with the engineer in a cab in front. In place of the huge boilers is an iron and steel tank containing the storage batteries. The whole weight is nearer the rail, thus bringing down the center of gravity and reducing the danger from oscillation."

As Rawolle was thus enlightening Cobb about the innovations made in the last century, the sleeper door opened, and a trainman entered and walked direct to their section and asked for Mr. Rawolle, saying he had a telegram for him, at the same time handing out the envelope.

Rawolle took it and thanked the man, who then left the car.

"He hit the right man squarely that time!" surprisedly exclaimed Cobb. "They seem to know you here."

"Not at all," replied Rawolle, smiling, while he tore open the envelope. "Every person on the train is known by name, and section, and car. Such is the system."

He opened and read the telegram.

"There!" he exclaimed, after a moment, extending the telegram to Cobb. "There is an order from the Secretary of State to stop at the Central Sea." And he and Lyman looked quizzingly at their companion, as he slowly took the telegram and read:

"WASHINGTON, 16, 18 D.
"*Albert Rawolle, on Central Pneumatic No. 3, east:*

"Telegram received. Stop at Cairo. Submarine boat Tracer ordered there to take you and Cobb through Central Sea.

"By order Secretary State.
"HARRY G. COLLINS, *Chief Clerk.*"

Cobb read it through twice ere he ventured any remark; then, handing it back while a troubled look overspread his countenance, he said:

"Cairo is in Illinois, at the junction of the Ohio with the Mississippi; but I fail to comprehend the import of the words 'Central Sea.' The submarine boat spoken of does not surprise me, for I would naturally expect that that which was almost an accomplished fact in 1887, would be an actual success at this late date."

"There is no Ohio River, or not as was in your time. The Ohio is now but a small stream flowing into the Central Sea," replied Rawolle.

"Again those words 'Central Sea;' what does it mean? Is there an inland sea?" and Cobb looked inquiringly at both of the others.

"There is," slowly spoke Rawolle.

"And a mighty big one, too," put in Lyman.

Cobb was highly educated and of a sanguine temperament; he neither doubted what seemed impossible, nor did he believe until the facts were clearly before his mind. He was perfectly cognizant of the physical geography of the United States, and did not understand under what conditions a great inland sea could have been formed, or maintained.

Settling himself back in his seat and breaking the circuit of the electric light to lessen the glare in their faces, Rawolle continued:

"I will give you some facts concerning this sea, for, now that you are one of a new generation, you have much to learn, and we cannot pass the hours between now and bed-time to better advantage. On the last day of August, 1916," he began, "at about 14 dial, or as they then said, 2 P. M., that which was taken, at the time, as the shock of a great earthquake, was felt by thousands of persons throughout the central portion of the United States. In less than two hours later, the nation was informed of the true nature of the shocks which followed each other in rapid succession. It was the explosion of natural gases deep down in the strata of the earth's crust, and the scene of the disturbances covered a vast area of territory. During the following week the shaking and trembling of the earth caused great destruction in many cities and towns not otherwise affected. Houses fell, the water supply failed, and other serious results were experienced. But throughout portions of the area now covered by the Central Sea, the scene was terrible, awe-inspiring, horrible. The earth heaved and sank; huge cracks opened, and flames hundreds of feet high shot into the air; thunder and lightning added to the horrors of the situation. The bursting of the earth's crust was attended by an appalling roar and crash, as if a million peals of thunder had combined in one grand effort to terrify mankind; then came a pall of dense, black smoke that wrapped the land in darkness. Consternation seized upon the people, and well it might, for when the full import of the disturbances was known, it was only then ascertained that a great cataclysm had befallen the nation. Without going too much into details, for you can later on gain a full knowledge of this great physical disturbance from the books published soon after its occurrence, I will explain but a few of the facts causing it. You are aware, Mr. Cobb, to what extent natural gas was used in the United States in 1887; that there were thousands of wells pouring out millions of cubic feet daily; that many of them showed pressure of from ten to twenty atmospheres. From the time you left the world, as it were, until August, 1916, gas wells were being sunk all over the country drained by the Ohio and its tributaries. Their number was way up in the thousands. Billions of cubic feet of natural gas were being consumed or flowing to waste daily. Pittsburgh alone used 300,000,000 cubic feet a day in its vast manufactories. The earth in the Ohio basin was honey-combed with the gas pockets and strata, and gas veins were struck in which the gas was under such pressure that the flow could not be checked by human hands. It was 14 dial, as I have said, on the last day of August, 1916, and the workmen in the large foundry of Dillenback & Co., at Lakeside, on the Ohio, some fifty miles below Pittsburgh, were tapping a huge melting of aluminum bronze for the purpose of casting the outer shell of one of the latest model guns of that period. But let me first describe the interior arrangements of the foundry, that you may fully grasp the situation as it then stood, and the cause of the results which followed. Natural gas was, and had been for a long time, the fuel used in these works. Up to 1914 the gas boring of Lakeside had furnished all the gas required. This well was of ten-inch bore, and reached a depth of 4,737 feet, but in the year mentioned the well had failed to furnish gas at any pressure. The standard pipe had been moved and an iron plate set over the mouth of the tube, on a level with the floor. Five hundred feet from this well a boring to 4,016 feet had struck a new stratum, giving vast quantities of gas at a pressure of five atmospheres. To revert back: Just as the tapping of the furnaces was made, the steam boiler of the crane engine, through some unaccountable cause, burst. The concussion shook the buildings, tore up the ground, displaced the iron plate over the disused gas well, and broke the aluminum furnaces, letting over one hundred tons of molten metal flow rapidly across the foundry floor. Recovering from the first shock and fright of the explosion, all efforts were at once made to arrest the flow of the liquid stream, or to divert its course away from the old well. That well, as all knew, still contained gas intermingled with common air, the mixture being of a very explosive nature. All perceived at a glance what would be the consequences if such a mass of molten metal should precipitate itself into the old well and fall over 4,500 feet into the interior of the earth's crust; the shock at bottom, the continuance of heat, the explosive medium through which it would pass, all were dangers to be dreaded. The gas strata were overlaid and underlaid by water and air strata; the breaking of one into another would cause a commingling of their constituent parts, and form explosive compounds of the most dangerous types. Human efforts failed to stem the fiery stream in its onward course across the foundry floor. With a bounding, hissing, and, as it were, victorious cry, the river of melted aluminum approached, reached and went plunging down into the old supply-pipe. Who could describe the terrible effect! Of all those hundreds of human beings employed in Dillenback's works, but two lived to tell the story of the catastrophe. These two men knew only one thing: that the earth seemed to shake to its very center, and they were hurled down among the debris of the fallen buildings, while sheets of fire almost scorched their very souls. Peal upon peal of thunder reverberated about them, and then darkness buried everything from their vision. Burned, bleeding, and nearly dead, these two men found themselves pinned down by the timbers of the works. Fire was upon every side; the timbers were burning, the heat was oppressive, and from a horrible death no man could save them. There was a higher Power, though, who had ordained that these two men should be witnesses of the full effects of this mighty effort of nature to overcome the grasping endeavors of man to accumulate wealth at the expense of reason. A sudden rush of waters from beneath them cooled their parching bodies, extinguished the fires about them, raised the mass of timbers which pinned them down, and gave them their liberty. You can read of this escape, as it is fully chronicled. This was the cause; now the effects. Are you tired?" seeing Cobb so quiet; "or would you like a drink of something to warm the inner man?"

Cobb had sat with scarcely a movement, save the heaving of his chest, as he listened to this terrible narrative. The last words of Rawolle seemed to awaken him.

"No, and yes," he slowly replied. "Let us take a glass of wine and retire. I wish to think this over before you finish. My head aches, and I need rest."

A few minutes later, all was quiet in the first sleeper of the Central Pneumatic No. 3, east.

It was 2:25 dial, or 25 minutes past 2, the next morning, when the Central Pneumatic arrived at Cairo.

Here Rawolle's party was met at the train by an officer from the government submarine boat Tracer, and conducted aboard that vessel, which lay at anchor in the stream. Cobb was informed that, as it was so early, he had better retire and take a little more rest, for they would not weigh anchor until 7 dial. Acquiescing, he was shown to his stateroom.

It was a cozy affair, indeed, that Cobb was ushered into—a little, but handsomely furnished room, containing all that one could desire in a thoroughly well-appointed apartment. Electric lamps threw a charming, subdued light over everything in the room, while an electric heater diffused a gentle warmth which was most agreeable this September morning. Retiring to rest, Cobb dreamed of nothing but pneumatic railways, submarine boats, and gigantic convulsions of nature.

It was about 7 dial when both Rawolle and Lyman came and awoke their guest, who, after a refreshing bath and a delicious breakfast, ascended to the upper deck of the Tracer.

The main deck of the vessel was of very small area amidship, some two feet above the water-line, and inclosed by an iron railing.

A beautiful scene presented itself to his view. The Tracer lay about half a mile from the docks of Cairo, and that city was just awakening to its daily round of bustle and activity. The stream was covered with shipping, some at anchor, while others were plying between the city and the opposite shore, a mile and a half away. Sailing craft there were a plenty, but no steamers, though there were many vessels moving swiftly through the water, yet showing no smoke or funnels.

This fact was immediately noted by Cobb, and inquiry made of Lyman, who stood near him, as to why there was no smoke visible.

"Neither coal nor wood is now used for marine propulsion," replied Lyman. "Lipthalite vapor, or lipthalene, is now the motive power of vessels without sails. I will show you some of this lipthalite, later on, in this vessel."

Turning his eyes from the busy and charming scene about him, Cobb's thoughts came back to his immediate surroundings. What was he standing upon? The small, water-flush deck of a metal submarine vessel, the total area of which could not exceed a thousand square feet. A number of peculiar openings, valves, and pipes abutted on the deck, and a single metal mast stood at the bows; but no smoke-stack or other accessories to propulsion were visible.

Surveying all these things, he was about to ask information concerning their use, when Lieutenant Sibley, the officer in command, made his appearance, and was introduced to him.

"I am sorry I was not aboard to welcome your arrival, last evening, Mr. Cobb," he began, in a courteous and pleasing tone of voice, "but I was detained in Central City, across the river, until early this morning. I hope you slept well, and are ready for the trip to Pittsburgh?"

"Not only ready, but anxious for it," was the reply.

In a few moments more, by order of the Lieutenant, the anchor was raised, and the Tracer moved up the stream, headed E. $\frac{1}{4}$ N.

As the vessel moved through the shipping, the national colors, which were displayed from its mast, were saluted by the dipping of flags and sounding of whistles.

A hoarse-toned marine whistle, almost at Cobb's feet, answered these salutations, and also caused that gentleman to jump back with a startled expression.

Drawing his hand from the whistle button, Lieutenant Sibley apologized for frightening him, saying:

"It did not occur to me that I had others aboard than those who are accustomed to these vessels."

The Tracer was a cigar-shaped vessel of two hundred feet in length by twenty beam, or middle diameter, and of nearly 1,000 tons displacement when submerged.

With an outer shell of aluminum bronze and an inner shell of the finest steel, the vessel combined great strength with a minimum amount of metal in its construction.

"Gentlemen, if you will follow me," said Lieutenant Sibley, "I will show you over the vessel."

Descending the companion-way, the entrance to which could be closed by an air-tight door, the party proceeded about the vessel.

Longitudinally and horizontally, from apex to apex of the cones, was a steel deck dividing the vessel into two equal parts. The first forty-five feet of each cone contained the tubes of compressed air and oxygen. There were in each end about 2,500 feet of five-inch steel tubes, one-half inch thick, containing over 4,500 cubic feet of air under a pressure of 1,500 pounds per square inch. This was sufficient, as Lieutenant Sibley explained, to sustain active life for the entire crew for two hours. "But we have other facilities," continued the Lieutenant, "by which the vitiated air is deprived of its carbonic acid, and then recharged with the lipthalene gas from the receivers and oxygen from the pipes, giving about eight hours of active life to the inmates of the vessel when totally deprived of air externally."

The store-rooms, mess-rooms, and quarters of the men were visited. Small though these rooms were, they were made with every convenience, and given every useful contrivance which this great age of invention could produce.

The Tracer was not a war vessel, but belonged to the Geographical Bureau, and was used in charting the Central Sea. Her complement was small: two engineers, two pilots, one electrician, cook, assistant cook, captain's boy, two helpers, and two officers. Everything was so admirably arranged and machinery played such a wonderful part in the power required to handle the vessel, that a larger force was not only unnecessary, but would have been detrimental to a satisfactory working of the vessel.

Cobb called attention to the steel partitions between the rooms, and asked why so much strength was required.

"There are," answered Lieutenant Sibley, "twelve partitions, dividing the vessel into twenty-six compartments. In case of accident to the outer shell, whereby water might gain ingress, that particular compartment can instantly be closed and the flow of water confined to it. Before going down into the engine-room, I will give you some idea of this remarkable vessel. The Tracer, when fully submerged, displaces 1,000 tons of water. The shell of the vessel is of $1\frac{1}{2}$-inch steel, covered externally by an aluminum armor of .3 of an inch in thickness, and weighs 570,000 pounds. The steel deck upon which we stand weighs 500,000; the steel partitions, braces, and iron-work weigh 195,000; the engines and machinery, 200,000; compressed air pipes, 125,000; the water cylinders, which you will soon see, weigh 100,000; all other parts, stores, lipthalite, etc., are allowed 50,000 pounds. Now, added to all this, is an immense aluminum-covered iron weight of 150,000 pounds attached to the bottom of the vessel, and which can instantly be freed and dropped from the ship into the sea, by simply breaking an electrical connection. This circuit is accessible from all parts of the vessel. Let us descend into the engine-rooms, and I will there explain why I have been so particular in giving you these weights."

Following the Lieutenant down the narrow ladder

into the depth below, Cobb, Rawolle, and Lyman were soon facing the powerful but small engines of the Tracer.

The room was large, clean, warm, and brightly illuminated by electricity. Here, Mr. Lochridge, the first engineer, was introduced by Lieutenant Sibley.

Cobb had seen the engines of many of the first-class vessels of his day, had noted their power and huge dimensions; but never before had he perceived such beautiful specimens of strength combined with size; nor did the finest workmanship he had ever seen approach to the perfection of the engines he saw beating and pulsating before him.

Cobb looked them carefully over before venturing any remark. He noted an absence of steam and heat, the peculiar construction of the boilers, and many other, to him, new inventions.

"I believe, Mr. Rawolle," he finally said, turning to him, "that you informed me last evening that no steam was used at the present day, but in its place, lipthalite?"

"That is our fuel and vapor nowadays," broke in Mr. Lochridge.

He led the way to two receivers, bearing some slight resemblance to the boilers of a steamer.

"Here are our boilers and furnaces combined," he continued; "and these," as he laid his hand upon two very peculiarly constructed frontal additions, which had quite a number of straight pipes running into the large receiver, "are our furnaces, if you choose to call them by such a designation; we call them generators. Lipthalite is our fuel and gas developer."

Mr. Lochridge stooped down and took from a case, containing many more, a stick of dark-brown material about four feet long by one inch in diameter, and handed it to Cobb for his inspection, saying:

"That is lipthalite. These rods are placed in those tubes, and, by proper mechanism, pushed through into the field of an arc light situated in the generator. Gas is evolved in great quantities, but the composition burns only while in the field of the arc. Little heat is developed. The gas is delivered to the cylinders in the same manner as was steam in your day."

"What is the volume of gas as compared with the solid base? and is it cheaper and as efficient as vapor of water?"

"I expected that question, Mr. Cobb," returned Mr. Lochridge, "and will explain it. One cubic foot of water, as you know, produces nearly 1,700 cubic feet of steam; one cubic inch of gunpowder makes about 1,500 cubic inches of carbonic acid and nitrogen gases; while one cubic inch of lipthalite will evolve 500 cubic feet of lipthalene, a combination of nitrogen, carbonic acid, and other gases. The ratio between water and lipthalite, evolved into gas, is as 1 to 500. In other words, to operate the engines of this vessel at a given speed for one hour, requires, of coal and water, one and thirty-one tons respectively; while of lipthalite, twenty-three pounds. Leaving out the question of water, of which there is a plentiful supply surrounding the vessel, the gain in a twenty-four hours' run for lipthalite over coal is as 1 is to 96; or one ton of lipthalite is used where ninety-six tons of coal would have been required."

"It is a wonderful discovery!" exclaimed Cobb, and a far-away, dreamy expression came into his eyes. For an instant his mind went back to the days, long years ago, when he had spent hours in his laboratory, at the Presidio, searching for this very same agent—the storage of great power in small volume—and his partial success in the discovery of meteorite. Then his thoughts led him to the remembrance that his new explosive had been sent to Washington. What had become of it? Lost, lost, years ago!

"Do you comprehend the advance in science that has been made in a hundred years?" and Rawolle broke his reverie by gently touching him on the arm.

"Can I help it? Could anyone have dreamed of such a power as this?"

Yes. He had dreamed of it; and many, many times. But too modest to venture the knowledge that his thoughts and work had been centered on such a grand invention, he turned to Mr. Lochridge, and abruptly asked:

"Is lipthalite turned into gas by explosion?"

"By no means," quickly returned that gentleman; "by inflammation, and inflammation alone, and not very fast, either. In our generators, here, it is at the rate of about two hundred and fifty feet of these sticks per hour."

"Strange that I should have worked on this very principle!" he said, half aloud; then turning to Lieutenant Sibley, he exclaimed:

"You spoke of water cylinders; where are they?"

"Under the grating, Mr. Cobb."

Mr. Lochridge raised the grated flooring, and showed three iron cylinders, each divided into halves, with piston-rods and cylinder-heads. They were about four feet in diameter by twenty-three feet long.

"These, gentlemen," he continued, "are connected by pipes with the outside of the vessel. Water can be admitted into any one or all of these cylinders, and, in two minutes, driven out by the pistons. Should these pistons fail, from any cause, to work, pumps connected with the cylinders could perform the same duty in ten minutes. I gave you the weights a few minutes ago; what did I make them?" taking a piece of paper and pencil from his pocket, and making a few notes. "Yes; 1,940,000 pounds, or just thirty tons less than our displacement. The water cylinders have a capacity of fifty tons. By allowing thirty tons of water to enter the cylinders, our weight is equal to our displacement, and we sink. Allowing all loss of weight aboard ship during a cruise, and which never exceeds twenty tons, we can always decrease our buoyancy and sink to the bottom, if necessary. Now, here," pointing to the left, and along the walls of the vessel, "are the dynamos for the electric lights, fans for circulating the fresh air, steering apparatus, electric heaters, exhaust pumps for expelling the vitiated air and drawing in the fresh, and many other inventions, the uses of which you can learn at your leisure."

The engine-room of the Tracer was indeed a curiosity-shop to Junius Cobb. Pipes in every direction; electric wires crossed and recrossed one another; peculiar machines occupied each side of the room, and a hundred other things, strange to him, were upon either side. Leaving the engine-room, Lieutenant Sibley led the way to the instrument-room of the ship. Here a new treat awaited Cobb.

Situated just at the junction of the main shell and the forward cone, was the pilot's, or instrument, room. In an easy-chair, in front of a box about two feet square, and resting on the table, sat Mr. Irwin, the first pilot of the Tracer. On either side of him, and fastened to the walls of the room, were a great number of delicate instruments, some of which were familiar to Cobb. At either side of the box on the table were several rows of push-buttons; to the left, a fine compass, and to the right, speaking tubes and bells.

"You met Mr. Cobb at breakfast, did you not, Irwin?" questioned Lieutenant Sibley, as the pilot arose and greeted the entrance of the party with a smile.

"Yes, I had that pleasure," he returned, bowing. "Have you been over the ship?" to Cobb.

"We have taken it all in, Mr. Irwin," said Lyman, answering for the party.

"How is the course? and where are we now?" asked the Lieutenant.

"It is now 9:35, and we are headed northeast by east. Cairo is to our rear ninety-five miles. We are over Princeton, thirty miles north of Evansville," was the reply.

"You may make Louisville. What time will we get there?"

Consulting his chart a moment, Mr. Irwin replied:

"Louisville is on our course now, and distant one hundred and eighty-eight miles. We will make it at 14:12."

"Now, Irwin, I wish you would explain the mysteries of your castle to Mr. Cobb, and then bring the gentleman to my cabin. You will excuse us a few minutes, will you not, Mr. Cobb? I have some official papers for Mr. Rawolle's inspection. Mr. Lyman, will you come along, too?" to that gentleman.

As they left the room, Mr. Irwin turned to Cobb, and held a few minutes' conversation regarding the remarkable experience of the latter; then, rising, he pointed to the right wall and said:

"These are instruments used aboard submarine vessels of to-day. There is a thermometer for interior temperature, that for exterior temperature; here are electric dials giving the humidity in various parts of the ship. These dials to the left show the motion of the fans, dynamos, and all other moving machinery aboard. The interior pressure is here noted," placing his hand upon a barometer, "and the exterior, there. The purity of the air is indicated by this little delicate meter. The speed of the vessel is shown on that reel, which is connected, electrically, with the log. These little bells," pointing to twenty-four little bells overhead, "will quickly give warning of the entrance of water into any of the chambers. The equilibrium of the ship is denoted automatically by this alcohol cross combined with a double pendulum. The lipthalene pressure is given here. The many buttons and tubes communicate to all parts of the ship. Those two buttons release the iron weight at the bottom of the vessel, and these twelve buttons regulate the entry and exit of the water in the six water cylinders. The speed is regulated here, and the vessel steered by this little wheel;" and he pointed out the various instruments as he mentioned their uses. Cobb carefully examined every instrument as it was mentioned to him. Turning to Mr. Irwin, he asked:

"But where is your steersman—your lookout, I mean? Cooped up in this little room, you can see nothing around the ship. Even on deck, especially in rough weather, you would be too low down to have much of a view of your surroundings."

"The explanation is most simple. Look into that box, if you please, and let your head fill the opening, to darken the interior."

He smiled as he noted Cobb's perplexed expression.

Obeying Mr. Irwin's request, Cobb fitted his face to the opening and gazed inside the box. He saw the sea rising and falling in its swell, vessels passing in various directions, the faint blue outlines of the shore to the northwest, and—click, the scene changes: now other vessels in view, and a clear circle of the horizon, denoting a great expanse of water. Again a clicking sound, and—

"My God!" he cried, starting back; "a ship! a ship is almost upon us!"

Like lightning, Irwin sprang to the camera and glanced in; then quickly reaching out his hand, his fingers touched a button, and the hoarse marine whistle of the Tracer thundered forth its warning; seizing the tiller-wheel, he threw it hard aport, and then, without pausing, pressed another button, and the large gongs of the ship pealed out their summons to its crew that danger was imminent. Even as the alarm sounded, came a shock, a shiver, a slight careening of the vessel, and as Irwin took his white face from the camera, the grateful exclamation:

"Thank God! we are safe! Look! the monster passes by!"

Into the camera Cobb again peered; the dark, black stern of a large freighter was passing to the southwest.

Lieutenant Sibley and the crew of the Tracer were quickly huddled at the door of the pilot's room.

"Lieutenant," said Irwin, with a salute, "I confess that we have had a very narrow escape from being run down by a heavy freighter. Explaining these instruments to Mr. Cobb, I failed to note the approach of the-vessel."

The alarm having subsided, the subject was fully discussed, and Mr. Irwin was exonerated by the Lieutenant. All parties then returned to their various occupations.

Mr. Irwin then turned to Cobb and said:

"It was very negligent of me not to carefully survey the field for approaching vessels. The Tracer carries but a single mast, and sits so low in the water, that these many merchant ships, with their sleepy crews, often fail to sight her until too late to make a proper clearing." Then returning to the subject upon which they had been speaking when Cobb's excited exclamation had burst forth, he continued:

"I see that you have understood the object of the little dark box on the table. It is a camera-obscura.

The single mast of the Tracer is of aluminum, strong, slight, and hollow, and rises to a height of twenty-eight feet. A lens at the top revolves by pushing this button; thus a perfect image of the surrounding water and all upon it is thrown on the white ground within the box. Sitting here and looking in the box, I note the proximity of objects and steer the vessel. The mast also serves to carry an arc light for night traveling, and our flag by day. Further, our air is drawn down through pipes in its interior; for, during heavy seas, we must have the air inlets far above the deck, which is constantly washed by the rollers."

Some further conversation was indulged in, and then Cobb thanked Mr. Irwin for his kindness, excused himself, and was soon seated, with Lieutenant Sibley, in the latter's cozy cabin.

Lunch having been disposed of, Rawolle, taking out his watch, remarked to Cobb: "In a few minutes we will be directly over Louisville, Kentucky; and in these few minutes, I will briefly explain the effects of the great cataclysm of 1916, as I promised to do: The gas strata of the Ohio basin," he began, "extending from above Pittsburgh to the Mississippi River, with pockets innumerable and ramifications in every direction, contained millions of millions of cubic feet of gas under varying pressures from nil to many atmospheres. The catastrophe at Dillenback's ignited the gas in what appeared to have been the main strata. Explosion followed explosion throughout the region now occupied by the Central Sea. The earth was rent and broken, and the great vacuums, caused by the annihilation of the gases, took away the support of the upper crust, and then atmospheric pressure completed the ruin. The earth sank and crushed into these voids until a new foundation was reached. In some sections the fall of the crust was frightful, terrific. In the vicinity of Cincinnati but one shock was felt, but that shock was terrible, horrible, annihilating. The earth sank 196 feet at one fall. Not a living soul escaped the shock of impact upon the underlying strata. The city was an inconceivable mass of ruins, and in two days, was covered with water. So it was over a region of 100,000 square miles, the earth sinking everywhere, but to different depths and with different rates of depression. Pittsburgh sank 377 feet, but so slowly that few lives were lost, though the destruction of property was very great. At the mouth of the Ohio the earth sank only one foot, increasing toward the east. Millions of lives were sacrificed and untold wealth lost, for the great depression commenced immediately to fill with the waters from the streams flowing into the Ohio basin, and from the underlying strata. Even the Mississippi turned its waters into the old mouth of the Ohio and flowed east, leaving but a small, shallow stream to flow in its old bed until augmented by the streams and rivers emptying into it below Cairo. Even with all these waters it was an insignificant river until it reached the Arkansas and received the mass of water from that river. But in 1918 the river was diverted back to its proper channel; though later on the dam was removed, owing to the rise in the Central Sea, and the natural outlet being at Cairo. This, in brief, Mr. Cobb, is the effect of a single accident in a gun factory, in 1916; though who can tell but that it might have occurred later on from some other cause?"

"But did not those who were not injured by the shocks and falling buildings have time to move their effects before the waters overtook them? for, surely, this immense sea did not fill up in a few days," ventured Cobb.

"Along the Ohio, from this side of Louisville to above Cincinnati, scarcely any property was saved. The depression was such that the submergence came very quickly. But this was not the case in the surrounding country. In one week the shocks were over and the earth quiet. People recovered from their fears a little, and looked about them. Later on they commenced to rebuild, and it was not until a year after that they found a new foe against which they could not combat: the country was below the level of any outlet, natural or artificial, and was filling up into an inland sea. Surveys were made, and in 1918 the true condition of the country ascertained. Then, and only then, was it found that the region now covered by the Central Sea was destined to be lost to mankind. Human ingenuity could not solve the problem of drainage. There was no drainage. Far below the bed of the Mississippi, the only possible outlet, the country was doomed to inundation. The survey was completed and the true limits established. All within that area began to be abandoned. Property, wherever possible, was removed; but the buildings, at least those which could not be taken apart and moved, still remain under the sea as monuments of a once densely populated area. To be sure, the removal was not rapid. The exact time was known, from the surveys made, when the waters would gain their maximum height, or reach to any particular point."

"Such an immense basin must have required a considerable time to fill up?" inquired Cobb.

"It did—years. It was a gala day at Cairo, and a day of rejoicing throughout the land, when, on the 14th of August, 1939, the Central Sea reached the dam at that city, and passed over in a gently increasing stream. The dam was removed, the channel opened, and navigation from the ocean to this immense body of water, through the mouth of the old Ohio River, was unobstructed."

"Why," exclaimed Cobb, in astonishment, "that was twenty-three years after the disturbances! It took longer to fill up than I had imagined."

"The area lost," continued Rawolle, "was about one hundred thousand square miles; the volume nearly one hundred and seventy-five trillion cubic feet. The water-shed of the Ohio produced ten billion cubic feet per day, all of which flowed into the Central Sea. The first two years the Mississippi discharged a like amount into the sunken area. It was estimated that over ninety trillion cubic feet of water were pushed up, so to speak, from the strata of the earth by the subsidence of the upper crust. Thus, one hundred trillion cubic feet of water rushed into the doomed basin of the Ohio in the first two years, making inundation very rapid during that time, and frightfully rapid during the first week. The Ohio water-shed supplied nearly four trillion cubic feet per year, which, to complete the seventy-five trillion necessary to fill the sea, took twenty-one years."

"This is a most wonderful occurrence, and did I not have ocular proof of its reality, I admit I should be loath to believe it a possibility;" and Cobb seemed lost in a reverie of the marvelous events which had transpired during his long sleep on Mt. Olympus.

The tinkling of a bell caused Lieutenant Sibley, who had been writing at his desk, to look up and say:

"I presume we are near Louisville."

Then, going to the tube, he answered Mr. Irwin, in the pilot-room, and was informed that the vessel was then over the city of Louisville.

The Tracer was soon brought to a rest, and Cobb witnessed the peculiar arrangements made for descending to the bottom of the sea. He watched every movement and noted every detail, and saw with what wonderful facility a thousand-ton ship could be made to obey a man's will.

The mast of the Tracer was dropped until its top rested upon the deck of the vessel, its top closing automatically to prevent the ingress of water. A large circular float containing air-valves, and attached to a long hose, was loosened from its fastenings on the deck. The water cylinders were opened, and as they partially filled, the vessel lost its superiority of displacement and began to sink; the large float, with its air-valves, and attached to the hose, remained upon the top of the water, permitting air to be drawn down into the vessel by suction. Thus a constant supply of fresh air was obtained without recourse to the compressed air in store. In fact, the latter was never used except in emergencies or when it was desired, as in the case of war, to keep the approach of the vessel a secret.

The sensation of falling was apparent, but it was indescribably peculiar; neither pleasing, nor yet distasteful—such a feeling as when, in his boyhood days, he had sat upon the board of a swing and let the "old cat die."

Passing with Lieutenant Sibley and the others into the pilot's room, he saw the ease with which the descent was regulated, and noted the instrument showing the depth of submersion.

Mr. Irwin pressed a button, and Cobb felt the tremor of a forward movement. The displacement being but a trifle less than the weight of the vessel, the movements of the ship were now regulated by its engines and double rudders.

Stepping to the side of the room, the Lieutenant threw open the steel covering of a bull's-eye, and then pressed the button near it. A brilliant flash shot out, and the rays penetrated the water for a considerable distance in every direction.

"There!" cried Lieutenant Sibley, with an involuntary wave of his hand. "Behold the city of the dead, Louisville!—Louisville, once such a grand city, now a silent, slime-covered, submerged testimony of nature's conquering power over man's puny will."

Cobb pressed his face against the glass and silently gazed upon the lifeless buildings and streets of the city. Even as they stood years ago, so stood many at that moment. Others were in ruins, with gaping walls and broken doors and windows, and all were covered with mud and slime and marine vegetation.

The streets were half-way up to the second stories, but the tops of the street-lamps could be discerned sticking out of the muddy sediment which had been deposited over everything.

Slowly the Tracer moved forward, and the whole expanse of the southeast side of this unfortunate, but once brilliant, city was presented to view.

What emotions filled that man's breast, with his eyes glued, as if fascinated by some unknown power, upon the spot he had, in years long since past, visited, looked upon, and walked in! With a sickening feeling of utter sadness at his heart, he turned away.

"God's ways are inscrutable," he sighed. A tear glistened in his eye as he cried: "No more! Let us ascend!"

At 24 dial the Tracer was at her moorings in Pittsburgh, and Cobb, Rawolle, and Lyman took the Chicago Pneumatic for Washington.

As he lay in his berth in the sleeper, his mind reverted back to the days when he had met his friends in social evenings of pleasure; to his old friend in Duke's Lane, and to the bright, lovely face of that man's daughter. Ah! how he longed for but an hour with them—an hour of true friendship and love; how he craved to listen to but a moment's innocent prattle of his girl-love. Alone among strangers, among a people far ahead of his time, he felt that he was looked upon as a curiosity, but not as one claiming sympathy and love as a relative or dear friend. Did the experiment come up to the ideal? Was he satisfied to die and live again? He asked these questions of himself. He meditated—reflected—and slept.

CHAPTER XI

It was 1:25 dial when the Chicago Pneumatic glided noiselessly into the switching section at Washington. Seizing their grips and coats, the party moved out on to the platform of the sleeper. In a moment the huge train had been raised by the hydraulic lift, and was soon standing in the depot of the capital of the United States.

What a beautiful and fairy-like scene presented itself to Junius Cobb! A depot of magnificent proportions, exquisite workmanship and finish, and possessing a hundred conveniences never dreamed of in his time. The great vaulted roof was set with thousands of electric lights which appeared like brilliant stars in the firmament. Thousands more, in every direction and in every conceivable place, made the vast chamber as bright as the midday sun.

At the barriers of the discharging section a great but orderly crowd was pushing and elbowing its way to a closer position at the gate. All Washington knew that Junius Cobb, the man of two centuries ago, would arrive on that particular train, and a great multitude had congregated to catch a glimpse of him.

As he passed through the gates, while the police

pushed back the crowd, he heard their exclamations and remarks:

"There he is!"

"Where?"

"There, with Commissioner Rawolle—on his left."

"I believe him to be a fake."

"Oh, he's a toola!"

"He has never slept a hundred years!"

"Isn't he a young man to have lived so long?"

"What's the matter with you? he didn't live, he just slept."

"They say he is an officer in the army yet."

"Well, people will be gulled!"

Thus were the expressions bandied about, and fell upon the ears of Cobb in a harsh and unpleasant manner. He was not flattered by the remarks he heard. Already, it seemed, there was a desire to doubt his identity.

As they neared the center of the hall, someone in the crowd cried: "Junius Cobb! Junius Cobb! Three cheers for Junius Cobb!" And the building rang and echoed back the salutation. Surely this was flattering. His reception, after all, was not without sincerity on the part of many of that vast throng.

A step or two more, and Cobb and Rawolle entered an electric drag, while Lyman bade them good-night, or rather good-morning, and hurried away to report.

Away, and at a rapid gait, sped the drag, its wheels of rubber giving no sound on the elastic pavement of the street, its headlight flashing out a brilliant beam, while ever and anon the driver caused a muffled-toned gong, whose sound was low and musical, to indicate the approach of the carriage.

Looking from the window on his side, Cobb saw to what extent street illumination had progressed in a hundred years. At every fifty feet, on either side, were arc lamps; and this at two in the morning, when those of the shops were extinguished. No gas lights were visible. It was a September morning, but the air was mild and balmy, and it seemed like a morning in early spring. Many people were upon the street, and the electric drags, with their flashing lights and musical gongs, were passing in every direction.

At exactly 1:42 dial the drag stopped under the arch of the entrance to the President's mansion, and Junius Cobb was received by the chief magistrate of the United States.

Emory D. Craft, President of the United States, was a tall, rotund, and pleasant gentleman of over sixty years of age. His head was massive, and his features square and clean-cut; his hair almost white, and a beard heavy and gray. A man of great perception, executive ability, true kindness, and wisdom, he ruled the greatest nation on earth as a loving father rules his household, with justice and firmness.

As Rawolle and Cobb alighted, he descended the steps, and, advancing, extended his hand to the former, exclaiming:

"I welcome you back, Mr. Rawolle."

"Thank you, sir; and let me present Mr. Junius Cobb."

"Mr. Cobb, I cannot express to you the pleasure of this meeting;" and the President shook the young man's hand heartily. "Be assured that your remarkable, nay, wonderful, case has been uppermost in my mind since first I became aware of your existence."

"Nor can I, Mr. President, express the gratification I feel in meeting and shaking the hand of the ،chief magistrate of this great nation, especially when that magistrate is ruling the country a hundred and forty years after my birth."

Cobb seemed proud of the fact that he, of all the world, could make such a statement.

A few moments later, the President and Cobb were sitting before a glowing, cheerful fire, engaged in earnest conversation.

Mr. Rawolle had been dismissed by the President, and had hastened to the welcome he knew awaited him from his wife and children.

"There, Mr. President," said Cobb, after a long recital of his life and the facts attending his entombment on Mt. Olympus, "you have the whole story. It is a remarkable one, is it not?"

"Stranger than any fiction I ever read," he exclaimed. "I can scarcely believe that I behold the intimate friend and contemporary of my great-grandfather in the person of one so young as you."

He looked at Cobb in wonder and awe.

"And are you the great-grandson of Hugh Craft, my dear old friend of 1887?" cried Cobb with joy, as if a new tie had been found to bind him to this new world.

"Yes; here is our family history." He arose and went to the cabinet, and returned with a large book. "Read it;" opening it and handing it to the other; "you will there see the history of your friend." He placed his finger on the page.

Cobb read slowly, and like one in a dream, this page of the history of the dead—this chronicle of the life of his chum and bosom friend.

"First Lieutenant, Captain, Major," he read, "killed at the battle of Ottawa, August 5, 1917."

He read it over twice; then suddenly turning to the President, he cried:

"A soldier's death! A noble ending to a noble man! But what battle is this in which he died?"

"'Tis a long story—too long for to-night," the President replied; "but, in brief, it was the decisive termination of English power in North America. Canada desired annexation to the United States; England opposed it. British troops were massed on Canadian soil, and she endeavored to prevent the loss of her colonies. War between the Canadians and the mother country followed. We looked on, but offered no assistance. It was not until the cry for freedom became a wail of misery and a piteous appeal for succor, that we interfered. We offered England $500,000,000 for the whole of her possessions in North America. The offer was refused with contempt. Indignation prevailed throughout the United States, and public opinion demanded that assistance be given to the suffering people in their struggle for freedom. Great Britain was notified by joint resolution of Congress of March 22, 1917, to evacuate Canada and all territory between the boundaries of the United States and parallel fifty-one degrees of north latitude. The demand was refused; and on April 2, in full Congress, war was declared against England. For twenty-five years, or from about 1890, this country had been building first-class ships of war, fortifying its coast and putting the nation in a condition to enforce its demands."

"They hadn't done much in my time," broke in Cobb, with a thought of the utterly defenseless condition of the country in 1887.

"No," continued the President; "but Congress, as you can see by referring to history, in 1890 awoke to the necessity of national protection. In 1917, we could and did enforce our demand. The war was short but terrible. England's great but slow floating fortresses were no match for our harbor vessels. She never gained entrance to a single port of note, but lost many of her finest ships in the attempt. On land, of course, the effect of our arms was more rapid. An army marched across the border, and the decisive battle of Ottawa was fought. Here was gathered all of England's force of occupation. On August 5, 1917, her army was utterly routed, and laid down its arms. With the loss of her American army, and the destruction of many of her finest iron-clads, England asked for terms. By the protocol of October 16th, England, in consideration of $250,000,000, relinquished, forever, all possessions on the continent of North America, together with all national property, fortifications, etc."

"And poor Craft never lived to see the fruits of his nation's courage," said Cobb.

"No; he died in the charge of his regiment." And then, after a pause: "But Hugh Craft still lives. I will introduce him to you to-morrow—do not ask any questions," as Cobb was about to interrupt him—"to-morrow, or rather to-day; and until then, you must sleep."

It was 4 dial when Cobb was shown to his apartments.

The next morning Cobb was awakened from a refreshing slumber by a voice singing:

> "He sleeps; he wakes; the hour is late.
> Arise, get up! the clock strikes eight."

Springing quickly from his bed, he glanced around the room. Again the song and words, and again he looked, but saw no one. Wondering much at the occurrence, he proceeded with his toilet.

At 8:45 he was with the President at breakfast, and had been introduced to Mrs. Craft and her lovely daughter, Mollie.

"Papa says he has taken complete possession of you, Mr. Cobb; and I am so glad, for I want you to tell me so much about those queer old days so long ago;" and she gave him a pleasant smile.

"We are delighted, dear Mr. Cobb, to have you with us. You must consider this your home now, for you have no other, you know;" and good Mrs. Craft spoke in a motherly tone of voice.

"And, of course, you will want a sister;" Mollie Craft cast her eyes down in a shy manner.

"Yes," said Mr. Craft, with evident pleasure and hope in his voice. "We want you to feel that you have not left all your friends in that distant age. We desire you to consider this your home as long as it shall please you to do so. My wife and I will endeavor to be a mother and a father to you; our daughter, a sister; our son, a brother."

Mollie Craft was a lovely girl of nineteen years—tall, dark, and robust. She was possessed of a clear skin, sparkling eyes, and beautiful teeth. She was accomplished, and a leader among the young ladies of her set. Her disposition was frank, kind, and retiring. No wonder that Cobb's eyes often wandered in her direction during that breakfast! It seemed to him that he had never before seen so lovely a face and figure, nor such charming ways as Mollie Craft was mistress of. Yes, there was one face that held just comparison with that before him; there was one figure that matched the symmetry of Mollie Craft; but, alas! she was no more! The queen was dead, but the princess lived! So passed the thoughts in his mind.

Adjourning to the President's library, for Mr. Craft loved to have his family about him while he smoked his after-breakfast cigar, the conversation proceeded with animation, but always with Cobb as the central figure.

>"A Captain in the army, a Colonel up a tree;
> Quite soon I'll be a Major, as you can plainly see."

As the words came forth in a free though quiet manner, a young man entered the door, stopped, and then, bowing, exclaimed:

"Pardon me; I did not know that you had company."

Junius Cobb looked up; then, starting from his seat with a white and perplexed expression, sprang toward the stranger, who, in astonishment, drew half back through the door.

"Hugh Craft! How came you here?"

Recovering himself, the man replied, but with embarrassment:

"Well! that's very good, indeed! Asking a man what he is doing in his own father's house!" and he gave a quiet, undecided laugh.

"Mr. Cobb, my son. Hugh, this is Mr. Junius

Cobb; you know who he is," with emphasis on the pronoun.

Junius Cobb rubbed his eyes in confusion. He comprehended the situation at once, and also remembered the President's words of the night before, when he said, "Hugh Craft still lives."

Hugh Craft bowed, and moved behind his sister's chair, and whispered:

"Is he dangerous?"

Cobb, as he turned around, overheard the words, and smiled.

"No, Hugh," he exclaimed; "not dangerous, but amazed. You are the exact image and counterpart of him who was my dearest and best friend, your—" he hesitated a moment—"your great-great-grandfather."

Hugh and Mollie looked bewildered, while Mr. Craft's face wore a smile. The situation was too comical, and all burst into a hearty laugh, Cobb joining the others.

"It is funny, is it not, to hear me talking of having been the friend and chum of this man's great-great-grandfather?"

A few moments and everything had been fully explained to Hugh, who had been absent a week, and had not heard that Cobb was at the executive mansion.

"Dear brother," said Mollie, as she put her arms about the young man's neck and kissed him, "I want you and Mr. Cobb to be brothers; to be to each other as your great-great-grandfather and he were long years ago."

"Hugh," said his father, "as you have returned so opportunely, you can take charge of Mr. Cobb—Junius, let us call him, if he does not object—until time for the reception. I have some work to attend to, and I know Junius will excuse me—will you not?" to him.

"Certainly. Do not let my presence interfere with your work; and let me thank you for calling me Junius. I hope you will always continue to do so."

For an hour these three—Hugh, Junius, and Mollie—sat and chatted. To Cobb it seemed very home-like and most pleasant, and his companions so kind and natural. Hugh was so like that other Hugh, and Mollie so charming and witty, that he scarcely realized, as Hugh looked at his watch and said that they had better dress, that an hour had passed away.

On their way to their rooms, Cobb suddenly said:

"By the bye, Hugh, I wish to ask you a question. This morning, as I was about to arise, I heard some-one singing in my room. It was not a very melodious voice, but nevertheless clear and distinct; something like 'Get up, arise; the hour is late!' Can you explain it?"

"Nothing easier. It was my old phonograph clock—one I picked up at a pawn-shop one day—a relic of fifty years back;" and he laughed at the thought of his friend's perplexity at hearing the words ground out of the machine.

"Why did I not think of that?" petulantly. "Why, they were just getting them out in 1887. Do you not have them now?"

"No; we have something better. The electric clock companies of every city run their wires to nearly every house in their towns, and to these wires are attached electric clocks. The resident buys the clock for five dollars, and pays twenty-five cents a month for its use. At the central station, a large clock of the finest make, and absolutely correct in its time, causes all the others to follow its movements. Thus every house has a dial which records correctly and requires no care. It is simple, cheap, and beneficial."

At the President's reception, at 11 dial, Junius Cobb was the lion of the hour. Senators gave him every attention; the foreign ambassadors treated him as a man of the greatest distinction; the army and navy laughed, chatted, and petted him.

Just after the introductions of the Senators, Tsunan-li, the Minister from China, and dean of the diplomatic corps, approached and bowed low to the President; the latter, also, bowing low, in acknowledgment of the salutation, said:

"O Sölal obik! Dälolsös obe nuikön mani yunik olse kela sava milagik de deil penunols, fuliko, nen dot." *

---

* "My Lord: Permit me, if you please, to present to you the young man of whose wonderful rescue from death you have been fully informed, no doubt."

As the President made the introduction, Cobb gave a slight start at hearing him speak in Volapük; then a smile of pleasure came over his face.

Bowing to the young man, the Minister expressed his pleasure at the meeting by saying:

"O Söl obik löfik! Panunob das pebinols bevü pedeilölsis balmil jöltum jölsevel, kaleda olsik. In ols logob oni, kel pegönom fa Confucius e Buddha god, in dat padälols denu getön luti lifa. Ogivols stimi obe fa visitöl obi ven plidos-la olsi kömön."*

Seeing the President about to translate the words of Tsu-nan-li, Cobb quickly interrupted him, and, smiling at his ability to meet at least one of the requirements of this new age, said:

"O Söl President, ed ols, Sölal obik! No stunolsös lilön obi gepükön in pük egebols. Lesevob, äs jen lefulnik, ut kel päbüsagos äyelos lemödik, das tim äkömomöv ven valik nets kulik äcälomsöv volapüki. Klödöl das et del no äbinom fago, ästudob at pük, ed adelo logob bizugi osa." †

An expression of astonishment overspread the

---

* "My dear sir: I am informed that you have been among the dead since 1887 of your calendar. I see in you one who has been favored by Confucius and the god Buddha, in that you are permitted again to receive the air of life. You will do me an honor by visiting me when it may please you to come."

† "Mr. President, and you, my Lord: Do not be astonished to hear me reply in the language you have employed. I recognize as an accomplished fact that which was prognosticated a great many years ago; that the time would come when all civilized nations would employ a universal language. Believing that that day was not far off, I studied this language, and to-day see the advantage of it."

faces of the other two gentlemen, and the President exclaimed, gleefully:

"Good enough, Cobb! There's one thing of the past equal to the present."

The others claiming attention, no more was said, and the throng of visitors met, were introduced to and passed the President and Junius Cobb.

A little later a party of officers were talking to Cobb near the grand stairway. Speculation was rife as to what his position in the army would be, knowing that he had been dropped for desertion years ago. The discussion was animated, though Cobb himself took no active part in it.

"Ah! Cobb, my boy," and a tall young man, in the full regimentals of a captain in the Second Cavalry —Cobb's old regiment—came forward and familiarly slapped him on the shoulder:

"I have been looking for you. Hugh informs me that you will undoubtedly be restored to your rank in the army; in fact, he says that they can't help giving you your commission again."

"Ah!" from Cobb, as he looked the other in the face.

"Yes," smiling. "And you will be my lieutenant, for I command your old troop of the Second. You will be a böd seledik (rare bird) to us in the Second, and, as I am ordered to join my regiment on the 10th of next month, I intend applying to have you ordered back with me."

Several smiled at the young captain's cool impudence, but Cobb simply bowed in recognition of the other's desire for his company to his regiment.

Captain Hathaway, of the Second Cavalry, was twenty-eight years of age, tall in stature, slight in build, and wearing a little, light mustache. With a glass in his eye, and a voice which sounded low and sweet, he was, with all his known cool impudence, a right clever fellow. But he had taken a dislike to Junius Cobb—and why?

"Yes, Mr. Cobb," taking up the army style of address to lieutenants, "I fear you will have to give up your good times here and join me. Of course they cannot refuse my request," with a new adjustment of his eyeglass.

"Mr. Hathaway—"

"*Captain*, sir; Captain Hathaway. You forget you are addressing your troop commander;" with dignity.

A flush overspread Cobb's face, and he bit his lip to keep from replying in hot terms to this uncalled-for insolence.

"Captain Hathaway, you will join your regiment before the 10th, and I will not be with you. Good morning." He turned on his heel and moved toward a group near the President.

With a laugh at the blank and crushed expression of the young Captain, the others sauntered away.

"Damme! but that's cool. Going to order his Captain to his regiment, eh! Going to get me out of the way and take my girl. Well, I guess not!" and he, too, moved off.

At lunch, after the reception and departure of the guests, Cobb laughingly referred to the little incident of the morning. The President expressed his disapprobation of the Captain's behavior, and told Cobb that he would give the young man a lesson in politeness.

According to their programme, the office of the Secretary of War was visited at 13:30 dial, and Cobb was introduced to Mr. Fowler, the urbane but quick-spoken Secretary. Here he learned much concerning himself, and a great deal in regard to the state of the nation for purposes of offense and defense.

"Yes," continued the Secretary, in answer to a question from Cobb, "your status has been investigated, and it is found that you were dropped from the army, as a deserter, December 1, 1904, under the provisions of section 1,229, Revised Statutes. But when the wonderful facts attending your return to life, and the existence and tenor of your leave of absence, given in 1887, had been fully laid before the Supreme Court, sitting in bank, yesterday, a decree was formulated that you have never been out of service—that is, legally. You, therefore, Mr. Cobb, revert back to your status as a Lieutenant in the Second Cavalry."

Cobb meditatively admitted that perhaps Captain Hathaway would, after all, take him back to the regiment on the 10th of the following month.

"But," and the Secretary looked inquiringly at the President, who nodded assent, "you would have been the ranking Major in the cavalry arm in 1918, the year you would have retired for age, according to the law at that date."

"Yes, you are quite right, Mr. Secretary, I would have been a Major; but I never expected to have been the senior. Promotion at that time was slow beyond measure—stagnated. Old men with grown-up families were still Lieutenants, while the majority of Captains were old, rheumatic, and unable to perform their duty. Lieutenants did all the work." Cobb seemed to revert back in disgust at the state of promotion in 1887.

"As you would have been retired as the ranking Major," slowly continued the Secretary, paying no attention to Cobb's remarks, but with a pleasant air at the news he was about to communicate, "the President has been guided by a sense of the justice due you, and has nominated you to the Senate as such, to rank at the head of the list. Further, as a vacancy exists in the grade of Lieutenant-Colonel, your promotion to that rank follows as a natural course. The Senate will confirm the nomination at 16 dial. Allow me, Colonel Cobb, to congratulate you," and the good old man clasped the hand of the new Lieutenant-Colonel; nor was the President slow in his congratulations. Both seemed to have taken a special interest in Cobb.

He, in his turn, expressed his sincere thanks for

their kindness to him, and was highly elated at the good fortune attending his new life.

"By the records," continued Mr. Fowler, "you are thirty-three years of age, for you entered the cataleptic state at that age; and it has been decided that the period of your inanimation shall not in any manner be counted against you. A Lieutenant-Colonel at thirty-three, the youngest in the army, you will one day command the army of the United States." And he smiled kindly, while the President looked admiringly upon his protégé.

Then, for an hour, the Secretary gave Colonel Cobb a brief history of the army during the hundred and odd years which had passed.

"We have, to-day," said he, "a population of over 500,000,000 of people, occupying sixty-eight States and nine Territories, covering the whole of North America from the Isthmus of Panama to the Arctic, and from the Pacific to the Atlantic Ocean."

"This is a vast and wonderful increase since the census of 1880," exclaimed Cobb. "Why, I remember, in 1887, that the most sanguine statistician estimated only 67,000,000 for the next census, that of 1890."

"True," returned the Secretary. "That was above the exact figure; if I remember correctly, it was only 64,987,504. But even that population was a trifle more than twenty-five per cent. increase upon the census of 1880. The ratio of increase since we were a nation of only 3,000,000, averaged about thirty per cent. until the year 1900. In 1910 it fell to twenty-two per cent., but the next census, that of 1920, showed an increase of thirty-four per cent. The reason for this great increase is found in the fact that in 1915 the United States acquired Mexico and all Central America, with its population of over 20,000,000 souls, and in 1917, after the conquest, the whole of British America, with 10,000,000 more. Our population was, by the census of 1920—counting in 30,000,000 people acquired—137,000,000. The increase since 1890 has averaged only 18.5 per cent. every ten years, or less than two per cent. a year."

"And is not the country somewhat crowded by this great mass of people?" inquired Cobb.

"By no means; there is room for double the number—yes, treble as many. The great States of Slave, Saskatchewan, Manitoba, Assiniboia, and west of the isothermal line of thirty-eight degrees are teeming with people engaged in agriculture."

"What is the strength of the army required to protect the country from internal violence, and for a cadre of a full army?" asked Cobb.

"Our army consists of 148,000 men only, comprising 70,000 infantry, 28,000 cavalry, and 50,000 artillery. The maintenance and distribution of this force is very different from what it was during the years when the country was new and sparsely inhabited. The artillery is along the sea-board, and is a full-paid army. The enlisted portion serve for three years at a time, and are paid at a fixed rate of $20 per month for the privates. The infantry and cavalry are distributed among the States; each State and the Territories of North and South Alaska, and Indian, has one regiment of infantry and a battalion of cavalry (400). The posts are near the great centers of the States, and from them the troops can be quickly transported to the scene of any disturbance. Each governor has authority to order out his State garrison for the preservation of life or property, or to quell riot or disorder in his State. The posts are large and handsome, and with fine and sufficient quarters for officers and men. The social standing of the soldier is equal to that of the citizen, except that, as a soldier, full and implicit obedience to his officers is required and maintained. The food is excellent, and well cooked and served; the uniform is of the best material. Now, Colonel, I will explain the system: The infantry and cavalry posts are schools for the instruction of the youth of the country. The period of service is three years, and the strength of each garrison strictly maintained. The regiments are recruited wholly from the State they are in, and do not leave that State to garrison other posts. This applies only to the enlisted portion of the army; the officers hold life positions, and are promoted lineally in their own branch of the service. They are moved from station to station every three years, but never returning to a station at which they had served before. The pay of the army of instruction, or 'Inland Army,' as it is named, is $5 per month per man, regardless of grade, and $100 upon discharge after three years of faithful service. Every year the State furnishes 500 young men who have passed the physical examination, and they are sworn into the service of the United States."

"But how are these men found? Do they voluntarily enlist?" broke in Cobb.

"Not all, though many do, in order to get their service in. Each State keeps a complete record of every male in its territory—his age, occupation, and physical condition. From a list of all those between twenty-one and twenty-four years of age, is selected, by chance, the yearly quota for military service, less the number of voluntary enlistments; and no one so selected can avoid the three years' service at the State post; nor do they try, I might add, for no excuse but physical incapacity will avail to free them from this duty to the State and Union. From every walk in life they come—the rich, the poor, the worker and the young man of leisure. If a son is the only support of a family, the State supplies a substitute. Except in time of war, they are never called upon again for military service. This is what makes the soldier the equal of the civilian. If a name is once selected and the man does not report, being at the time a resident of the State, he is declared a deserter, and punished as such. To their officers these men are obedient and respectful; with the civilian, they are sons of the State, and their duty honorable in the extreme. Desertion is almost unknown; but when it does occur, the offender receives the fixed punishment of twenty years in the government island prison."

"And the government pays these men?" asked Cobb.

"No; the pay proper and subsistence is paid by the State, but everything else is furnished by the government."

"And their duties, what are they?"

"They are taught all the duties of a soldier; they make marches from point to point, and diffuse a military feeling among the people; they learn to ride, to use their arms, and to become able, if the time occurs, to impart this instruction to others. They are a guard against interior violence in the State, and their presence tends to keep alive that little spark of military ardor which should never be allowed to die, even in a country deemed ever so secure from foreign invasion."

"A system both great and useful!" exclaimed Cobb. "But how are the artillery regiments kept full?"

"By enlistment only. The applications far exceed the demands. The majority come from the Inland Army, from those who are poor and from those who have taken a fancy to a military life."

"And the officers—how are they appointed?"

"They are taken from the non-commissioned officers who have completed their three years' service and are desirous of becoming officers. From the number of non-commissioned officers of each regiment competing, the five who lead in the examinations are sent to the United States military school and pursue a three years' course of study. From this class, in the order of their standing, are filled the vacancies existing on New-Year's-Day of each year, the remainder of the class being discharged."

"Will you tell me what kind of arms are now used?" asked Cobb.

"For infantry, the service rifle and milag cartridge; for cavalry the same, but shorter and lighter, besides a pistol using the milag cartridge of calibre 35. The artillery use nothing but the heavy guns, which are of different styles and for different purposes. Some are for lipthalene, others for lipthalene and meteorite, and still others using meteorite alone."

"What! did I understand you to say meteorite?" and Cobb looked at the Secretary with a surprised and earnest expression, while his hand nervously grasped the back of his chair.

"Yes; certainly. Is there anything strange in the name, that you should look at me so doubtingly?"

"No; I suppose not," settling back in his chair.

"But you appeared very much surprised."

"Yes?"

"Yes; have you seen this explosive? But no; you could not have seen it. It did not come to the notice of the government until after your time."

"Will you show me one of these milag cartridges?"

"Certainly."

He rang a bell and ordered a box of milag cartridges sent to him in the office. When the Secretary had received them, he gave one to Cobb, saying:

"This small bullet does not look much like a cartridge, does it?"

Cobb took it and carefully examined it.

It was precisely similar to those he had sent to Washington in 1887. Smiling to himself, he turned his eyes first upon the President and then upon the Secretary.

"When did you say these were invented?" he asked, in an unconcerned manner.

"I can soon tell you."

Rising and taking a book from the shelf, he quickly found the history of the milag cartridge, and read:

"'Milag cartridge; from the Volapük word *milag*, "wonderful" A cartridge using meteorite as an explosive; usual charge for 40 calibre, one and one-third grains; initial velocity, 3,562; range, four miles. Meteorite was discovered in 1899, and the formula sold to the government by John Otis, chief clerk to the Chief of Ordnance.'"

"Chief of Ordnance?" broke in Cobb, quickly.

"Yes; Chief of Ordnance. But have you read this?"

"No, sir."

"But there certainly is some mystery here!" exclaimed the President, highly interested in the conversation.

Cobb took his penknife from his pocket, and slowly opening it, said:

"If I cut this black cement in the base of the bullet, I come to the meteorite; am I correct?"

"Yes."

"And it is white." And he cut the cement carefully away and disclosed the little disc of fulminate and the white explosive surrounding it.

"Strange!" cried both of the others together, surprised that he should know the color of an explosive invented after his time.

"Have you any nitric acid?" asked Cobb.

"Yes; here is a little," and Secretary Fowler handed him a small bottle containing the nitric acid used in testing at the War Department.

Dipping a twisted paper into the liquid, Cobb let fall a single drop of the acid on the explosive in the bullet; then moving toward the window, which he threw open, he struck a match and said:

"If I understand this meteorite, it will, upon the application of flame, dissipate itself in vapor, but not explode."

'Hold, Colonel!" cried Mr. Fowler, in great alarm,

as he and the President drew back. "It will explode and tear your hand into pieces."

It was too late. Holding his hand containing the bullet well out through the window, he touched the flame to the cartridge. A slight flash from the fulminate followed, and then the meteorite disappeared in a colorless gas. Holding aloft the empty bullet, he exultingly cried:

"Was I not right when I claimed a knowledge of this explosive?"

Then Junius Cobb explained how he had discovered this compound; how he had transmitted it to the Chief of Ordnance in 1887, and the restrictions he had placed upon that office regarding the sealed packet containing the formula. Time passed, and he had been dropped for desertion, but the sealed packet still remained in the office of the Chief of Ordnance. It had been opened, and a subordinate in that office had stolen his secret, sold it to the government, and reaped immense reward and honor. But Cobb had no ill-feeling against the man; he had died long years ago; and what did this theft avail him at that moment?

"You are a wonderful man, my dear Colonel; and I believe that, in the dim past, you conceived the idea of many of our greatest inventions of to-day."

President Craft arose from his seat as he spoke.

Thanking Secretary Fowler for his kindness, Cobb turned to the President and asked:

"Is it time to take our departure?"

"Yes, Colonel." Then, turning to the Secretary, he said: "By the way, Mr. Fowler, be so kind as to have an order made out directing Captain Hathaway, Second Cavalry, to report to Colonel Cobb to-night for orders; send it at once."

"Sir, I will attend to it immediately."

"Then, Mr. Fowler, we will say good afternoon."

"Good afternoon, gentlemen;" and then to Cobb: "Come and see me, Colonel, whenever you feel inclined."

In fifteen minutes they were back at the executive mansion.

After partaking of a cup of coffee, as was the President's custom at that hour, they entered the drag again, and were rapidly propelled toward the Capitol.

Cobb noticed the handsome exterior of the buildings, their beautiful architecture and harmonious coloring.

Pennsylvania Avenue was, indeed, a beautiful thoroughfare. Its buildings were large and grand; great hotels, clubs, bazars, churches, and theatres were thrown together in one complex but magnificent order. Over the sidewalk, on either side, and also covering the cross-streets, was a glass canopy supported by pillars of the same material, handsomely carved and finished. The windows and doors were grand in their size; and what seemed strange and dangerous to Cobb, no sash was to be observed; nothing but great panes of glass, some white and clear, others of various hues.

The streets and walks were as clean as a parlor floor, and no obstructions were to be seen upon them. The pavement was of a soft gray tint, and like a felt blanket in its appearance. The sidewalks were laid in tessellated work of all the hues of the solar spectrum. Statues and works of art were everywhere observable. Great trees ranged on either side, while beautiful plants and green grass plats surrounded many of the buildings.

As the rays of the sun in the west fell upon the buildings, they were reflected back to the opposite side of the street, again and again reflected, and the eye of Cobb beheld the parallel lines of Pennsylvania Avenue adorned with millions of sparkling, dancing lights, meeting at the farther end in one great diamond whose lustre could almost compare with the sun itself.

Ah! what a grand sight!—worthy of a life of inanimation for a thousand years. Cobb feasted his eyes on the beauty of the scene. Lost in the ecstasy of the moment, he was rudely awakened to a sense of the reality by the President remarking:

"It is a grand sight, is it not?"

"Yes! yes, indeed! Grand beyond expression!"

"This street, Colonel Cobb, is said to be the handsomest in the world."

"I can well believe it! I cannot conceive of one that could be more beautiful."

"And yet, Colonel, it is all glass."

"Glass?"

"Yes; plain, cheap, common glass."

'You mystify me! You do not mean to tell me that these magnificent buildings are built of glass?"

"The buildings, walks, streets, and nearly everything visible to your eye is of glass."

President Craft enjoyed the look of amazement and incredulity which overspread the other's face.

"Surely you are jesting with me! Glass is no substance for any of these purposes."

"Remember," slowly, "you are in the year 2000. That which was impossible, unheard of, to you in 1887, may be possible and common with us to-day."

"True! I find I must accept as possible every theory and proposition advanced, until it is, by undeniable evidence, totally disproved. But blame me not if doubt sometimes arises. Will you stop the drag a moment?"

"Certainly," was the puzzled answer.

Turning his head to the driver in the rear, he ordered the drag stopped at the curb.

In front of the entrance to the Dom Kanitöl Legletik (Grand Opera House), by the side of two tall and elaborately carved pillars covered with fine and thread-like filigree work, the drag came to a standstill. Without a word of explanation, Cobb sprang from his seat, walked up to the nearest pillar and dashed the heel of his boot against a beautiful rose of pure white. A look of triumph came into his eyes. They might make it to appear like glass, but it was not glass! The beautiful rose lay crushed against its stem, its delicate petals bent and twisted, and its leaves flattened together.

The President comprehended the young man's motive, and smiled. As Cobb again entered the drag, the President said, but kindly:

"You have destroyed that beautiful glass rose, and because you doubted me."

"Blame me not for doubting, kind sir, nor blame me for investigating. Without investigation we could never arrive at a certain knowledge of the truth or falsity of any proposition."

"And you have investigated?"

"Yes."

"And proved—"

"That glass is not the component part of that pillar," with confidence.

"One word will dispel that illusion." Mr. Craft spoke very deliberately.

"Speak it, then, I pray you," with greater astonishment than ever.

"Malleability!"

Like a flash of lightning, the conviction of the truth of the President's words fell upon the doubting man's mind. Malleable glass! that *ignis-fatuus* which had caused men's minds to turn from reason to insanity; had caused chemists and philosophers throughout the known world to struggle for years and years, and finally go down to their graves with their hopes unfulfilled; that art which was said to have been known in the third century, during the reign of Tiburon—had been again discovered and made known to mankind.

"And is all of this of malleable glass?" still with wonder.

"All. The art has been known for over fifty years. It is common glass, composed of silica, lime, barytes, etc., to which is added nitrate of zesüd and coloring matter. It is cheaper than wood or any of the metals, is about the weight of copper, and has its strength and malleability. It is made into every conceivable form and shape, and has almost entirely taken the place of the cheaper metals where temper and extreme rigor are not desired. It never tarnishes, decays, or breaks. When exposed to the inclemencies of the weather, it is as bright to-day as it was yesterday, or years ago."

Wonderful, indeed, were the inventions of the twentieth century!

At 16:5 dial the President's electric drag glided evenly and noiselessly out of Pennsylvania Avenue, rounded the corner, and stopped at the grand entrance to the Dom Lon, or Capitol, of the United States.

An hour was passed in visiting the three houses of Congress, and Cobb carefully noted the working of the national legislature.

On the way home, the President said:

"There is a Senate of 136 members, or two from each State, presided over by the First Vice-President; two lower houses of 400 and 280 members, respectively, presided over by the Second and Third Vice-Presidents. The Smadom, or lower house, is that body in which are introduced all bills of a private nature whatsoever—such as claims or appeals for money, position, justice, rights and franchises. If approved in this house they go to the Senate, and are usually approved by that body. In the Gledom, or upper house, originate all bills for the good of the nation at large. The system of committees, as of old, is a component part of the machinery of this house. The functions of the Senate, with the restrictions imposed upon it by the creation of a third house, have undergone few changes since your time."

"Are there any changes in the method of electing Senators, Representatives, and chief magistrate?"

"Yes; the President's term of office is five years, taking office on New-Year's-Day of every year divisible by five without a remainder—that is, it commenced in 1940. In the October of the year preceding the taking of office, the governors of all the States assemble at a designated place and nominate four candidates for each office. The two houses of Representatives meet on the first day of November, and proceed to elect, from the nominees, the President and Vice-Presidents."

"Then, I take it that a Republican house would surely elect a Republican, and vice versa?" said Cobb.

"There is no Republican or Democratic party, nor any two parties, as formerly. One party, the American, rules this country. No diversity of opinion exists as regards the welfare of the nation. No policy from the candidates for the Presidency is called for, or expected. To-day there are no great questions to split the nation with contention."

"But may not the choice of the people be defeated, where the election is in the hands of so few?"

"Again experience teaches that you are wrong. Under the old system the people had a choice between two men; now the nation has a choice from four men. The extent and population of the country being so enormous, individual voting would necessitate long and arduous work in counting and verifying the vote. Were the two distinct parties in the field, our method might—mind you, I say might—work disadvantageously to one party or the other. The fairness of the system now in vogue consists in the celerity of the election after nomination, and in the number of nominees. No man can tell beforehand upon whom will fall the nominations given by sixty-eight men, high in social and civil standing, and who come together from every part of this great country—men who are, as a rule, unacquainted with one another. Even if collusion brought about a certain nomination, who could tell that that nominee would be elected by the two houses? The nomination takes place October first, and certified copies, signed by every governor present, though he may have voted against the nominee, are delivered by the three governors oldest in years to each of the three Vice-Presidents of the United States. On the first day of November the names are presented, and the balloting commences in both houses simultaneously, and continues until an election is completed by that house. The record is sent to the Senate, and that body counts and verifies the vote of the two houses, and announces the result."

"Very simple, after all," remarked Cobb. "But has it always worked well?"

"Perfectly."

"How long have you been in office, Mr. President?"

"Since last New-Year's-Day."

"Will you get the nomination again, do you think?"

"No; assuredly not. One of the most strictly followed laws of the United States is that no man can hold the same elective office twice. This law applies to all national and State offices, but not to others below that dignity."

"Does this law not tend to deprive the State and nation of the services of tried and capable men?"

"Colonel, this nation is great; vast. There are

thousands upon thousands of men fully as capable as those in office, ready to take their turn."

"And federal appointments, the patronage of the party, as it was formerly called—how are they made?"

"Wholly upon competitive examination; not in scientific branches of learning, but upon the duties required, together with a common-school education."

"And the term of office?"

"In many positions it is during active life; in others for ten years, or less periods. But in all cases the period is known, and removals never take place without cause having been given by the incumbent: this cause is never political."

"I see we are at the door," reluctantly said Cobb, as the drag came to a standstill before the entrance to the executive mansion, "so will ask you no more questions to-day—but the subject is one of great interest to me."

After dinner, as Cobb and Hugh were lounging about and smoking their cigars, the President came into the room and handed the former the evening paper, remarking:

"You have not seen a paper to-day. Here is the American: you will find all the news in it."

Moving toward the door, the President turned around, and added:

"By the bye, Junius, Captain Hathaway will report to you this evening for orders; dispose of him as you please," and he passed out into the hall.

"Don't mind me, Junius," said Hugh; "read your paper. I'll look at the society news in it—there is no such nonsense in yours," drawing out the "Washington Report" from his pocket.

CHAPTER XII

Leaning back in his chair, and sending upward clouds of smoke from his fragrant cigar, Cobb unfolded the paper, and glanced at the title-page.

"Hello! The 'Daily American,'" he said to himself. "Another copy of the paper I saw in San Francisco."

Opening it, he observed the same peculiarities which had attracted his attention before, the same headings for the columns, the same want of regularity in the spacing at the ends of the lines, and the same scarcity in the variation of the type used. Glancing at the date, he read:

"'America, September 19, 2,000.' This is the 19th," he mused; "surely this paper could not have come from San Francisco, or its vicinity, since its issue." He would ask Hugh, in a moment, to explain it. Hardly knowing where to commence, he took the first column, and read:

"FROM EUROPE.

"LONDON, 19, 10 D.—Congress adjourned to-day out of respect to the memory of Albert Victor Guelph, formerly Prince of Wales, and ex-Senator of the Republic, who died at 2 D., aged eighty-five years. Albert Victor Guelph was the son of Albert Victor Christian Edward, the last reigning sovereign of

Great Britain, and was born at Windsor Castle, April 5, 1915. Upon the downfall of the monarchy, in 1918, the King retired, with his son, to France. In 1955 Albert Guelph returned to England, by permission of the government, and became a citizen of the republic. He became a Senator in 1962, and retired to private life in 1980."

"BERLIN, 19, 8 D.—A great fire is raging at this hour in die Strasse unter den Linden. At 2 D. smoke was seen issuing from the rear windows of the Berlin Art Gallery, and at this hour the building is doomed to destruction. The Berlin Art Gallery was one of the finest buildings in the city, and was, before the institution of the United States of Germany, the palace of the German monarchs. The last Emperor to occupy this palace was William II. grandson of that great and beloved Emperor, William I. By the dethronement of William II., in 1903, all the States which had formed the confederation united under the title of the United States of Germany."

"ST. PETERSBURG, 19, 9 D.—An imperial ukase has been promulgated granting self-government to all Siberia. By this ukase the Russian Empire loses nearly one-half of its territories. The separation is the outcome of the bitter internal war between the mother country and the distant colonies. Since the discontinuance of exiling to Siberia, which was abolished in 1895, soon after the exposé to the world of the pernicious system and the atrocities practiced by the officials, and after the general amnesty ukase of that year, Siberia has grown in wealth and population to such an extent that self-government comes as a matter of right. Mutual offensive and defensive alliance only is stipulated."

"PARIS, 19, 4 D.—Le Roi est mort. Vive le Roi! The King, Louis XX. is dead. Louis Charles Philippe, great-grandson of Louis Philippe Robert, Duc d'Orleans, and afterward King Louis XVIII., expired at 23 dial of yesterday, after a prolonged and severe sickness. Louis Auguste Stanislaus, Dauphin of France, takes the throne as Louis XXI. Louis Philippe Robert, great-grandfather of Louis XX., ascended the throne in 1894, and reigned until 1917, when the republic was again declared, and Louis XVIII. fled to Naples. After thirteen years the monarchy was reëstablished, and continued until 1951. For twenty-three years did poor France struggle along without the pomp and glitter of an imperial rule; but the strain was too much, and in 1974 the deceased Emperor was summoned to the throne of his forefathers. He proved himself a good sovereign, giving France peace and prosperity."

"ROME, 19, 5 D.—The Republic of Italy has sent a telegram of condolence upon the death of the French King."

"MADRID, 19, 5 D.—The Republic of Granada [Spain and Portugal] has sent telegrams of sympathy to the new King of the French."

"FROM ASIA.

"PEKING, 18, 22 D.—By a royal edict, Li Hung Tsoi, the Emperor, has decreed that, 'in view of the fact that the good subjects of Tien-tze have for ages worn the emblem of a once distasteful slavery under the Hiong-un, it is now decreed that the ban-ma shall at once be cut from the head of every one of our male subjects, and the chang-mor no longer worn.' [Ban-ma is the long braided hair worn by all Chinese, and called by us 'the queue.' Chang-mor is long hair.—EDITOR.]"

And then Cobb read on and pondered upon the changes which had taken place, and which he here saw recorded as newspaper items. England, once so proud as a kingdom, now a republic; Germany following in the wake; Spain and Portugal and Italy numbered in the fold. And France! alas! poor France! up and down, changeable as a weather-vane; who could expect a stable government? La belle France! to-day a republic; to-morrow a monarchy!

Turning over the pages of the paper, his eyes lighted up with renewed interest. Though his interest was great as he read of kingdoms falling and new ones building up, here was the page that aroused his old-time enthusiasm. Yes; he was a crank—a crank of the veriest pronounced type, and he knew it as he folded out the paper in his eagerness to read:

"Boston, 18, 18 D.—The game to-day was a fine exhibition of pitching and fielding. Neither side could score until in the last innings 'Michael,' that descendant of the only Mike of the nineteenth century, got his wagon-tongue square against the sphere, and sent it skyward outside of the field.

"The score:

"Innings—	1	2	3	4	5	6	7	8	9
Boston.............	0	0	0	0	0	0	0	0	1
New York..........	0	0	0	0	0	0	0	0	0

"Errors: none. 2 b. hits: none. 3 b. hits: none. Home run: Michael Kelley. Batteries: for Boston, Clarkson and 'Ginty' Carroll; for New York: Keefe and Ewing. Double plays: Boston, 5; New York, 4. Umpire: Sheridan. Time of game: 1:20."

"The same grand game," he murmured, "is still the national sport. It could never die! No, never!"

He read on and on. Everything was of interest to him in his new life. He read of himself, of his arrival in Washington, and of his every act during the previous day.

Letting the paper fall from his hand, he aroused Hugh from the perusal of the society columns of the "Washington Reporter" by exclaiming:

"This paper is a great affair, is it not?" nodding toward the paper which had fallen to the floor by his chair.

"A very newsy paper indeed, Junius," Hugh answered; "in fact, it is the only paper of general news in the United States."

"How is that? Are there not other newspapers besides this?"

"Oh, plenty. But all others are published for local interests, and rarely circulate outside of their city or township."

"And you mean to tell me that this paper is the newspaper of the whole country? It must be quite stale ere it reaches many portions of this nation.

"Not at all. It is simultaneously printed in over five hundred different cities, and no copy has to be sent far to reach its subscriber. For instance: this copy is printed in this city; the copies for New York, in New York; and those for San Francisco, in that town."

"But the heading reads: 'America, September 19, 2000?'"

"That is the original paper. At America, the type is set and form made from which copies are taken and reprinted throughout the nation."

"You astonish me; pray explain yourself."

"America," and Hugh wheeled his chair closer to Cobb, "is a small town on the Central Sea, in the old State of Kentucky. All the news of the world is telegraphed to this place, and set in form for printing. Copies of this form are then transmitted by telegraph to every city which is to reproduce the paper—a very simple operation."

"Yes," dubiously; "very simple, indeed!"

"But let us not discuss the subject now; I will

take you to America, and show you the whole system."

And the subject of the "Daily American" rested.

At this moment Captain Hathaway entered the room, bowing to both of the gentlemen.

"Good evening, Hugh," he exclaimed, extending his hand. Then to Cobb: "Good evening, Mr. Cobb."

"Colonel, sir; *Colonel* Cobb. You forget you are addressing your superior officer.

As Hugh spoke, he gave the other a severe look, as if to say, "How do you like it?"

The story of young Hathaway's discourtesy toward Cobb that morning had been told him.

Captain Hathaway blushed, and turning toward Cobb, said, apologetically:

"I am cognizant of your good fortune and new rank. I congratulate you. You will pardon my rudeness to you this morning, will you not, Colonel Cobb? Some time I will explain why I so far forgot myself," and he dropped his eyes to the floor.

"Captain Hathaway, let it be forgotten," frankly extending his hand. "Let us be friends, not enemies."

Hathaway grasped the hand and wrung it with a sincere grasp of friendship. Then, saluting Cobb, he reported to him for orders.

"You are under orders to join your regiment, are you not?"

"Yes, sir."

"Do you wish to go?"

"Well, to tell you the truth, there is every reason for wishing to remain; but they will not allow me to do so," sadly.

"Who will not?"

"The President; for I have applied to him personally."

"It is rather early for me to go against the wishes of the President," and he looked at Hugh; "but you are directed to report to me for orders, and I must give them to you."

"And I must join." Hathaway spoke in a resigned manner.

"And you will stay in Washington until further orders," looking at him kindly.

"Colonel, I thank you."

Cobb had made one more friend.

After an hour at the club, the trio parted; Hathaway to his hotel, and Cobb and Hugh to their rooms.

That night, as he lay upon his bed, Cobb dreamed of Mollie Craft and her radiant beauty, and of Marie Colchis, his child love. The faces of both came in visions before him. He seemed translated to a dark and dreary region, and wandered about sad and alone. No human soul greeted his approach. Alone and desolate of heart, he pursued his way. At last, after ages of misery, he came upon a solitary grave in the desolate waste. Stunted and gnarled, a solitary oak grew at its foot. A headboard, worn and battered by the elements, lay, torn up from its setting upon the ground. A rivulet of water, small and silent in its course, flowed away and sank into the sand.

Moving forward, he read the inscription on the moldy board:

"Junius Cobb and the heart of Marie Colchis."

With a flood of tears, he threw himself upon the mound, and cried aloud in his anguish:

"O, Marie! Marie! my own, my darling! Oh! come; come to me ere I die!"

A bright light overspread the earth; the desolation seemed to vanish, and all nature assumed its grandest garb. Rising from the grave, he beheld an angel approaching, and leading by the hand a woman in robes of white. Nearer and nearer they drew to his wondering gaze. In the angel's face he recognized the fair and lovely countenance of Mollie Craft.

"Look up! Behold!" cried the angelic form.

Its companion's face was raised, and forth she stretched her hands.

With a wild cry of joy, he sprang forward, and was clasped in the arms of Marie Colchis. He saw her ecstatic beauty, her heavenly eyes, her form divine, and felt that she was his once more. Then the voice of the angel, in sweet, harmonious tones, spoke forth the words:

"A bride I bring thee, O sorrowing soul! Those whom God hath made as man and wife, no chance of fate can set apart. Though years and years have fled and passed, yet life shall once again renew her heart!"

CHAPTER XIII

Weeks passed, and Junius Cobb still remained the guest of the President. He investigated the many marvelous subjects which presented themselves to his view. He studied and learned, and became familiar with his new life. He visited New York and other large cities in his vicinity, and noted their growth and progress. He was astonished to find New York a city of over four millions of people, and covering nearly two hundred square miles of territory.

He visited the great tunnels which connect East and West New York to the city proper, Brooklyn and Jersey City having become a corporate part of New York City. The double streets of the city were a wonderful realization of what the needs of a great commercial center will demand of its people. From One Hundredth street south, and over the whole island from the East to the North River, was a double street—a city on top of a city. The lower streets were the originals, and were paved with roughened glass. On one side, covered, and just below the street level, were the great sewers of the city. The height from lower to upper street was twenty feet. In the center of Lower Broadway, Lower Fourth, Sixth, and Ninth Avenues (for such the under streets were designated), and below the level of the pavement, was a double tunnel carrying the rapid-transit electric trains. These trains were composed of light, cylindrical cars, about ten feet in diameter; they had no windows, light being obtained from electricity. The air was received through ventilators, a steady stream of pure, fresh air being kept circulating through the tunnels by immense fans. Automatic indices gave warning of the different stations. The normal speed of these trains was forty miles per hour, and stops were made at every half-mile between Three Hundred and Fifty-third street and the Battery, East New York (Brooklyn); and West New York (Jersey City). Handsome stations along the line, connected by hydraulic lifts with the upper-street stations, enabled the passengers to quickly take the surface lines to all parts of the city. All vehicles devoted to business purposes were confined to the lower streets, and all merchandise, also, was here received and shipped. In the roof of the street were the water-pipes, electric light, telephone, power, and other wires—all easy of access. Like the lower, the upper streets and sidewalks were of glass, which was molded into huge blocks, these resting on steel girders running across and down the streets. The sidewalks were light gray, and the street light steel-color. The thickness of these blocks of glass was four inches, and the light transmitted to the under-street had nearly its natural intensity. On the upper streets, light electric cars ran in every direction, stopping whenever desired. These surface trains were peculiar in that they sat two feet above the pavement, held aloft and in position by two wide but thin rods of steel passing through a slot in the street, the trucks for the cars running upon a roadbed just under the center of the street, or in the roof of the lower street. Upon inquiry, he was informed that the reasons for the elevation of the cars and the subterranean roadway were to avoid accidents; as a person who was so unfortunate as to be struck by a train would be knocked down but passed over by the elevated car without much injury, the steel bars having rounded guards in front to push any object aside. Cobb observed that the entrances to all of the houses, stores, theatres, churches, hotels, etc., were on the upper streets; and also, that access to the lower streets was obtained at every street-corner by flights of broad steps. He noticed that the streets and sidewalks were perfectly clean, and that an air of care, attention, and good order seemed to prevail. Light carriages to horses, electric drags, and such lighter vehicles as are used for transportation of persons only, were alone permitted upon the upper streets. At short distances upon either side of the street were electric lamps, while at one of the corners of each cross-street was a combination post of fine and handsome make. At the base it was about two feet square, decreasing in size to about eight inches at a height of six feet, the whole surmounted by a white glass shaft, twenty-five feet in length. These posts were for a variety of purposes. The lower part contained the carbons, materials, etc., for the electric lights which were placed upon the top; the next compartment was for the reception of mail matter; above these two were the fire-alarm and police boxes, while on either side were the hydrant nozzles. Just under the lamp were the names of the two streets and the ward of the city. The street name was also set into the sidewalk under foot, in different colors—two names on each corner. Red names indicated a north direction; white, east; blue, south; and green, west.

Asking Hugh, who was with him, if they had any improved method of removing the snow during the winter—for he remembered with what difficulty the streets of New York had been cleared of their snow in his time—he was informed that very little snow fell in New York, or, in fact, along the coast as far north as Maine.

"How is that?" exclaimed Cobb, in surprise. "You haven't changed the seasons, have you?"

'Yes," nonchalantly.

"What!"

"We have changed the possibility of a frightful winter into the reality of a very even and uniform temperature," he continued.

"What haven't you done?"

"Well, we haven't made a California climate by

our work, but we have vastly decreased the severity of our Eastern winters," he laughingly replied.

"And how have you accomplished this great change?" Cobb asked.

"Here is the Metropolitan Club," as they came to a grand edifice near Union Square; "let us go in, have a bottle of wine, and I will explain the methods pursued to work this beneficial change of climate."

"Do you know," asked Hugh, as he filled two glasses with champagne, after they had become seated in one of the reception-rooms of the club; "do you know why New York and the coast to Nova Scotia is so much colder than the Pacific coast of equal latitude?"

"Certainly. On the Pacific, we have the Kuro Sivo, or Japanese current, touching the coast; while on the Atlantic the Gulf Stream is driven off the coast from about the mouth of the James River, by an arctic current coming around Newfoundland and flowing close to the coast."

"Exactly. And if this arctic current could be checked, or driven off, then what?"

"Why, the Gulf Stream would bring its waters close to the shore, and the temperature would be raised."

"That's it, precisely. And that is just what we have done."

"How have you done this, pray?"

"The waters of the arctic current," said Hugh, as

he lighted a fresh cigar, and settled himself back in his chair, "come down Davis Strait with icy chillness and sweep around Newfoundland, over the banks and along the eastern coast. This is the main current. By the northerly point of Newfoundland projecting, as it does, into the Atlantic, a second or minor current is evolved which passes through the Straits of Belle Isle. This current, three miles wide by twenty-five fathoms deep, flows at a rapid pace through the Gulf of St. Lawrence, and turns sharp around Cape Breton and flows south. Its icy waters, as they reach the Gulf Stream, chill the latter for miles along the coast, finally disappearing under the stream about the mouth of the James River. If it was not for this minor current, the Gulf Stream would touch our eastern shores to the banks of Newfoundland; of course, more or less chilled by the arctic current, which would impinge upon and sink under the Gulf Stream off the southwest extremity of the banks. Knowing this, we have closed up Belle Isle Strait, save a ship passage."

"That must have been a huge undertaking," remarked Cobb.

"Yes, it was. But it was done, nevertheless."

"How?"

"By very hard and costly work, and very little science. On the southern coast of Labrador, near the straits, are large and vast quarries of granite. Thousands upon thousands of tons of this were quarried out, and when winter came and Belle Isle Straits were frozen over, a double track was laid across the straits, on the ice; large holes cut through, and the granite blocks brought and thrown into the water. Accurate charts were made of each year's work, so that the material should always fall upon the same line. In four years the work was finished. The sediment brought down by the arctic current soon filled all the interstices, and to-day the dam is perfect, preventing any entrance of the waters of Davis Strait into the Gulf of St. Lawrence, except through a narrow channel for the passage of vessels. Four hundred million cubic feet of material was used in this work."

Thus, little by little, did Cobb learn of the reasons and wherefores of the many innovations and changes which he constantly saw about him. The days came and passed; Cobb finding delight in the society of Mollie Craft, and pleasure and instruction in that of Hugh, her brother.

And then, when alone, came the dream wherein the angel had led Marie Colchis to him and had spoken the prophetic words. Words prophetic of what? he asked himself. Long and long did he ponder over the vision. His was a nature to love and to desire love in return. To him, woman was an angel, a being divine. Desolate and alone, his heart demanded a companion. He admired Mollie Craft; did he love her? And when he asked the question of himself, he could give no satisfactory reply. But of one fact he felt assured: if he loved her, he loved his lost Marie more. Yet she his Marie, was dead: was it wrong for him to seek for a companion to soothe the desolation of his heart, especially one embodying such virtues as Mollie Craft? May not the vision have been given for such an interpretation? he argued: he did not know.

One day in the latter part of November, as he and Mollie were sitting by the cheerful fire in the private parlor of the executive mansion, he looked intently into her eyes, and sadly asked:

"Do you not think me sad at times, Mollie?"

He called her Mollie, and she called him Junius; such was the President's request, as he considered Junius Cobb his adopted son.

"Yes, Junius; and it often pains me to think that, perhaps, we are not doing all that we ought to make your life happy."

"Would you do more if you could?" and he fixed his eyes with a loving expression upon hers, which fell at his glance.

"I am sure, Junius, that never was a sister—" and she emphasized the word—"more ready and willing to make a brother happy, than I."

"Were you ever in love, Mollie?" He jerked the words out as if fearful of the answer she might give.

"Why! what a question!"

"But were you?" he persisted.

"Now, Junius, that is not fair, to ask a girl such a question. Were you ever in love?" She laughed, but anxiously awaited his answer.

"Yes." He spoke slowly and with an absent air. "Twice have I known what it was to love a woman."

A tear seemed to glisten in his eye as his memory carried him back a hundred years.

"Twice?" inquiringly

"Yes; or rather might I say, once to love a woman, and once to love a child."

"You surprise me greatly, Junius. Will you not make a confidant of me and tell me all about your loves?" and she put her hand upon his shoulder.

That touch, so gentle and light, sent a thrill of pleasure through his heart. He turned and seized her hands in his, and looked long and lovingly into her eyes.

"Can man forswear his soul?" he cried, harshly, while his tight grasp of her hands gave her pain.

"Do not hurt me, Junius!" she cried, trying to free her hands. He released her, and sat down in his chair.

"I did not mean to hurt you, Mollie. I am torn by contending passions of right and wrong. My soul is athirst. I long to quench its burning fires, but dare not speak my thoughts. Alone in a new world, I am barren of kith or kin to fill the aching void in my heart. And, though knowing this, yet am I bound by chains of honor, respect and manly devotion from speaking the words which might, perchance, secure me that greatest of God's blessings to man, a woman's love."

He bowed his head, and remained silent.

Mollie Craft was no child, no affected schoolgirl, nor hardened society woman. She was a true, noble-hearted being, and read this man's secret without his lips framing its confession: he loved her.

With sorrow in her voice, she said:

"Junius, you are not alone in the world. You have a father, mother, brother, and sister, though not of the same blood, yet are they as loving as your own relatives could be."

"I know," he returned; "but my heart craves more—a being like you, Mollie, to love me and be loved by me in return."

It was out. He had avowed his love but not in such passionate terms as one would have used if a reply had been expected. He meant not to ask her heart and hand; he merely told her what his heart craved.

She made no answer; gave no reply.

Then, with a burst of increased sadness, Cobb continued:

"I crave this love, Mollie, but cannot ask for it. I have already given my pledge to a woman—have promised to marry none but her."

"Then, Junius, you should not break that promise," and a relieved expression came over the fair face.

"But she can never be mine; she is dead!" and the strong man bowed his head and wept like a child.

Going up to him, she put her arms about his neck, and kissed him on the forehead, then silently left the room.

As the dial in the executive mansion sounded the hour of 22 that night, a figure wrapped in a black cloak stole silently from the rear entrance of the building, through the gardener's gate and into the conservatory. An instant later and a tall man had clasped her in his arms, and lovingly pressed her to his heart.

"Ah, Lester, you are waiting for me," looking up into his manly face.

"Yes, dearest; waiting and watching. These moments by your side, stolen though they are, become the happiest in my life. Ah, Mollie! would that you could be with me forever. Why must I thus always beat about the bush to seek your society?"

Reluctantly he released her, but held one dainty hand in his, as he led her to a wicker seat just beside the daisy rows at the lower end of the conservatory and seated himself by her side.

Throwing her large black cloak over the back of the seat, Mollie turned her great blue eyes toward her lover.

"Why must you seek me thus stealthily, Lester, you ask? You know."

Her eyes dropped, and a shade of shame overspread her fair face.

"Yes, I know. For you have told me that your father has taken a dislike to me in particular, and against all army officers as suitors for your hand in general. But he can find no cause to be prejudiced against me—at least, none that I am aware of," looking into her eyes inquiringly.

"No, Lester," quickly returned the girl, "he can certainly find no stain upon your character, else his daughter would not have entered here to-night to meet you." This with a proud knowledge that, wrong as she was in disobeying her father's wishes, she was conscious of the nobleness of her lover's character.

"'Tis the old story, Lester," she continued, after a moment—"a father's ambition. Papa *is* ambitious, but his ambition no longer centers in himself, but in his children. Reaching, as he has, to the highest position within the gift of the nation, he hopes to see his children, when he descends from his station, still moving onward and upward toward renown, popularity, and—and—O Lester, I hate to say it—wealth."

She hung her head as if ashamed to confess that her father for a moment considered pecuniary matters in connection with the disposal of her hand.

Taking her hand in his, he calmly said:

"Mollie, I blame him not. 'Tis a father's first duty to seek the welfare of his children. But, darling," drawing her toward him, "though I have not wealth, yet have I my pay as a Captain in the army, a sum sufficient to enable me to provide a cozy, happy home for us. Do you not think it would be cozy and happy?" looking tenderly into her eyes, which had been raised and turned upon him as he spoke.

"Ah, Lester, to me, yes," she returned, petting the hand that held hers. "I am your promised wife, Lester—promised by me, but not by my father. Let us hope, dearest, that time will make some change in his determination to find a suitor of greater wealth; he could *not* find one more noble," blushing sweetly at the confession.

Lester Hathaway drew her closer to him, and kissed her rich, red lips in appreciation of her kind and loving words.

"We will hope," he said, as she modestly drew away. "I dislike, dearest, as much as you, to have our meetings clandestine, but I could not live throughout the day without at least a moment of your sweet society. You do not blame me, Mollie, do you?" lovingly pressing the hand that lay in his.

"Of course not, Lester, if you say so; for I believe you to be the very soul of truth," she returned, smiling archly.

"And when I avow that no fairer woman ever lived, that my heart beats but in love for you, that I adore you, Mollie, you believe me sincere, do you not, dearest?" and his arm stole gently about her slender waist, drawing her unresisting form closer to his heart.

"Lester, my own, I do; and your love is reciprocated with all the depth of my heart." She spoke with truth and pathos.

Raising her face to his, he looked into her eyes.

"You will marry none other than me? You will wait until I can claim you from your father? Speak, dearest."

"I will," came the words, lowly but lovingly spoken.

He kissed her lips even as the words were uttered.

"Now, Lester, I have something to communicate to you," continued Mollie, as Hathaway finally released her. "Mr. Cobb half proposed to me today," and she related the whole conversation. "Now, Lester; I could not tell him I was engaged. He loves me, I can see it; but he is laboring under the restrictions which an honorable heart has imposed. If he succeeds in holding to his sense of duty, he will never ask me to be his wife; if he wavers, I may expect an open declaration. Be not angry with him, Lester. He knows not our relations; for if he did, his lips would be sealed forever. I know the honorable and true heart that beats within his breast."

"What will you do? You should not have encouraged his love," reprovingly said Hathaway.

"I, Lester? I did not encourage it. I tried from

the first to teach him that I could be only a sister to him. I know not what to do! If I had a handsome, jolly girl friend to come and remain with me for a month or two, perhaps his thoughts and love might be transferred to her."

"You have never seen my sister, dearest; but I think she would meet all the requirements, exactly," with an air of pride.

"O Lester! papa wouldn't like to have your sister come as a guest at the house, and be compelled to keep the brother out; and, besides, he might fear her influence in your behalf; and she might help your case, too," with a sly glance.

"That would be terrible intriguing, wouldn't it?" laughing. "But couldn't she come as somebody else? your friend, for instance, at school?"

"Capital! That's it! I will introduce her as Miss Marie Colchester, my old chum at Weldon. Send for her, Lester; and when she comes I will meet her at the hotel and instruct her in her duties."

"I will send for her to-morrow."

"But I had forgotten; is she engaged, or in love?"

"Neither; I am positive of it."

"And you will send for her to-morrow?"

"Yes, my darling. She will be here by the 20th of the month."

"Good! And now, Lester, you may have just one kiss, and I must go."

She put up her lips, and raised on the tips of her toes to meet his kiss.

"Oh!—oh!—don't smother me, Lester," disengaging herself.

"Will I see you here to-morrow evening?" he anxiously asked.

"I don't know; but you can come," laughing as she passed through the door.

CHAPTER XIV

The evening following his interview with Mollie found Cobb in better spirits and more cheerful. He had not seen her since the day before, as she had complained of a slight indisposition and had remained in her room.

Seated in the library of the President, and in his accustomed place—for Cobb came nearly every evening to hear Mr. Craft discourse on the topics of the day, and to narrate, in his turn, the events contemporary with his former existence—he reminded his friend that he had promised to explain the law system of the present day, and to discuss its merits and defects.

"And right happy I am, my dear boy," returned the President, "to sit and chat with you on these subjects, which, in many cases and under many phases, may strike you as being worthless, absurd, and detrimental to a just definition of the principles of sound common law."

"You will hardly surprise me by any innovation upon the law of my time," said Cobb; "knowing, as I do, that the age is progressing. It could not have taken a retrograde movement in common law—not the law itself, but its definition and interpretation in the courts."

"The laws of the land have been greatly modified and simplified. No longer are the bickerings, snarlings, personal abuse and ungentlemanly conduct of the opposing counsel permitted in the courts. Decorum is strictly observed, and justice—pure, plain justice, as far as it is possible for human minds to discern it—is meted out to the culprit at the bar, the defendant or the appellant in the case."

"If such is now the condition of your courts and your law, you are worthy of man's sincere praise and thanks. The farce daily enacted in the courts of 1887 was a disgrace to an enlightened and civilized community."

"The root of the innovation was the substitution of a plain and simple code of laws for the cumbrous shelves of State and national codes existing during your time. There is now one universal code of laws for the nation, whole or integral. Every crime known to man is laid down fully and plainly, and one, and only one, punishment ordained for the guilty."

"But does this not work more harshly against those of otherwise good reputation than against the habitual criminal?"

"Possibly. But to avoid that greatest of evils —the giving of different sentences for exactly the same crimes, and committed under almost similar conditions—the universal code was established. Now every man knows exactly the punishment fixed for those guilty of any particular crime. There is no such thing as irrelevant testimony. The desire of justice is to know every circumstance connected with the commission of the crime. Yet limits to the continuance of testimony in certain directions are fixed. The desire now is not to defeat the just endeavors of man to obtain his rights—not to punish the accused because he is accused, but to quickly dispense justice to all. The most radical change in the dispensing of justice is the discontinuance of the jury system in vogue up to 1926—a system faulty in the extreme; a system where twelve men of widely different characters, education, religious principles, and ideas of justice, were expected to each and individually concur in one particular finding, and where a single dissenting voice required the trial to be held again, before a similar enlightened jury, or the accused discharged. In fact, during the jury system, it was the endeavor of counsel to impanel a jury of ignoramuses, a jury of men who had not read of the events of the day, or if they had read them, then of such infantile, idiotic minds as to have reached no conclusion upon the case whatever. That system is obsolete, thank God! Outside of the police courts, which have a single judge who hears and determines the case, and whose powers are very limited, we have the Dom Cöda, or house of justice, in which all cases are tried in which the punishment does not exceed a certain fixed standard. This house is presided over by three judges, and to them is the testimony given, by them heard, and by them is judgment rendered. They are lawyers, and understand the law. Next comes the Gledom Cöda, or superior court, presided over by five judges. Here are heard the highest criminal cases. The Legledom Cöda, or supreme court, is the highest in the State, and is presided over by nine judges. There are Doms Cöda and Gledoms Cöda for civil cases, likewise."

"But suppose one is dissatisfied with his trial; what then?"

"He appeals it, as formerly; but with this knowledge and understanding: If the higher court finds him guilty, the penalty fixed by the lower court is doubled, provided such a sentence is possible."

"Humph! I should think guilty people would hesitate about appealing."

"Indeed they do. It is not often that an appealed case is decided against the appellant; and for the very reason you have advanced, that if guilty, they stand by the finding given in the lower court."

"Does not this system give opportunities for bribery and jobbery?"

"The opportunities may exist, but the practice is one of the rarest crimes known in the calendar. The punishment for conviction of bribery of, or corruption in, a judge, is life imprisonment in the government prisons; and to the person accomplishing it, a similar sentence; while to attempt it is a twenty years' offense."

"Severe punishments, compared with those of former times," was Cobb's remark.

"Yes, very severe. But a good government needs and demands a good and true corps of judges to settle, justly, the individual disputes of its people, and to protect them in their lives, liberty and property."

"I should imagine that the system is very expensive—the salary of so many judges?"

"Not nearly as expensive as the summoning of jurors, their per diem pay, the delays in justice, and the many incidentals of cost in trials in former years. One Dom and one Gledom Cöda serves for 15,000 people. The salary lists are $12,000 and $25,000, respectively; or three dollars per capita to insure justice. The judges serve until seventy years of age, unless removed for incapacity or for commission of crime. The lease of office is thus, practically, for life, the salary high, the honor great, and self-interest makes the man honest."

"I think it a good innovation," exclaimed Cobb.

"No doubt you would like to hear of the prison system as it exists to-day; for it is directly connected, of course, with the law?"

"Certainly. I have wondered if there was any change."

"Each State has its own prison, wherein are incarcerated all convicts whose sentence is less than five years. All others are sent to the government prisons. Of these latter prisons, there are ten, situated in various parts of the country, but all on islands and isolated from communication with the world except by government vessels. The island of Anticosti, in the Gulf of St. Lawrence, is the main Eastern prison; then, there are those of Tiburon, in the Gulf of California; Great Abicos, among the Bahamas; Charlotte's Island, in the Pacific Ocean, and others. These are prisons belonging to the government, and no convicts are sent to them whose sentence is less than five years. Here are manufactured every conceivable thing needed by the government, and for which it would have to pay cash, did it not make it itself. Great ship-yards, from which are turned out magnificent vessels of war; foundries, in which immense and powerful guns are fabricated; looms and workshops for the clothing of the army and navy; factories for boots, shoes, furniture, ironware, and thousands of other articles that the various departments of the government require. In fact, the manufactured articles are few that the government has to buy by contract. The raw material, however, is purchased and sent to the prisons, and there fabricated into the articles needed. As no convict comes with less sentence than five years, ample time is available in which to teach him such a trade as will give to the government the greatest benefit from his labor. The working system of the prisons is admirable in the extreme. The convicts are well fed and clothed, and required to work a given number of hours, only, a day, depending upon the fatigue of the labor. Good conduct remits four days in each month, or fifty-two days in each year; extra work, when available, is furnished to them, and credited at the rate of the number of hours of that particular service per day, as so many days of their sentence served. This system prevails in all of the State prisons, but, of course, upon a minor scale. In them only such articles are manufactured as are required and used by the State governments."

"How about pardons from these prisons?" inquired Cobb.

"The President alone has the power of pardoning from national prisons; the governors, from State prisons. At each prison is a Legledom Cöda, and a pardon is never issued except this court has examined the case and recommended it. The Legledom Cöda of each prison also tries all cases of infraction of the laws of the prison, and fixes the punishment for the same. As a matter of fact, few, very few, pardons are given, and then only when it is apparent from subsequent evidence that an injustice has been done a man."

"What are considered among the gravest crimes?"

"Murder, perjury, rape, receiving of bribes, or giving of same, corruption in office, arson, mayhem, premeditated and willful. These are all life imprisonment offenses, and there is no reduction of sentence for any reason."

"But does not this convict labor compete with the labor of the masses?" asked Cobb.

"How can it? If the government needs a million dollars' worth of manufactured articles, one of two courses must be pursued to obtain them: either to buy or manufacture. If they are bought, the people are taxed to pay for them; if they are manufactured by convict labor, the tax-payers save just that amount of money, while a punishment is inflicted upon the worthless class by causing it to labor without reward."

"True; but in my time the people howled and railed against convict competition. Now, turning from the subject, tell me if there are many labor troubles at the present day."

"None worthy of the name. A great and just law was advocated, in 1920, by that eminent jurist, Attorney-General William Bean, of Pennsylvania, and passed the next year, that it should be unlawful for any firm or corporation carrying on any manufacture, to accumulate in any one calendar year a profit in excess of twenty per cent. on the actual money invested, and exclusive of that invested in the plant. Full provision was made in the bill for examination of accounts, books, etc. The bill further provided that each person, firm, etc., should regulate the price of the labor employed by them. Then further laws were enacted against combined strikes, intimidation of the employed, etc. It was a wise bill, and has worked advantageously ever since it was passed by Congress."

"But I fail to see its benefits to the laborer," dubiously returned Cobb.

"In this way, Junius. Twenty per cent. interest on the money invested is enough to satisfy any man, and cause him to advance capital and embark in manufactures. Now, if the wages of his laborers are fixed by him, he can increase them just as much as his income is greater than twenty per cent.; he must do it or cut down supply. He actually divides the surplus over twenty per cent. among his men. If competition is great and the profits less, he must cut the wages or increase the output to save his percentage; but if he is willing to accept fifteen per cent., or ten per cent., then the wages remain the same as before. But if he desires to cut the wages, it is his right by the law; the laborer may work for it, or not. As a truth, though, wages are better now than ever, while the price of articles has fallen nearly twenty-five per cent. below that of 1920."

"Are there any laws relating to the holding of real estate?" Cobb asked. "I remember quite an agitation on that subject during the '80s."

"Yes; one general law only: no individual not a citizen can hold land in the United States; and no one citizen can hold, in his own name, more than 640 acres, or one square mile."

"A good and wise law. In my time, vast tracts of land were held by individuals and corporations, both domestic and foreign."

"It was so until the Bean bill of 1920. One year after the passage of that bill was given to foreigners to dispose of their real estate, and five years given the citizen to bring his holdings within the limit of the law."

"I think I was informed by Mr. Rawolle that the government owns all of the railroads in the country?" inquiringly.

"Yes, all; and likewise the telegraph system. Furthermore, each city owns its own water supply and electric-light plant. It will thus be seen that the people, and not the capitalist, own and govern the country."

"What is the rate of taxation—national and municipal?"

"There is no national taxation except on tobacco and liquors. Municipal taxation is really the only burden, if it can be called a burden, which the people bear. That taxation is very low indeed, and is levied under certain equitable laws. The revenue of the nation is derived from customs, liquor, tobacco, and the excess of receipts over expenditures of the railroads, telegraph and postal service."

"And how about the rates of postage?"

"The rate per mile for railroad traveling is one cent, the rate for telegraphic messages is one cent per word, and letter postage one cent per ounce, throughout the United States."

"Is the nation in debt?"

"No; the nation owes not a dollar. The last of what we call the great debt was paid in 1979. It would have been paid long before that time had it not been that an enormous outlay was required to gain possession of the railway system of the country."

"What did you pay for the telegraph system? That must have taken another immense sum."

"The rights of the sympathetic telegraph system were purchased in 1892, for five millions of dollars, and that system caused all of the surface lines to be abandoned in a few years."

"The sympathetic system, did you say?" and Cobb showed more interest than he had evinced in the President's dry recital of the law of the country.

"That is the name of it," Mr. Craft replied.

"Does it differ much from the Morse system?"

"Many would not understand your question, Junius. You must remember that the system has been in operation for over a hundred years; few persons know any other. Fortunately, I can answer your question, for I have studied the subject. There is practically no difference between the two systems, save in one respect—"

"And that respect is—" interrupted Cobb.

"That there is no wire, metal, or tangible connection of any kind between the instruments."

"What! no wire! How, then, does the current pass?"

"We do not know!"

"Well! that is very strange! A telegraph system, and its principle unknown!"

"It is just as I tell you. We know how it works, but not why."

"And was the principle never divulged by the inventor?"

"Never."

"Surely, he taught you how to make the instruments?"

"Oh, yes; or the system would have been of little worth," and Mr. Craft smiled at the utter amazement of his listener.

"But I can conceive of no instrument being made by human hands for a specific purpose, unless the principle upon which it was constructed was fully known," and Junius Cobb shook his head as if doubting the statement of the other.

"The sympathetic telegraph is, however, a manifest success," continued the President. "It works over miles of country and in every direction, and at each station records the pulsations of the heart of its mate, wheresoever on the face of the earth that mate may be."

"By whom was this wonderful instrument invented? Surely, his name will live forever!"

"Ah, Junius, you are right! The name of Jean Colchis will—why, Junius! what is the matter?"

Cobb had sprung from his chair as the old name, so dear to him, was uttered. He moved anxiously toward the President, and seized him by the arm, while an expression of hope, of fond remembrance, came into his eyes.

"O, tell me," he cried. "Tell me of this Jean Colchis! of his daughter! It was he, you have said! There never was but one Jean Colchis! It must be he—my master!"

"Calm yourself, Junius," hurriedly exclaimed Mr. Craft, as he gently laid his hand upon the young man's shoulder. "Did *you* know Jean Colchis?" in a wondering tone.

"Ah! did I? He was my master! It was he, Mr. Craft, who invented the power that brought me to this new life!" Tears came into his manly eyes as he remembered his benefactor and his lovely daughter.

"I know nothing of him," sadly returned Mr. Craft. "He was, and has passed out of life. He lives now but in history and the minds of the American people." A dimness came into his eyes as he witnessed the emotion of the other.

"Where is the evidence of his skill, of his ingenuity? Where can I behold the work of his loved mind?"

"If you desire, Junius, you shall visit the great theatre of action of hundreds upon hundreds of his wonderful instruments—the city of America, on the Central Sea."

Cobb had heard the announcement of his old master's wonderful achievement in the sciences with astonishment not unmixed with joy.

He thought, now the good old man will have money, fame, and distinction; his daughter, the dear little Marie, would be advanced to her rightful place among womankind, and no longer be hidden in Duke's Lane, unknown and unsought. Unsought! Then came a feeling of jealousy at his heart. Men would seek the heart and hand of his little fiancé. Would they succeed? Would she quickly forget him, and receive with pleasure the advances of other suitors? Then, with a grim smile, he bade his heart have no fear; Marie Colchis was no more. It mattered not what she had done; she was dead to him forever. He would live in the remembrance of her childish yet womanlike love.

It was past midnight when Cobb and the President separated, each to his bed; the latter to slumber, the former to lie in a mournful remembrance of former days and former friends.

The next few days were passed by Cobb as the others had been, in the gaining of a knowledge of the world as he now found it. Much of the excitement caused by his advent had passed; much of the curiosity of mankind in his appearance among them had vanished. He settled down to a life similar to the rest. To Mollie Craft he was kind and polite, but not passionate. He still believed her the magnet toward which fate was drawing him; but he awaited the propitious moment to tell her of his belief, of his love. She was kind and sisterly to him; nothing more.

It was near the first of December that a new face, a sweet, girlish face of innocence and simplicity, came across the path of his life.

Marie Colchester had arrived at the executive mansion as the one dear friend of Mollie Craft during her school-days at Weldon. As she was presented to mamma and papa Craft, she blushed at the knowledge of the deception she was practicing; but she had promised her brother and his fiancé to obey their wishes.

A tall girl, with blonde hair, majestic form, round and plump, with eyes melting in their expression of artlessness and innocence, Marie Colchester was one who would easily conquer the heart of a susceptible man. In the parlor they met for the first time, Junius Cobb and she.

"My brother, Marie. Junius, let me make you acquainted with my dear old schoolmate, Marie Colchester. I want you to be the best of friends," and she moved toward the piano, and listlessly tapped the ivory keys.

"Oh, I am sure we will, will we not, Mr. Cobb?" exclaimed Miss Colchester, with a winning smile. "You know everybody has heard of you, and I feel it a great honor to know one who has lived in two lives."

For a moment Cobb stood with a perplexed expression, and gazed intently at her; the name had startled him. She raised her face, and met his gaze, then, blushing, dropped her eyes to the floor.

"You do not answer, Mr. Cobb?" she ventured. "Are you displeased at meeting me?"

Recovering himself in a moment, he quickly returned:

"Pardon me. My thoughts were far away."

"Not very complimentary to me," with a merry laugh. "But, then, if you will tell me of whom you were thinking, and her name, for I know it must be a woman, I will forgive your ungallantry," with bewitching naiveté.

"Marie Colchis," he slowly answered, with his thoughts still far away.

"How funny! almost my own name. Now you have aroused my curiosity. Who is this divinity that can hold your thoughts so enthralled when am near?" and again she laughed as she emphasized the pronoun.

"She was my affianced wife!"

The words came as if from the depths of his heart.

Marie Colchester saw she had touched a tender chord in his memory. Casting aside all semblance of levity, she approached him and laid her white, small hand upon his arm.

"Forgive me," she said; "I did not wish to bring sad memories to your mind."

Mollie Craft slyly watched them both, as she

stood at the piano, apparently deeply absorbed in the music copy on the stand.

"Good! They will be friends," she murmured.

Such was the meeting of Junius Cobb and Marie Colchester.

CHAPTER XV

The month of Finis had passed, and it was Old-Year-Day; to-morrow would be New-Year's-Day, A. D. 2001.

In the conservatory, among the roses, geraniums and violets, with scissors and twine in their hands, were Marie and Mollie. As fresh and bright as the flowers about them, they chatted and laughed as they clipped the buds and fashioned the floral pieces which were to grace the private room of the executive mansion on the morrow.

New-Year's-Day was a great day, in this new era of time. It was a day upon which all toil ceased, and all hearts were made glad by the exchange of good wishes and good cheer.

The President held a great reception from 9 until 11 dial, and after that hour devoted the afternoon to his family and intimate friends. In the evening the day was crowned by a magnificent ball; such had been the custom for years in Washington on New-Year's-Day.

With deft fingers, the two girls made the pretty floral pieces: one for papa and mamma; one each for Hugh and Junius; and Lester was to have one— Mollie said two—sent to his hotel.

"Well, if you send him two, I shall send another

to Hugh," cried Marie, with a pretty, threatening gesture.

"Marie Colchester, you are in love!" and Mollie stopped in her work to note the effect of her words.

"Oh!" prolonged and low from her companion.

"Yes, you are," teasingly.

"O Mollie Craft! How can you ever say such a thing?" and the blushes overspread her whole face.

"You are a little traitor," with a show of anger.

Marie looked up as if uncertain of her friend's meaning, but the twinkle in the latter's eye satisfied her that no belligerent intentions were premeditated.

"How so, Mollie?" demurely, as she clipped a japonica rose from its stalk.

"How so? Didn't I ask you to come here and win the love of Junius Cobb so as to free me from the pain of seeing his love for me unreturned? Didn't you agree to throw yourself away for Lester's sake and mine? Didn't you tell me that you knew he couldn't help loving you, and that his heart would soon be lying at your feet like a—a—a sponge-cake stepped upon by an elephant? There!"

"O Mollie! I didn't say all that!" cried Marie, in confusion.

"Yes, you did; you know you did," shaking her scissors at the other.

"Well, haven't I tried to make him love me? Oh, I am so ashamed! Trying to make a man love me, and he won't show the least little bit of love," and she hid her face in her hands, in apparent distress.

"That's all put on, miss; as if I couldn't see. You were not here a week before you had that great big brother of mine dancing after you as if tied to your apron-strings," and Mollie looked severely at the culprit.

"But, Mollie, I couldn't help it. He would come—and come, and stay—and stay—and—and—I didn't know you objected—and I'll go away to-morrow," and the poor girl burst into a flood of tears, and sank beside the floral tribute to her lover.

In an instant Mollie was by her side, her white arms clasped around the sobbing girl, and the kisses checking the rain of tears.

"There, there, Marie, my own true girl!" she coaxingly said, "I was only teasing you. I would not, indeed I would not, have said it if I had thought you would have believed me in earnest. I am proud of my brother's choice; I want you for a sister."

"And you are not angry with me for not loving Mr. Cobb?" looking up beseechingly.

"No, dear girl. I love Junius, for he is a noble though a silent man. It would have given me great pleasure to have seen him love and marry you, Marie, for you will be a prize to your husband; but, to be my brother's wife, that is better still," and she kissed the red, quivering lips of the girl, and gently raised her form from the ground.

Thus another scheme devised by human minds had failed.

Hugh Craft had been won by the innocence and loveliness of this girl; had given her his whole heart, and had received hers, with its wealth of love, in return. Their love plighted, and sitting by his side one afternoon in the conservatory, whither he had led her to enjoy, unmolested, her sweet society, she had told him the story of her coming, her identity and her relationship to Lester Hathaway. And then, under his promise of secrecy, she had told him of Lester's infatuation and semi-engagement to Mollie. Loving this woman as he did, he could find no fault with his sister for loving the brother; but in deference to Marie's wishes, he had refrained from informing his sister and her lover that their secret was known.

It was New-Year's night, and the grand ball-room of the executive mansion was a scene of beauty and splendor. Incandescent lights hung in huge festoons from the ceiling; beautiful women and brilliant uniforms mingled in one grand, gorgeous panorama.

Out from the moving multitude came Hugh Craft, with Marie leaning on his arm. Pausing at the grand stairway to the supper-room, Hugh sent word to Lester and Mollie to meet him in the conservatory.

A few minutes later they were joined by Mollie and her lover, who found them standing under the rose arbor at the lower end of the conservatory. As they approached, Hugh left the side of Marie, and, confronting Lester, addressed him in a tone of severity:

"You have made love to my sister, sir!"

Mollie uttered a little scream, and clung to the arm of Lester, while Marie stood mute in astonishment at the scene.

"I repeat it, sir," continued Hugh, in harsh and severe tones; "you have been guilty of engaging yourself to my sister."

For a moment Lester Hathaway stood looking at the other, not knowing what answer to make. His sister must have told Hugh of his secret, he thought; then, boldly:

"And you, sir, have made love to *my sister!*"

Hugh was surprised at the retort, for he did not know of the interview between the two girls, of the day before, nor that Mollie had told Lester all about it.

"I admit it," he smilingly said.

"And so do I," returned Lester, as the twinkle in Hugh's eye gave him the assurance that there was no anger in his words.

"You want her, Lester?"

"And you want her, Hugh?"

So rapidly had the words been spoken that the girls had had no time to speak.

"Yes; and you?"

"Want her forever."

"Then, Lester, let us trade sisters," and he laughed heartily as he saw the comical expression which came over Mollie's face as she realized the situation.

"You are real mean, Hugh, to scare us that way. Look at poor Marie; she doesn't know yet if you are in earnest or not," and Mollie looked toward the girl.

"She knows now," as he clasped her in his arms and kissed her lips.

"Oh!" exclaimed Mollie.

Then these lovers sat and discussed their hopes and plans. Sympathy, deep and true, was expressed for Junius Cobb; for it had been noticed by all that an appearance of sadness was ever in his face. He seemed devoid of energy and all desire for amusement. He cared not for the society of women; even Mollie received far less attention from him than formerly; not that she believed he thought any less of her, but that he never did actually love her. In her kind heart, she suggested to the others that they combine their forces, and endeavor to arouse him from the apathy into which he certainly was sinking. Each gladly agreed to do all in her power to make the man forget his former life and enter into the enjoyment of the present. With their hearts bearing nothing but respect and friendship for Junius Cobb, they left the conservatory, and returned to the ball-room

The night passed, and it was January 1, 2001.

At breakfast, Hugh told Cobb that he intended to

take him to America, as the President had promised that he should be made acquainted with the system of the sympathetic telegraph, and also with the methods pursued in publishing the "Daily American."

Cobb's face brightened up, and he expressed his pleasure at the prospect of gaining a knowledge of these wonderful inventions.

Accordingly, at 14 dial the two young men took the Chicago Pneumatic, and reached Pittsburgh at 16:50 dial. Here the Tracer, in which Cobb had crossed the Central Sea in the preceding September, and which had been ordered to report to Captain Craft, was boarded, and Cobb again met Lieutenant Sibley and his assistants.

Putting to sea as soon as the baggage had arrived from the train, the Tracer was headed southwest by west, and quickly made the offing.

At 3:10 dial the next morning the vessel came to anchor in the harbor of America. It was 7 dial before Lieutenant Sibley would awaken his guests, and nearly 9 dial when Mr. Doane, the superintendent of the telegraph system, presented himself, under an order from the Secretary of State to render every service to his visitors.

The city of America lay just a mile from the shores of the Central Sea, upon a nearly level plain about six miles long by three in width. The Kentucky hills in the background, with their magnificent scenery, the great sea in front and the beautiful streets and houses, made the scene appear to Cobb like an enchanted city of the Arabian Nights.

Landing at the dock, an electric drag quickly took the party to the beautiful residence of Mr. Doane.

A few minutes later, after meeting the charming wife of their host, Cobb and Hugh were ushered into the library by Mr. Doane, who again expressed the pleasure which he felt at meeting the man of whom the world had been talking for the past four months.

"I can assure you," he exclaimed, "we see it here. Thousands of telegrams have passed through the United States—I should say the Central Office—in which your name was the prominent subject."

"I ought to feel flattered at such world-wide reputation," returned Cobb, modestly; "but I am tired of it, and wish to be a man born in the period."

The conversation continued, and the object of Cobb's visit to the city was fully explained.

Stepping to a book-case, Mr. Doane took a large book from a shelf, and, opening it upon a table, displayed a map of the city of America and its immediate vicinity.

"There is a map of the city, Mr. Cobb," he said, "and you can follow me as I explain to you the reasons why the city has been so laid out, and in such an extraordinary fashion. America is a city of about 125,000 souls. The plan of the city is very peculiar indeed, but made with the one view of bringing the employés of the system into little communities near the place of their occupation. It resembles a portion of a great checkerboard, eight squares long by six in breadth. Each square is a half-mile in length and breadth, and has an area of one-quarter of a square mile. Four of these squares is called a section, making twelve sections, or twelve square miles in the city. Each section is divided into eight triangles of equal shape and area by diagonals from its corners. Thus there are in the city five great streets, each four miles in length, extending from one extreme to the other, or east and west; seven streets two miles in length running north and south, and the diagonal streets. Electric cars run on all the streets except the diagonals. All of these streets are 200 feet wide, and paved with gray glass. Each triangle is cut into streets of 100 feet in width, running north and south for the north and south triangles, and east and west for the others, and contain about 400 houses. Thus there are in each section 3,200 houses for employés. Each house occupies an area of fifty feet front by 100 feet in depth. In the center of each section is a beautiful but small park. Four large, grand buildings of six stories each face this park, occupying the apices of the eight triangles.

"These buildings are the workshops, or site of occupation, of the inhabitants of that particular section. Thus a community of 3,200 families live and work in each section. For further benefit to the people, each two triangles of a quadrant is combined under the title of 'square.' Each square, therefore, has its own diagonal street, meeting the other diagonals of the section in the center, or place of occupation. Again, as each square is a smaller community of the section, it has its own shops, stores, etc. All of these places of business are located midway on the diagonals, and are styled the 'bazar.' There is allowed in each bazar, only one store for each particular trade; for instance, there is but one grocer, baker, market, etc., through the whole list of trades. There are, also, restaurants and club-rooms for men and women, libraries, churches and school-houses located on these streets. So complete is the system that the residents have little need of ever going outside their square to have their wants properly attended to. All of the stores in the city, except the grocers, bakers, and markets, are under control of the authorities; and the articles offered for trade have to be of the best, while the schedule of prices is so regulated that only a certain minimum profit can be made. The excepted trades are directly under the charge of competent officials, and the articles sold at cost. The houses for the operators, on the main streets, are all six-room cottages, while those on the cross-streets contain only five rooms. They are built in various and different designs, and all are provided with heat and light by electricity. They are covered with ornamental slabs of various colored glass, which give them durability against the weather, and exquisite beauty. Each section is under the direct supervision of a governor and two assistants, and all disputes and controversies arising among the people are settled and judged by them. No person is allowed to settle or remain in the city without special authority from the superintendent and council of the system. The cars are free to all people; so, also, is the rent of the houses to the operators, the only requirement being that each occupant shall keep his house in good repair. Every expenditure for the welfare of the city is paid out of the receipts of the system, thus leaving nothing to be demanded of the employés save the cost price of their subsistence. You will see from the map, Mr. Cobb, that there are ten sections having their central offices, while the two interior sections of the city, and wherein we now are," and he placed his finger upon the spot, "have one between them. This central spot, with its parks and great buildings, is called 'The United States,' to distinguish it from the other centers of operations; which are named, in order, from left to right, around to point of beginning: 'Islands,' 'Indias,' 'Asia,' 'Africa,' 'East,' 'Australia,' 'Continent,' 'Britain,' 'South America,' and 'West.' In each section 2,000 operators move down to the central offices each morning at 8 dial, making 20,000 telegraph operators, besides 2,000 in the central section of the whole system, who daily work the keys that flash the millions of messages over the world. This vast throng of employés moves, easily and without impediment, down the cross-streets of their triangles into the diagonals of their squares, and thence to their work. By the system of squares, no employé has a greater distance to walk to his work than the length of the hypotenuse of the triangle whose base and altitude is a half-mile in length; or a little less than three-quarters of a mile. One-half of the number of operators go to their dinner at 12 dial, and the other half at 13 dial. At 20 dial, they are relieved, and 10,000 others take their place until 8 dial the next morning. Their work is clean and light; but the hours are long, as it is not practicable to have three sets of operators. Now, for the amusement of the city, there are theatres, dancing-halls, clubs, boating and sea-bathing, libraries, gymnasiums, and many other means of recreation. The greater portion of the operators are married, and live happy and contented in their positions. The finer houses, on the main streets, are given to those longest in service, as a reward for their services. The salary of an operator is sixty dollars per month, and promotion is by competition. I may have wearied you, Mr. Cobb, by going into details as I have," Mr. Doane said, apologetically; "but in order to understand this vast system of communication, with its ramifications extending to every known part of the globe, it is necessary that you should learn how the working force is set in motion and how continued."

"On the contrary, Mr. Doane, you have not wearied me at all," replied Cobb. "I can assure you I take special delight in everything tending to better the condition of the working classes. How much better could capital have been employed in my day in building up communities like this, instead of accumulating vast wealth to be fought over by contending heirs."

"This, Mr. Cobb," continued Mr. Doane, "is the condition of life and the surroundings of these thousands of men who daily tick the thoughts and wishes of mankind from every part of the known earth. Now, if you are ready, we will take the drag and visit one of the sectional offices, and you can see the actual working of the system."

It was but a few minutes' ride from Mr. Doane's residence to the nearest sectional headquarters, and they were soon entering the beautiful park surrounding the four large buildings which faced toward the center. Cobb noticed the air of order and cleanliness which pervaded everything, and the lack of hubbub which might be expected in the vicinity of four buildings holding 2,000 employés.

Ascending by the elevator to the first floor, they were ushered into "The State of New York," as the floor was designated in the system.

The scene that met the eye of Cobb was unique in the extreme. Row upon row of little tables, at each of which sat an operator, extended from one end of the room to the other. In front of each line of tables an endless belt was carrying little folded papers, and dropping them through a chute in the floor. At one extremity of the room was a number of pipes vomiting forth an unceasing stream of small metal cases, which were quickly seized and deposited in boxes near at hand. A stream of assistants were busy handing these cases to the operators at the tables. A humming sound, low and musical, pervaded the room as the hundred and more instruments clicked forth their messages.

"This is the 'State of New York,'" explained Mr. Doane. "There are 140 operators in this room, working direct with the central office of the State of New York. Upon the next floor is 'New England,' and above that, 'Pennsylvania,' and so on, each floor being devoted to the work with the central office of a particular State or States." Mr. Doane then enlightened Cobb on the work of the system. In each State of the United States, and each nation of the various divisions of the world, was located a central office; these central offices worked direct with some floor of the buildings in the sectional offices. For instance: the section designated "East," contained the operators who worked with the central offices of the Eastern States. "South America" worked with the central offices of all the countries of South America. From the central office of a State or nation, the message was sent direct to the town or city of destination, if in that State or nation.

"To understand the system," said Mr. Doane, "let us follow the course of a message from St. Petersburg to San Francisco. The operator at St. Petersburg sends it to the central office of his county by his sympathetic instruments. From that central office it is sent to the section in this city designated 'Continent;' there it is received, and sent to 'The World,' or central office, by pneumatic tubes. At 'The World' it is assorted from the hundreds dropping from the tubes, and sent in a tube to the 'West' section. Here it is received, and sent to the floor named 'California,' handed to an operator, and transmitted to the central office of California, and by them to the city of San Francisco. The time of transit of such a message of twenty words, from St. Petersburg to San Francisco, is thirty minutes."

"Quick work, that!" exclaimed Cobb, admiringly.

"But a more peculiar illustration of the system," continued Mr. Doane, "is exemplified in the sending of a message from Portland, Oregon, to Vancouver, Washington. These cities are but fifteen miles apart; yet the message from the former city is sent to its central office, thence to the 'West' section in this city, thence by tube to the next floor, thence to the central office of Washington, and thence to Vancouver. Now I will show you the instruments," and he motioned them to follow him to the lower end of the room.

Here Cobb for the first time examined the great invention of his old friend and master, Jean Colchis.

On a table were set an ordinary relay, sounder and key, instruments which were familiar to Cobb, who had thoroughly studied the electric telegraph system of his day. The relay only differed from those used in former years in that it had no large and heavy armature in front of its poles, but in its place was a small, bright needle swinging on a vertical pivot. The short end of the needle was held by two delicate springs, pulling in opposite directions. The needle was metallically connected through a local battery to an ordinary sounder, and thence the current was carried to a little stud near the extreme end of the short arm of the needle.

The relay was connected through its keys to another local battery.

If the key was closed—that is, pressed down so as to form a metallic connection—the relay magnets were magnetized by its local battery, and the little needle was drawn toward them by their attraction, until the short arm of the needle rested against the little stud. This touching of the needle to the stud closed the circuit of the second local battery, and the sounder armature answered to the influence. If the key was opened, the circuit was broken, the needle was drawn back by its little spring and the local current of the sounder disrupted. With the exception of the needle, the whole apparatus was precisely similar to that employed in telegraphing in 1887.

Cobb examined it carefully and noted its delicacy

and the care exercised in its protection from external forces by being covered with a glass globe and surrounded by helices in opposite directions.

Mr. Doane watched his expression, and smiled at his perplexity.

"Simple, isn't it?" he asked.

"Yes, in construction," returned Cobb; "but its theory of action upon the distant instrument is to me a total mystery, I must confess."

"But easily explained, in so far as how it acts, but not why it performs its work," Mr. Doane answered. "The needle which you see has a mate, and that mate is in the California office. These needles are made in pairs, and, by a wonderful process, made sympathetic. No two pairs are charged with the same sympathy; consequently, no other needle of the whole system of instruments will affect this save that single one in California. The instruments of each pair are most carefully set up at their different stations, so that the needles shall point to the true north; thus the needles are exactly parallel to each other. When the instrument is not in use, the key is left open, and the needle is held back by its spring. Now, if the California operator should close his key, he would cause his needle to be attracted toward the relay magnets; this movement of his needle exerts a sympathetic influence upon the needle in this instrument. *It endeavors to parallel itself to its mate.* It moves to the right, overcoming the power of its spring, and, touching the stud, closes the circuit, and the sounder records the fact. Opening his key in California, both needles move back by the tension of their springs, and the sounders are demagnetized. The sympathy of these two needles to place themselves in a parallel position, or, more properly, the repulsion of the poles of each from those of the other, is the secret of the sympathetic telegraph system."

"A wonderful, grand invention!" burst from the lips of Cobb, as he comprehended the almost human action of the two needles. "How could mortal man have discovered such a secret of nature!"

"Yes, Junius; it is wonderful!" echoed Hugh.

"How many pairs of these sagacious little instruments have you in the system?" asked Cobb, after a silence.

"In the United States, 280,000; in the world, 450,000. But more are needed very much, and have been for years," returned Mr. Doane.

"Well, why don't you make them?" inquiringly.

"Ah! there's where the trouble is! Since 1963 no instruments have been made. The secret is lost!"

"Lost! The secret is lost! How could it be possible to lose the secret of such a discovery as this?" and a look of incredulity expressed the doubts he entertained.

"It is a fact, nevertheless, Mr. Cobb; a fact coupled with sorrow to me in many ways. But let us take the drag and return to the house, as it is near luncheon; I will tell you of the accident as we ride along." A shade of sorrow came over his face as he spoke.

As the drag sped along the grand avenue toward the beautiful home of the superintendent, Cobb listened to the old man's story concerning the loss of the secret of Jean Colchis' great invention.

"My grandfather," commenced Mr. Doane, "was the first superintendent of the sympathetic telegraph system. In 1892, when the wonderful discovery of Jean Colchis, of whom you no doubt have heard—"

"And with whom he was on terms of the closest friendship," broke in Hugh, in a matter-of-fact sort of way.

"Knew Jean Colchis! personally knew the inventor of the system I have been explaining to you!" cried Mr. Doane, in astonishment.

"Yes," from Cobb.

"Ah, yes! I had forgotten your status in this life. You have lived a hundred years; why may you not have known him?" murmured the old man, as if reasoning with some doubt in his mind as to Cobb's sincerity of expression. "You must tell me of him," with an eager look; "for I reverence the name of him who conceived this wonderful agent of communication, and placed its power subject to the will of man. To-night, to-night, Mr. Cobb, you must tell me of yourself and of him."

"With pleasure, Mr. Doane," returned Cobb.

"Be it so. And now I will go on with my story,"

continued the superintendent. "As I was saying, in 1892, when Jean Colchis made his discovery, the government bought the invention from him, and selected my grandfather, who was a Major in the army, to be the superintendent of the system. I do not know what were the terms of sale, or what were the conditions imposed, excepting that only one man was to know the secret of sympathizing the needles; that that man was never to commit the secret to writing or to tell it to any living soul until at death's door; then it was to be transmitted to only one other, verbally. It is believed that this great stipulation on the part of Jean Colchis was to prevent France from reaping any benefit from his discovery, as he was said to have been an exile from that country."

Cobb smiled as he uttered the latter words, for the political secrets of Colchis were fresh in his memory.

"For thirty-seven years my grandfather sympathized, in his laboratory, all the needles used in the system. Upon his death-bed, in 1929, at the ripe age of eighty-five, he communicated the secret to his son, who was his assistant in the system. The government made my father superintendent to succeed my grandfather. I was born in 1937, and at twenty years of age became my father's assistant. It was his intention to leave the secret with me; but, from a stroke of paralysis preventing speech and motion, he died on the 6th of September, 1963, and the secret died with him. On account of my knowledge of the system I was, upon the death of my father, immediately appointed superintendent, and have occupied the position ever since."

"And has no effort been made to rediscover this secret?" asked Cobb.

"Oh, yes. Scientists throughout the world have worked assiduously, but without success. The government has standing rewards of five millions of dollars for the lost secret."

They had reached the house, and the drag stopped at the door.

CHAPTER XVI

After lunch a visit was made to the offices of the "Daily American," the great newspaper of the country. The establishment was situated at the southeastern corner of the city, just outside of section "South America."

The making of the form and printing of this great paper was explained by Mr. McGregor, the manager.

The items of news and interest from all parts of the world were received at the "World" building by the sympathetic telegraph, and then transmitted by tube to the chief of copy at the office of the paper. Here it was assorted and given to the typewriters. Type, as used in the nineteenth century, had no place in the form of this paper.

Each compositor sat before a machine which appeared to Cobb very like a Yost type-writer, and printed his copy on slips about as long and twice as wide as the columns of an ordinary newspaper.

The paper was prepared, by immersion in certain chemicals, to undergo a change of texture and composition upon the passage of an electric current of 400 volts. The letter arms of the type-writers were connected with the batteries, and whenever, in printing, a letter was struck upon the paper, the current passed through to the metallic bed, leaving a silver-gray print of the character on the paper.

These strips, or columns of the paper, as they proved to be, were set together to form sheets or pages of the "Daily American."

A little instrument, having a pointer with 100 metallic hairs, each about an inch in length, and each connected by an insulated wire to a sympathetic instrument, was placed on the outer edge of the sheet of paper, which lay flat and smooth upon a copper bed. The 100 little points were so set that they just touched the paper, but not each other; and their arrangement was such that, as the machine traveled over the sheet from bottom to top, every part of the paper for a width of two inches was touched by some one of these points.

Now, the current of electricity which passed through the slips of paper when printed, had not left the letters in clear color, but had changed the metallic composition in the paper into metallic letters.

Another, and one of the most important factors in this new process, was that the letter was metallic clear through the paper, the reverse side of the sheet showing a perfect type-form.

The "Daily American" was printed simultaneously in one hundred cities of the country, and from these cities delivered by train as in former days. Of course it was necessary that each city should have its own type-form, but the size of the paper precluded the possibility of sending such a vast amount of matter to each place and there putting it in type-form.

The difficulty was overcome by each city having a little 100-pointed instrument, similar to the one at the main office of the paper, the wires of which were connected to mates to the 100 sympathetic instruments in the home office; for the special work the needles had been sympathized in 100 sets of 100 needles each.

At 2:45 dial by the time at America, each sub-office had great sheets of paper saturated with the metallic chemicals used to prepare the home-form, spread perfectly flat upon copper beds, and the little traveler in position at the lower left-hand corner of the sheet.

At precisely 3 dial the operator at America touched the key of a sympathetic instrument, and the traveler on his sheet of paper passed rapidly down the entire page. At every sub-office the traveler performed a similar journey, being regulated by a main sympathetic instrument. When the travelers reached the end of the page, they automatically returned to the point of starting, excepting that they moved the width of the 100 points, or two inches, to the right. This was repeated until every particle of the paper necessary for a whole edition had been completely passed over.

The principle, as Cobb learned, was this: The home sheet having metallic letters, and the copper bed being connected with a battery, whenever a point of the traveler touched a letter a current passed to the point, thence to the relay, which caused the sympathetic needle to move to the right. At the sub-office, the mate of this needle also moved to the right and closed the circuit of the local battery; a current then passed down to a point of the traveler —which point was a mate to one of the points in the home traveler—and thence through the prepared paper, changing the composition into a fine metallic line. Whenever the points of the home traveler passed off of a metallic letter the current for that particular point or points was broken, as the paper had been rendered non-conductive after its receipt from the type-writers.

The result was that each sub-office had an exact copy of the original form, made up of thousands of little, fine lines, but so close together as to form perfect letters. These forms were quickly placed in rapid-acting plating baths, and the top surface, or that side over which the traveler passed, plated with aluminum. In thirty minutes the forms were covered by a sheet of metal which held every letter that had been made in the paper by the electrical change of the chemical, rigidly in position; the letters being formed clear through the paper. The forms were now flattened, and then bent over rollers for the great rotary presses. The last act in the manipulation of these forms was then accomplished by decomposing and removing all the paper which had not been transformed into metal. The result of all these operations was that a printing cylinder was obtained exactly similar to the one at the home office. The paper was then printed and distributed as in former times.

Cobb studied all these details very carefully, and left the establishment with feelings of astonishment at the progress made in a hundred years.

"We must have an early breakfast, Junius," said Hugh, that evening, "for we are to take the Tracer across the sea and visit the metropolis."

"The metropolis?" echoed Cobb, with a look of surprise.

"Yes."

"I do not think that I care about going to New York again; not for the present, anyway," said the other.

"Well, did I say anything about going to New York?" returned Hugh, carelessly.

"But you spoke of visiting the metropolis."

"So I did."

"There can be but one metropolis in a country."

"True," smiling.

"And that must be New York for this country."

"And that is not New York for this country." This with a decided emphasis. "I am going to take you to Chicago; to the metropolis of the United States; to the greatest city on earth."

He noted the expression of wonder which came over the other's face.

"And do you mean to tell me that Chicago is a greater city than New York? Chicago, an inland town, to compete with and excel New York, a seaport city?" and Cobb shook his head as if he doubted the possibility of the truth of such an assertion. "Why, you have told me that New York has over four million inhabitants; has Chicago more than that number?"

"Yes," returned Hugh; "nearly double that number. By the census finished last June, Chicago had, at that date, 7,345,906 souls living within its corporate limits."

"Come, Hugh," pettishly exclaimed Cobb, "that's a little too strong. I remember that it was estimated, in 1887, that Chicago would have about 1,500,000 in 1890, and if that estimate was correct, this vast population given by you could never have been obtained through ordinary growth."

"Nor was it, Junius. The growth was extraordinary," lightly returned the other.

"Humph! So I should say. Why, it is equivalent to a gain of 53,000 persons every year since 1890. Such a rapid growth for so many years is an absurdity."

"As you please; have it so. But let me enlighten you a little. In 1910 the population of Chicago was 1,800,000—a rapid but fair growth for a city possessing the surrounding country, energy, resources, and natural attractions of Chicago. But it was after the year 1916, and for the next ten years that Chicago, as well as many other towns and cities in the West, received the greatest addition to its population. After the great cataclysm of 1916 the vast numbers of people who were driven from their homes by the rising of the waters over the doomed area of the Ohio basin, sought temporary shelter in all the towns and cities surrounding the Central Sea. As time progressed and showed the future destruction that would be wrought as the waters rose, the people emigrated in great numbers. The movement was westward, only a small portion going East or to the South. The great cities of Chicago, St. Louis, Minneapolis, St. Paul, and Kansas City received vast additions; but of them all, Chicago, being the nearest and largest, gained the most. From a million and three-quarters, in 1910, that city had over four million in 1930. The rest of her immense population has been gained through natural increase and immigration, being at the rate of about 50,000 per year, or less than one and-a-half per cent. increase."

"And Chicago is now the metropolis of the United States," mused Cobb. Then aloud: "Yes, it was to be. The condition and extent of this great republic were factors to cause a westward movement, not only of the center of population, but of the location, even, of the metropolis of the nation."

"Now, Junius, go to bed and get a good sleep; we will rise early in the morning," said Hugh, rising from his chair.

"All right; anything to keep me interested," returned Cobb. "I must have excitement. I feel blue and down in the mouth the instant my interest flags."

"O, pshaw, man! you ought not to feel that way. You'll come around all right in time; you mark my words," and Hugh sauntered off to his room.

It was 17:25 dial the next day, when Cobb and Hugh arrived in Chicago, on the Southern Pneumatic. Taking a drag at the Central Station, they soon reached and were comfortably domiciled in "The World," the great and magnificent hotel of the metropolis.

"The World" was but one of the many grand and luxuriously appointed hostelries of that great city, but it was nevertheless the leading one. The building was situated upon Michigan avenue, facing the Lake Front. Built entirely of metal and glass, it was absolutely fire-proof; its frontage was one mass of ornamentation in all the colors of the spectrum, yet harmoniously blended. There were 3,000 rooms for guests, each provided with bath, telephone, electric light, dumb-waiters, etc. The parlors were upon the eighth floor; while above them, and covering the entire block, were magnificent gardens, covered by a glass canopy thirty-five feet above the floor.

Here rare flowers bloomed every day in the year, the temperature being uniform; the immense and lofty roof being made to slide in panels, by electricity, thus allowing the natural temperature of the outside air to prevail, when sufficiently high not to be detrimental to the plants. At night the grandeur of the scene was superb when lighted by the electric lamps.

After an hour for their toilet and lunch, Cobb and Hugh passed out and around the eastern part of the city bordering the lake, and here Cobb observed the wonderful growth and curious innovations over his time.

Like New York, the city was a double one, over its central portion, appropriate descents being situated at short intervals for passing from the upper to the lower streets. The great avenues, such as Michigan, Wabash, State, First, Fifth, and Seventh, were provided with rapid-transit trains, in tunnels crossing the river below its surface, and running south to Five Hundred and Tenth street. Electric surface roads were used for cross-transportation, and were similar to those which he had already seen.

The city was divided into four great divisions; or, as they were styled, zenods. Each zenod had its own post-office, court-house, police, city prison, and all the machinery necessary in the operation of a complete city. The zenods were governed by a lieutenant-mayor and a council of fifteen members; the city, as a whole, was governed by a mayor and a supreme council of thirty-nine members.

Cobb ascertained from Hugh that it had been found utterly impossible to properly provide for the welfare and advancement of such a great population unless the work was divided, and to that end the four zenods, with their respective municipal corporations, with a supreme head and upper house, had been created.

For three days Cobb and Hugh passed about the great city, the one observing and the other explaining the many wonderful things to be seen.

Chicago was indeed a remarkable city, not only in its vast population, quadruple government, extent of territory and unprecedented increase, but in the application of every known adjunct to man's welfare, comfort, and benefit.

Leaving "The Wonderful City" and its vast progress for a future and thorough investigation, the two friends took the 23 dial pneumatic for Niagara.

CHAPTER XVII

It was 2 dial the next morning, when Cobb and Hugh reached Niagara. The night was beautiful, but the weather cold, and it was with pleasure that the two men reached the hotel, and ensconced themselves by the side of a real coal fire, as Cobb called it.

The stillness of the night was a source of surprise to Cobb, as he heard not that thundering, deafening roar of the mighty cataract which had always heretofore greeted him upon his arrival at the falls.

The next morning Cobb and Hugh were up early, and, after a hearty breakfast, proceeded in the direction of the old inclined railways where Cobb had so often, in former years, made love and talked nonsense to the pretty girls of Niagara.

A different sight met his eyes as he neared the balcony where formerly the best view of the grand falls was to be obtained. Niagara was still a mighty cataract, but not half the volume of water which had passed over its precipitous edge in former days now flowed over the walls of rock. Where formerly the great mass of surging, foamy floods rushed out over the top to a distance of fifty feet, and fell in one unbroken blue sheet into the boiling torrent below, now was a lighter sheet of white and broken water.

Two artificial streams, one on either side of the river, below the falls, the beds for which had been carved out of the precipitous banks which marked the erosive power of the stream, carried an immense flow seven miles down the river.

Along the banks, and from one hundred to seventy-five feet below the canals, were rows of houses of similar construction and color. From every house, in either line, poured forth a torrent of water which rushed and leaped down the rocks to the stream below. Electric wires and huge cables were to be seen in every direction.

Turning back from the novel scene in front of him, Cobb moved nearer the edge of the balcony, and looked over towards the base of the falls. Great masses of ice rose from the depths below, half obscuring his view; but the field was clear enough for him to ascertain that a new order of phenomena had taken place since his last advent there. It seemed as if a hundred gigantic mouths in the face of the cliff were belching forth mighty torrents of seething, foamy water.

Passing down the stairs to the first landing, which was sixty feet below the brink of the falls, he and Hugh came to the gate of a tunnel in the walls under the falls. The gatekeeper, after a few words from Hugh, touched an electric bell, and a young man who answered the summons was directed to show them about the works.

Niagara Falls had, indeed, undergone a most remarkable change in a hundred years. The face of the cliff, from the Canadian, or "Ontario" side, as it was then termed, clear around to the city, had been pierced by huge tunnels, ten feet in diameter, extending under the rapids above for a distance of 1,000 feet. There were two rows of these tunnels; the first row was 120 feet below the top of the falls, and the tunnels were twenty feet apart. The next row was cut over the walls between the lower tunnels, and was ninety feet below the edge of the falls. Again, above this line, was a row of smaller tunnels, five feet in diameter and 100 feet apart. From the two rows of large tunnels mighty jets of water were pouring out, and breaking into foam as they reached the waters coming from over the cliff.

Cobb and Hugh passed into the tunnel, which was brilliantly lighted by electricity, dry, and much warmer than the outer air. Moving onward, they soon came to the great chambers of the cliff.

"Here, Cobb," said Hugh, as they entered the first chamber, "here are the first dynamos. This whole cliff, from the front to 1,000 feet in rear, is honeycombed with these chambers. Each chamber has a turbine wheel and a set of dynamos, and receives its water-supply through shafts drilled straight up through the roof into the waters of the rapids above. The water, after working the turbines, is discharged into the great tunnels which you saw emptying from the face of the rock. Of the mighty body of water flowing over the falls, only a portion could be used in this manner, as it was not deemed wise to make more than two rows of tunnels; but to gain as much power from the water as possible, the two lines of dynamo houses along the banks, which you saw from above, were constructed. The little tunnels are for air circulation, and fans are continually moving the air through the whole labyrinth of chambers. There are, in the face of this rock, 200 tunnels, in two rows of one hundred each, and extending back 1,000 feet, or forty miles in total length. Over each tunnel are chambers, twelve by twenty feet, with ten-foot walls between, or thirty chambers along the line of each tunnel.

"Each chamber has a fifteen-inch shaft tapping the water-supply above. Now, the descent of the water is at the rate of 3,840 feet per minute, the fall is sixty feet, and the weight of a cubic foot of water 62.5 pounds: thus the horse-power of each shaft is exactly 400, and the flow-off, in area, one square foot. As there are thirty of these chambers to each discharge tunnel, then an area of thirty square feet flows from a seventy-eight-square-foot escape. But the volume of water from the shafts, owing to its increased velocity, would soon overflow the discharge tunnels if level; to obviate this, they are inclined as much as possible. Four hundred horse-power turbines in each chamber, coupled to dynamos, give 350 electrical horses. As there are 6,000 chambers in the rock, the output, in electricity, is equivalent to 2,100,000 electrical horse-power; this, added to the power generated by the fourteen miles of dynamos along the river, which have 3,650 wheels, brings the whole power utilized up to three and a quarter millions of electrical horses. This mighty current is carried by great copper cables to all parts of eastern United States, and used for every conceivable purpose where power is required."

"You seem to be pretty well posted in this matter," was all Cobb could say, as Hugh gave him this array of figures.

"I am. I was on a board of engineer officers in connection with the water-power of these falls, some years ago," he replied.

"How long have these works been in operation?"

"About fifty years."

"So long?"

"Yes."

"Is it a private concern?" inquired Cobb.

"Oh, bless you, no. It cost too much money to put it into operation. The government expended over two hundred millions of dollars in building the works; but they have paid for themselves almost twice over."

"And this is the source of the great electrical supply—"

"For the Eastern States of the nation," interrupted Hugh; "but it is only a portion of the power used. The water-power everywhere is converted into electricity, and sent over the country."

"And steam isn't used any more?" hesitatingly.

"To be sure, it is; in the great timber districts, and where fuel, which otherwise would go to waste, is plentiful, steam engines are still used."

After a thorough inspection of the great center of electrical supply, the two returned to their hotel, and made preparations to leave Niagara and visit New England, and especially Boston and Providence, "the places I love so dearly," said Cobb. "I must once more visit the scenes of my childhood, and note their advancement."

So away they went to pass a week, intending to be in Washington by the 10th of January.

CHAPTER XVIII

It was the third morning after Cobb and Hugh had started for America, that Marie Colchester, or, as she should be called, Marie Hathaway, had said to Mollie:

"I wish I could see some of those peculiar contrivances which Mr. Cobb used in his sepulchre, in San Francisco."

"And why may we not?" Mollie had returned. "He is away, and we can take a peep into his room without a living soul but ourselves knowing it."

So it was that these two girls stole silently into Cobb's bedroom, and noted, with feminine curiosity, every detail of a man's private apartments.

With a guilty feeling, they opened bureau and chiffonier drawers, peered into boxes, and finally opened the doors of the wardrobe. None of the wonderful inventions for prolonging life, which they had expected to find, were discernible. Then into the closet, to the left of the bed, they looked. An old trunk, an iron box, some old boots, and a bundle of clothing, were all that met their view.

"Humph! We haven't discovered much, Marie," dolefully exclaimed Mollie. "Hugh's room looks just like this. Nothing but clothing, old boots and shoes and such traps," and she seized the old clothing in the corner, and threw it disdainfully to the side of the closet.

"Hello! What's this?" she slowly exclaimed, as a hollow rod of copper fell to the floor at her feet.

Stooping down, she cautiously picked it up and examined it. Marie was looking over her shoulder, brought there by her exclamation.

"There's writing on it, Mollie!" Marie cried. "There; on the side!"

Mollie turned it over, and saw the words, dim and blurred by time:

"To Junius Cobb. Important!"

"In God's name, do not delay in opening this cylinder!"

With palpitating hearts and bated breath, the two girls stood with their eyes glued upon the inscription. Finally, Mollie, in a solemn voice, said to her companion:

"Junius has never seen this. It has been mislaid. It is our duty to send it to him at once."

"But you do not know where they will go from America," referring to Hugh and Cobb.

"True," sadly. "We may not see them for a week or more. What shall we do?" in a tone of inquiry.

"Why, put it where he will see it when he returns," answered Marie, as if there was no doubt of the propriety of the action.

"But it says not to delay in opening it," persisted Mollie.

"Yes," slowly; "it does." Then, after a pause: "Why not open it, Mollie? Maybe we may become like the good genii in the fairy tales, who always helped the poor, unfortunate prince who was about to lose his sweetheart."

"Oh, I dare not," and Mollie shook her head.

"But you must; we cannot leave it now," the other returned.

"But dare I?"

It was evident that Mollie's curiosity would overcome her scruples.

"Of course, you dare. We may do some good. At least," hesitatingly, "it will do no harm to see what that cylinder contains."

So they argued the point, and finally left the room bearing the cylinder with them.

An hour later, in the sanctity of Mollie's bedroom, and with the aid of a file which she had procured, the cylinder was opened. From it Mollie drew forth, cautiously, and with a sense of fear, a tightly-rolled paper. The cylinder was only half an inch in diameter by ten inches in length, and the rolled paper, when spread out, was simply a letter containing a few words, yet with writing as fresh as if spread upon its surface only a short time since.

With heads together, and wonder in their hearts, they read:

"To you, Junius Cobb, is ordained the task of freeing from a living tomb a woman of rare beauty and angelic disposition of heart. Lose not a moment! A delay of a day will cost you a year of sorrow! Hasten to your duty, and God be with you! On the island of Guadalupe, in the Pacific Ocean, in latitude 29 degrees 15 minutes north, and longitude 41 degrees 16 minutes west, is entombed a woman whose return to life may gladden your heart, or be a curse to your existence. Listen, and heed well these instructions: From the town of Noniva, on the island, travel southwest, nineteen miles, to the deep canyons of the dry fork of the Ninta River; pass up this fork until you come to a tall and slender rock which the superstitious natives have named the 'Finger of God.' Set your chronometer with the exact time of the meridian, and when your time shall indicate the hour of four o'clock in the afternoon of January 6th, note carefully the spot where the shadow of the 'Finger of God' rests on the gray, steep rock of the eastern side of Ninta Creek. Along a shelving ledge on the face of the cliff, pass to the spot and look for the two letters 'J. C.,' cut in the wall. Into the lower point of the letter J, which will show a small hole, drive a steel rod until twenty inches have passed into the rock. A door of solid granite will open, and you will be at the mouth of a cavern. Enter, and learn the rest."

A feeling of awe came over the hearts of the two girls, as they read this weird communication.

Again and again they read the letter, and pondered long over its contents.

"What does it mean?" gasped Marie.

But Mollie was of a more practical turn of mind. She saw it to be an order for the deliverance of a human being—a woman. Casting aside her feelings of superstition which the reading of the letter had at first inspired, she commenced to debate in her mind what was the true meaning of the instructions so minutely given. Taking the letter again in her hand, she carefully read it over.

"Ah! this letter is very old!" she exclaimed; then pointing her delicate finger to a line, she cried: "Do you see that? 'four o'clock in the afternoon,' it says. It has been years and years since the time of day has been designated as 'o'clock.' This paper must be very old!"

"Yes; it must be very old," agreed Marie, in a low voice, reverently looking at the letter.

"And here! this must be important! The shadow must be seen on January 6th of any year," and she again read the letter. "Junius must go at once, or another year will have to be passed before a trial can be made." Then, musing a moment, she exclaimed: "It is even less time than I thought, for if this paper is as ancient as we believe, then January 6th is really January 5th, for in old times, New-Year's-Day was January 1st."

"Yes?" from Marie.

"Yes," sadly. "It is plain that we cannot get

word to Junius in time for him to reach Guadalupe by that day." Then starting up with fire in her eye, she cried: "Why not make the attempt ourselves?"

"Oh!" prolonged, and in amazement, by Marie. "We dare not!"

"And why dare we not, Miss Timidity?" retorted Mollie, scornfully.

"Because we are only poor, weak women; it would take men, great, big men, to perform this terrible task."

"Oh, pshaw! you are a timid little mouse; that's what you are, Marie Hathaway. I am going to rescue this woman, and you are going with me," grandly. "Now, don't say a word," as the other attempted to speak. "You go immediately and get everything ready for our journey; we will leave for San Diego to-night, at 19 dial, for I remember that San Diego is in latitude 33, or thereabouts; and that should be the place from which to take a lipthalener."

"Truly, Mollie?" with a look of consternation in her eyes.

"Yes; truly! Now, Marie; have some courage. Will you go with me and aid me? or must I go alone?" and she put her arms lovingly about the girl's waist.

"If you really and truly mean it, dear Mollie, I will do as you wish, and go with you; but it's an awful undertaking," shaking her head.

Thus was it decided by these two young women to go thousands of miles to an unknown island, seek the location of an isolated cavern, and bring back to life the prisoner therein entombed.

An hour after, and Mollie came into the library, where her father was engaged in writing. Stealing softly up to him, she put her plump white arms about his neck, and kissed his forehead reverently.

"What is it now, pet?" he said, laying down his pen.

"Father, dear; I wish to visit aunt Lora in San Francisco; can I go?" looking him in the eyes.

"Why, yes; I suppose so. You may go next week if you can get ready."

"Not next week, papa. I want to go to-night; on the Central Pneumatic."

"What?" he exclaimed. "To-night! And why this haste, my daughter?" and he gave her a deep, searching look.

"Father, have I been a good, true daughter to you?" and her deep blue eyes looked straight into his.

"In truth you have, my daughter," and he kissed her cheek, so close to his lips.

"Then, my dear father, I beg of you one great kindness, one great confidence in my sincerity, honesty, and truthfulness. Grant me permission to go West to night with Marie Colchester; grant me a short time to remain, give me a thousand dollars, and ask me not to tell you the reasons for my strange request and actions."

"My daughter, this is very strange!" and he arose from his chair, took her hands in his, and drew her toward him. His eyes looked into hers with an earnest expression. Steadily, and with an honest eye, she returned his gaze.

"Do you, indeed, make this request?" he slowly added.

"Father, I do," she replied.

"Answer me one question. Has Lester Hathaway any connection with this undertaking?"

"As God sees me, he has not," she firmly replied.

"My daughter, you shall go as you desire, and may God watch over you. Now see your mother and inform her, and then prepare for your journey."

She again kissed him, and left the room.

At 19 dial the two girls, clad in traveling-dresses, and with grips in their hands, entered the depot, and were soon cozily ensconced in the fourth sleeper of the Central Pneumatic, No. 5, west.

"What will Lester say when he does not find me in the conservatory to-night?" sighed Mollie.

"And what will Hugh say when he returns and finds me gone?" and another deep sigh could have been heard.

"But I left a letter for him," with a sly glance toward the other.

"And I left a note for Hugh," glancing toward Mollie. Their eyes met, and a smile lighted up both faces.

"Oh! you did?" from Mollie,

"Ah! you did?" retorted Marie.

On rushed the train. Miles upon miles were left behind them, and the hours sped by. They should be at El Paso at 6:30 dial the next morning, and at San Diego at 10 dial. It would be nearly 11 dial before they would be able to search for a vessel to take them to Guadalupe.

The time was passing, and it was with a troubled mind that Mollie surveyed the route and the time at her command. With beating hearts, the two girls watched the hours pass as the train rushed along to the Pacific; eagerly did they look for the approach of the city by the sea.

It was 12 dial when the train reached the city of San Diego. Quickly disembarking, the girls entered a drag, and were rapidly propelled to the Great Pacific. Once within the office of the hotel, Mollie excitedly asked for information as to what lipthaleners were in the port.

"None, madame," was the calm reply of the clerk. Her heart sank within her bosom at the words. "There are none but sailing vessels in the harbor; will madame have use for one of them?" continued the man, noticing her agitation.

"No; and yes—I cannot tell. Show us a room and serve breakfast there, and at once," was the impatient reply.

During their breakfast, the two girls discussed the situation, but without arriving at any solution as to how they would reach Guadalupe Island.

Having partaken of a light repast, they proceeded to the docks to find some means of transportation to the island. Not a lipthalener was in port, and but few sailing vessels. To her inquiries, Mollie was informed that the island was 120 leagues southwest, and no sailing vessel could make the voyage in less than three days, with the best of winds; and that the chances were that it would take five.

Disheartened, she and Marie turned back to the hotel.

Fate was against them, and they would not be able to rescue the imprisoned girl ere another year had come and passed. Would the woman live through another year? Would she not die, if yet alive? *Was* she yet alive? Such were the questions Mollie asked herself.

Often and often she went out on the porch, and scanned the horizon for the approach of a lipthalener.

Sixteen dial came, and found poor Mollie in a fever of anxiety. I no lipthalener came into port before 20 dial, her case was hopeless. It was 350 miles to Guadalupe Island, and she must be there at 10 dial the next day, in order to have sufficient time to reach Ninta Creek and make her preparations. Discouraged, she sat and buried her face in her hands, while Marie, in sympathy, put her arms about her, and tried to comfort the sinking heart.

Hark! What was that sound? Like a flash of lightning, Mollie was on her feet.

"Did you hear it, Marie?" she cried, excitedly.

"Yes; what was it?" the other replied with equal excitement.

"There! there! Do you hear it? There it is again!" and the girl danced for very joy.

The hoarse, rolling sound of a marine whistle was plainly heard by both.

"A lipthalener! A lipthalener!" they both cried, and rushed out on to the porch.

Coming around the fortress point was a magnificent cruiser of about 3,000 tons. Her black hull and raking, yardless masts proclaimed her calling; the flag at the peak, the glorious stars and stripes, proclaimed her nationality. Off the lower dock, and a half-mile from it, she came to anchor, and her great hull swung around with the tide.

"Come, Marie; no time is to be lost!" and Mollie rushed into the parlor, seized her hat, and quickly made her way to the dock.

For a dollar, a boatman gladly took them in his little craft, and rowed to where the lipthalener lay quietly at her anchors.

"Ahoy! On deck! Is the captain on board?" cried the boatman, as he held off by a hook against the side of the big vessel.

"You'll think so, you lubber, if he sees that hook in his vessel," came the response from the port bows. "Heave off and lie to, and I'll report," and the man and voice disappeared

A moment after, a man in the uniform of the United States navy, appeared at the companion-way and cried:

"Ahoy! What's wanted?"

"Two ladies wish to come aboard and speak to the captain, sir," replied the boatman, touching his hat in a nautical fashion.

"Very well. Heave to on the starboard side."

A few minutes later Mollie and Marie were in the captain's cabin of the San Francisco, and had asked its commander to take them to Guadalupe Island.

"But, ladies," replied Captain Gordon, a bluff but kind-hearted old gentleman of fifty-five years, "this is rather an unusual request upon the United States navy, and comes from a very unusual source; yes, a very unusual source indeed, but a very charming source, I must confess," and he bowed gallantly to the two girls.

"I know it, Captain; but the case is one of life or death: I must be in Guadalupe Island at 10 dial to-morrow." Mollie looked beseechingly at him as she spoke.

"I wish I could accommodate you, ladies; but I fear it is impossible."

Mollie's heart almost ceased to throb as she heard these words.

"I am here for dispatches," continued the captain, "and expect to leave for San Francisco to-morrow morning."

"But," pleaded Mollie, "it will only take a half-day to make the run—"

"And a half-day back again," interrupted the captain, "is a whole day. Why, my children, I might be court-martialed if I were to do this thing."

"But, if I promise that you not only will not be court-martialed, but will receive the commendation of the President, and the Secretary of the Navy, will you go?'

"If you could guarantee this, ladies, why, damn me!—I beg your pardon—I would do it, just to please two such lovely girls as honor my cabin by their presence to-day; but, of course, you cannot do it."

"But I can!" cried Mollie, "and your promise is given. I am Miss Mollie Craft, the President's daughter: in his name, I guarantee approval of your action."

The beautiful girl arose from her chair, and stood proudly before the old sailor.

Without moving a muscle of his face, Captain Gordon slowly said:

"Pardon me, ladies, but any woman could have uttered those words."

Crushed, and with a sinking feeling at her heart, Mollie nearly fell at his feet. He doubted her, and she had nothing to prove her identity.

Deliberately came the words:

"Have you anything to prove your relationship to the President?"

"Alas, nothing!" she cried, and the tears filled her eyes.

"No letter in which you are recognized?" he kindly asked.

Ah! Stay! Hope again rose within her soul. Quickly thrusting her hand into her pocket, she drew out a letter. Nervously she broke the seal, and glanced over its contents. A ray of sunshine came into her tear-bedimmed eyes, her bosom heaved for a moment, and then she became calm. Handing the letter to the captain, she said:

"The letter is to my aunt, in San Francisco, and was written by my father just before my departure."

Captain Gordon took the letter, and, instantly recognizing the executive heading, slowly read:

"WASHINGTON, January 3, 2001.

"DEAR LORA:

*　　*　　*　　*　　*　　*

"She is the only daughter I have, sister, and you must watch over her carefully. We cannot afford to lose our Mollie.

*　　*　　*　　*　　*　　*

"Affectionately, your brother,

"EMORY D. CRAFT."

As he finished reading the letter, Captain Gordon rose from his chair, advanced toward Mollie, and extended his hand.

"You will pardon my doubts, will you not, Miss Craft?" he asked; "but men in official positions must protect themselves. I no longer doubt your identity; the San Francisco is at your command," and he bowed low to her.

"I thank you, Captain Gordon, and you will not lose by this kind act."

Mollie's eyes were again flowing with tears, but now tears of joy.

"When do you desire to start, Miss Craft?"

"At once," she cried.

"Return, then, dear ladies, and get your effects. I will leave the port in half an hour."

Thirty minutes sped by, and Mollie and Marie were again on board the San Francisco. Then came the orders to weigh anchor, much to the astonishment of all the crew, and the vessel moved slowly toward the fortress at the point of the harbor.

As the San Francisco approached the north water battery, the sound of a gun was heard, and the flag on the battery-staff was dipped twice, then a red streamer was run up the staff, and a boat put off from the mole.

"Hard aport, Mr. Navigator, and stop the ship," cried the captain, who was standing on the bridge by the side of Mollie, who had been invited there as the commander of the vessel for a day.

Slowly the great ship ceased on her course, and awaited the little craft, which came rushing through the water, propelled by a lipthalene screw.

"The dispatch boat, sir," said the officer of the deck, touching his cap.

"So I perceive," returned the captain. "You will receive the dispatches and cast her off, as we must not delay.'

"Very well, sir; and the officer again saluted, and passed to the companion-way.

A moment later the dispatches had been received, and handed to Captain Gordon. Breaking the port seal, he read the dispatch; then, hesitating a moment, he handed it to Mollie, and noted the sudden paleness of her face as she slowly reached forth her hand and took it.

With a feeling of impending evil, she read the paper:

"WASHINGTON, January 4, 15 D.
"*To Captain Gordon, U. S. L. San Francisco, San Diego, Cal.*

(Due at and hold.)

"Proceed to San Francisco at once. Make no delays. C. SCOFIELD,
"*Secretary of Navy.*"

With a beating heart and a quivering lip, the girl handed it back.

"And you will obey this order?" she slowly asked.

"It is imperative," he replied.

Almost out of the harbor, almost away from the chance of a telegram, she had become happy and cheerful once more. Now it was changed: this man would not dare, no matter how she prayed, to violate such an order.

Bursting into tears, a woman's resource to relieve her overcharged heart, she looked into his face, and again asked:

"And you will obey these instructions?"

"Damn it; no! I—pardon me, I—I—well, damn it! the course of this vessel will not be changed; she goes to Guadalupe Island. There!" blowing as if from some great exertion, and wiping his forehead in a vigorous manner. "If they dismiss me from the service for it, you shall perform your mission on that island," and the good old man walked to the extremity of the bridge to hide his agitation, and escape the thanks which Mollie was about to shower upon him.

The sea was rough, and the southwest winds blowing a small gale, a combination that told on the speed of the San Francisco, swift as she was. The 350 miles became nearly 450, and it was not until 4 dial the next day, that anchors were cast in the harbor of Noniva, Guadalupe Island.

Mollie Craft had had a long conversation with the ship's surgeon, Dr. Town, the day previous, and had shown him the mysterious letter, and asked his assistance; the doctor had readily consented to aid her by all means in his power.

Captain Gordon gave Mollie until 20 dial to return to the vessel before shaping his course for San Francisco.

CHAPTER XIX

At 8 dial that bright day of January 5, 2001, an expectant and anxious party left the deck of the San Francisco, and landed at the mole of Noniva. The Doctor had two men from the ship to carry the stretcher—he was a thoughtful man, and always had a stretcher along for emergencies—and the tools and such things as he believed might be needed. In the town, saddle mules were obtained, and the party of five quietly left the vicinity, as if for a day's camping in the hills.

The journey was through a broken and thickly-wooded country, and the traveling slow and tedious. It was long past the meridian when the party reached and passed up the dry bed of the Ninta River, and nearly 15 dial when "The Finger of God," which all recognized from the description furnished by the natives of Noniva, was reached.

The gray cliffs on either bank of the river were steep and rugged. Huge festoons of tropical growth covered them from top to bottom, and stunted pines stood nodding their crested heads among the rocky crevices. Already the shadow of the rock was creeping up the eastern bank, and by its position the pathway ledge was easily found.

Leaving the two seamen at the base of the rock, Dr. Town, with the tools which he had brought, and followed by the two girls, carefully made his way up the narrow, overhanging ledge, and stood near the point of the dark shadow on the face of the rock. With watch in hand, which he had set to the meridian of Guadalupe, he awaited the time of 16 dial, or 4 P. M., as recorded by the author of the letter of instructions.

The minutes passed slowly—too slowly for the two girls, who stood by his side. Their feelings were wrought to a fever heat; their hearts beat a tattoo within their bosoms, and a fear of some dreadful revelation possessed their souls.

The shadow crept on; the sun was going down to its bed in the ocean, which spread out in every direction. On moved the shadow; it had reached a dense cluster of mountain-ivy, which completely hid the rock from view: the hour was 15:55 dial.

Seizing a large knife from his bundle of tools, the doctor sprang quickly to the spot, and with dispatch, cleared away the evergreen, exposing the solid rock of the cliffs. With his eyes upon his watch, he noted the passing moments.

"Sixteen dial!" he cried, and placed the point of his knife at the end of the shadow of the "Finger of God."

Carefully marking the spot, he diligently searched for the letters mentioned in the communication. Not a trace of a letter was visible; the virgin rock lay bare, and undefiled by human hands Above, below, and on either side, his search was equally unsuccessful, and as he communicated the result of his examination to Mollie and Marie, consternation seized upon them. Could it be that they had been deceived, and that the contents of the letter were false, and made for some purpose of alluring Junius Cobb to this spot? They looked at each other in bewilderment.

Suddenly the doctor exclaimed:

"Ah! It may be that!"

"What, doctor?" they both cried, excitedly.

But the doctor made no reply; he was climbing up the cliff, straight up from the knife-mark in the rock. With the celerity of a man intensely excited, he cut and slashed away the ivy, and threw it into the ravine; then, looking at his watch, he noted that twenty-five minutes had passed since the shadow of the rock had reached the point which he had marked. Noting the variation of the shadow from the vertical for these twenty-five minutes, he drew his knife slowly and carefully up the face of the cliff, from the mark which he had made to where the shadow of the "Finger of God" then rested, the knife describing the path of the shadow.

Turning to Mollie, who had been watching his movements in wonder, he said:

"If the instructions are correct, then will the characters 'J. C.' be found near the line which my knife has described; for the letter, if true, as I have remarked, was written a long time ago, and the Finger of God' was taller then than it is to-day, as the elements must have worn many inches from its top in the course of a great number of years; its shadow was higher up the cliff, at any particular hour of the day, at a remote period, than it is to-day. Now come and examine closely along the line I have described."

With diligence and care, all three scanned the face of the rock, scraped away the mold, and sought to find the key to the mysterious cavern.

Suddenly Mollie gave a scream—an exultant scream—and cried:

"Here it is! Here it is! I have found them!"

Crowding about her, the other two saw before them the letters in the rock. Small, discolored, and covered with a green moss, it was a wonder they had been discovered at all. Yes, there they were, "J. C." Leaning over, Dr. Town took his penknife and carefully dug the moss away from the point of the J, and exposed the hole mentioned in the letter.

There was no farce, no falsehood in the communication, after all;. at least, not as regards the letters "J. C." and the hole in the J. The decisive moment had arrived.

Putting the point of the steel rod, which he had brought along for the purpose, into the hole, the doctor drove it in to its full length. A creaking, cracking sound followed, and the rock in front of them sank into the side of the cliff, leaving exposed a doorway about six feet high by three in width. Involuntarily all started back as the yawning, dark passage was exposed, and a cry of alarm escaped the lips of Marie.

The opening had been made, but the interior was dark and unknown.

"I will go in," said the doctor, "and explore the place; I will return, and inform you if it is safe."

"Oh, I am not afraid," returned Mollie; "certainly there can be nothing there to harm us."

"Oh, but there may be!" broke in Marie.

"Go in, doctor; we will follow you," not heeding Marie's alarm.

Dr. Town lighted a lantern, and, followed by the girls, passed in through the opening. A passage of some fifteen feet in length hewed into the solid rock, led them into a large chamber with a high and arched roof. As the light of the lantern threw its rays about the room, its contents were plainly discernible by all.

The walls were draped with beautiful silks and plushes; chandeliers were suspended from the arched roof; costly chairs with embroidered cushions were upon every side; books and works of art lay upon the massive center-table and about the room. A thousand objects of beauty and richness adorned the large chamber.

As they walked across the room, a light cloud of dust rose at their feet as the carpet gave way in its rottenness. Reaching out her hand, Mollie took a book from the table, and was about to open it, when it fell to the floor in a mass of rotten fibre. A beautiful picture hanging on the wall, its oil coloring still fresh and its gilded frame yet bright and handsome, was accidentally struck by the doctor, and came tumbling to the ground, in a heap of decayed wood and canvas. The table, with all its beautiful ornaments, was but a phantom; for, as they endeavored to move it to one side, it fell to the floor in ruins. Time and nature had caused such decay that it seemed to need but the touch of man to change the vision of enchantment into a scene of ruin and chaos.

There was no moisture, no mold; but apparently a dry-rotting process had been at work for years, and the destructible articles of the chamber were ready to fall in pieces at the least shock.

From the first chamber opened a second, to the left, and here was found what appeared to have been a kitchen. Utensils of all kinds were scattered about as if left where they had been last used; dishes of finest china lay broken on the floor, where also lay the once beautiful sideboard, now fallen by its weight and rottenness; decay worse than was found in the first chamber pervaded the place. A large oil-stove in one corner, and glass bottles with seals upon them, gave evidence of the methods which had been pursued in this the culinary department of the establishment.

From this room a long passage opened to the right, and led deep into the cliff. With feelings of awe, not unmixed with terror on the part of Marie, the three moved forward. The light flashed upon the dark, rocky walls, and was absorbed in their dingy gray.

Moving cautiously forward, a dozen steps brought them to a third chamber, small and low. Mollie, who was close in rear of the doctor, glanced in as the light penetrated the darkness of the room. With a scream, she drew back, shuddering with fear, and clasped Marie in her arms:

"A skeleton!" she cried. "A coffin!"

The fear was contagious; Marie sank to the ground, trembling like a leaf, and, in her fall, dragged Mollie with her. There they lay, frightened, and with chattering teeth.

"Come, young ladies," brusquely said the doctor, "there is nothing to be afraid of. Scared at a skeleton, eh? I thought you had more nerve," to Mollie.

"But it was so sudden," she gasped; "and it seems so terrible."

"Well, there is nothing to fear," as he assisted them to their feet.

"O Mollie! Let us go!" cried Marie.

"Stuff and nonsense!" broke in the doctor. "Let us fathom this mystery. We will go in."

In the center of the chamber and on a high bier, covered with black velvet, which fell in great folds to the floor, lay a golden casket. It bore no ornamentation, save the beading of silver about its edges. Its top was of glass, and a wreath of the most exquisite flowers lay near the head. On the four corners of the great black pall were sprigs of immortelles, and at the head of the casket, a wreath of orange blossoms. The floor of the chamber was of slabs of white marble, skillfully laid and joined together.

At the side of the room, upon a low couch, lay the skeleton of a human being; the grinning skull was turned upon one side, with its yawning, eyeless sockets turned toward the casket in the center of the chamber.

The garments which had been worn in life, still clung about the form, and showed it to have been a man. Upon a small table, at the head of the couch, stood a bronze lamp, from which the oil had long since passed into vapor; a paper lay by its side, and at the foot of the couch stood an iron box.

Reverently they moved toward the casket, and, with feelings wrought up to the highest pitch, looked through the glass top. Again did the girls cry out in their wonder and awe; and the doctor, accustomed though he was to sights of death, pressed his hand to his head, and stared with eyes almost starting from their sockets.

Within the casket, upon the whitest silk, lay the form of a woman of wondrous beauty—a form of the most exquisite shape, a face of the rarest mold; hair of the fairest golden blonde, and hands and feet as delicate and small as a girl's. Naked from her feet to her loins, and exposing a bust of wondrous form, she lay among the folds of the white silk lining. A swathing of bandages covered the abdomen, and the mouth was wrapped in cloth. By her side lay a golden saucer, and another, filled with a black substance, lay at her head.

Silently they stood and gazed upon the motionless form. Within her casket she lay in death before them, but such a death as none had ever seen before. The eyelids closed, the face as white as the driven snow, the hands folded upon her bosom, it seemed to all that sacrilege had been committed by intruding within the sacred precincts of her tomb.

The awe-inspiring silence was at last broken by the voice of the doctor, who had recovered himself, and whose thoughts had come back again to the duty of the present.

"This is a most remarkable discovery, ladies," he slowly said; "but we should look for a further solution of the mystery. We can do nothing by standing here and gazing at this wondrous vision."

Laying his hand on the pall near the head of the casket, the velvet fell in dust and rags to the floor, and the sprig of immortelles, striking the marble slab, became mashed and battered. Picking up the flowers, he examined them carefully.

"Why, they are made of gold and silver and precious stones," he exclaimed, in astonishment.

Then they examined the three remaining sprigs, and the wreath of orange blossoms at the head of the casket; all were of the finest gold and silver, and diamonds were the petal-points of the flowers. Wondering much, the doctor then took those from the top of the casket, and found them, likewise, of the same precious materials. But in removing the last bunch of flowers, a discovery had been made. Where the wreath of golden flowers had lain, was now seen a silver plate, covered with engraved letters.

"Perhaps we have a clue to the identity of the beautiful woman who lies in this casket," exclaimed the doctor, as he threw the rays of the light upon the plate on the top of the casket.

Crowding close to him, all three read the words cut in the silver plate:

"MY DAUGHTER: To God I trust thee; into His keeping I give thee. O Junius! If thou hast, in years past and numbered in the great cycle of time, loved, and loved with steadfast heart, then arise and rescue that love from oblivion; but—and search thy heart to its utmost depths—if such love has never been, or is past and gone, turn back again, and leave to eternal rest the being who lies entombed before you—my daughter, Marie Colchis.

"Within the second chamber are batteries and means of obtaining heat, and fluids of life-giving principles. Cause the chamber to be warmed, arrange the batteries for current, and prepare the nourishment which you will find in the glass jars. When all is ready, cover your nostrils well, break the top glass of the casket, quickly seize the form therein lying, and bear it to the second chamber.

"Once within the warmth of that room, tear off the bandages, and apply the poles of the battery to the heart, in front, and over the fifth rib, in the back. Let the current come with all its force. If it be God's will, the form will shake, will quiver, open its eyes, will breathe, and become a living woman once again. Nourishment and care are all that will be required to complete the resurrection. Within the folds of the bandages over the heart lies a golden case containing a letter which is to be read by my daughter alone. Give it to her when she is recovered, and may God be with you.

"JEAN COLCHIS."

"Ah!" sighed Mollie, with tears in her eyes; "I see it all—I know it all!" Then, with all semblance of fear vanished from her heart, she cried:

'To work, doctor! To work!"

Dr. Town was a man quick to grasp a situation. He did not stop to wonder or ask questions. To be sure, he was very much surprised at what he saw, and at Mollie's exclamation, but he was prepared to rescue a woman therein entombed—this from a knowledge of the contents of the letter found in the copper cylinder, and which Mollie had shown him. Wasting no time in speculation, the instructions engraved upon the tablet on the top of the casket were carefully followed out. Returning to the second chamber, they commenced their work. Oil was found in the sealed bottles, and put into the stove, whose asbestos wick would still perform its functions. The stove was soon aglow with a bright flame, and its warmth diffused about the chamber. The batteries were ready for adjustment, and only required the dropping of the carbons into the electropoion fluid. The bottles of beef extract and fluids of nourishment were opened, and their contents prepared upon the stove. Clothing from their own persons was prepared by the two girls, as none could be found about the place.

When all was ready, the doctor prepared to break the glass top of the casket.

"Remain here," he said to them, "and I will bring her to you;" then, modestly: "and you shall strip off the bandages and cover her form; but leave bare her bosom and back."

Having given his instructions, he proceeded to the chamber wherein Marie Colchis lay.

A moment of silence followed, then a crash was heard, and the doctor came staggering into the room with the drooping, lifeless form of Marie Colchis in his arms. Laying her upon a bed, which had been improvised from their wraps, he cried, as he turned away:

"Quick! Strip off the bandages, and tell me when you are ready!"

A moment later, when the girls had performed

their work and had called upon him to come, he was by their side, and had adjusted the copper plates; then, pushing down the carbons into the batteries, he seized her hand and placed his finger on her pulse. As the current of electricity passed through her heart, there was a spasmodic contraction of the muscles of the body, a quivering of the flesh, a gasp, and her lovely bosom rose and fell as the air was inhaled and expelled; then the lips parted, and a low, deep sigh escaped, her eyes opened, and she lived.

"What is it?" she asked, in a quiet, weak voice.

"Hush! You must not speak; you are ill," hastily said the doctor. "Drink this, and you will feel better," and he put the cup of liquid to her lips.

Mechanically the girl obeyed the order, and drank the warm broth; then, closing her eyes, she became motionless, save a slight rising and falling of the bosom in breathing. Gently throwing aside her clothing, the doctor commenced a brisk rubbing of the legs, arms, and body along the spine. The heat of the fire, together with the friction of the rubbing, soon caused a free circulation of the blood, which had but barely moved through her arteries and veins for years. The color came slowly to her face, her breathing became stronger, she was receiving back the life which had been on the point of leaving her body. Once more the eyes opened, and she spoke, but in a stronger voice:

"Who are you? Where is my father?"

Marie, dear girl," cried Mollie, bending over her, while tears of joy fell from her eyes, "we are your friends, your dearest friends. You are ill now; do not speak or ask questions. All will be made known to you soon."

Dressing her in warm clothing taken from their own bodies, they bore her to the litter which the doctor had ordered brought to the door of the cavern.

An hour later the whole party was en route to Noniva. The litter was strung between two mules, with a man on each side to steady it, while Mollie and Marie followed, mounted on their mules. The doctor led the way down the creek, across the country to the town. Mollie had the little gold case which had been found among the bandages, Marie the golden flowers, and the doctor carried the iron box in front of him on the saddle.

It was 2 dial the next day when the party reached Noniva, as they had been compelled to travel very slowly. A fear that the lipthalener had departed caused Mollie much uneasiness, for they should have been back at 20 dial. But, no; as they entered the town, they saw the San Francisco's lights streaming over the waters. Captain Gordon had not found it in his heart to leave until the girls had joined the vessel.

Two days later, bidding a kind farewell to Captain Gordon and Dr. Town, the girls, with their charge, and the things brought from the cavern, left the deck of the cruiser in the Bay of San Francisco. Landing at Mission street dock, a drag was taken, and the home of Mollie's aunt Lora soon reached.

The weeks followed, and by careful nursing from her two faithful attendants, Marie Colchis regained her health, strength and beauty.

The letter in the golden case had been read by all the girls, and long and earnest were the conversations which had followed. Marie learned of the resurrection of her lover, and of his entrance into the family of the President; she became fully informed concerning the period of time it was in the world's history, and all the details attending her own lifeless sleep and miraculous return to the world of the living. It seemed but a day since she was with her father in the cavern on Guadalupe Island; it was but a moment that her thoughts had been away from her lover.

With all the fire and passion of her former life not decreased, but increased, by long years of patient waiting, she longed for the time when she could meet him, could see him, and hear his loved voice. She had been told of his apparent lack of interest, his seemingly moody ways, and his careworn and sad expression of countenance. She felt the cause; she knew it: he still loved his little girl-wife of Duke's Lane.

And she? Ah, God! she worshiped him!

CHAPTER XX.

It was the 10th of January when Cobb and Hugh returned from their visit to New England and reached the city of Washington.

Hugh was not at all pleased to find Marie gone; as for Cobb, it mattered not whether Mollie was there or not. To be sure, he admired the girl; loved her, but as a brother. All the passion which he had first thought to be in his heart for his friend's sister had vanished into a simple brotherly regard.

"Hello!" cried a familiar voice as Hugh came from the executive mansion that evening.

"Hello, Lester!" exclaimed Hugh, extending his hand. "Glad to see you back, old man."

"I can't say that I'm glad to get back. The girls are gone, father says," returned Hugh, in a woe-begone tone of voice.

"Yes," laconically.

"Given us the slip, eh?"

"Looks very much that way."

"Did she leave any word for you?"

"Yes; a short letter. Gone to visit her aunt in San Francisco, or some other seaport, I believe," answered Lester, dubiously.

"Father says she went in a great hurry; don't know

the cause of her sudden departure. Looks funny, doesn't it?" inquiringly.

"Very," knowingly.

"Bad, eh?" with a scowl.

"Horrible!"

"Well, you hear me, young man; when your sister walks off on an unknown journey and to be gone an unknown time, she generally comes back and finds me on an equally unknown voyage, and having about as much idea when that voyage will end as a jackass knows about Sunday;" and he thrust his hands savagely into his coat-tail pockets, and assumed the air of a man perfectly indifferent as to what the world liked or disliked.

"And when your sister forgets that she has an affianced husband dodging about your father's back door every night to catch but a moment's happiness in her society, why—she'll come back and find me off on a pleasure trip, somewhere," and poor Lester faced the other, and mingled his disgust at the state of affairs with that of his friend.

"Let us clear out, and not come back until they have experienced the same disappointment as we do now—that is, if our absence will affect them that way," with a dubious shake of his head.

"I'll do it, Hugh! I'll go to-morrow!" cried Lester, with an injured expression on his face.

"Then, it's agreed. We'll get Cobb and take the Orion and skip to—well, anywhere, so we don't get back here under two months." Hugh whistled an air of satisfaction at the thought of the misery he was going to bring to the heart of Marie Hathaway.

That evening Cobb was informed of Hugh's intention of starting the next day in the Orion, and making a tour of the United States.

"Ah, Hugh; why say the United States? say the world! Let us go far, far away; to the north pole, for instance," and Cobb looked his friend in the face, sadly, but yet with an anxious hope that his proposition would be accepted. "Yes, to the north pole," he continued. "No living man has been there, even in this great age of progress, so you have informed me."

"It is impossible, Junius. We cannot reach it," returned Hugh.

"It is funny! I have seen your aërial ships, large and stanch; why can't you go in one of them?"

"Yes, our aërial ships are large and stanch; but it would be foolhardy to attempt to reach the pole in one of them. We, of course, depend on their lightness to overcome gravitation; now, the lightest gas we can get is hydrogen, and this we use. With our vessels filled with this gas, we have no trouble in making from twenty to fifty, and even a hundred miles per hour, according to the wind. But here comes in the greatest factor in aërial navigation: how to make up the gas discharged in changing altitudes and lost by exudation through the skin of the balloon. In nearly every great city large quantities of hydrogen are kept in store for filling the balloons of such vessels as may arrive and require replenishment. So long as a vessel is kept within a day's journey of one of these cities, it is easy to keep sufficient gas in the balloon, and thus to travel from point to point; but as there are no hydrogen works north of latitude fifty-four degrees fifteen minutes, and as the distance from there to the pole is over 2,200 miles, and the same distance back again, and as, again, the speed of an aërial ship depends upon the direction of the wind, and its velocity—the maximum speed in a perfectly tranquil atmosphere being only forty-five miles per hour—it will easily be seen that a period of one hundred hours, and perhaps very many more, would elapse ere the ship could return to the starting point. As a fact, the loss of hydrogen will be so great that, unless replenished, the vessel will lose its carrying power ere thirty hours have passed. Thus you see, Junius, it is impossible to use the aërial ship to reach the pole."

"But can you not carry material to keep your supply of hydrogen up to the amount required?" asked Cobb, eagerly.

"No. The amount would be too great to manufacture in the time which would be at one's command; besides, the apparatus would be too heavy for the balloon to carry."

"Then, I understand that, if you could manufacture this gas in sufficient quantities on the ship, and by light apparatus, you could go anywhere?" Cobb spoke the words slowly, as if lost in some deep thought.

"Certainly," replied Hugh. "But that is a discovery which I doubt much will ever be accomplished!"

"Perhaps."

"Perhaps?"

"Yes, I said perhaps," returned Cobb, with a complaisant smile. Then, inquiringly: "Will you show me your finest aërial ship to-morrow?"

"Of course you will see it if we start to-morrow, as we have agreed."

"But do not agree to start to-morrow. Show me your ship, as I have not seen them closely, and I will be ready to start soon after."

"Well, if you wish it, Junius, I will do so; but I do not understand the reason for your request."

"You will see," quietly returned Cobb.

It was about 10 dial the next day when Cobb accompanied Hugh to the dock house of the large government aërial ship Orion. The vessel stood in the navy yard at Washington, covered by an immense canvas shed. Her gas bags were uninflated, and lay in great folds along the central support.

The vessel was 377 feet long, and was built in a very peculiar manner. The balloon part of the vessel was in the form of a huge cigar, through the center of which extended a rod 380 feet long, with trusses to keep it rigid. The cones of the balloon were covered with aluminum shields, which extended toward the center to a distance of sixty feet. Light rods joined these two shields to each other, thereby bracing the whole vessel. Depending from the central rod, by stiff hangings, and just under the gas envelope, was the car, built of bamboo, canvas. and aluminum rods. The car was 100 feet in length and 15 wide, and had an area of 1,500 square feet; the flooring was of the lightest material consistent with safety. The rear point of the cone carried a wind propeller of forty-six feet in diameter; the forward cone had four rudders working from the point of the cone back to a distance of thirty feet, and set in pairs—one pair vertical, and the other horizontal. There was a small lipthalene engine in the center of the ship coupled to the propeller. Within the car were fourteen state-rooms, parlor, instrument-room, kitchen, dining-room, and cabin, besides the pilot's room in front, and the engine-room in the center. The balloon, when inflated, was 377 feet from point to point of the cones, and 100 feet in diameter. Its displacement of air was 2,000,000 cubic feet, or 153,000 pounds, under the pressure of one atmosphere. Inflated with hydrogen, it had a carrying capacity of seventy tons. The silk bag was covered with a peculiar coating, which made it almost impervious to change of texture, yet soft and pliable. The weight of the whole ship was fifty-two tons, the engines and machinery three tons more; making the whole weight, without passengers or freight, fifty-five tons. Five tons was the usual weight carried, as the gas bag was only about six-sevenths full at rising, in order to allow for the expansion of the gas as the elevation increased. The cabin was aft, and the state-rooms near the center; all were furnished handsomely, and with everything requisite for one's comfort, but of the lightest material.

Through the center of the great gas bag a silk shaft led to a platform on the very top of the balloon. This was the lookout's station, and communication with the pilot was by telephone. The vessel was lighted and heated by electricity, supplied from storage batteries of great power, though small in volume. The cooking was by electricity likewise, and owing to the inflammability of the hydrogen gas, fire was not permitted aboard the ship.

Cobb surveyed the vessel very carefully, examining every part, and looking at every detail of the mechanism of the machinery. The gas bag was critically inspected, and then the area of the deck measured. With a smiling, satisfied air, Cobb turned to Hugh, and said: "It rests with you, Hugh, whether this vessel take us to the north pole or simply makes a tour of the States."

"You astonish me!" exclaimed Hugh. "You certainly will not ask me to make an attempt which others have declared impossible?"

"I mean to ask you to do it," calmly replied the other.

"But I certainly will not grant your request," with a decided movement of the head.

"But you will not only grant my request, but you will, with me, reach the pole before a week has passed." There was a quiet, cool assurance in his words that gave Hugh a feeling that the man was not talking at random, but had some grand scheme in view, which, to him, gave promise of success. Feeling this to be the case, he framed his next words accordingly: "Tell me what you mean? How is this to be accomplished? Explain yourself."

Without replying to the questions, Cobb simply asked: "Will you get the authority for a few simple changes in the construction of this vessel? Can you do this?"

"Yes; I think I can; that is, if it is to improve the ship."

"Then, get that permission, and have the changes made, a list of which I will give you this evening; they can be finished by day after to-morrow. Also, have 10,000 pounds of meteorite and 200 gallons of nitric acid put aboard the vessel, and 2,500 pounds of meteorite and fifty gallons of acid near at hand. Increase your supply of lipthalite sufficiently to run the engines twenty-five days."

"But will you not be adding too much weight for buoyancy?" suggested Hugh.

"How much will the hydrogen which is used to

inflate that bag weigh?" asked Cobb, pointing to the folded envelope.

"Well," replied Hugh, thinking a moment, "the capacity is two million cubic feet, and a cubic foot of air weighs nearly eight hundredths of a pound; that would give about 160,000 pounds. Assuming the specific gravity of air at one, that of hydrogen would be sixty-nine thousandths, and the weight about 11,000 pounds."

"Correct," said Cobb, who had made a mental calculation of the weight. "Now I ask you to put on the vessel 12,000 pounds of meteorite and acid. Very well; if your ship can take care of 6,000 of these pounds, I will reduce the weight of the gas in the bag to 5,000 pounds, thus providing for the other 6,000 pounds."

"But you cannot do it!" cried Hugh. "Hydrogen is the lightest gas known; you cannot reduce its weight."

"I can." Cobb looked calmly into the face of his friend.

"You, perhaps, think you can," insinuated Hugh.

"I know I can," firmly replied the other.

"Then the changes shall be made."

"And day after to-morrow, at 12 dial, we sail for the north pole?" asked Cobb. "Is it to be so?"

"As you wish, Junius."

Their plans being settled, they returned to the executive mansion, where Hugh immediately sought his father, and told him of his interview with Cobb, and what the latter had promised to do. He then asked for the order permitting the changes in the Orion.

Without evincing any surprise, the President wrote the order, and gave it to him, adding:

"I think I know where he will get this new gas. I saw it demonstrated in the Secretary's office last September."

"And I am to go with him, you understand?" anxiously asked Hugh.

"Well, as to that, if he has found a method of manufacturing the gas as it is needed, I see not the slightest objection, for you know that has been the only difficulty, heretofore, in making the voyage. Yes, my son, go, and let another laurel be added to the family name."

When Cobb read the "Daily American" the next morning he was surprised to come across a notice to the world of his proposed voyage. He had said nothing to anyone, and could only account for the item by reasoning that the order to the Secretary, and which Hugh had shown him, had read:

" * * * These changes must be completed by the 12th instant, at 12 dial, as Colonel Cobb and Captains Craft and Hathaway will start for the north pole at that hour. * * * "

The paper gave the news, and commented upon the proposed undertaking as follows:

"WASHINGTON, 10, 18 D.—Orders have been received at the War Department to have the aërial ship Orion put into shape for a long and extended voyage. It is currently reported at the Capitol that Lieutenant-Colonel Junius Cobb, Second Cavalry, the man of '87, as he has become known, intends to make the attempt of reaching the pole in an airship. His companions will be Captains Craft and Hathaway, of the army; the former officer a son of the President of the United States. This will be the seventh trial to reach the pole since the invention of the air-ship. The first four who competed for the honor returned in disgrace, their vessels failing to reach the sixty-ninth parallel of north latitude ere they were compelled to turn back on account of loss of gas. The other two adventurers, Pope, in the Star, in 1985, and Capron, in the Highflyer, in 1993, have never been heard from. The problem is one utterly without solution; the air-ship is not destined to ever reach the pole.

"The foolhardy attempt now about to be made will not only end in disaster to the gentlemen engaged in it, but will bring sorrow to the nation by the loss to the President of his only son."

Rather discouraging, that," said Cobb to himself, as he laid the paper aside. "Strange how much these newspaper men know! They haven't changed a particle since the days of old."

The work progressed upon the Orion, and the sound of hammers was heard all the day. A long silken pipe had been connected to the gas bag, and terminated near a small, bell-shaped aluminum receiver. The poles of the storage batteries had been joined to a dozen pairs of carbon points within this receiver, and a series of long pipes projected from its base. Two huge safety-valves had been placed in the top of the great gas bag, and additional escape provided. It was 9 dial of the 12th of January, and great crowds of people filled the streets, covered the house-tops, and jammed themselves into every available place from which a view could be had of the departure of the Orion. At the dock of the vessel the President, Secretaries, foreign ministers, and other notables were assembled to witness the departure of the man who had promised to reach the pole and return.

The huge silken bag still lay inert and motionless against the aluminum support, no attempt having been made to fill it. The baggage had been placed on board; the stores, the meteorite, and nitric acid were carefully in place, and the crew, consisting of two pilots, a cook, cabin boy, and two engineers, were standing near the vessel.

A moment later Junius Cobb appeared, and by his side walked Craft and Hathaway. Their appearance was greeted by cheer upon cheer from the vast concourse of people. Slowly approaching the big ship, they mounted the ladders to the side, and stood upon the deck of the Orion. Throwing off his coat, Cobb at once commenced his work. The meteorite was in sticks four feet long and an inch in diameter, and much resembled the sticks of lipthalite used on the Tracer. Taking a glass cylinder five feet in length by one in diameter, he filled it nearly full of nitric acid, and then placed a bunch of the meteorite rods in the liquid. Waiting but a moment, he withdrew them, and then put one into each of the ten pipes of the receiver, placed springs against their ends, and closed the caps. Having thus charged the receiver, he stepped back, and touched a push-button, and turned on the current to the carbons inside.

Slowly at first, then faster, rose fold upon fold of the gas bag of the Orion; the gas was generating. The crowd cheered. For two hours the process was continued, until the Orion just balanced at her moorings; then and only then, Cobb ceased to fill the receiver. The 2,500 pounds of meteorite and fifty gallons of nitric acid, which had been brought as an extra supply, had been nearly all consumed, and over 1,500,000 cubic feet of meteorlene filled the great gas bag to within one-seventh of its capacity.

Stepping down the ladders, Cobb and his two companions bade good-bye to their friends. The crew went aboard, and then the three officers followed. At 11:57 the receiver pipes were again charged, and the electric current turned on; the great ship tugged hard at her cables, and swayed in the air.

"Cast off!" thundered the words from Cobb, and the hawsers whirled through the guards, and came tumbling to the ground. The vessel rose swiftly and gracefully in the air; the dial marked 12.

High up in the cold winter air, and swiftly, the noble ship rose; and soon the tooting of whistles and the cheers of the people became but faint murmurings in the depths below.

"Admiral," reported Hugh, making a grave salute, and with a twinkle in his eye, "the barometer shows 8,000 feet."

The fact was apparent that a great elevation had already been attained, for the temperature had fallen and a decided cold feeling was experienced by all.

"That is sufficient, Commodore," returning the other's salute, and smiling at his new title. "Be kind enough to have the course laid northeast by east, and discharge gas to keep at about this altitude;' and Cobb passed into his state-room, and donned a heavy overcoat.

As the engines commenced their work the great propeller turned rapidly on its axis, and the Orion, describing a great circle, took a course which would soon bring her over Newfoundland.

Rapidly they passed over the country; the towns and cities, the rivers and lakes, lay far below them, and the scene was like some gigantic panorama.

Emerging from the cabin, Cobb walked to the port bows, where Hugh and Lester were leaning on the rail, and commenting on the grand scenery over which they were being swiftly whirled. An expression of satisfaction overspread his face, and a fire of ambition sparkled in his eye.

"Would that I were never more compelled to descend to earth!" he cried. "Would that I could ever remain thus far away from civilization and society!" and a sad, mournful expression succeeded the former brightness of his countenance.

"Say not so, dear Junius," and Hugh took the other's hand in his. "I am sure there is a bright future in store for you. I feel it; I know it!"

"I am not a part of those below," and he jerked his thumb toward the earth dimly outlined far below them. "I am not a part of that people. No solitary tie, save that of new-found friendship, binds me to them, or them to me, Hugh," and he pressed the hand that held his. "If I but had the love of her long since dead, long since gone to her heavenly home, then all would be changed. I would live again, would laugh and jest, and be another man. Alas, it is not to be," and tears filled his eyes, and became crystals of ice in the freezing temperature that pervaded the air about them.

"Brace up, my dear Colonel!" interposed Lester. "Accept the world as you find it! The sun of a week hence may shine on a people shouting your praise to the end of the earth."

"What care I for praise!" savagely returned the man, as he turned upon the other; then in a kinder tone, he said, "Forgive me, Lester; I know your heart is in the right place." Twice he crossed the deck in moody silence. "Enough," he cried, at length, as he stopped in front of them. "Let fate work its decree." Then turning once more from his friends, his emotion gave utterance to the feelings of his heart: "I abide the time of death, and a return to thee, O Marie, my darling, my girl wife!" Once more he faced them, and in harsh tones exclaimed: "It is over! Let us to business now; we are bound for the pole! For your sakes I hope we return."

It was 1,500 miles to the banks of Newfoundland, and nearly 5 dial the next day, when the Orion was poised a thousand feet above the Atlantic. Below, plowing her way through the water, was one of the latest transatlantic passenger lipthaleners. Eight hundred and fifty feet in length by a beam of only forty-six feet, the huge spindle rushed through the water with a speed of over forty miles an hour. Sounding the great whistle of the Orion, Cobb threw over a small parachute, to which was attached a bundle of papers of the 12th inst. The lipthalener sounded her whistle in salutation, ceased her course, and sent a launch to pick up the papers. Again sounding the whistle as a parting salute, Cobb ordered gas, and the Orion rose, and was soon hidden in the clouds. The course was then laid due east.

CHAPTER XXI

It was 20 dial.

High up in the air and swiftly sped the Orion.

At the bow rail stood Junius Cobb and Hugh. Each was silent, his thoughts far away; the one in the present, and the other in a former, period of the world's time. How their thoughts contrasted! Hugh, bright in his hopes for the future, meditated on the renown and glory that would attach to them all should their great undertaking prove successful. And then, was she not now informed of his mission? and was she not watching and praying for his safe return?

Ah! was he not to be envied?

But the other—Junius—how ran his thoughts? Back, back years before, he was wandering, among old scenes and old friends so dear to his heart. His head bowed upon his arm, he gave no heed to his friend's presence.

On, on they sped; the whir of the propeller alone breaking the awful silence that surrounded them. The night advanced; the darkness came upon them.

"Are you not too cold, Junius?" asked Hugh, after watching for a moment his companion, and noticing a slight tremor of his form.

The words, though lowly spoken, fell upon the ear of the other as if a voice from the unknown world had shouted out his doom; so still was all about them that a whisper even seemed to vibrate back until it had swelled into a harsh, discordant cry.

With a quick, shaking movement, Cobb raised his head, and turned toward the speaker: "What is it, Hugh? you spoke to me, did you not?"

"Yes; I asked if you were not cold. For ten minutes have we stood here in this freezing temperature, each busy with his own thoughts."

"Yes; I am cold," came the reply. "And, cold as my body may be, my dear friend, my heart is colder. I would that I could shake off these depressing feelings, but my mind will wander. Even now I thought how easily, how swiftly, and painlessly man could from this air-ship terminate a distasteful and annoying existence. Yes," looking into the other's eyes, "yes, one has but to throw himself over this rail, and life passes from him without a pang."

"And do you call that a painless death, being crushed upon the earth below into a shapeless mass?" asked Hugh, with a shudder, glancing over the rail.

"Yes, Hugh. Death from falling from a great height is perfectly painless. Let me explain it," warming to the subject, and losing some of his melancholy in the prospective discussion of a scientific theme. "Let me tell you why such is the case. We are now 10,000 feet above the ocean, are we not?"

"So I read the barometer, a quarter of an hour ago," answered Hugh.

"Well, no matter; let us assume that we are at that elevation. Now, what would be our velocity falling from this point upon reaching the surface of the earth below?"

"Really, I could not answer that question without working it out," the other returned.

"Well, it would be just 802 feet per second," said Cobb. "And that velocity at 500, 1,000 and 5,000 feet below us would be 179, 253, and 567 feet, respectively, per second. A human being falling is, for an instant, convulsed by a terrible, awful feeling; not a feeling of pain, but rather a feeling of apprehension. This fear, this apprehension, is but momentary, I say; it lasts during the first second of the descent only, or for a distance of about sixteen feet. After this first second the senses become confused, circulation of the blood is retarded, a feeling of rest, a sense of pleasure, pervades the whole soul. This state of ecstasy, which it should really be called, increases as the velocity of descent is accelerated, until the mind can no longer enjoy the delightful sensation, but loses all knowledge, all thought, all feeling, and insensibility ensues. This condition of the senses is produced when the velocity of the body has attained a rate of 400 feet a second, or at the fourteenth second of descent—about 2,480 feet below the point of starting. The cause of this is, that the lungs no longer perform their function; they fail to take in the quantity of air, and consequently the oxygen necessary to fully renovate the blood. The velocity being so great, the air is pushed aside by the falling body, and fails to surround that portion of the body not directly in the line of descent, with air at the normal pressure. The air supply being thus diminished, the blood leaps through the veins, rushes to the brain, and the mind knows no more. A human body of 175 pounds weight falling from this height—10,000 feet—would reach the earth at the end of the twenty-fifth second, and would have, at that moment, a velocity of 802 feet per second."

"There would not be much resemblance to a human being left," ejaculated Hugh, intently interested, and looking over the rail as if he already saw the body falling toward the earth. "No." Cobb shook his head in a decided manner. "No; I should say hot. The body would strike the earth with a force of 146,000 foot pounds per second, and would become but a shapeless, pulpy mass." He ceased speaking a moment, as if lost in thought, then quickly added: "But enough of this subject. Let us take a turn on the forward deck, and then retire to the cabin."

The two men moved forward, and crossed to the starboard side of the Orion. Here the air was a trifle warmer, or, rather, the wind caused by their forward movement was less strong and piercing. The great perpendicular rudders of the vessel were inclined two degrees to the left to overcome the northern currents, which came strong and cold.

It was now 21 dial, and the earth below seemed

covered by a black pall. Around them were silence and darkness. No moon was visible, and the gloom below was only relieved by the beautiful sky, with its thousands of twinkling stars above them.

Stopping at the rocket box, just to the right of the rudder chains, Cobb laid his hand upon the rail, and gazed fixedly into the depths below; and then, raising his eyes toward the horizon, he pointed his finger forward, and exclaimed: "Hugh, what are those bright lights away off in the ocean, and this one, almost under us?"

Hugh looked in the direction indicated, and also leaned over the rail, and noted a beautiful, brilliant light almost underneath the Orion. Hesitating a moment, he cried:

"Why, Junius, those are the Atlantic stations. We can see one—two—three of them. Yes, I am sure; and there is one behind us," pointing to a light directly in their rear. "Yes, they are the stations. That one behind us must be the first one, and this underneath, the second, from Newfoundland; that would agree with our position, which, I take it, is about a hundred miles east of the land."

"Atlantic stations! Do you mean that these lights are on stationary vessels in the ocean?" asked Cobb, intently gazing at the bright lights.

"Yes; those are ocean stations for the relief of distressed vessels and shipwrecked people. You see the lights; this one under us, and the one toward the west, and those two to the east. Ah! there is another!

see it? away down on the horizon. That makes five. By Jove! I doubt if ever before five of these lights have been seen at the same time by one person!" with a pleased expression on his face.

Cobb viewed for a moment the brilliant light, which was apparently gently swaying to right and left just beneath him, and then his eyes passed along the line made by the others. The second light was quite bright also, but the third seemed faint. The fourth light appeared as a star lying just on the edge of the ocean. Indeed, were it not for the fact that the Orion lay exactly in the line of the stations, and for the further fact that no stars were visible so low down toward the horizon, the light might not have been noticed at all.

"How far apart are these stations?" he asked.

"They are placed at intervals of fifty miles," returned the other.

"Then, that light away down near the horizon is nearly 150 miles from us?"

"Yes."

"And our elevation now is 10,000 feet, you say?"

"So I observed it, as I told you, some fifteen or twenty minutes ago."

Then, after a moment's silence, Cobb exclaimed: "We are rising. We cannot be less than 12,500 feet above the ocean."

"How do you make that out, Junius?" asked Hugh. "I don't think we have ascended 2,500 feet since my last observation."

"It is easily answered," said the other. "The curvature of the earth and the refraction of light necessitate an elevation of 1,430 feet for one to see an object on the surface at a distance of fifty miles. To see this light, distant 150 miles, our altitude must be at least 11,500 feet."

"Yes?"

"Yes Let us go inside, and see if I am not correct, and then I want you to tell me about these stations," touching the other on the arm, and then moving aft.

Once in the cabin, the barometer was consulted, and found to read 19.29 inches, or an elevation of 11,581 feet. Cobb again asked his friend to enlighten him concerning this new invention, the lights of which he had seen twinkling and scintillating away toward the east.

"I cannot tell you much, Junius, for I am not well posted on the subject. These transatlantic life-stations are set on a line extending from St. John's, Newfoundland, to Land's End, England, or nearly on the fiftieth parallel of north latitude. Perhaps there may be something relating to the subject among the books in the chart-room. Excuse me but a moment, and I will look." Saying which, he arose and passed out to the pilot's house. A moment later he returned, bearing a pamphlet in his hand.

"Here we are, my boy," he exclaimed, as he shut the door behind him. "Here's quite a history of these stations. I found it among the nautical almanacs and charts in the pilot's room.

Opening the first page, Hugh displayed three wood-cuts of one of the transatlantic life-stations. The first cut showed the station in its normal position upon the surface of the ocean; the second showed it partially submerged, during a storm, and the third gave a cross-section of its interior. Handing the book to Cobb, he said: "You can read it yourself, for everything is explained therein, I think." The other took the pamphlet, and settling himself back in his chair, read of this wonderful adjunct to a safe traveling of the great Atlantic highway to Europe.

There were, across the Atlantic Ocean, from Newfoundland to England, thirty-eight marine life-saving stations. These stations were, in all respects, similar; a full description of one answered for all. In the pamphlet which Cobb read, were given the details of Station No. 14, situated in longitude 37 degrees 5 minutes west, and latitude 49 degrees 50 minutes north. He read:

"HISTORY OF THE TRANSATLANTIC LIFE-SAVING SERVICE.

"In 1923 a joint commission of Great Britain, France and the United States, met in the city of Washington for the purpose of devising some means toward making travel across the Atlantic Ocean more safe and sure than was possible under the circumstances at the time. Vessels of the finest description and of great tonnage were traversing a well-known route continuously. Accidents had occurred, which it seemed could not have been prevented, whereby a great number of lives had been sacrificed and vast property lost.

"Great factors in the calling together of this commission were a series of terrible accidents in the years 1919, 1920, and in the fall of 1922.

"On the 15th of July, 1919, at 23 dial, or as they then reckoned time, 11 o'clock P. M., the City of New York was struck by lightning, in latitude 49 degrees 10 minutes, and longitude 31 degrees 14 minutes. Despite the endeavors of a well-trained crew and every facility for extinguishing fire, the vessel burned and sunk; 2,167 souls who were aboard of her at the time took to the boats. Of this number 914 only were rescued, or ever heard of. Those who were rescued had sailed over 450 miles before being picked up. The supposition is that the distance from land was too great for them to overcome with the limited amount of water and food aboard the boats, and had land, or some station, been within reasonable distance from the scene of the accident, all would have been saved.

"A most peculiar case was that of the City of Providence in 1920. This vessel was one of the finest of the American transatlantic passenger steamers, 600 feet in length, with a tonnage of 16,000. She left the Mersey on October 7 of that year, with 3,465 souls on board. On the morning of the 9th, at 4:12 dial, a terrible accident occurred; two of the thirty-six boilers burst, the concussion causing nine more to explode. The vessel was torn almost asunder, her bulkheads broken, and the water poured into the ship. Her engines were wrecked, and the engine-room flooded. A vessel of ordinary construction would have sunk immediately, but the Providence, having every improvement, and a great number of water-tight compartments, continued to float. Torn and broken, she lay upon the ocean perfectly helpless.

"The strange but sad continuation of this disaster follows:

"The City of Providence, making the trip across the ocean, as she usually did, in four days, carried provisions for but eight days. After the explosion the ship drifted at the mercy of the currents and wind.

"It was four weeks after the disaster when she was found by vessels sent out to look for her, in latitude 44 degrees 12 minutes, and longitude 31 degrees 16 minutes. Seven boats' crews had left her to seek aid; her passengers had been cut down to rations, and finally every vestige of food had been consumed, and starvation and thirst commenced their deadly work. Out of that host of people on the Providence when she sailed, only fifty-four lived to tell of the terrible disaster. Four of the boats were never heard from, and only twenty-seven persons were found alive on the ship. During all these weeks that the Providence drifted about, she twice crossed the line upon which the life-stations are now situated. Had these stations then been in existence, every soul on board of the ill-fated vessel would probably have been saved. How it could be that a vessel of the Providence's size could have escaped the notice of the hundreds of ships passing in that latitude is a problem none can solve; that she did, is a fact, for no report of her was ever made until she was sighted by the relief vessel sent out to search for her.

* * * * * *

"These terrible disasters, taken in consideration with the great advantages which would accrue were there stations at intervals across the ocean, led to the creation of the commission.

"The commission met on the 19th day of June, 1923, and made proposals for plans for these stations. On the 11th of December of that year the commission selected, from the plans submitted, those of Mr. Cyril Louis, of California.

"These plans were for a huge cylindrical vessel, sitting upright in the water, and surmounted by a tower one hundred feet above the water line. The vessel proper was a cylinder; its base, a plane; its top, the frustum of a cone, surmounted by a tower upon a tower. The cylinder was eighty-three feet in length to the water line, the cone nine feet high, the first tower fifty-one feet above the frustum of the cone, and the second tower forty feet above this. The cylinder was made of boiler iron in three layers of one-inch plates, and covered on the outside with aluminum plates a quarter of an inch thick; the diameter was thirty feet, and the vessel was divided into eight stories by floors of one-inch steel. The first, or lower, and second chambers were fourteen feet high; the next twelve; the four following, ten; while the top chamber, under the cone, was twelve feet to the frustum. All of these chambers, except the first, were divided into water-tight compartments by steel bulkheads. The second chamber had eight compartments; the third, two; the fourth, fifth and sixth, four; the seventh and eighth two. The first, or main tower extended down through the cylinder to the top of the third chamber, and was eight feet in diameter. It was necessary to pass through this tube to gain entrance to any of the floors. Access to the different compartments of each floor was by means of doors closing water-tight. The chambers were for use as follows: the first contained 10,000 cubic feet of fine sand—1,300,000 pounds—or so much of it as was needed to bring the surface of the water to within three feet of the cone. This chamber was peculiarly constructed; water-holes permitted free access to the surrounding water, causing the sand to be saturated. Ten capped openings in the bottom were manipulated from the engine-room and office, and by means of which any amount of sand could be quickly dropped from the chamber into the ocean, thus decreasing the weight and increasing the buoyancy.

"The second chamber was the water-chamber, and was divided into eight separate compartments. Water could be admitted into any one, or all, by suitable levers worked in the engine-room. Pipes from each compartment were connected to the pumps in the engine-room, thus permitting of the compartment being quicky emptied of its water. The capacity of the eight compartments was 10,000 cubic feet, or 64,000 pounds of water.

"The third chamber was the engine-room. Here was all of the machinery used in operating the station: The main engines for the pumps (pipes from which ran to every compartment in the cylinder), for the fans for circulating fresh air; dynamos for electric lighting, pumps of the condensers, and, last, the three propellers, which were situated on the outside, on a level with the engine-room floor—two at 180 degrees apart, their faces parallel to the diameter of the cylinder, and the other at right angles to them and ninety degrees from either. These propellers were used to prevent any rotary motion of the cylinder.

"Until lipthalite had been discovered—and it is now used—petroleum was the fuel for these engines, the vapors escaping through a tube extending to near the top of the first tower. Within the engine-room was a set of dials and bells which would give instant warning of the entrance of water into any compartment, tubes and telephones to all parts of the vessel; dials for pressure, submergence, state of electricity; levers for opening sand and water ports, etc. The fourth and fifth chambers were for stores and material.

"The sixth contained the kitchen, mess, etc.

"The seventh was the dormitory, while the eighth was the officers' cabin and office. Natural light was admitted into the last two chambers through bull's-eyes.

"The office was provided with every instrument necessary in operating the station, and from it the sand and water ports could be opened.

"The first tower was eight feet in diameter, tapering to five feet at the top, and fifty-one feet high. It was made of two-inch steel rings, six feet wide, firmly riveted together, the whole covered by aluminum plates.

"The entrance to the vessel was through the tower, at the top of the frustum. A spiral stairway led to a port at the top, through which the upper balcony was reached. Bull's-eyes admitted light to the interior during the day.

"The upper tower was forty feet high in the clear, setting down fifteen feet in the first tower, and was twenty inches in diameter, of one-inch cast steel. The interior of this tower was divided into a central pipe of ten inches diameter, surrounded by four pipes in the quadrants of its area. The central pipe was used for raising the electric lamp, of 25,000 candle power; the other pipes were, two for the engines, to carry off the vapors, etc., one for receiving fresh air into the vessel, and the other for carrying off the vitiated air.

"Upon the side of the cone was a complete life

raft, provisioned and ready for instant use, and so fastened that it could be launched at a moment's notice.

"The station was anchored by a three-inch cable, pivoted at both ends to prevent twisting. In the center of the cable were electric wires terminating at the bottom of the ocean in a large coil. This coil was laid upon one of the old Atlantic cables which had been abandoned after the invention of the sympathetic telegraph.

"In the office were a set of instruments, and communication was by induction to the cable below, and thence to each end and to each station.

"The normal submergence of the vessel was to within three feet of the cone. The exceptional, or rough weather, submergence was to within two feet of the top of the tower.

"The weights were as follows:

	Pounds.
Shell of vessel	1,200,800
Cone	106,000
First tower	163,000
Second tower	12,000
Seven floors	176,000
Bulkheads	100,000
Bracing and iron-work	100,000
Engines and machinery	200,000
Stores for 100 persons (six months)	75,000
Stores for vessels	50,000
Cable	260,000
Total weights	2,442,000

"The normal displacement of the vessel was 57,225 cubic feet, or 3,664,000 pounds. This displacement, less the weights, gave an excess of 1,200,000 pounds, which was compensated for by the sand in the sand-chamber—the capacity of that chamber being 1,300,000 pounds.

"During stormy and rough weather, to decrease the pressure of the winds and waves upon the towers, and to increase the stability of the vessel, water could be admitted into the water-chambers, and the vessel would sink until the water line was within two feet of the top of the first tower, for the displacements to be overcome were:

	Pounds.
Three feet of the shell	135,000
Cone	180,000
First tower	149,000
Total	464,000

"The capacity of the water-chamber being 677,000 pounds, there was a large excess over this displacement; this excess was to compensate for loss of weight by stores being used, taken out, etc.

* * * * * *

"The station carries a flag at its peak, by day, with its station number thereon; at night it shows a 25,000 candle-power light; its interior, also, is lighted by electricity.

* * * * * *

"The plans of Mr. Louis were accepted, and in less than three years a line of thirty-eight stations were placed across the Atlantic Ocean.

* * * * * *

"It was agreed between the nations that each should contribute a third of the cost ($12,000,000), and that salvage for person and property, at a fixed and just rate, should be demanded from every nation whose flag may be succored by one of these stations; and further, that should war intervene between any of the nations contracting, the line of stations should remain unmolested, and should not be used for purposes of war."

Cobb dropped the pamphlet by his side, and pondered over the great invention of which he had just read, and which he had seen.

"And have no accidents ever happened to these stations from ice-floes, collisions, or faulty construction?" he finally asked, turning toward Hugh.

"I believe there has been but one noteworthy accident," the other returned. "An immense ice-floe caused Station No. 5 to slip her cable, and run away—an easy matter for her, as her propellers give her a speed of about five miles an hour. Of course her cable was lost; but she was saved, and was picked up and reset by the lipthalener which continuously plies along the line."

It was now nearly 23 dial, and Cobb arose, and consulted the speed dial of the Orion.

"Hugh," he said, "please have the course changed to due north; we are nearly on the fortieth meridian, and should now make direct for Cape Farewell."

The other passed up to the pilot's house.

CHAPTER XXII

The cold was increasing, and the snug, warm cabin of the Orion was a most acceptable substitute for the frost-covered deck of the vessel. At 7 dial breakfast was laid, and the three officers partook of a hearty meal; then lighting their cigars—the necessity for fires aboard the vessel being removed by the substitution of meteorlene for hydrogen—they lay back and enjoyed the hour.

"Why did you bring so much meteorite and acid?" suddenly asked Lester.

"Because," answered Cobb, "I wished to have enough to meet all emergencies which may arise. I have enough to fully inflate the balloon four times."

"Do you intend to make direct for the pole from Cape Farewell?" broke in Hugh.

"No. I wish to satisfy myself about the northern extremity of Smith's Sound first. I shall pass west when on the eightieth parallel of latitude."

"Can you explain why it is that the pole has never been reached by land parties?" inquired Lester.

"My opinion," replied Cobb, "is that they have never proceeded upon the proper course. I think that Smith's Sound leads the waters of an immense polar ocean into Baffin's Bay; that the sea is a moving sea of ice, and that any northward progress upon it would be more than counterbalanced by its southward movement. I have long believed that the only route lay along the backbone of Greenland."

"Well," with satisfaction, "we can soon ascertain the truth or fallacy of your hypothesis," exclaimed Hugh.

"Yes; for we will pass up on the fortieth meridian of longitude to the eightieth parallel; this course will take us over the central length of Greenland," and Cobb blew a cloud of smoke about him, and closed his eyes in meditation.

At precisely 4:15 dial the following day the Orion stood poised above the southern extremity of Greenland. The earth below them lay like a white sheet, extending as far to the north as the eye could reach; the waters to the south were covered with floating ice, while great, towering icebergs were visible in many directions. The cold had become very great, and it was necessary to change their clothing for fur. But, despite the freezing atmosphere, they were warm and cozy in the ship. Hugh had worked hard during the two days given him to complete their arrangements; the canvas exterior of the car had been given a thorough coating of heavy varnish, and the interior lined with blankets throughout, while heavy, thick carpets covered all the floors. The electric heaters, except in the pilot's house and three staterooms, had been replaced by oil-stoves of superior heating properties. Ten barrels of oil had been placed on board, and one hundred cells of storage battery added to the plant. With these wise provisions and the forethought to provide an abundance of the warmest flannel, and fur clothing for all, the severity of the weather had little effect upon the welfare and comfort of those aboard the Orion.

A strong wind was blowing off the coast, and the vessel made but little headway; the barometer marked 26.64 inches, and the elevation was 3,200 feet.

"Lester," said Cobb, after a pause, and looking through the frosted window, "I wish you would increase the gas; we must rise above this current of air, or we will be blown off the coast."

Hathaway passed out, and filled the receivers, and soon the Orion was rapidly ascending. Watching the barometer carefully, Cobb soon put his lips to the speaking-tube, and called to Lester: "That will do." The barometer registered 18.2 inches, and the elevation had been increased to 13,000 feet, striking a strong current which immediately took the vessel swiftly due north.

Cape Farewell was in latitude sixty degrees, and on the forty-fourth meridian from Greenwich. It was over 1,200 miles to the eightieth degree, from which Cobb intended to move west to Smith's Sound.

The days had become shorter and shorter as they progressed northward.

"It's a bad time of the year," said Hugh, "to make the voyage. The cold will be intense, and there will be no sun north of the seventy-fourth degree after to-day."

"Yes; I know it," returned Cobb. "But we will have the aurora, and that will give a sufficiency of light for all our purposes."

In the steady, strong northerly current, the Orion made rapid progress. The great glaciers of Southern Greenland were passed, and then the chain of mountains which traverses the land from north to south were reached. Keeping exactly along the backbone of the range, the Orion speed northward.

On either side great canyons opened toward the west and east; immense rivers of ice and slow-moving glaciers extended toward the sea. The land was white with snow, save here and there where the black rocks of the mountains broke through. A barren, dreary waste was upon every side, and a scene of utter desolation presented itself to these few mortals far up in the clouds.

Still the vessel moved northward; degree after degree was passed, and it was 12 dial when they reached the seventy-fifth degree of latitude. The sun lay like a ball of fire upon the plain of snow to the south, its disc just visible as it seemed to rest on the horizon. The three officers stood at the rail, and raised their fur caps in salutation.

"Good-bye, old Sol; good-bye to your bright light!" cried Cobb, as he waved his cap. "It will be many an hour—days, even, and perhaps years, ere your face is seen by us again!"

"Let us say days only, Junius," the others exclaimed, together. "We hope soon to see its glorious face again."

"Perhaps!" With this single word, Cobb turned and entered the cabin, where he spread out before him a chart of the arctic regions, and examined it intently. Five degrees more and he would turn to the west!

Dinner was soon announced, and eaten with a relish, as the bracing air had given each a good appetite. The sunlight had given place to twilight, and that, in turn, had been followed by night. The stars shone out with brilliancy, and studded the heavens in every direction. The Orion, being in an upper current, moved with surprising evenness. The pole-star was high in the sky, and the great bear directly over their heads.

It was 18 dial by their chronometers, and they should be near the eightieth parallel.

"Hugh," said Cobb, rising from his chair, "will you take the latitude from Polaris? Never mind the refraction; I want it only to within a few minutes." Hugh took the sextant, and left the cabin, while Cobb turned to Hathaway, and remarked: "Lester, this is a very comfortable room, this one of ours in the arctic regions, is it not?"

"Indeed, it is," the other replied.

"And we are going north, to the extremity of the earth?"

"I understand such to be your intention."

"It would be sad for you and Hugh if we never returned!"

"I do not think of it in that light," smilingly returned his companion, as he lighted a fresh cigar. "There is no reason why we should not return, and return in a halo of glory."

"I hope so."

At this moment Hugh came, and announced that he made the latitude 79 degrees 55 minutes. Seven minutes later the course of the Orion was laid due west.

On the 17th of January, at 1 dial, the vessel lay to over Napoleon Island. From this point they proceeded due north, Cobb carefully watching the earth below them. For three degrees the course of Smith's Sound was plainly visible, then it terminated in a great sea of floating ice to the north. "As I thought," he murmured: "There is no road to the pole from the continent of North America."

At 6 dial the Orion's course was still due north.

Returning to the cabin, breakfast was served, and all enjoyed the good things which had been prepared, and, also, the warmth of the interior. As the hour of 10 dial drew near, Cobb took the sextant, and passed out of the cabin, and stationed himself at the rail near the pilot's house. There, with instrument in hand, he carefully watched Polaris rise toward the zenith as the ship moved north. Suddenly he dropped the instrument to his side, and cried, in a quick, sharp voice: "Ninety degrees to the right; quick!"

The Orion turned in a graceful curve, and bore due east.

At 16 dial Cobb again came on deck and consulted his sextant. After a moment he laid aside the instrument, and took his watch in his fur-covered hand, and noted the revolution-counter on the side of the pilot's house. "We are moving due east on the parallel of 83 degrees 24 minutes," he replied to Hugh and Lester, as the two men came from the cabin and inquired why he was consulting his watch, "and if I am not mistaken, will be on the meridian of 40 degrees 46 minutes in five minutes," and he put the telescope to his eye and intently examined the earth below them. "Ha! As I thought!" he suddenly cried, excitedly: "Stop her! Stop her! Stop the engines!"

The pilot threw over the electric switch, and the great propeller gradually ceased to revolve. Jumping quickly to the escape-valve, Cobb carefully allowed the gas to escape, and the Orion began gently to settle. Hugh and Lester looked at the man in amazement. Was he crazy? Why was he thus descending into a barren, icy plain miles yet from the pole?

"Make ready, Hugh, to alight," cried Cobb. "I will explain all afterward."

The Orion touched the snowy plain. Still discharging gas that the vessel might not ascend when relieved of the weight of himself and companions, he pointed to a cone of rocks standing high and bare above the snow, some four hundred yards away.

"That is why I have landed," he quietly said: "Come; follow me, and I will explain."

Stepping down the ladders, the three men made their way over the snow toward the spot pointed out, and found a pile of rocks about thirty feet high standing on the shore of the icy sea. As Lester and Hugh examined the monument, Cobb, saying nothing, commenced to pull aside the stones. A moment later and he had unearthed an old rusty meat-can, and was excitedly tearing it open. Its contents was a letter. Without waiting to hear the questions which he knew the two men were about to ask, he said: "This is the cairn left by Brainard and Lockwood in 1882. This is the spot, 83 degrees 24 minutes north latitude, and 40 degrees 46 minutes west longitude, which they reached on that day, memorable in history, when the highest latitude on the globe was reached by a human being."

"And you knew that a letter would be found in that cairn?" inquired Lester, with intense surprise.

"I was told so by Brainard," Cobb answered, with quiet unconcern.

"And you personally knew the man who left that letter here in this desolate waste?" incredulously broke in Hugh.

"Intimately."

Cobb then detailed all the circumstances attending

Lat. 83° 24' North Long 40° 46' West

~~Copy of Record left in Cairn at Farthest~~

I left Fort Conger, Discovery Harbor, April 3rd, 1882, with party of twelve men and equipment consisting of one dog-sledge and team and four Hudson Bay sledges. Four of the party broke down in crossing the straits and were sent back. Two of the sledges also became useless and another, a large sledge, was substituted for them. Thus equipped the party left the base of supplies (which we had in mean time established at the Boat Camp, Newman Bay) April 16th and reached Cape Bryant April 27th. Near the Black Horn Cliffs the large sledge referred to broke a runner, and at Cape Bryant the two remaining Hudson Bay sledges were unable to go farther, being worn out. Here the rest of the party turned back while I continued on with the dog team, Sergeant David L. Brainard, General Service, U. S. Army, and Frederick Christiansen (Eskimo)

Cape Britannia was reached May 4th and this cape May 13th, 1882. Here I turn back, starting tomorrow the 15th instant. All well at this date.

        J. B. Lockwood
        2d Lieutenant 23d Infantry
        U.S. Army.

the fit-out of the Greely expedition, and his personal acquaintance with Brainard and Lockwood. He narrated that they had reached this memorable spot on the 13th of May, 1882, and could go no farther, as a great sea washed the shore in front of them—the time being summer. Opening the letter which he had taken from the meat-can, he read to his astonished friends:

"Now!" he exclaimed, as he raised the letter aloft; "now, in honor to the men who suffered, and to Lockwood, who perished, the record of their search for the pole shall not rest here, but shall continue its journey, even to the pole itself, and be laid upon the pivotal axis of this mighty globe."

An hour later the Orion was bearing due north, and the three officers were sitting in the warm cabin discussing the cairn, the letter, and the Greeley expedition of 1880.

Higher and higher rose Polaris to the zenith; onward, mile after mile, flew the ship. The cold outside had become intense, and the spirit thermometer registered 86 degrees F. The aurora filled the heavens about them as if a huge, circular tent of brilliantly colored stripes of fire had been pitched above them. No moisture in the air, no sound, save the whir of the propeller, as it rapidly revolved and sent the vessel forward. Below was ice—ice—and nothing more.

So intense was the cold that, as Cobb unthinkingly touched his bare moist hand to the sextant which had been brought in by the boy, the skin and flesh were burnt as by a red-hot iron.

"It was 18 dial when we left the cairn, in latitude 83 degrees 24 minutes," said Cobb, after a pause in the conversation, "and the distance to the pole was just 458 miles. Our speed has been uniform, and at the rate of forty-three and-a-half miles per hour, we should cover the distance in ten hours thirty-one minutes and forty-eight seconds, and at thirty-one minutes forty-eight seconds past 4 dial ought to be directly over the pole."

Indeed, Cobb was perfectly correct in his reckoning, for at the hour mentioned the Orion was brought to a standstill, and then gently dropped to the earth below. Excitedly jumping down the ladders, the three men sprang out upon the snow, and, in one voice, exultingly exclaimed: "The pole! the pole! the north pole!"

True, it was the vicinity of the north pole of the earth, but it was not until after five days of hard work and intricate calculations that the exact spot through which the axis of the earth passed, had been located.

The record showed the exact time of locating this spot to be 12 dial, January 23, 2001.

Then was erected, from such materials as could be spared from the Orion, a monument to mark the spot. A hollow aluminum rod was driven deep through the snow into the earth underneath, and within it were placed letters and papers, and a portion of the documents found in the cairn in latitude 83 degrees 24 minutes.

Their task completed, they contemplated their achievement; a dreary waste, with snow in every direction, contained within its center the evidence of their wonderful discovery; and that evidence was a single monument of boxes, barrels, metals, and whatever else could be spared from the Orion to mark the north point of the earth's axis! Surely this was little reward for the years of arduous toil and physical suffering of mankind, for the vast sums expended and for the hundreds of human lives which had been sacrificed in the vain ambition of discovering the polar axis of the earth!

The Orion lay about a hundred yards from the monument which had been erected, with her great gas bag nearly empty. A large tent, however, had been set up exactly over the pole to shelter them from the cold winds as they made their observations.

On the morning of the 24th of January the three men proceeded to the tent for the last time. Hugh carried a large box in his arms, and Lester had a storage battery well wrapped in warm flannels.

"It will be gladsome news to your father, Hugh, if you can send a message to him from here," said Cobb. as they entered the tent.

"Indeed, it will!" joyously returned the other. "I will soon have my instruments in position, and then for word from home!" He beamed with the thought, for might he not hear from Marie? Of course he would! They certainly would tell him where she was, and if she and Mollie were well!

Hugh had brought a set of sympathetic instruments with him, the mate to which was in the office of the President's private secretary. He had cautioned that gentleman to watch at a certain hour of each day for his signals. That hour had been designated as 11 to 12 dial.

Setting his instruments on the top of the little monument, Hugh worked assiduously to get an answering click from the office in Washington, but without success. In every conceivable position that he laid the needle the result was the same— no influence from its Washington mate. Disgusted, he arose from his work, and debated the situation in his mind.

"Ah!" he suddenly exclaimed, pointing to the needle. "I see it now! The needle is directly over the pole, and moves in the plane of the equator, while every other needle of the whole system of the sympathetic telegraph points to the north star." As he spoke, he seized the instrument, and carefully turned it on its side until the needle moved in a vertical plane; then fixing it solidly, he brought the needle into a perfectly vertical position, and raised his hands from the instrument.

"Ah!" burst sharp and quick from all. "Click— click—click," and the needle seemed to fondly pat the little brass stud on its right. "Hurrah! we've got him!" cried Hugh, and wild with excitement, he sprang to the key and called, "W—W—W." Again the joyful click, and the "I—I—I—W" of the Washington operator was heard by all. For an hour the instruments clicked, and message upon message had been sent to the President and others in the great, busy world far to the south of them; and from these messages word had been flashed to all the known nations of the globe of the great success—the discovery of the north pole by three American officers.

At last came the words, through the instrument:

"Your father says Mollie and Marie are in San Francisco yet, and have sent word for you to join them there as soon as possible. They have a surprise in store for Mr. Cobb. He says you are not to delay at the pole, but proceed direct to San Francisco, to your aunt's. Your father further says that, as Captain Hathaway has made such a record for himself with you and Mr. Cobb, he may call upon him, on his return, in regard to a little matter which has been, heretofore, an unpleasant subject between them."

Hugh smiled as he translated the message, and looked with a glad expression into the eyes of Lester. That gentleman, as he comprehended the meaning of the message, danced a hornpipe in the snow, and cried, with ecstasy: "She'll be mine at last!"

"Let us be up and away!" exclaimed Hugh, as he

gave the final answers to the Washington operator. "On to San Francisco, Lester! on to our girls, is our cry!"

"Then, take your bearings, Hugh, for Behring Strait," directed Cobb. "It will be necessary for us to go that way to replenish our supply of lipthalite at Port Clarence, or else trust to the currents part of the way."

A puzzled expression came over the face of the other, and he seemed lost in a quandary. "Easy enough to say, 'Take your bearings,'" he returned, "but how? I will be hanged if I know one meridian from another here. In fact, we are on all of them."

"Don't you know in which direction south is?" asked Lester, with a laugh.

"Of course, I do. But do you know in which direction the meridian of ten degrees runs, for that is the meridian which passes through Behring Strait?"

In fact, it was quite a puzzling question to answer. All the meridians centered at the pole, and the time there was the apparent time of every meridian on the globe. Standing on the pole, it seemed absolutely impossible for one to know if he were facing London or Washington, or any particular point on the earth's surface. Hugh scratched his head in perplexity.

"Take the needle," calmly said Cobb.

"Yes; but it don't point north any more; it poinas somewhere south," he answered.

"And where may that south point be?" inquiringly.

"Why, the north magnetic pole of the earth, of course," with a glimmer of perception.

"And that pole is where?"

"In Boothia Felix."

"Exactly; in 70 degrees 6 minutes north latitude, and 96 degrees 50 minutes 45 seconds west longitude, on the west coast of Boothia, facing Ross Straits. Your needle points there; so all you have to do is to lay off 73 degrees 9 minutes 15 seconds to the right, and you have the course to Port Clarence, North Alaska."

The Orion was again made ready, the gas bag filled, a last adieu given to the north pole of the earth, and the three friends mounted the ladders, touched the electric button of the engines, and sped swiftly down the one hundred and seventieth meridian of longitude.

CHAPTER XXIII

It was the 11th of February, warm and bright, in that delightful climate of California. In the handsome residence of Mrs. Morse, on California street, reclining in a large arm-chair, sat Marie Colchis. A book lay upon the floor, where it had fallen from her hand, and she lay among the cushions with a far-away, dreamy expression in her eyes. Nearly five weeks had elapsed since she left the Island of Guadalupe and came with her two friends to San Francisco.

Care and attention and the best of nursing had saved the girl from the fever which first threatened to make her recovery slow and uncertain. She had regained her health, her flesh and beauty; her skin was exceeding fair, but the whiteness was set off by the rich red of her cheeks and lips.

Recovered from death, among friends who loved her, and expecting every moment the arrival of the one of all men whom she had ever loved, whom she adored now, she lay dreaming of the time when she should be clasped in his arms.

Marie had been informed of everything concerning Junius Cobb. She knew of his apparent infatuation with Mollie, and of his subsequent disinclination for the society of either her or Marie Hathaway. Mollie had told her of the time when he had called her by name in such words of love and endearment, and Marie believed that his heart was hers yet. She was informed of his journey to the pole, of his safe arrival there, and knew that he was expected in San Francisco at any moment.

"Oh that the time would soon come!" she had cried in her heart many times. "Will he know me? Will he still love me?" she had asked herself; "and then, if not, I shall die!" she would murmur sadly, while the beautiful eyes would fill with tears.

"They are coming, Marie! They are coming!" screamed Mollie, rushing into the room. "They are at the door!"

Marie started from her chair, gasped, and pressed her hand to her heart. He was at the door! he whom she loved, and from whom she had been separated for over a hundred years!

"Remember, Marie, your promise; you are Leona Bennett;" and with this parting instruction, Mollie shot to the door just in time to be clasped in the arms of Lester Hathaway, who was leading the way for Cobb. Hugh had stopped in the hall, hugging the plump little form of Marie Hathaway.

A moment later Mollie led Cobb toward Marie, who was standing by the window at the side of the room.

"Leona, this is our friend, Mr. Cobb, of whom you have heard us speak. Junius, my cousin, Leona Bennett."

Mollie smiled slyly, and gave Marie a knowing look.

Cobb bowed low, and then, looking up, hesitated as if lost in admiration of the beautiful face before him. Ere a word could be spoken by either, Lester and Hugh were brought forward and presented.

"You must have thought me rude, Miss Bennett," said Cobb, a little later, as he and Marie sat near each other, "not to have expressed the pleasure which I could not but feel at meeting one so beautiful as yourself."

"I, equally, was unable to more than acknowledge the introduction; for you know the others were upon us, and we had no time," and she smiled charmingly upon him, while her eyes seemed to have a longing, craving expression. "You have had a most remarkable experience in life, Mr. Cobb," she added, after a pause.

"Yes," sadly. "And many times I have wished my fate had ordained it otherwise; but now, Miss Bennett, it would be ungallant, and," with a searching look, "untrue, to say that I do, for I have met you."

"Ah, you are like all men, ever ready with a compliment."

"But it seems as if I was drawn to you by some power I cannot express," he continued, looking deep into her eyes.

"Do I remind you of some old friend, some old

love?" she banteringly asked, though it was easy to perceive that she longed for an affirmative reply.

"That is just what puzzles me, Miss Bennett. It seems as if your face was familiar, and yet I could never have met you before."

"Are you sure?" She looked up with one of those expressions of childhood days when she had clung to him and begged him to come again to her in Duke's Lane.

His eyes scanned her; his thoughts traveled back many years. "How like Marie Colchis was that expression," he said to himself; yet he gave no utterance to his thoughts.

"She was dead, dead long years ago!" Then, aloud, he slowly said: "Yes; I am sure."

"Then, how can you account for the power of attraction which draws you to me?" she persisted.

"I know not its cause," he smilingly returned, "unless it be that perhaps all men are similarly attracted. I am but mortal, Miss Bennett, and consequently cannot resist the loadstone of so much grace and loveliness."

Thus they met, and thus they talked. He knew her not, nor did she reveal her identity. She wished to test the man she loved; and why? Ask a woman!

Two weeks passed, and still they all remained in San Francisco; but the next day was to see them on their way to Washington; the President had sent an imperative summons for all to join him at once.

Junius Cobb had seen Marie every one of these

days; had walked and driven and been her escort everywhere. In fact, he had been by her side during every moment that propriety would allow. A new life seemed opened to him; he laughed and chatted like the gayest; he was witty and bright, and the old expression of sorrow had vanished from his face.

He seemed to live in her smiles, to be supremely happy in her presence. He was in love; this time he knew it. Did he ever think of little Marie Colchis? Yes, often and often, and the divinity he now worshiped seemed to him as if risen from the soul of her, and that in loving the former he still maintained his allegiance to the latter. Leona, to him, was his old love Marie. He could not explain the semblance, yet he saw that it existed. He loved Leona Bennett; he thought of Marie Colchis.

Sitting by her side that evening, in the small, cozy library, whither he had gently led her, and whither she had gladly, willingly gone, he quietly said, "Miss Bennett, you return to Washington to-morrow?"

Turning her large blue eyes upon him, she asked, "And do you not go, too, Mr. Cobb?"

"It all depends," he answered, nervously.

"Why, I thought it was all settled. Mollie told me that you were to go. Have you changed your mind, Mr. Cobb?"

"I dislike to return to Washington," he continued, not heeding her question, "unless I can do so with a lighter heart than I took away with me when I left."

"You ought to go there with the greatest pleasure. Your name is famous throughout the world," and she looked proudly upon him; proud of the man she loved.

"But fame is not all that man craves," he returned.

"What more can man desire than a name great to the world; a name honored, respected and loved?" Her eyes had dropped, while his were fastened upon her with love intense.

"Love." He whispered the word lowly and sweetly in her ear as he bent over her drooping form.

Raising her eyes, now full of all that deep love of her aching, patient heart, she met his ardent gaze.

"And can you not have that?" she asked, in tones so low as to be almost inaudible.

"Miss Bennett," he sadly returned, "mine is a peculiar position. Listen but a moment, and let me tell you my history."

Junius Cobb then narrated his meeting with Marie Colchis; how he had loved her, but as a child; how he had promised to be her husband, and how he had forsaken her to gratify his ambition. He told her how this love of his little Marie had come to him in all its intensity since his return to life, yet he knew that she was lost to him forever. He informed her of his supposed love for Mollie

Craft, and of his sudden discovery that his heart could never be given to her. He related the vision he had wherein Marie had been led to him by an angel. And during all this recital his listener had sat, with tears in her eyes, but a holy feeling of adoration for the man who had remembered her with such love. It was only by a supreme effort that she refrained from declaring herself and falling into the arms of this noble man.

"Miss Bennett—Leona," gently and slowly; "since my eyes have beheld you, I have seen but one form, have known but one name—Marie Colchis. Yours is the face, the voice, the grace and loveliness that would have been hers at your age. It seems that in your form reposes her soul; that through your eyes beams her sweet and loving nature. Never could two beings be more alike."

As he spoke the words, Marie's overflowing heart gave vent to its fullness in a deep sob.

"I know, Leona," proceeded Cobb, as he noticed her agitation, "that you feel sad at the recital of my story; your great heart—her heart—responds in sympathy to the sufferings of others. I feel that the vision of her coming has been realized; that though departed from this earth and among the angels in heaven, she has sent her soul, her form, her mortal being, back again to earth that I might meet my just reward—life or death. Marie Colchis—for by that name are you henceforth in my heart—I love you, I adore you. Is it to be life or death?"

Amid the sobs which came from her heart, she asked: "And will I always be Marie Colchis to you, Junius? Will you always bear me the love you profess for that other?"

"Yes; a thousand times yes," he cried, as he arose and took her hand in his. "As my life, will I love you; as my life do I now adore you. O Marie, my darling, my own. Will you give me life? Can you love me in return, for her sake?" pleadingly, as he gently turned the beautiful face toward him and looked into her tear-bedimmed eyes.

Her heart was overflowing; the flood-gates of her love, so long closed and barred, were about to break asunder; her soul had passed out into his keeping. With a passionate cry, she threw her arms about him, and wept tears of joy. Gently he drew her closer to him, and kissed her lips; kissed away the tear-drops in her eyes.

"You love me, my own, my darling!" he cried. "Tell me that you do."

"O Junius; as I love my God!" Again the tears of joy and happiness flowed fast and furious from her eyes.

"And you reproach me not that I see in you my former love?"

"No. No more is my name Leona Bennett. To you, my own, my noble heart, it shall ever be Marie Colchis. By that name alone shall you henceforth know me, love me, and be my husband." Thus she spoke the truth, yet kept the promise she had made.

CHAPTER XXIV

"Home again, at last," gleefully exclaimed Mollie, as the double drag brought the whole party from the depot to the executive mansion.

The President and Mrs. Craft met them at the private entrance, and gave to each a cordial welcome. Marie Colchis was received by the old people as a beloved niece, for Mollie had, in a letter written some weeks before to her father, partially explained the situation of Marie, whom she wished to be called Leona Bennett.

Once in the house, the several members, excepting Mollie, went directly to their rooms to change their traveling clothes; but she, taking her father by the hand, asked him and her mother to give her a few moments of their time, as she had something of importance to relate. Once in the library, she knelt at her father's feet, and related the whole story concerning Marie Colchis. She told of finding the letter in Cobb's room, and of her journey to Guadalupe Island, and the rescue of the girl; she dwelt upon all the wonderful incidents of the finding of the cavern and its contents; and then she told him of the letter which was found with Marie, and the relations which had existed between Marie and Junius Cobb, years ago; that Junius was ignorant of Marie's identity, but was in love with her, and had asked her to marry him.

The iron box which was found in the cavern, and which was now in the trunk, was next spoken of. Finally, she admitted to her parents her love for Lester, and his adoration of her, and asked for their consent to their union. "And this is not all, dear papa and mamma," she said: "Marie Colchester is Marie Hathaway, Lester's sister; I brought her here to win the love of Junius, but it was not to be, for"—and she hesitated—"for she is engaged to Hugh."

It was several minutes ere Mr. and Mrs. Craft could grasp the whole situation, the revelations had come so fast and free; but, finally, the old man took his wife's hand in his, and slowly, but with a smile of pleasure, said: "Mamma, we were young once."

Mollie accepted the words and expression of his face as evidence that a happy termination would end the hide-and-seek courtship of herself and Lester; she kissed them both, and ran to communicate the good news to her lover.

It was evening of that day. A happy, jolly, bright party was congregated in the private parlor of the executive mansion. In the corner, by the great mirror, sat Junius Cobb and Marie Colchis, his eyes drinking in the beauty of her being, and his thoughts wrapped in a contemplation of her grace and loveliness. On the sofa, across from them, sat

Hugh and Marie Hathaway; Lester was alone in a big arm-chair near the window, while Mollie stood in the center of the room under the electric lights, bright, radiant and vivacious.

"Three spooney couples!" she cried. "No; I mean two and a half—and you are the half, Lester," slyly turning her head toward him. "Six hearts beating as one; all in unison, but none engaged. He is coming, papa is coming; and I advise some young gentlemen whom I could name to step boldly to the front and ask—well, I think I'll say no more, but I pity you. Papa holds his daughters in an iron fist," and she clenched her little hand to emphasize her words.

A moment later and the President and his wife entered the room, and all arose to meet them.

"Be seated, my children," he kindly said. "For the first time in my life I feel that I have three beautiful daughters and three noble sons. I have asked you to meet me here that I might bring complete happiness to three pairs of loving hearts. I know all your secrets, dear children; everything is known to me."

He paused. An expression of surprise came over the face of Hugh, while anxiety was depicted in Lester's countenance. Marie Colchis turned her eyes upon the speaker, but said nothing. As for Cobb, he thought it all quite natural, as, no doubt, Marie had told her uncle of his proposal.

"I will not keep you long in suspense. You,

Lester," and he turned toward him. "Love my daughter. You have asked for her hand more than once. I know she returns that love; and as her happiness is next my heart, I will not bring sorrow to her by refusing your request." He stepped forward, and took the hand of Mollie, whose cheeks were red with blushes, and led her to where Lester stood, having risen from his chair. "Lester, take her; she is yours. Be a good, kind husband to her, is all I ask."

Lester took the fair girl in his arms, and imprinted the first lawful kiss upon her lips.

"And now," continued Mr. Craft, "as two hearts are thus made happy, let me seek another pair. Hugh; stand up, my son."

Hugh arose, gently raising Marie Hathaway from the sofa, and moved toward his father. "Father," he said, "here is another pair."

Marie hung her head in confusion, but Hugh was bold and fearless.

"I know all about you two also," said Mr. Craft, smiling. "I am more than satisfied to receive such a daughter as you, Marie Hathaway." The girl started as her name was pronounced, and a guilty blush mantled her cheek at the thought of the deception she had practiced upon this good old man. "Unto my son I give you, if it be your wish that he should become your husband."

He paused. Marie made no reply, save to pass

her hand through Hugh's arm, and nestle closer to his heart.

"Hugh, take her, and bless God for the prize which you have received." Hugh led the girl away with joy in his heart.

"Junius"—the President spoke the word low, and with more embarrassment than he had used in addressing the others—"I know not how to commence. She who stands by your side is not my niece, but my daughter," and he took Marie Colchis' hand in his, and drew her toward him. "She is my daughter; no blood makes the tie, but that of love has given her to me. She stands before you alone in this life. No father or mother, brother or sister, or relative has she in the wide world." The tears were now falling from Marie's eyes, and she clung closer to her adopted father. Hugh and Lester looked on in silence but wonder. "She has come," he continued, "like a radiant star in our universe, and from a remote period of time. She lived years ago—a hundred or more. Do not start, Junius," as the other moved a step, and stood gazing on Marie's face with a look of partial recognition. "Like you, she lived, and died, and lived again. The same methods which were used to prolong your life were used to give life again to this fair girl. The hand that assisted at your interment prepared the casket wherein his daughter has lain for over a century. She is—"

The wild excitement of Cobb's soul, paralyzed

for a moment by the words of the other, now broke forth in a hoarse, pathetic cry—"Marie Colchis!" and he rushed forward, and almost crushed the fair form in his strong arms. Regardless of all present, he kissed her face, her lips—kissed her with all the depth and passion of a man receiving back from death the being divine of his heart.

When Cobb's feelings had calmed sufficiently for him to realize the situation, the President led him and Marie to their chairs. "Take her, Junius; God has ordained it!" he said, with a choking sensation in his throat. Without letting too long a pause ensue, he drew from his pocket a paper, unfolded it, and said: "Listen, my children, to the last words of that girl's father, Jean Colchis."

In a low tone he read:

"GUADALUPE ISLAND, December 15, 1897.

"JUNIUS: To you I leave these words! Dead though thou art, yet a voice tells me that you will live again. In this chamber, with the inanimate body of my darling daughter lying beside me, I write my last words to mortal man.

"From the day you left us, and for years after, the heart of Marie has lain like a stone in her bosom; no feeling but that of love for you has gained entrance there.

"Wealth poured in upon me, and I endeavored by its aid to surround her with life, luxury and change of scene, hoping thus to turn her thoughts into other channels than of you. It was in vain! Sad and sorrowful she passed the days and years in hope of your return.

"I did not tell her that you had entered into a state of inanimation from which you would not awake until years had passed. I could not crush her heart! The days came and went, and no change took place. I felt that she was dying of a broken heart. As the conviction forced itself upon me, I prayed to God for help. Long and long I debated the situation. The knowledge was apparent that she would die ere many days had passed unless means were promptly taken to remove the sorrow in her heart on account of your prolonged absence. What should I do? I had assisted in your preparations for a future existence; I knew of the methods you had taken to continue life in your body.

"'Junius can never return to my daughter,' I cried, in the agony of my soul. Why not send that daughter to him?' If you lived, she might again live, through the means I might employ. If you did not survive the ordeal, then it were better that she, also, should die. I argued with myself; I won. I sought for a spot where no human being would find the resting place of my beloved daughter until the time should arrive for her deliverance. I selected the island of Guadalupe, far from the busy world. I prepared the chambers and made them beautiful.

"My daughter came, and for nearly a year we lived in quiet but sad community. But, alas! it was of no avail! I saw her dying before my eyes. I resolved to subject her to a living death, in the hope that she might live again and be happy.

"I have prepared her body, even as you had told me yours was to be prepared. I inclose her fair form in a golden coffin, as a fitting receptacle for one so true and noble. With immortelles for her death, should she die, I surround the casket; with orange blossoms at her head, in the hope of future life and of her marriage to you, I lay her to rest.

"In an iron box at the foot of her coffin you will find my last testament, and the dowry I bequeath my daughter. I have prepared everything for this moment. That you might know this place, I put the letter into the copper cylinder; I bored through the walls of your tomb, and pushed in the case; and when I heard it fall on the floor of your sepulchre, I sealed up the hole. I knew if you lived again you would rescue your Marie. I felt, that if you died, it was better that she died also.

"The time has come! I lay this letter upon the snowy bosom of her who loved you as never woman loved a man. O God! can mortal know the anguish that seizes my heart as I am about to seal the lid which closes her sweet face in a living tomb!

"When these words are read by thee, O my daughter, if ever thine eyes shall brighten again in life, my bones will lie bare and naked at the foot of thy coffin. Good-bye, my darling daughter. I close the lid! I seal thy fate!

"JEAN COLCHIS."

Without allowing the sadness of the moment to weigh upon their feelings, the President stepped to the door, and soon returned, followed by a servant bearing the little iron box which Dr. Town had carried on his saddle from Guadulupe Island, and which Mollie had surrendered to her father.

Soon it had been opened, and its contents exposed to view. A bundle of papers was on top, and these the President took out and gave to Cobb.

He took them, and opened the first paper: it was the will of Jean Colchis, giving to Junius Cobb, on the day of his marriage to Marie Colchis, all money due from the government of the United States on the contract of sale of the invention of the sympathetic telegraph. The second paper examined was the original contract for the transfer of this invention to the government in consideration of $5,000,000 paid down and a perpetuity of one-half of one per cent. on the gross earnings derived from its use.

"Why!" exclaimed the President, as Cobb read the contract, "you will be one of the richest men in the country. As near as I remember, there are over a hundred millions of dollars lying unclaimed in the Treasury on this contract."

The third paper found was the formula for making the needles used in the invention, sympathetic.

"Ah!" cried Cobb. "This is most important! Not but that the wealth given Marie and me is most acceptable; but now," and he held up the paper, "now the world will again know and make use of the secret of sympathizing the needles."

"And you forget another thing, Junius," broke in Hugh. "You are five millions of dollars richer by that paper, as that is the reward offered by the government for the discovery of the lost secret."

The last paper in the box was then read:

"That the wealth which I possess may descend to my daughter unimpaired by time and change, I have converted the $5,000,000 which the government paid me for my invention into the sack of stones underneath this paper. J. C."

Cobb reached his hand into the box, and withdrew a silken bag. Opening it, he poured the contents upon the table.

All started with exclamations of astonishment at the sight; and well they might. The center of the table seemed ablaze with a million sparkling, dancing rays of light. Five million dollar's worth of precious stones lay before them—the dowry of Marie Colchis.

"Junius," said the President, laying his hand upon the young man's shoulder, "wealth has rolled in upon you by millions, but above all the wealth you have received is the fair prize you have won, your future wife," and he kissed the blushing face of Marie. "One more gift I can add to the many you have received," and he drew from his pocket a folded paper bearing the great seal of the Navy Department upon it. "Your commission as Admiral of the Aërial Navy of the United States," and he handed the paper to Junius Cobb. "Your discovery of meteorlene has revolutionized warfare, and you soon will command a powerful fleet of aërial war ships."

Cobb bowed low as he accepted the paper, and expressed his gratitude to the President for this additional proof of his generosity.

"I was not far wrong," exclaimed Hugh, grasping his hand, "when I saluted you as Admiral, on board of the Orion."

"No, Hugh," returned Cobb; "and I wish I had not been, when I returned it to you as my Commodore."

"And you were not, Junius," laughed the President, as he drew another paper from his pocket. "Your commission as Commodore in the Aërial Navy, Hugh," handing him the paper.

"And what does my hubby get?" cried Mollie, pouting her pretty lips.

"A colonelcy in the army for distinguished service during the war," and the President smiled as he took a third paper from his pocket and gave it to Lester.

"And now," said Cobb, after a pause, "as wealth

more than I can use has been heaped upon me, I wish to add my mite to the happiness of the moment. Hugh," and he took up the third paper from the bundle on the table, "here is the secret of the sympathetic telegraph; it is worth five million dollars. Take it, and divide it between yourself and Lester, as a wedding gift from me."

Then Marie stepped forward, and filled her two hands with glittering stones from the pile on the table. "Take these, my dear sisters," she said, as she poured them into the laps of the two astonished girls; "take these as a bridal gift from Marie Colchis."

THE END

Utopian Literature

AN ARNO PRESS/NEW YORK TIMES COLLECTION

Adams, Frederick Upham.
President John Smith; The Story of a Peaceful Revolution. 1897.

Bird, Arthur.
Looking Forward: A Dream of the United States of the Americas in 1999. 1899.

[Blanchard, Calvin.]
The Art of Real Pleasure. 1864.

Brinsmade, Herman Hine.
Utopia Achieved: A Novel of the Future. 1912.

Caryl, Charles W.
New Era. 1897.

Chavannes, Albert.
The Future Commonwealth. 1892.

Child, William Stanley.
The Legal Revolution of 1902. 1898.

Collens, T. Wharton.
Eden of Labor; or, The Christian Utopia. 1876.

Cowan, James.
Daybreak. A Romance of an Old World. 1896. 2nd ed.

Craig, Alexander.
Ionia; Land of Wise Men and Fair Women. 1898.

Daniel, Charles S.
AI: A Social Vision. 1892.

Devinne, Paul.
The Day of Prosperity: A Vision of the Century to Come. 1902.

Edson, Milan C.
Solaris Farm. 1900.

Fuller, Alvarado M.
A. D. 2000. 1890.

Geissler, Ludwig A.
Looking Beyond. 1891.

Hale, Edward Everett.
How They Lived in Hampton. 1888.

Hale, Edward Everett.
Sybaris and Other Homes. 1869.

Harris, W. S.
Life in a Thousand Worlds. 1905.

Henry, W. O.
Equitania. 1914.

Hicks, Granville, with Richard M. Bennett.
The First to Awaken. 1940.

Lewis, Arthur O., editor
American Utopias: Selected Short Fiction. 1790–1954.

McGrady, Thomas.
Beyond the Black Ocean. 1901.

Mendes H. Pereira.
Looking Ahead. 1899.

Michaelis, Richard.
Looking Further Forward. An Answer to *Looking Backward* by Edward Bellamy. 1890.

Moore, David A.
The Age of Progress. 1856.

Noto, Cosimo.
The Ideal City. 1903.

Olerich, Henry.
A Cityless and Countryless World. 1893.

Parry, David M.
The Scarlet Empire. 1906.

Peck, Bradford.
The World a Department Store. 1900.

Reitmeister, Louis Aaron.
If Tomorrow Comes. 1934.

Roberts, J. W.
Looking Within. 1893.

Rosewater, Frank.
'96; A Romance of Utopia. 1894.

Satterlee, W. W.
Looking Backward and What I Saw. 2nd ed. 1890.

Schindler, Solomon.
Young West; A Sequel to Edward Bellamy's Celebrated Novel "Looking Backward." 1894.

Smith, Titus K.
Altruria. 1895.

Steere, C. A.
When Things Were Doing. 1908.

Taylor, William Alexander.
Intermere. 1901.

Thiusen, Ismar.
The Diothas, or, A Far Look Ahead. 1883.

Vinton, Arthur Dudley.
Looking Further Backward. 1890.

Wooldridge, C. W.
Perfecting the Earth. 1902.

Wright, Austin Tappan.
Islandia. 1942.